Collected Short Stories
Featuring
Doctor John Thorndyke
Volume 3

Collected Short Stories Featuring Doctor John Thorndyke

Thirteen Criminal Investigations of an
Edwardian Forensic Scientist

Volume 3

R. Austin Freeman

LEONAUR

Collected Short Stories Featuring
Doctor John Thorndyke
Thirteen Criminal Investigations of an Edwardian Forensic Scientist
Volume 3
by R. Austin Freeman

FIRST EDITION IN THIS FORMAT

Leonaur is an imprint
of Oakpast Ltd

ISBN: 978-1-916535-94-7 (hardcover)
ISBN: 978-1-916535-95-4 (softcover)

http://www.leonaur.com

Contents

The Touchstone

It happened not uncommonly that the exigencies of practice committed my friend Thorndyke to investigations that lay more properly within the province of the police. For problems that had arisen as secondary consequences of a criminal act could usually not be solved until the circumstances of that act were fully elucidated and, incidentally, the identity of the actor established. Such a problem was that of the disappearance of James Harewood's will, a problem that was propounded to us by our old friend, Mr. Marchmont, when he called on us, by appointment, with the client of whom he had spoken in his note.

It was just four o'clock when the solicitor arrived at our chambers, and as I admitted him he ushered in a gentlemanly-looking man of about thirty-five, whom he introduced as Mr. William Crowhurst.

"I will just stay," said he with an approving glance at the tea-service on the table, "and have a cup of tea with you, and give you an outline of the case. Then I must run away and leave Mr. Crowhurst to fill in the details."

He seated himself in an easy chair within comfortable reach of the table, and as Thorndyke poured out the tea, he glanced over a few notes scribbled on a sheet of paper.

"I may say," he began, stirring his tea thoughtfully, "that this is a forlorn hope. I have brought the case to you, but I have not the slightest expectation that you will be able to help us."

"A very wholesome frame of mind," Thorndyke commented with a smile. "I hope it is that of your client also."

"It is indeed," said Mr. Crowhurst; "in fact, it seems to me a waste of your time to go into the matter. Probably you will think so too, when you have heard the particulars."

"Well, let us hear the particulars," said Thorndyke. "A forlorn hope has, at least, the stimulating quality of difficulty. Let us have your outline sketch, Marchmont."

The solicitor, having emptied his cup and pushed it towards the tray for replenishment, glanced at his notes and began: "The simplest way in which to present the problem is to give a brief recital of the events that have given rise to it, which are these: The day before yesterday—that is last Monday—at a quarter to two in the afternoon, Mr. James Harewood executed a will at his house at Merbridge, which is about two miles from Welsbury. There were present four persons: two of his servants, who signed as witnesses, and the two principal beneficiaries—Mr. Arthur Baxfield, a nephew of the testator, and our friend here, Mr. William Crowhurst.

The will was a holograph written on the two pages of a sheet of letter-paper. When the witnesses signed, the will was covered by another sheet of paper so that only the space for the signatures was exposed. Neither of the witnesses read the will, nor did either of the beneficiaries; and so far as I am aware, no one but the testator knew what were its actual provisions, though, after the servants had left the room, Mr. Harewood explained its general purport to the beneficiaries."

"And what was its general purport?" Thorndyke asked.

"Broadly speaking," replied Marchmont, "it divided the estate in two very unequal portions between Mr. Baxfield and Mr. Crowhurst. There were certain small legacies of which neither the amounts nor the names of the legatees are known. Then, to Baxfield was given a thousand pounds to enable him either to buy a partnership or to start a small factory—he is a felt hat manufacturer by trade—and the remainder to Crowhurst, who was made executor and residuary legatee. But, of course, the residue of the estate is an unknown quantity, since we don't know either the number or the amounts of the legacies.

"Shortly after the signing of the will, the parties separated. Mr. Harewood folded up the will and put it in a leather wallet which he slipped into his pocket, stating his intention of taking the will forthwith to deposit with his lawyer at Welsbury. A few minutes after his guests had departed, he was seen by one of the servants to leave the house, and afterwards was seen by a neighbour walking along a footpath which, after passing through a small wood, joins the main road about a mile and a quarter from Welsbury. From that time, he was never again seen alive. He never visited the lawyer, nor did anyone see him at or near Welsbury or elsewhere else.

"As he did not return home that night, his housekeeper (he was a widower and childless) became extremely alarmed, and in the morning she communicated with the police. A search-party was organised, and, following the path on which he was last seen, explored the wood—which is known as Gilbert's Copse—and here, at the bottom of an old chalk-pit, they found him lying dead with a fractured skull and a dislocated neck. How he came by these injuries is not at present known; but as the body had been robbed of all valuables, including his watch, purse, diamond ring and the wallet containing the will, there is naturally a strong suspicion that he has been murdered. That, however, is not our immediate concern—at least not mine. I am concerned with the will, which, as you see, has disappeared, and as it has presumably been carried away by a thief who is under suspicion of murder, it is not likely to be returned."

"It is almost certainly destroyed by this time," said Mr. Crowhurst.

"That certainly seems probable," Thorndyke agreed. "But what do you want me to do? You haven't come for counsel's opinion?"

"No," replied Marchmont. "I am pretty clear about the legal position. I shall claim, as the will has presumably been destroyed, to have the testator's wishes carried out in so far as they are known. But I am doubtful as to the view the court may take. It may decide that the testator's wishes are not known, that the provisions of the will are too uncertain to admit of administration."

"And what would be the effect of that decision?" asked Thorndyke.

"In that case," said Marchmont, "the entire estate would go to Baxfield, as he is the next of kin and there was no previous will."

"And what is it that you want me to do?"

Marchmont chuckled deprecatingly. "You have to pay the penalty of being a prodigy, Thorndyke. We are asking you to do an impossibility—but we don't really expect you to bring it off. We ask you to help us to recover the will."

"If the will has been completely destroyed, it can't be recovered," said Thorndyke. "But we don't know that it has been destroyed. The matter is, at least, worth investigating; and if you wish me to look into it, I will."

The solicitor rose with an air of evident relief.

"Thank you, Thorndyke," said he. "I expect nothing—at least, I tell myself that I do—but I can now feel that everything that is possible will be done. And now I must be off. Crowhurst can give you any details that you want."

When Marchmont had gone, Thorndyke turned to our client and asked, "What do you suppose Baxfield will do, if the will is irretrievably lost? Will he press his claim as next of kin?"

"I should say yes," replied Crowhurst. "He is a businessman and his natural claims are greater than mine. He is not likely to refuse what the law assigns to him as his right. As a matter of fact, I think he felt that his uncle had treated him unfairly in alienating the property."

"Was there any reason for this diversion of the estate?"

"Well," replied Crowhurst, "Harewood and I have been very good friends and he was under some obligations to me; and then Baxfield had not made himself very acceptable to his uncle. But the principal factor, I think, was a strong tendency of Baxfield's to gamble. He had lost quite a lot of money by backing horses, and a careful, thrifty man like James Harewood doesn't care to leave his savings to a gambler. The thousand pounds that he did leave to Baxfield was expressly for the purpose of investment in a business."

"Is Baxfield in business now?"

"Not on his own account. He is a sort of foreman or shop-manager in a factory just outside Welsbury, and I believe he is a good worker and knows his trade thoroughly."

"And now," said Thorndyke, "with regard to Mr Harewood's death. The injuries might, apparently, have been either accidental or homicidal. What are the probabilities of accident—disregarding the robbery?"

"Very considerable, I should say. It is a most dangerous place. The footpath runs close beside the edge of a disused chalk-pit with perpendicular or over hanging sides, and the edge is masked by bushes and brambles. A careless walker might easily fall over—or be pushed over, for that matter."

"Do you know when the inquest is to take place?"

"Yes. The day after tomorrow. I had the subpoena this morning for Friday afternoon at 2.30, at the Welsbury Town Hall."

At this moment footsteps were heard hurriedly ascending the stairs and then came a loud and peremptory rat-tat at our door. I sprang across to see who our visitor was, and as I flung open the door, Mr. Marchmont rushed in, breathing heavily and flourishing a newspaper.

"Here is a new development," he exclaimed. "It doesn't seem to help us much, but I thought you had better know about it at once." He sat down, and putting on his spectacles, read aloud as follows: "A new and curious light has been thrown on the mystery of the death of Mr. James Harewood, whose body was found yesterday in a disused chalk-pit near Merbridge. It appears that on Monday—the day on which Mr. Harewood almost certainly was killed—a passenger alighting from a train at Barwood Junction before it had stopped, slipped and fell between the train and the platform. He was quickly extricated, and as he had evidently sustained internal injuries, he was taken to the local hospital, where he was found to be suffering from a fractured pelvis.

"He gave his name as Thomas Fletcher, but refused to give any address, saying that he had no relatives. This morning he died, and on his clothes being searched for an address, a parcel, formed of two handkerchiefs tied up with string, was found in his pocket. When it was opened it was found to contain five watches, three watch-chains, a tie-pin and a number of banknotes. Other pockets contained a quantity of loose money—gold and silver mixed—and a card of the Welsbury Races, which were held on Monday. Of the five watches, one has been identified as the one taken from Mr. Harewood; and the bank-notes have been identified as a batch handed to him by the cashier, of his bank at Welsbury last Thursday and presumably carried in the leather wallet which was stolen from his pocket.

"This wallet, by the way, has also been found. It was picked up—empty—last night on the railway embankment just outside Welsbury Station. Appearances thus suggest that the man, Fletcher, when on his way to the races, encountered Mr. Harewood in the lonely copse, and murdered and robbed him; or perhaps found him dead in the chalk-pit and robbed the body—a question that is now never likely to be solved."

As Marchmont finished reading, he looked up at Thorndyke. "It doesn't help us much, does it?" said he. "As the wallet was found empty, it is pretty certain that the will has been destroyed."

"Or perhaps merely thrown away," said Thorndyke. "In which case an advertisement offering a substantial reward may bring it to light."

The solicitor shrugged his shoulders sceptically, but agreed to publish the advertisement. Then, once more he turned to go; and as Mr. Crowhurst had no further information to give, he departed with his lawyer.

For some time after they had gone, Thorndyke sat with his brief notes before him, silent and deeply reflective. I, too, maintained a discreet silence, for I knew from long experience that the motionless pose and quiet, impassive face were the outward signs of a mind in swift and strenuous action. Instinctively, I gathered that this apparently chaotic case was being quietly sorted out and arranged in a logical order; that Thorndyke, like a skilful chess-player, was "trying over the moves" before he should lay his hand upon the pieces.

Presently he looked up. "Well?" he asked. "What do you think, Jervis? Is it worth while?"

"That," I replied, "depends on whether the will is or is not in existence. If it has been destroyed, an investigation would be a waste of our time and our client's money."

"Yes," he agreed. "But there is quite a good chance that it has not been destroyed. It was probably dropped loose into the wallet, and then might have been picked out and thrown away before the wallet was examined. But we mustn't concentrate too much on the will. If we take up the case—which I am inclined to do—we must ascertain the actual sequence of events. We have one clear day before the inquest. If we run down to Merbridge tomorrow and go thoroughly over the ground, and then go on to Barwood and find out all we can about the man Fletcher, we may get some new light from the evidence at the inquest."

I agreed readily to Thorndyke's proposal, not that I could see any way into the case, but I felt a conviction that my colleague had isolated some leading fact and had a definite line of research in his mind. And this conviction deepened when, later in the evening, he laid his research-case on the table, and rearranged its contents with evident purpose. I watched curiously the apparatus that he was packing in it and tried—not very successfully—to infer the nature of the proposed investigation. The box of powdered paraffin wax and the spirit blow-pipe were obvious enough; but the "dust-aspirator"—a sort of miniature vacuum cleaner—the portable microscope, the coil of Manila line, with an eye spliced into one end, and especially the abundance of blank-labelled microscope slides, all of which I saw him pack in the case with deliberate care, defeated me utterly.

About ten o'clock on the following morning we stepped from the train in Welsbury Station, and having recovered our bicycles from the luggage van, wheeled them through the barrier and mounted. During the train journey we had both studied the one-inch Ordnance map to such purpose that we were virtually in familiar surroundings and immune from the necessity of seeking directions from the natives. As we cleared the town we glanced up the broad by-road to the left which led to the race-course; then we rode on briskly for a mile,

12

which brought us to the spot where the footpath to Merbridge joined the road. Here we dismounted and, lifting our bicycles over the stile, followed the path towards a small wood which we could see ahead, crowning a low hill.

"For such a good path," Thorndyke remarked as we approached the wood, "it is singularly unfrequented. I haven't seen a soul since we left the road." He glanced at the map as the path entered the wood, and when we had walked on a couple of hundred yards, he halted and stood his bicycle against a tree. "The chalk-pit should be about here," said he, "though it is impossible to see. He grasped a stem of one of the small bushes that crowded on to the path and pulled it aside. Then he uttered an exclamation.

"Just look at that, Jervis. It is a positive scandal that a public path should be left in this condition."

Certainly Mr. Crowhurst had not exaggerated. It was a most dangerous place. The parted branches revealed a chasm some thirty feet deep, the brink of which, masked by the bushes, was but a matter of inches from the edge of the path.

"We had better go back," said Thorndyke, "and find the entrance to the pit, which seems to be to the right. The first thing is to ascertain exactly where Harewood fell. Then we can come back and examine the place from above."

We turned back, and presently found a faint track which we followed until, descending steeply, it brought us out into the middle of the pit. It was evidently an ancient pit, for the sides were blackened by age, and the floor was occupied by a trees of some of considerable size. Against one of these we leaned our bicycles and then walked slowly round at the foot of the frowning cliff.

"This seems to be below the path," said Thorndyke, glancing up at the grey wall which jutted out above in stages like an inverted flight of steps. "Somewhere hereabouts we should find some traces of the tragedy."

Even as he spoke my eye caught a spot of white on a block of chalk, and on the freshly fractured surface a significant brownish-red stain. The block lay opposite the mouth of an artificial cave—an old wagon-shelter but now empty and immediately under a markedly overhanging part of the cliff.

"This is undoubtedly the place where he fell," said Thorndyke. "You can see where the stretcher was placed—an old-pattern stretcher with wheel-runners—and there is a little spot of broken soil at the top where he came over. Well, apart from the robbery, a clear fall of over thirty feet is enough to account for a fractured skull. Will you stay here, Jervis, while I run up and look at the path?"

He went off towards the entrance, and presently I heard him above, pulling aside the bushes, and after one or two trials, he appeared directly overhead.

"There are plenty of footprints on the path," said he, "but nothing abnormal. No trampling or signs of a struggle. I am going on a little farther."

He withdrew behind the bushes, and I proceeded to inspect the interior of the cave, noting the smoke-blackened roof and the remains of a recent fire, which, with a number of rabbit bones and a discarded tea-boiler of the kind used by the professional tramp, seemed not without a possible bearing on our investigation. I was thus engaged when I heard Thorndyke hail me from above and coming out of the cave, I saw his head thrust between the branches. He seemed to be lying down, for his face was nearly on a level with the top of the cliff.

"I want to take an impression," he called out. "Will you bring up the paraffin and the blower? And you might bring the coil of line, too."

I hurried away to the place where our bicycles were standing, and opening the research-case, took out the coil of line, the tin of paraffin wax and the spirit blowpipe, and having ascertained that the container of the latter was full, I ran up the incline and made my way along the path. Some distance along, I found my colleague nearly hidden in the bushes, lying prone, with his head over the edge of the cliff.

"You see, Jervis," he said, as I crawled alongside and looked over, "this is a possible way down, and someone has used it quite recently. He climbed down with his face to the cliff—you can see the clear impression of the toe of a boot in the loam of that projection, and you can even make out the shape of an iron toe-tip. Now the problem is how to get down to take the impression without, dislodging the earth above it. I think I will secure myself with the line."

"It is hardly worth the risk of a broken neck," said I. "Probably the print is that of some schoolboy."

"It is a man's foot," he replied. "Most likely it has no connection with our case. But it may have, and as a shower of rain would obliterate it we ought to secure it." As he spoke, he passed the end of the cord through eye and slipped the loop over his shoulders, drawing tight under his arms. Then, having made the line fast to the butt of a small tree, he cautiously lowered himself over the edge and climbed

14

down to the projection. A soon as he had a secure footing, I passed the spare cord through the ring on the lid of the wax tin and lowered it to him, and when he had unfastened it, I drew up the cord and in the same way let down the blowpipe. Then I watched his neat, methodical procedure. First he took out a spoonful of the powdered, or grated, wax and very delicately sprinkled it on the toe-print until the latter was evenly but very thinly covered.

"Next he lit the blowlamp, and as soon as the blue flame began to roar from the pipe, he directed it on to the toe-print. Almost instantly the powder melted, glazing the impression like a coat of varnish. The flame was removed and the film of wax at once solidified and became dull and opaque. A second, heavier, sprinkling with the powder, followed by another application of the flame, thickened the film of wax, and this process, repeated four or five times, eventually produced a solid cake. Then Thorndyke extinguished the blowlamp, and securing it and the tin to the cord, directed me to pull them up. "And you might send me down the field-glasses," he added. "There is something farther down that I can't quite make out."

I slipped the glasses from my shoulder, and opening the case, tied the cord to the leather sling and lowered it down the cliff; and then I watched with some curiosity as Thorndyke stood on his insecure perch steadily gazing through the glasses (they were Zeiss 8-prismatics) at a clump of wallflowers that grew from a boss of chalk about half-way down. Presently he lowered the glasses and, slinging them round his neck by their lanyard, turned his attention to the cake of wax. It was by this time quite solid, and when he had tested it, he lifted it carefully, and placed it in the empty binocular case, when I drew it up.

"I want you, Jervis," Thorndyke called up, "to steady the line. I am going down to that wallflower clump."

It looked extremely unsafe, but I knew it was useless to protest, so I hitched the line around a massive stump and took a firm grip of the "fall."

"Ready," I sang out; and forthwith Thorndyke began to creep across the face of the cliff with feet and hands clinging to almost invisible projections. Fortunately, there was at this part no overhang, and though my heart was in my mouth as I watched, I saw him cross the perilous space in safety. Arrived at the clump, he drew an envelope from his pocket, stooped and picked up some small object, which he placed in the envelope, returning the latter to his pocket. Then he gave me another bad five minutes while he recrossed the nearly vertical surface to his starting-point; but at length this, too, was safely accomplished, and when he finally climbed up over the edge and stood beside me on solid earth, I drew a deep breath and turned to revile him.

"Well?" I demanded sarcastically, "what have you gathered at the risk of your neck? Is it samphire or edelweiss?"

He drew the envelope from his pocket, and dipping into it, produced a cigarette-holder—a cheap bone affair, black and clammy with long service and still holding the butt of a hand-made cigarette—and handed it to me. I turned it over, smelled it and hastily handed it back. "For my part," said I, "I wouldn't have risked the cervical vertebra of a yellow cat for it. What do you expect to learn from it?"

"Of course, I expect nothing. We are just collecting facts on the chance that they may turn out to be relevant. Here, for instance, we find that a man has descended, within a few yards of where Harewood fell, by this very inconvenient route, instead of going round to the entrance to the pit. He must have had some reason for adopting this undesirable mode of descent. Possibly he was in a hurry, and probably he belonged to the district, since a stranger would not know of the existence of this short cut. Then it seems likely that this was his cigarette tube. If you look over, you will see by those vertical scrapes on the chalk that he slipped and must have nearly fallen. At that moment he probably dropped the tube, for you notice that the wallflower clump is directly under the marks of his toes."

"Why do you suppose he did not recover the tube?"

"Because the descent slopes away from the position of the clump, and he had no trusty Jervis with a stout cord to help him to cross the space. And if he went down this way because he was hurried, he would not have time to search for the tube. But if the tube was not his, still it belonged to somebody who has been here recently."

"Is there anything that leads you to connect this man with the crime?"

"Nothing but time and place," he replied. "The man has been down into the pit close to where Harewood was robbed and possibly murdered, and as the traces are quite recent, he must have been there near about the time of the robbery. That is all. I am considering the traces of this man in particular because there are no traces of any other. But we may as well have a look at the path, which, as you see, yields good impressions."

We walked slowly along the path towards Merbridge, keeping at

16

the edges and scrutinising the surface closely. In the shady hollows, the soft loam bore prints of many feet, and among them we could distinguish one with an iron toe-tip, but it was nearly obliterated by another studded with hob-nails.

"We shan't get much information here," said Thorndyke as he turned about. "The search-party have trodden out the important prints. Let us see if we can find out where the man with the toe-tips went to."

We searched the path on the Welsbury side of the chalk-pit, but found no trace of him. Then we went into the pit, and having located the place where he descended, sought for some other exit than the track leading to the path. Presently, half-way up the slope, we found a second track, bearing away in the direction of Merbridge. Following this for some distance, we came to a small hollow at the bottom of which was a muddy space. And here we both halted abruptly, for in the damp ground were the clear imprints of a pair of boots which we could see had, in addition to the toe-tips, half-tips to the heels.

"We had better have wax casts of these," said Thorndyke, "to compare with the boots of the man Fletcher. I will do them while you go back for the bicycles."

By the time that I returned with the machines two of the footprints were covered with a cake each of wax, and Thorndyke had left the track, and was peering among the bushes. I inquired what he was looking for.

"It is a forlorn hope, as Marchmont would say," he replied, "but I am looking to see if the will has been thrown away here. It was quite probably jettisoned at once, and this is the most probable route for the robber to have taken, if he knew of it. You see by the map that it must lead nearly directly to the race-course, and it avoids both the path and the main road. While the wax is setting we might as well look round."

It seemed a hopeless enough proceeding and I agreed to it without enthusiasm. Leaving the track on the opposite side to that which Thorndyke was searching, I wandered among the bushes and the little open spaces, peering about me and reminding myself of that "aged, aged man" who—

Sometimes searched the grassy knolls,
For wheels of hansom cabs.

I had worked my way nearly back to where I could see Thorndyke, also returning, when my glance fell on a small, brown object caught among the branches of a bush. It was a man's pigskin purse; and as I picked it out of the bush I saw that it was open and empty.

With my prize in my hand, I hastened to the spot where Thorndyke was lifting the wax casts. He looked up and asked, "No luck, I suppose?"

I held out the purse, on which he pounced eagerly. "But this is most important, Jervis," he exclaimed. "It is almost certainly Harewood's purse. You see the initials, 'J. H.,' stamped on the flap. Then we were right as to the direction that the robber took. And it would pay to search this place exhaustively for the will, though we can't do that now, as we have to go to Barwood, I wrote to say we were coming. We had better get back to the path now and make for the road. Barwood is only half-an-hour's run."

We packed the casts in the research-case (which was strapped to Thorndyke's bicycle), and turning back, made our way to the path. As it was still deserted, we ventured to mount, and soon reached the road, along which we started at a good pace toward Barwood.

Half-an-hour's ride brought us into the main Street of the little town, and when we dismounted at the police station we found the Chief Constable himself waiting to receive us, courteously eager to assist us, but possessed by a devouring curiosity which was somewhat inconvenient.

"I have done as you asked me in your letter, sir," he said. "Fletcher's body is, of course, in the mortuary, but I have had all his clothes and effects brought here; and I have had them put in my private office, so that you can look them over in comfort."

"It is exceedingly good of you," said Thorndyke, "and most helpful." He unstrapped the research-case, and following the officer into his sanctum, looked round with deep approval. A large table had been cleared for the examination, and the dead pickpocket's clothes and effects neatly arranged at one end.

Thorndyke's first proceeding was to pick up the dead man's boots—a smart but flimsy pair of light brown leather, rather down at heel and in need of re-soling. Neither toes nor heels bore any tips or even nails excepting the small fastening brads. Having exhibited them to me without remark, Thorndyke placed them on a sheet of white paper and made a careful tracing of the soles, a proceeding that seemed to surprise the Chief Constable, for he remarked, "I should hardly have thought that the question of footprints would arise in this case. You can't charge a dead man."

Thorndyke agreed that this seemed to be true; and then he proceeded to an operation that fairly made the officer's eyes bulge. Opening the research-case—into which the officer cast an inquisitive glance—he took out the dust-aspirator, the nozzle of which he inserted into one after another of the dead thief's pockets while I worked the pump. When he had gone through them all, he opened the receiver and extracted quite a considerable ball of dusty fluff. Placing this on a glass slide, he tore it in halves with a pair of mounted needles and passing one half to me, when we both fell to work "teasing", it out into an open mesh, portions of which we separated and laid—each in a tiny pool of glycerine—on blank labelled glass slides, applying to each slide its cover-glass and writing on the label, "Dust from Fletcher's pockets."

When the series was complete, Thorndyke brought out the microscope, and fitting on a one-inch objective, quickly examined the slides, one after another, and then pushed the microscope to me. So far as I could see, the dust was just ordinary dust—principally made up of broken cotton fibres with a few fibres of wool, linen, wood, jute, and others that I could not name and some undistinguishable mineral particles. But I made no comment, and resigning the microscope to the Chief Constable—who glared through it, breathing hard, and remarked that the dust was "rummy-looking stuff"—watched Thorndyke's further proceedings. And very odd proceedings they were.

First he laid the five stolen watches in a row, and with a Coddington lens minutely examined the dial of each, Then he opened the back of each in turn and copied into his notebook the watch-repairers' scratched inscriptions. Next he produced from the case a number of little vulcanite rods, and laying out five labelled slides, dropped a tiny drop of glycerine on each, covering it at once with a watch-glass to protect it from falling dust. Then he stuck a little label on each watch, wrote a number on it and similarly numbered the five slides.

His next proceeding was to take out the glass of watch No. 1 and pick up one of the vulcanite rods, which he rubbed briskly on a silk handkerchief and passed across and around the dial of the watch, after which he held the rod close to the glycerine on slide No. 1 and tapped it sharply with the blade of his pocket-knife. Then he dropped a cover-glass on to the glycerine and made a rapid inspection of the specimen through the microscope.

This operation he repeated on the other four watches, using a fresh rod for each, and when he had finished he turned to the open-mouthed officer. "I take it," said he, "that the watch which has the chain attached to it is Mr. Harewood's watch?"

"Yes, sir. That helped us to identify it." Thorndyke looked at the watch reflectively. Attached to the bow by a short length of green tape was a small, rather elaborate key. This my friend picked up, and taking a fresh mounted needle, inserted it into the barrel of the key, from which he then withdrew it with a tiny ball of fluff on its point. I hastily prepared a slide and handed it to him, when, with a pair of dissecting scissors, he cut off a piece of the fluff and let it fall into the glycerine. He repeated this manoeuvre with two more slides and then labelled the three "Key, outside," "middle" and "inside," and in that order examined them under the microscope.

My own examination of the specimens yielded very little. They all seemed to be common dust, though that from the face of watch No. 3 contained a few broken fragments of what looked like animal hairs—possibly cat's—as also did the key-fluff marked "outside." But if this had any significance, I could not guess what it was. As to the Chief Constable, he clearly looked on the whole proceeding as a sort of legerdemain with no obvious purpose, for he remarked, as we were packing up to go, "I am glad I've seen how you do it, sir. But all the same, I think you are flogging a dead horse. We know who committed the crime and we know he's beyond the reach of the law."

"Well," said Thorndyke, "one must earn one's fee, you know. I shall put Fletcher's boots and the five watches in evidence at the inquest tomorrow, and I will ask you to leave the labels on the watches." With renewed thanks and a hearty handshake he bade the courteous officer adieu, and we rode off to catch the train to London.

That evening, after dinner, we brought out the specimens and went over them at our leisure; and Thorndyke added a further specimen by drawing a knotted piece of twine through the cigarette-holder that he had salved from the chalk-pit, and teasing out the unsavoury, black substance that came out on the string in glycerine on a slide. When he had examined it, he passed it to me, The dark, tarry liquid somewhat obscured the detail, but I could make out fragments of the same animal hairs that I had noted in the other specimens, only here they were much more numerous. I mentioned my observation to Thorndyke. "They are certainly parts of mammalian hairs," I said, "and they look like the hairs of a cat. Are they from a cat?"

"Rabbit," Thorndyke replied curtly; and even then, I am ashamed to admit, I did not perceive the drift of the investigation.

The room in the Welsbury Town Hall had filled up some minutes before the time fixed for the opening of the inquest, and in the interval, when the jury had retired to view the body in the adjacent mortuary, I looked round the assembly. Mr. Marchmont and Mr. Crowhurst were present, and a youngish, horsey-looking man in cord breeches and leggings, whom I correctly guessed to be Arthur Baxfield. Our friend the Chief Constable of Barwood was also there, and with him Thorndyke exchanged a few words in a retired corner. The rest of the company were strangers.

As soon as the coroner and the jury had taken their places the medical witness was called. The cause of death, he stated, was dislocation of the neck, accompanied by a depressed fracture of the skull. The fracture have been produced by a blow with a heavy weapon, or by the deceased falling on his head. The witness adopted the latter view, as the dislocation showed that deceased had fallen in that manner.

The next witness was Mr. Crowhurst, who repeated to the court what he had told us, and further stated that on leaving deceased's house he went straight home, as he had an appointment with a friend. He was followed by Baxfield, who gave evidence to the same effect, and stated that on leaving the house of the deceased he went to his place of business at Welsbury. He was about to retire when Thorndyke rose to cross-examine.

"At what time did you reach your place of business?" he asked.

The witness hesitated for a few moments and then replied, "Half-past four."

"And what time did you leave deceased's house?"

"Two o'clock," was the reply.

"What is the distance?"

"In a direct line, about two miles. But I didn't go direct. I took a round in the country by Lenfield."

"That would take you near the race-course on the way back. Did you go to the races?"

"No. The races were just over when I returned."

There was a slight pause and then Thorndyke asked, "Do you smoke much, Mr. Baxfield?"

The witness looked surprised, and so did the jury, but the former replied, "A fair amount. About fifteen cigarettes a day."

"What brand of cigarettes do you smoke, and what kind of tobacco is it?"

21

"I make my own cigarettes. I make them of shag."

Here protesting murmurs arose from the jury, and the coroner remarked stiffly, "These questions do not appear to have much connection with the subject of this inquiry."

"You may take it, sir," replied Thorndyke, "that they have a very direct bearing on it." Then, turning to the witness he asked, "Do you use a cigarette-tube?

"Sometimes I do," was the reply.

"Have you lost a cigarette-tube lately?"

The witness directed a startled glance at Thorndyke and replied after some hesitation, "I believe I mislaid one a little time ago."

"When and where did you lose that tube?" Thorndyke asked.

"I—I really couldn't say," replied Baxfield, turning perceptibly pale.

Thorndyke opened his dispatch-box, and taking out the tube that he had salved at so much risk, handed it to the witness. "Is that the tube that you lost?" he asked.

At this question Baxfield turned pale as death, and the hand in which he received the tube shook as if with a palsy. "It may be," he faltered. "I wouldn't swear to it. It is like the one I lost."

Thorndyke took it from him and passed it to the coroner. "I am putting this tube in evidence, sir," said he. Then addressing the witness, he said, "You stated that you did not go to the races. Did you go on the course or inside the grounds at all?"

Baxfield moistened his lips and replied, "I just went in for a minute or two, but I didn't stay. The races were over, and there was a very rough crowd."

"While you were in that crowd, Mr Baxfield, did you have your pocket picked?"

There was an expectant silence in the court as Baxfield replied in a low voice: "Yes. I lost my watch."

Again Thorndyke opened the dispatch-box, and taking out a watch (it was the one that had been labelled 3), handed it to the witness. "Is that the watch that you lost?" he asked.

Baxfield held the watch in his trembling hand and replied hesitatingly, "I believe it is, but I won't swear to it."

There was a pause. Then, in grave, impressive tones, Thorndyke said, "Now, Mr. Baxfield, I am going to ask you a question which you need not answer if you consider that by doing so you would prejudice your position in any way. That question is, When your pocket was picked, were any articles besides this watch taken from your person?

Don't hurry. Consider your answer carefully."

For some moments Baxfield remained silent, regarding Thorndyke with a wild, affrighted stare. At length he began falteringly, "I don't remember missing any thing—" and then stopped.

"Could the witness be allowed to sit down, sir?" Thorndyke asked. And when the permission had been given and a chair placed, Baxfield sat down heavily and cast a bewildered glance round the court. "I think," he said, addressing Thorndyke, "I had better tell you exactly what happened and take my chance of the consequences. When I left my uncle's house on Monday, I took a circuit through the fields and then entered Gilbert's Copse to wait for my uncle and tell him what I thought of his conduct in leaving the bulk of his property to a stranger. I struck the path that I knew my uncle would take and walked along it slowly to meet him. I did meet him—on the path, just above where he was found—and I began to say what was in my mind. But he wouldn't listen.

"He flew into a rage, and as I was standing in the middle of the path, he tried to push past me. In doing so he caught his foot in a bramble and staggered back, then he disappeared through the bushes and a few seconds after I heard a thud down below. I pulled the bushes aside and looked down into the chalk-pit, and there I saw him lying with his head all on one side. Now, I happened to know of a short cut down into the pit. It was rather a dangerous climb, but I took it to get down as quickly as possible. It was there that I dropped the cigarette-tube. When I got to my uncle I could see that he was dead. His skull was battered and his neck was broken.

"Then the devil put into my head the idea of making away with the will. But I knew that if I took the will only, suspicion would fall on me. So I took most of his valuables—the wallet, his watch and chain, his purse and his ring. The purse I emptied and threw away, and flung the ring after it. I took the will out of the wallet—it had just been dropped in loose—and put it in an inner pocket. Then I dropped the wallet and the watch and chain into my outside coat pocket.

"I struck across country, intending to make for the race-course and drop the things among the crowd, so that they might be picked up and safely carried away. But when I got there a gang of pickpockets saved me the trouble; they mobbed and hustled me and cleared my pockets of everything but my keys and the will."

"And what has become of the will?" asked Thorndyke.

"I have it here." He dipped into his breast pocket and produced a folded paper, which he handed to Thorndyke, who opened it, and having glanced at it, passed it to the coroner.

That was practically the end of the inquest. The jury decided to accept Baxfield's statement and recorded a verdict of "Death by Misadventure," leaving Baxfield to be dealt with by the proper authorities.

"An interesting and eminently satisfactory case," remarked Thorndyke, as we sat over a rather late dinner. "Essentially simple, too. The elucidation turned, as you probably noticed, on a single illuminating fact."

"I judged that it was so," said I, "though the illumination of that fact has not yet reached me."

"Well," said Thorndyke, "let us first take the general aspect of the case as it was presented by Marchmont. The first thing, of course, that struck one was that the loss of the will might easily have converted Baxfield from a minor beneficiary to the sole heir. But even if the court agreed to recognise the will, it would have to be guided by the statements of the only two men to whom its provisions were even approximately known, and Baxfield could have made any statement he pleased. It was impossible to ignore the fact that the loss of the will was very greatly to Baxfield's advantage.

"When the stolen property was discovered in Fletcher's possession it looked, at the first glance, as if the mystery of the crime were solved. But there were several serious inconsistencies. First, how came Fletcher to be in this solitary wood, remote from any railway or even road? He appeared to be a London pickpocket. When he was killed he was travelling to London by train. It seemed probable that he had come from London by train to ply his trade at the races. Then, as you know, criminological experience shows that the habitual criminal is a rigid specialist. The burglar, the coiner, the pickpocket, each keeps strictly to his own special line Now, Fletcher was a pickpocket, and had evidently been picking pockets on the race-course.

"The probabilities were against his being the original robber and in favour of his having picked the pocket of the person who robbed Harewood. But if this were so, who was that person? Once more the probabilities suggested Baxfield. There was the motive, as I have said, and further, the pocket-picking had apparently taken place on the race-course, and Baxfield was known to be a frequenter of race-courses. But again, if Baxfield were the person robbed by Fletcher, then one of the five watches was probably Baxfield's watch. Whether it was so or not might have been very difficult to prove, but here came in the single illuminating fact that I have spoken of.

"You remember that when Marchmont opened the case he mentioned that Baxfield was a manufacturer of felt hats, and Crowhurst told us that he was a sort of foreman or manager of the factory."

"Yes, I remember, now you speak of it. But what is the bearing of the fact?"

"My dear Jervis!" exclaimed Thorndyke. "Don't you see that it gave us a touchstone? Consider, now. What is a felt hat? It is just a mass of agglutinated rabbits' hair. The process of manufacture consists in blowing a jet of the more or less disintegrated hair on to a revolving steel cone which is moistened by a spray of an alcoholic solution of shellac. But, of course, a quantity of the finer and more minute particles of the broken hairs miss the cone and float about in the air. The air of the factory is thus charged with the dust of broken rabbit hairs; and this dust settles on and penetrates the clothing of the workers. But when clothing becomes charged with dust, that dust tends to accumulate in the pockets and find its way into the hollows and interstices of any object carried in those pockets.

"Thus, if one of the five watches was Baxfield's it would almost certainly show traces where this characteristic dust had crept under the bezel and settled on the dial. And so it turned out to be. When I inspected those five watches through the Coddington lens, on the dial of No. 3 I saw a quantity of dust of this character. The electrified vulcanite rod picked it all up neatly and transferred it to the slide, and under the microscope its nature was obvious. The owner of this watch was therefore, almost certainly, employed in a felt hat factory. But, of course, it was necessary to show not only the presence of rabbit hair in this watch but its absence in the others and in Fletcher's pockets; which I did.

"Then with regard to Harewood's watch. There was no rabbit hair on the dial, but there was a small quantity on the fluff from the key barrel. Now, if that rabbit hair had come from Harewood's pocket it would have been uniformly distributed through the fluff. But it was not. It was confined exclusively to the part of the fluff that was exposed. Thus it had come from some pocket other than Harewood's and the owner of that pocket was almost certainly employed in a felt hat factory, and was most probably the owner of watch No. 3.

"Then there was the cigarette-tube. Its bore was loaded with rabbit hair. But its owner had unquestionably been at the scene of the crime. There was a clear suggestion that his was the pocket in which the stolen watch had been carried and that he was the owner of watch No. 3. The problem was to piece this evidence together and prove definitely who this person was. And that I was able to do by means of a fresh item of evidence, which I acquired when I saw Baxfield at the inquest. I suppose you noticed his boots?"

"I am afraid I didn't," I had to admit.

"Well, I did. I watched his feet constantly, and when he crossed his legs I could see that he had iron toe-tips on his boots. That was what gave me confidence to push the cross-examination."

"It was certainly a rather daring cross-examination and rather irregular, too," said I.

"It was extremely irregular," Thorndyke agreed. "The coroner ought not to have permitted it. But it was all for the best. If the coroner had disallowed my questions we should have had to take criminal proceedings against Baxfield, whereas now that we have recovered the will, it is possible that no one will trouble to prosecute him."

Which, I subsequently ascertained, is what actually happened.

A Wastrel's Romance

The lingering summer twilight was fast merging into night as a solitary cyclist, whose evening-dress suit was thinly disguised by an overcoat, rode slowly along a pleasant country road. From time to time he had been overtaken and passed by a carriage, a car or a closed cab from the adjacent town, and from the festive garb of the occupants he had made shrewd guesses at their destination. His own objective was a large house, standing in somewhat extensive grounds just off the road, and the peculiar circumstances that surrounded his visit to it caused him to ride more and more slowly as he approached his goal.

Willowdale—such was the name of the house—was, tonight, witnessing a temporary revival of its past glories. For many months it had been empty and a notice-board by the gate-keeper's lodge had silently announced its forlorn state; but tonight, its rooms, their bare walls clothed in flags and draperies, their floors waxed or carpeted, would once more echo the sound of music and cheerful voices and vibrate to the tread of many feet. For on this night the spinsters of Raynesford were giving a dance; and chief amongst the spinsters was Miss Halliwell, the owner of Willowdale.

It was a great occasion. The house was large and imposing; the spinsters were many and their purses were long. The guests were numerous and distinguished, and included no less a person than Mrs. Jehu B. Chater. This was the crowning triumph of the function, for the beautiful American widow was the lion (or should we say lioness?) of the season. Her wealth was, if not beyond the dreams of avarice, at least beyond the powers of common British arithmetic, and her diamonds were, at once, the glory and the terror of her hostesses.

All these attractions notwithstanding, the cyclist approached the vicinity of Willowdale with a slowness almost hinting at reluctance;

and when, at length, a curve of the road brought the gates into view, he dismounted and halted irresolutely. He was about to do a rather risky thing, and, though by no means a man of weak nerve, he hesitated to make the plunge.

The fact is, he had not been invited.

Why, then, was he going? And how was he to gain admittance? To which questions the answer involves a painful explanation.

Augustus Bailey lived by his wits. That is the common phrase, and a stupid phrase it is. For do we not all live by our wits, if we have any? And does it need any specially brilliant wits to be a common rogue? However, such as his wits were, Augustus Bailey lived by them, and he had not hitherto made a fortune.

The present venture arose out of a conversation overheard at a restaurant table and an invitation-card carelessly laid down and adroitly covered with the menu. Augustus had accepted the invitation that he had not received (on a sheet of Hotel Cecil notepaper that he had among his collection of stationery) in the name of Geoffrey Harrington-Baillie; and the question that exercised his mind at the moment was, would he or would he not be spotted? He had trusted to the number of guests and the probable inexperience of the hostesses. He knew that the cards need not be shown, though there was the awkward ceremony of announcement.

But perhaps it wouldn't get as far as that. Probably not, if his acceptance had been detected as emanating from an uninvited stranger.

He walked slowly towards the gates with growing discomfort. Added to his nervousness as to the present were certain twinges of reminiscence. He had once held a commission in a line regiment—not for long, indeed; his "wits" had been too much for his brother officers—but there had been a time when he would have come to such a gathering as this an invited guest. Now, a common thief, he was sneaking in under a false name, with a fair prospect of being ignominiously thrown out by the servants.

As he stood hesitating, the sound of hoofs on the road was followed by the aggressive bellow of a motor-horn. The modest twinkle of carriage lamps appeared round the curve and then the glare of acetylene headlights. A man came out of the lodge and drew open the gates; and Mr. Bailey, taking his courage in both hands, boldly trundled his machine up the drive.

Half-way up—it was quite a steep incline—the car whizzed by; a large Napier filled with a bevy of young men who economized space by sitting on the backs of the seats and on one another's knees. Bailey looked at them and decided that this was his chance, and, pushing forward, he saw his bicycle safely bestowed in the empty coach-house and then hurried on to the cloak-room. The young men had arrived there before him and, as he entered, were gaily peeling off their overcoats and flinging them down on a table. Bailey followed their example, and, in his eagerness to enter the reception-room with the crowd, let his attention wander from the business of the moment, and, as he pocketed the ticket and hurried away, he failed to notice that the bewildered attendant had put his hat with another man's coat and affixed his duplicate to them both.

"Major Podbury, Captain Barker-Jones, Captain Sparker, Mr. Watson, Mr. Goldsmith, Mr. Smart, Mr. Harrington-Baillie!"

As Augustus swaggered up the room, hugging the party of officers and quaking inwardly, he was conscious that his hostesses glanced from one man to another with more than common interest.

But at that moment the footman's voice rang out, sonorous and clear—

"Mrs. Chater, Colonel Grumpier!" and, as all eyes were turned towards the new arrivals, Augustus made his bow and passed into the throng. His little game of bluff had "come off," after all.

He withdrew modestly into the more crowded portion of the room, and there took up a position where he would be shielded from the gaze of his hostesses. Presently, he reflected, they would forget him, if they had really thought about him at all, and then he would see what could be done in the way of business. He was still rather shaky, and wondered how soon it would be decent to steady his nerves with a "refresher." Meanwhile he kept a sharp look-out over the shoulders of neighbouring guests, until a movement in the crowd of guests disclosed Mrs. Chater shaking hands with the presiding spinster. Then Augustus got a most uncommon surprise.

He knew her at the first glance. He had a good memory for faces, and Mrs. Chater's face was one to remember. Well did he recall the frank and lovely American girl with whom he had danced at the regimental ball years ago. That was in the old days when he was a subaltern, and before that little affair of the pricked court-cards that brought his military career to an end. They had taken a mutual liking, he remembered, that sweet-faced Yankee maid and he had danced many dances and had sat out others, to talk mystical nonsense which, in their innocence, they had believed to be philosophy. He had never seen her since. She had come into his life and gone out of it again, and he had forgotten her name, if he had ever known it. But here she was, middle-aged now, it was true, but still beautiful and a great personage withal. And, ye gods! what diamonds! And here was he, too, a common rogue, lurking in the crowd that he might, perchance, snatch a pendant or "pinch" a loose brooch.

Perhaps she might recognise him. Why not? He had recognised her. But that would never do. And thus reflecting, Mr. Bailey slipped out to stroll on the lawn and smoke a cigarette. Another man, somewhat older than himself, was pacing to and fro thoughtfully, glancing from time to time through the open windows into the brilliantly-lighted rooms. When they had passed once or twice, the stranger halted and addressed him.

"This is the best place on a night like this," he remarked; "it's getting hot inside already. But perhaps you're keen on dancing."

"Not so keen as I used to be," replied Bailey; and then, observing the hungry look that the other man was bestowing on his cigarette, he produced his case and offered it.

"Thanks awfully!" exclaimed the stranger, pouncing with avidity on the open case. "Good Samaritan, by Jove. Left my case in my overcoat. Hadn't the cheek to ask, though I was starving for a smoke." He inhaled luxuriously, and, blowing out a cloud of smoke, resumed: "These chits seem to be running the show pretty well, h'm? Wouldn't take it for an empty house to look at it, would you?"

"I have hardly seen it," said Bailey; "only just come, you know."

"We'll have a look round, if you like," said the genial stranger, "when we've finished our smoke, that is. Have a drink too; may cool us a bit. Know many people here?"

"Not a soul," replied Bailey. "My, hostess doesn't seem to have turned up."

"Well, that's easily remedied," said the stranger. "My daughter's one of the spinsters—Granby, my name; when we've had a drink, I'll make her find you a partner—that is, if you care for the light fantastic."

"I should like a dance or two," said Bailey, "though I'm getting a bit past it now, I suppose. Still, it doesn't do to chuck up the sponge prematurely."

"Certainly not," Granby agreed jovially; "a man's as young as he feels. Well, come and have a drink and then we'll hunt up my little girl." The two men flung away the stumps of their cigarettes and headed for the refreshments.

The spinsters' champagne was light, but it was well enough if taken in sufficient quantity; a point to which Augustus? and Granby too—paid judicious attention; and when he had supplemented the wine with a few sandwiches, Mr. Bailey felt in notably better spirits. For, to tell the truth, his diet, of late, had been somewhat meagre. Miss Granby, when found, proved to be a blonde and guileless "flapper" of some seventeen summers, childishly eager to play her part of hostess with due dignity; and presently Bailey found himself gyrating through the eddying crowd in company with a comely matron of thirty or thereabouts.

The sensations that this novel experience aroused rather took him by surprise. For years past he had been living a precarious life of mean and sordid shifts that oscillated between mere shabby trickery and downright crime; now conducting a paltry swindle just inside the pale of the law, and now, when hard pressed, descending to actual theft; consorting with shady characters, swindlers and knaves and scurvy rogues like himself; gambling, borrowing, cadging and, if need be, stealing, and always slinking abroad with an apprehensive eye upon "the man in blue."

And now, amidst the half-forgotten surroundings, once so familiar; the gaily-decorated rooms, the rhythmic music, the twinkle of jewels, the murmur of gliding feet and the rustle of costly gowns, the moving vision of honest gentlemen and fair ladies; the shameful years seemed to drop away and leave him to take up the thread of his life where it had snapped so disastrously. After all, these were his own people. The seedy knaves in whose steps he had walked of late were but aliens met by the way.

He surrendered his partner, in due course, with regret—which was mutual—to an inarticulate subaltern, and was meditating another pilgrimage to the refreshment-room, when he felt a light touch upon his arm. He turned swiftly. A touch on the arm meant more to him than to some men. But it was no wooden-faced plain-clothes man that he confronted; it was only a lady. In short, it was Mrs. Chater, smiling nervously and a little abashed by her own boldness.

"I expect you've forgotten me," she began apologetically, but Augustus interrupted her with an eager disclaimer.

"Of course I haven't," he said; "though I have forgotten your name, but I remember that Portsmouth dance as well as if it were yesterday; at least one incident in it—the only one that was worth remembering. I've often hoped that I might meet you again, and now, at last, it has happened."

"It's nice of you to remember," she rejoined. "I've often and often thought of that evening and all the wonderful things that we talked about. You were a nice boy then; I wonder what you are like now. What a long time ago it is!"

"Yes," Augustus agreed gravely, "it is a long time. I know it myself; but when I look at you, it seems as if it could only have been last season."

"Oh, fie!" she exclaimed. "You are not simple as you used to be. You didn't flatter then; but perhaps there wasn't the need." She spoke with gentle reproach, but her pretty face flushed with pleasure nevertheless, and there was a certain wistfulness in the tone of her concluding sentence.

"I wasn't flattering," Augustus replied, quite sincerely; "I knew you directly you entered the room and marvelled that Time had been so gentle with you. He hasn't been as kind to me."

"No. You have gotten a few grey hairs, I see, but after all, what are grey hairs to a man? Just the badges of rank, like the crown on your collar or the lace on your cuffs, to mark the steps of your promotion—for I guess you'll be a colonel by now."

"No," Augustus answered quickly, with a faint flush, "I left the army some years ago."

"My! what a pity!" exclaimed Mrs. Chater. "You must tell me all about it—but not now. My partner will be looking for me. We will sit out a dance and have a real gossip. But I've forgotten your name—never could recall it, in fact, though that didn't prevent me from remembering you; but, as our dear W. S. remarks, 'What's in a name—'"

"Ah, indeed," said Mr. Harrington-Baillie; and apropos of that sentiment, he added: "Mine is Rowland—Captain Rowland. You may remember it now."

Mrs. Chater did not, however, and said so. "Will number six do?" she asked, opening her programme; and, when Augustus had assented, she entered his provisional name, remarking complacently: "We'll sit out and have a right-down good talk, and you shall tell me all about yourself and if you still think the same about free-will and personal responsibility. You had very lofty ideals, I remember, in those days, and I hope you have still. But one's ideals get rubbed down rather faint in the friction of life. Don't you think so?"

"Yes, I am afraid you're right," Augustus assented gloomily. "The wear and tear of life soon fetches the gilt off the gingerbread. Middle

32

age is apt to find us a bit patchy, not to say naked."

"Oh, don't be pessimistic," said Mrs. Chater; "that is the attitude of the disappointed idealist, and I am sure you have no reason, really, to be disappointed in yourself. But I must run away now. Think over all the things you have to tell me, and don't forget that it is number six." With a bright smile and a friendly nod she sailed away, a vision of glittering splendour, compared with which Solomon in all his glory was a mere matter of commonplace bullion.

The interview, evidently friendly and familiar, between the unknown guest and the famous American widow had by no means passed unnoticed; and in other circumstances, Bailey might have endeavoured to profit by the reflected glory that enveloped him. But he was not in search of notoriety; and the same evasive instinct that had led him to sink Mr. Harrington-Baillie in Captain Rowland, now advised him to withdraw his dual personality from the vulgar gaze. He had come here on very definite business. For the hundredth time he was "stony-broke," and it was the hope of picking up some "unconsidered trifles" that had brought him.

But, somehow, the atmosphere of the place had proved unfavourable. Either opportunities were lacking or he failed to seize them. In any case, the game pocket that formed an unconventional feature of his dress-coat was still empty, and it looked as if a pleasant evening and a good supper were all that he was likely to get. Nevertheless, be his conduct never so blameless, the fact remained that he was an uninvited guest, liable at any moment to be ejected as an impostor, and his recognition by the widow had not rendered this possibility any the more remote.

He strayed out onto the lawn, whence the grounds fell away on all sides. But there were other guests there, cooling themselves after the last dance, and the light from the rooms streamed through the windows, illuminating their figures, and among them, that of the too-companionable Granby. Augustus quickly drew away from the lighted area, and, chancing upon a narrow path, strolled away along it in the direction of a copse or shrubbery that he saw ahead.

Presently he came to an ivy-covered arch, lighted by one or two fairy lamps, and, passing through this, he entered a winding path, bordered by trees and shrubs and but faintly lighted by an occasional coloured lamp suspended from a branch.

Already he was quite clear of the crowd; indeed, the deserted condition of the pleasant retreat rather surprised him, until he reflected that to couples desiring seclusion there were whole ranges of untenanted rooms and galleries available in the empty house.

The path sloped gently downwards for some distance; then came a long flight of rustic steps and, at the bottom, a seat between two trees. In front of the seat the path extended in a straight line, forming a narrow terrace; on the right the ground sloped up steeply towards the lawn; on the left it fell away still more steeply towards the encompassing wall of the grounds; and on both sides it was covered with trees and shrubs.

Bailey sat down on the seat to think over the account of himself that he should present to Mrs. Chater. It was a comfortable seat, built into the trunk of an elm, which formed one end and part of the back. He leaned against the tree, and, taking out his silver case, selected a cigarette. But it remained unlighted between his fingers as he sat and meditated upon his unsatisfactory past and the melancholy tale of what might have been. Fresh from the atmosphere of refined opulence that pervaded the dancing-rooms, the throng of well-groomed men and dainty women, his mind travelled back to his sordid little flat in Bermondsey, encompassed by poverty and squalor, jostled by lofty factories, grimy with the smoke of the river and the reek from the great chimneys. It was a hideous contrast. Verily the way of the transgressor was not strewn with flowers.

At that point in his meditations he caught the sound of voices and footsteps on the path above and rose to walk on along the path. He did not wish to be seen wandering alone in the shrubbery. But now a woman's laugh sounded from somewhere down the path. There were people approaching that way too. He put the cigarette back in the case and stepped round behind the seat, intending to retreat in that direction, but here the path ended, and beyond was nothing but a rugged slope down to the wall thickly covered with bushes. And while he was hesitating, the sound of feet descending the steps and the rustle of a woman's dress left him to choose between staying where he was or coming out to confront the newcomers. He chose the former, drawing up close behind the tree to wait until they should have passed on.

But they were not going to pass on. One of them—a woman—sat down on the seat, and then a familiar voice smote on his ear.

"I guess I'll rest here quietly for a while; this tooth of mine is aching terribly; and, see here, I want you to go and fetch me something. Take this ticket to the cloak-room and tell the woman to give you my little velvet bag. You'll find in it a bottle of chloroform and a packet of cotton-wool."

"But I can't leave you here all alone, Mrs. Chater," her partner expostulated.

"I'm not hankering for society just now," said Mrs. Chater. "I want that chloroform. Just you hustle off and fetch it, like a good boy. Here's the ticket."

The young officer's footsteps retreated rapidly, and the voices of the couple advancing along the path grew louder. Bailey, cursing the chance that had placed him in his ridiculous and uncomfortable position, heard them approach and pass on up the steps; and then all was silent, save for an occasional moan from Mrs. Chater and the measured creaking of the seat as she rocked uneasily to and fro. But the young man was uncommonly prompt in the discharge of his mission, and in a very few minutes Bailey heard him approaching at a run along the path above and then bounding down the steps.

"Now I call that real good of you," said the widow gratefully. "You must have run like the wind. Cut the string of the packet and then leave me to wrestle with this tooth."

"But I can't leave you here all—"

"Yes, you can," interrupted Mrs. Chater. "There won't be any one about—the next dance is a waltz. Besides, you must go and find your partners."

"Well, if you'd really rather be alone," the subaltern began; but Mrs. Chater interrupted him.

"Of course I would, when I'm fixing up my teeth. Now go along, and a thousand thanks for your kindness."

With mumbled protestations the young officer slowly retired, and Bailey heard his reluctant feet ascending the steps. Then a deep silence fell on the place in which the rustle of paper and the squeak of a withdrawn cork seemed loud and palpable. Bailey had turned with his face towards the tree, against which he leaned with his lips parted scarcely daring to breathe. He cursed himself again and again for having thus entrapped himself for no tangible reason, and longed to get away. But there was no escape now without betraying himself. He must wait for the woman to go.

Suddenly, beyond the edge of the tree, a hand appeared holding an open packet of cotton-wool. It laid the wool down on the seat, and, pinching off a fragment, rolled it into a tiny ball. The fingers of the hand were encircled by rings, its wrist enclosed by a broad bracelet; and from rings and bracelet the light of the solitary fairy-lamp, that hung from a branch of the tree, was reflected in prismatic sparks. The hand was withdrawn and Bailey stared dreamily at the square pad of cotton-wool. Then the hand came again into view. This time it held a small phial which it laid softly on the seat, setting the cork beside it. And again the light flashed in many-coloured scintillations from the encrusting gems.

Bailey's knees began to tremble, and a chilly moisture broke out upon his forehead.

The hand drew back, but, as it vanished, Bailey moved his head silently until his face emerged from behind the tree. The woman was leaning back, her head resting against the trunk only a few inches away from his face. The great stones of the tiara flashed in his very eyes. Over her shoulder, he could even see the gorgeous pendant, rising and falling on her bosom with ever-changing fires; and both her raised hands were a mass of glitter and sparkle, only the deeper and richer for the subdued light.

His heart throbbed with palpable blows that drummed aloud in his ears. The sweat trickled clammily down his face, and he clenched his teeth to keep them from chattering. An agony of horror—of deadly fear—was creeping over him? a terror of the dreadful impulse that was stealing away his reason and his will.

The silence was profound. The woman's soft breathing, the creak of her bodice, were plainly—grossly—audible; and he checked his own breath until he seemed on the verge of suffocation.

Of a sudden through the night air was borne faintly the dreamy music of a waltz. The dance had begun. The distant sound but deepened the sense of solitude in this deserted spot.

Bailey listened intently. He yearned to escape from the invisible force that seemed to be clutching at his wrists, and dragging him forward inexorably to his doom.

He gazed down at the woman with a horrid fascination. He struggled to draw back out of sight—and struggled in vain.

Then, at last, with a horrible, stealthy deliberation, a clammy, shaking hand crept forward towards the seat. Without a sound it grasped the wool, and noiselessly, slowly drew back. Again it stole forth. The fingers twined snakily around the phial, lifted it from the seat and carried it back into the shadow.

After a few seconds it reappeared and softly replaced the bottle—now half empty. There was a brief pause. The measured cadences of the waltz stole softly through the quiet night and seemed to keep time with the woman's breathing. Other sound there was none. The place was wrapped in the silence of the grave.

Suddenly, from the hiding-place, Bailey leaned forward over the back of the seat. The pad of cotton-wool was in his hand.

The woman was now leaning back as if dozing, and her hands rested in her lap. There was a swift movement. The pad was pressed against her face and her head dragged back against the chest of the invisible assailant. A smothered gasp burst from her hidden lips as her hands flew up to clutch at the murderous arm; and then came a frightful struggle, made even more frightful by the gay and costly trappings of the writhing victim. And still there was hardly a sound; only muffled gasps, the rustle of silk, the creaking of the seat, the clink of the falling bottle and, afar off, with dreadful irony, the dreamy murmur of the waltz.

The struggle was but brief. Quite suddenly the jewelled hands dropped, the head lay resistless on the crumpled shirt-front, and the body, now limp and inert, began to slip forward off the seat. Bailey, still grasping the passive head, climbed over the back of the seat and, as the woman slid gently to the ground, he drew away the pad and stooped over her. The struggle was over now; the mad fury of the moment was passing swiftly into the chill of mortal fear.

He stared with incredulous horror into the swollen face, but now so comely, the sightless eyes that but a little while since had smiled into his with such kindly recognition.

He had done this! He, the sneaking wastrel, discarded of all the world, to whom this sweet woman had held out the hand of friendship. She had cherished his memory, when to all others he was sunk deep under the waters of oblivion. And he had killed her—for to his ear no breath of life seemed to issue from those purple lips.

A sudden hideous compunction for this irrevocable thing that he had done surged through him, and he stood up clutching at his damp hair with a hoarse cry that was like the cry of the damned.

The jewels passed straightaway out of his consciousness. Everything was forgotten now but the horror of this unspeakable thing that he had done. Remorse incurable and haunting fear were all that were left to him.

The sound of voices far away along the path aroused him, and the vague horror that possessed him materialized into abject bodily fear. He lifted the limp body to the edge of the path and let it slip down the steep declivity among the bushes. A soft, shuddering sigh came from the parted lips as the body turned over, and he paused a moment to listen. But there was no other sound of life. Doubtless that sigh was only the result of the passive movement.

Again he stood for an instant as one in a dream, gazing at the huddled shape half hidden by the bushes, before he climbed back to the path; and even then he looked back once more, but now she was hidden from sight. And, as the voices drew nearer, he turned, and ran up the rustic steps.

As he came out on the edge of the lawn the music ceased, and, almost immediately, a stream of people issued from the house. Shaken as he was, Bailey yet had wits enough left to know that his clothes and hair were disordered and that his appearance must be wild. Accordingly he avoided the dancers, and, keeping to the margin of the lawn, made his way to the cloakroom by the least frequented route. If he had dared, he would have called in at the refreshment-room, for he was deadly faint and his limbs shook as he walked. But a haunting fear pursued him and, indeed, grew from moment to moment. He found himself already listening for the rumour of the inevitable discovery.

He staggered into the cloakroom, and, flinging his ticket down on the table, dragged out his watch. The attendant looked at him curiously and, pausing with the ticket in his hand, asked sympathetically: "Not feeling very well, sir?"

"No," said Bailey. "So beastly hot in there."

"You ought to have a glass of champagne, sir, before you start," said the man.

"No time," replied Bailey, holding out a shaky hand for his coat. "Shall lose my train if I'm not sharp."

At this hint the attendant reached down the coat and hat, holding up the former for its owner to slip his arms into the sleeves. But Bailey snatched it from him, and, flinging it over his arm, put on his hat and hurried away to the coach-house. Here, again, the attendant stared at him in astonishment, which was not lessened when Bailey, declining his offer to help him on with his coat, bundled the latter under his arm, clicked the lever of the "variable" on to the ninety gear, sprang onto the machine and whirled away down the steep drive, a grotesque vision of flying coat-tails.

"You haven't lit your lamp, sir," roared the attendant; but Bailey's ears were deaf to all save the clamour of the expected pursuit.

Fortunately the drive entered the road obliquely, or Bailey must have been flung into the opposite hedge. As it was, the machine, rushing down the slope, flew out into the road with terrific velocity; nor did its speed diminish then, for its rider, impelled by mortal terror, trod the pedals with the fury of a madman. And still, as the machine whizzed along the dark and silent road, his ears were strained to catch the clatter of hoofs or the throb of a motor from behind.

He knew the country well, in fact, as a precaution, he had cycled over the district only the day before; and he was ready, at any suspicious sound, to slip down any of the lanes or byways, secure of finding his way. But still he sped on, and still no sound from the rear came to tell him of the dread discovery.

When he had ridden about three miles, he came to the foot of a steep hill. Here he had to dismount and push his machine up the incline, which he did at such speed that he arrived at the top quite breathless. Before mounting again he determined to put on his coat, for his appearance was calculated to attract attention, if nothing more. It was only half-past eleven, and presently he would pass through the streets of a small town. Also he would light his lamp. It would be fatal to be stopped by a patrol or rural constable.

Having lit his lamp and hastily put on his coat he once more listened intently, looking back over the country that was darkly visible from the summit of the hill. No moving lights were to be seen, no ringing hoofs or throbbing engines to be heard, and, turning to mount, he instinctively felt in his overcoat pocket for his gloves.

A pair of gloves came out in his hand, but he was instantly conscious that they were not his. A silk muffler was there also; a white one. But his muffler was black.

With a sudden shock of terror he thrust his hand into the ticket-pocket, where he had put his latch-key. There was no key there; only an amber cigar-holder, which he had never seen before. He stood for a few moments in utter consternation. He had taken the wrong coat. Then he had left his own coat behind. A cold sweat of fear broke out afresh on his face as he realised this. His Yale latch-key was in its pocket; not that that mattered very much. He had a duplicate at home, and, as to getting in, well, he knew his own outside door and his tool-bag contained one or two trifles not usually found in cyclists' tool-bags. The question was whether that coat contained anything that could disclose his identity. And then suddenly he remembered, with a gasp of relief, that he had carefully turned the pockets out before starting.

No; once let him attain the sanctuary of his grimy little flat, wedged in as it was between the great factories by the river-side, and he would be safe: safe from everything but the horror of himself, and the haunting vision of a jewelled figure huddled up in a silken heap beneath the bushes.

With a last look round he mounted his machine, and, driving it over the brow of the hill, swept away into the darkness.

PART 2. MUNERA PULVERIS
(Related by Christopher Jervis, M.D.)

It is one of the drawbacks of medicine as a profession that one is never rid of one's responsibilities. The merchant, the lawyer, the civil servant, each at the appointed time locks up his desk, puts on his hat and goes forth a free man with an interval of uninterrupted leisure before him. Not so the doctor. Whether at work or at play, awake or asleep, he is the servant of humanity, at the instant disposal of friend or stranger alike whose need may make the necessary claim.

When I agreed to accompany my wife to the spinsters' dance at Raynesford, I imagined that, for that evening, at least, I was definitely off duty; and in that belief I continued until the conclusion of the eighth dance. To be quite truthful, I was not sorry when the delusion was shattered. My last partner was a young lady of a slanginess of speech that verged on the inarticulate. Now it is not easy to exchange ideas in "pidgin" English; and the conversation of a person to whom all things are either "ripping" or "rotten" is apt to lack subtlety. In fact, I was frankly bored; and, reflecting on the utility of the humble sandwich as an aid to conversation, I was about to entice my partner to the refreshment-room when I felt someone pluck at my sleeve. I turned quickly and looked into the anxious and rather frightened face of my wife.

"Miss Halliwell is looking for you," she said. "A lady has been taken ill. Will you come and see what is the matter?" She took my arm and, when I had made my apologies to my partner, she hurried me on to the lawn.

"It's a mysterious affair," my wife continued. "The sick lady is a Mrs. Chater, a very wealthy American widow. Edith Halliwell and Major Podbury found her lying in the shrubbery all alone and unable to give any account of herself. Poor Edith is dreadfully upset. She doesn't know what to think."

"What do you mean?" I began; but at this moment Miss Halliwell, who was waiting by an ivy-covered rustic arch, espied us and ran forward.

"Oh, do hurry, please, Dr. Jervis," she exclaimed; "such a shocking thing has happened. Has Juliet told you?" Without waiting for an answer, she darted through the arch and preceded us along a narrow path at the curious, flat-footed, shambling trot common to most adult women. Presently we descended a flight of rustic steps which brought us to a seat, from whence extended a straight path cut like a miniature terrace on a steep slope, with a high bank rising to the right and declivity falling away to the left. Down in the hollow, his head and shoulders appearing above the bushes, was a man holding in his hand a fairy-lamp that he had apparently taken down from a tree. I climbed down to him, and, as I came round the bushes, I perceived a richly-dressed woman lying huddled on the ground.

"She was not completely insensible, for she moved slightly at my approach, muttering a few words in thick, indistinct accents. I took the lamp from the man, whom I assumed to be Major Podbury, and, as he delivered it to me with a significant glance and a faint lift of the eyebrows, I understood Miss Halliwell's agitation. Indeed—for one horrible moment I thought that she was right—that the prostrate woman was intoxicated. But when I approached nearer, the flickering light of the lamp made visible a square reddened patch on her face, like the impression of a mustard plaster, covering the nose and mouth; and then I scented mischief of a more serious kind.

"We had better carry her up to the seat," I said, handing the lamp to Miss Halliwell. "Then we can consider moving her to the house." The major and I lifted the helpless woman and, having climbed cautiously up to the path, laid her on the seat.

"What is it, Dr. Jervis?" Miss Halliwell whispered.

"I can't say at the moment," I replied; "but it's not what you feared."

"Thank God for that!" was her fervent rejoinder. "It would have been a shocking scandal."

I took the dim lamp and once more bent over the half-conscious woman.

Her appearance puzzled me not a little. She looked like a person recovering from an anaesthetic, but the square red patch on her face, recalling, as it did, the Burke murders, rather suggested suffocation. As I was thus reflecting, the light of the lamp fell on a white object lying on the ground behind the seat, and holding the lamp forward, I saw that it was a square pad of cotton-wool. The coincidence of its shape and size with that of the red patch on the woman's face instantly struck me, and I stooped down to pick it up; and then I saw, lying under the seat, a small bottle. This also I picked up and held in the lamplight. It was a one-ounce phial, quite empty, and was labelled "Methylated Chloroform." Here seemed to be a complete explanation of the thick utterance and drunken aspect; but it was an explanation that required, in its turn, to be explained. Obviously no robbery had been committed, for the woman literally glittered with diamonds. Equally obviously she had not administered the chloroform to herself.

There was nothing for it but to carry her indoors and await her further recovery, so, with the major's help, we conveyed her through the shrubbery and kitchen garden to a side door, and deposited her on a sofa in a half-furnished room.

Here, under the influence of water dabbed on her face and the plentiful use of smelling salts, she quickly revived, and was soon able to give an intelligible account of herself.

The chloroform and cotton-wool were her own. She had used them for an aching tooth; and she was sitting alone on the seat with the bottle and the wool beside her when the incomprehensible thing had happened. Without a moment's warning a hand had come from behind her and pressed the pad of wool over her nose and mouth. The wool was saturated with chloroform, and she had lost consciousness almost immediately.

"You didn't see the person, then?" I asked.

"No, but I know he was in evening dress, because I felt my head against his shirt-front."

"Then," said I, "he is either here still or he has been to the cloak-room. He couldn't have left the place without an overcoat."

"No, by Jove!" exclaimed the major; "that's true. I'll go and make inquiries." He strode away all agog, and I, having satisfied myself that Mrs. Chater could be left safely, followed him almost immediately.

I made my way straight to the cloakroom, and here I found the major and one or two of his brother officers putting on their coats in a flutter of gleeful excitement.

"He's gone," said Podbury, struggling frantically into his overcoat; "went off nearly an hour ago on a bicycle. Seemed in a deuce of a stew, the attendant says, and no wonder. We're goin' after him in our car. Care to join the hunt?"

"No, thanks. I must stay with the patient. But how do you know you're after the right man?"

"Isn't any other. Only one Johnnie's left. Besides—here, confound it! you've given me the wrong coat!" He tore off the garment and handed it back to the attendant, who regarded it with an expression of dismay.

"Are you sure, sir?" he asked.

"Perfectly," said the major. "Come, hurry up, my man."

"I'm afraid, sir," said the attendant, "that the gentleman who has gone has taken your coat. They were on the same peg, I know. I am very sorry, sir."

The major was speechless with wrath. What the devil was the good of being sorry; and how the deuce was he to get his coat back—

"But," I interposed, "if the stranger has got your coat, then this coat must be his."

"I know," said Podbury; "but I don't want his beastly coat."

"No," I replied, "but it may be useful for identification."

This appeared to afford the bereaved officer little consolation, but as the car was now ready, he bustled away, and I, having directed the man to put the coat away in a safe place, went back to my patient.

Mrs. Chater was by now fairly recovered, and had developed a highly vindictive interest in her late assailant. She even went so far as to regret that he had not taken at least some of her diamonds, so that robbery might have been added to the charge of attempted murder, and expressed the earnest hope that the officers would not be foolishly gentle in their treatment of him when they caught him.

"By the way, Dr. Jervis," said Miss Halliwell, "I think I ought to mention a rather curious thing that happened in connection with this dance. We received an acceptance from a Mr. Harrington-Baillie, who wrote from the Hotel Cecil. Now I am certain that no such name was proposed by any of the spinsters."

"But didn't you ask them?" I inquired.

"Well, the fact is," she replied, "that one of them, Miss Waters, had to go abroad suddenly, and we had not got her address; and as it was possible that she might have invited him, I did not like to move in the matter. I am very sorry I didn't now. We may have let in a regular criminal? though why he should have wanted to murder Mrs. Chater I cannot imagine."

It was certainly a mysterious affair, and the mystery was in no wise dispelled by the return of the search party an hour later. It seemed that the bicycle had been tracked for a couple of miles towards London, but then, at the cross-roads, the tracks had become hopelessly mixed with the impressions of other machines and the officers, after cruising about vaguely for a while, had given up the hunt and returned.

"You see, Mrs. Chater," Major Podbury explained apologetically, "the fellow must have had a good hour's start, and that would have brought him pretty close to London."

"Do you mean to tell me," exclaimed Mrs. Chater, regarding the major with hardly-concealed contempt, "that that villain has got off scot-free?"

"Looks rather like it," replied Podbury, "but if I were you I should get the man's description from the attendants who saw him and go up to Scotland Yard tomorrow. They may know the Johnny there, and they may even recognise the coat if you take it with you."

"That doesn't seem very likely," said Mrs. Chater, and it certainly did not; but since no better plan could be suggested the lady decided to adopt it; and I supposed that I had heard the last of the matter.

In this, however, I was mistaken. On the following day, just before noon, as I was drowsily considering the points in a brief dealing with a question of survivorship, while Thorndyke drafted his weekly lecture, a smart *rat-tat* at the door of our chambers announced a visitor. I rose wearily—I had had only four hours' sleep—and opened the door, whereupon there sailed into the room no less a person than Mrs. Chater, followed by Superintendent Miller, with a grin on his face and a brown-paper parcel under his arm.

The lady was not in the best of tempers, though wonderfully lively and alert considering the severe shock that she had suffered so recently, and her disapproval of Miller was frankly obvious.

"Dr. Jervis has probably told you about the attempt to murder me last night," she said, when I had introduced her to my colleague. "Well, now, will you believe it? I have been to the police, I have given them a description of the murderous villain, and I have even shown them the very coat that he wore, and they tell me that nothing can be done. That, in short, this scoundrel must be allowed to go his way free and unmolested."

"You will observe, doctor," said Miller, "that this lady has given us a description that would apply to fifty *per cent.* of the middle-class men of the United Kingdom, and has shown us a coat without a single identifying mark of any kind on it, and expects us to lay our hands on the owner without a solitary clue to guide us. Now we are not sorcerers at the Yard; we're only policemen. So I have taken the liberty of referring Mrs. Chater to you." He grinned maliciously and laid the parcel on the table.

"And what do you want me to do?" Thorndyke asked quietly.

"Why sir," said Miller, "there is a coat. In the pockets were a pair of gloves, a muffler, a box of matches, a tram-ticket and a Yale key. Mrs. Chater would like to know whose coat it is." He untied the parcel with his eye cocked at our rather disconcerted client, and Thorndyke watched him with a faint smile.

"This is very kind of you, Miller," said he, "but I think a clairvoyant would be more to your purpose."

The superintendent instantly dropped his facetious manner.

"Seriously, sir," he said, "I should be glad if you would take a look at the coat. We have absolutely nothing to go on, and yet we don't want to give up the case. I have gone through it most thoroughly and can't find any clue to guide us. Now I know that nothing escapes you, and perhaps you might notice something that I have overlooked; something that would give us a hint where to start on, our inquiry. Couldn't you turn the microscope on it, for instance?" he added, with a deprecating smile.

Thorndyke reflected, with an inquisitive eye on the coat. I saw that the problem was not without its attractions to him; and when the lady seconded Miller's request with persuasive eagerness, the inevitable consequence followed.

"Very well," he said. "Leave the coat with me for an hour or so and I will look it over. I am afraid there is not the remotest chance of our learning anything from it, but even so, the examination will have done no harm. Come back at two o'clock; I shall be ready to report my failure by then."

He bowed our visitors out and, returning to the table, looked down with a quizzical smile on the coat and the large official envelope containing articles from the pockets.

"And what does my learned brother suggest?" he asked, looking up at me.

"I should look at the tram-ticket first," I replied, "and then—well, Miller's suggestion wasn't such a bad one; to explore the surface with the microscope."

"I think we will take the latter measure first," said he. "The tram-ticket might create a misleading bias. A man may take a tram anywhere, whereas the indoor dust on a man's coat appertains mostly to a definite locality."

"Yes," I replied; "but the information that it yields is excessively vague."

"That is true," he agreed, taking up the coat and envelope to carry them to the laboratory, "and yet, you know, Jervis, as I have often pointed out, the evidential value of dust is apt to be under-estimated. The naked-eye appearances? which are the normal appearances—are misleading. Gather the dust, say, from a table-top, and what have you? A fine powder of a characterless grey, just like any other dust from any other table-top. But, under the microscope, this grey powder is resolved into recognisable fragments of definite substances, which fragments may often be traced with certainty to the masses from which they have been detached. But you know all this as well as I do."

"I quite appreciate the value of dust as evidence in certain circumstances," I replied, "but surely the information that could be gathered from dust on the coat of an unknown man must be too general to be of any use in tracing the owner."

"I am afraid you are right," said Thorndyke, laying the coat on the laboratory bench; "but we shall soon see, if Polton will let us have his patent dust-extractor."

The little apparatus to which my colleague referred was the invention of our ingenious laboratory assistant, and resembled in principle the "vacuum cleaners" used for restoring carpets. It had, however, one special feature: the receiver was made to admit a microscope-slide, and on this the dust-laden air was delivered from a jet.

The "extractor" having been clamped to the bench by its proud inventor, and a wetted slide introduced into the receiver, Thorndyke applied the nozzle of the instrument to the collar of the coat while Polton worked the pump. The slide was then removed and, another having been substituted, the nozzle was applied to the right sleeve near the shoulder, and the exhauster again worked by Polton. By repeating this process, half-a-dozen slides were obtained charged with dust from different parts of the garment, and then, setting up our respective microscopes, we proceeded to examine the samples.

A very brief inspection showed me that this dust contained matter not usually met with—at any rate, in appreciable quantities. There were, of course, the usual fragments of wool, cotton and other fibres derived from clothing and furniture, particles of straw, husk, hair, various mineral particles and, in fact, the ordinary constituents of dust from clothing. But, in addition to these, and in much greater quantity, were a number of other bodies, mostly of vegetable origin and presenting well-defined characters in considerable variety, and especially abundant were various starch granules.

I glanced at Thorndyke and observed he was already busy with a pencil and a slip of paper, apparently making a list of the objects visible in the field of the microscope. I hastened to follow his example, and for a time we worked on in silence. At length my colleague leaned back in his chair and read over his list.

"This is a highly interesting collection, Jervis," he remarked. "What do you find on your slides out of the ordinary?"

"I have quite a little museum here," I replied, referring to my list. "There is, of course, chalk from the road at Raynesford. In addition to this I find various starches, principally wheat and rice, especially rice, fragments of the cortices of several seeds, several different stone-cells, some yellow masses that look like turmeric, black pepper resin-cells, one 'port wine' pimento cell, and one or two particles of graphite."

"Graphite!" exclaimed Thorndyke. "I have found no graphite, but I have found traces of cocoa—spiral vessels and starch grains—and of hops—one fragment of leaf and several lupulin glands. May I see the graphite?"

I passed him the slide and he examined it with keen interest. "Yes," he said, "this is undoubtedly graphite, and no less than six particles of it. We had better go over the coat systematically. You see the importance of this?"

"I see that this is evidently factory dust and that it may fix a locality, but I don't see that it will carry us any farther."

"Don't forget that we have a touchstone," said he; and, as I raised my eyebrows inquiringly, he added, "The Yale latchkey. If we can narrow the locality down sufficiently, Miller can make a tour of the front doors."

"But can we?" I asked incredulously. "I doubt it."

"We can try," answered Thorndyke. "Evidently some of the substances are distributed over the entire coat, inside and out, while others, such as the graphite, are present only on certain parts. We must locate those parts exactly and then consider what this special distribution means." He rapidly sketched out on a sheet of paper a rough diagram of the coat, marking each part with a distinctive letter, and then, taking a number of labelled slides, he wrote a single letter on each. The samples of dust taken on the slides could thus be easily referred to the exact spots whence they had been obtained.

Once more we set to work with the microscope, making, now and again, an addition to our lists of discoveries, and, at the end of nearly an hour's strenuous search, every slide had been examined and the lists compared.

"The net result of the examination," said Thorndyke, "is this. The entire coat, inside and out, is evenly powdered with the following substances: Rice-starch in abundance, wheat-starch in less abundance, and smaller quantities of the starches of ginger, pimento and cinnamon; bast fibre of cinnamon, various seed cortices, stone-cells of pimento, cinnamon, cassia and black pepper, with other fragments of similar origin, such as resin-cells and ginger pigment—not turmeric. In addition there are, on the right shoulder and sleeve, traces of cocoa and hops, and on the back below the shoulders a few fragments of graphite. Those are the data; and now, what are the inferences? Remember this is not mere surface dust, but the accumulation of months, beaten into the cloth by repeated brushing—dust that nothing but a vacuum apparatus could extract."

"Evidently," I said, "the particles that are all over the coat represent dust that is floating in the air of the place where the coat habitually hangs. The graphite has obviously been picked up from a seat and the cocoa and hops from some factories that the man passes frequently, though I don't see why they are on the right side only."

"That is a question of time," said Thorndyke, "and incidentally throws some light on our friend's habits. Going from home, he passes the factories on his right; returning home, he passes them on his left, but they have then stopped work. However, the first group of substances is the more important as they indicate the locality of his dwelling—for he is clearly not a workman or factory employee. Now rice-starch, wheat-starch and a group of substances collectively designated 'spices' suggest a rice-mill, a flour-mill and a spice factory. Polton, may I trouble you for the Post Office Directory?"

He turned over the leaves of the "Trades" section and resumed: "I see there are four rice-mills in London, of which the largest is Carbutt's at Dockhead. Let us look at the spice-factories." He again turned over the leaves and read down the list of names. "There are six spice-grinders in London," said he. "One of them, Thomas Williams & Co., is at Dockhead. None of the others is near any rice-mill. The next question is as to the flour-mill. Let us see. Here are the names of several flour millers, but none of them is near either a rice-mill or a spice-grinder, with one exception: Seth Taylor's, St. Saviour's Flour Mills, Dockhead."

"This is really becoming interesting," said I.

"It has become interesting," Thorndyke retorted. "You observe that at Dockhead we find the peculiar combination of factories necessary to produce the composite dust in which this coat has hung; and the directory shows us that this particular combination exists nowhere else in London. Then the graphite, the cocoa and the hops tend to confirm the other suggestions. They all appertain to industries of the locality.

"The trams which pass Dockhead, also, to my knowledge, pass at no great distance from the black-lead works of Pearce Duff & Co. in Rouel Road, and will probably collect a few particles of black-lead on the seats in certain states of the wind. I see, too, that there is a cocoa factory—Payne's—in Goat Street, Horsleydown, which lies to the right of the tram line going west, and I have noticed several hop warehouses on the right side of Southwark Street, going west. But these are mere suggestions; the really important data are the rice and flour mills and the spice-grinders, which seem to point unmistakably to Dockhead."

"Are there any private houses at Dockhead?" I asked.

"We must look up the 'Street' list," he replied. "The Yale latch-key rather suggests a flat, and a flat with a single occupant, and the probable habits of our absent friend offer a similar suggestion." He ran his eye down the list and presently turned to me with his finger on the page.

"If the facts that we have elicited—the singular series of agreements with the required conditions—are only a string of coincidences, here is another. On the south side of Dockhead, actually next door to the spice-grinders and opposite to Carbutt's rice-mills, is a block of workmen's flats, Hanover Buildings. They fulfil the conditions exactly. A coat hung in a room in those flats, with the windows open (as they would probably be at this time of year), would be exposed to the air containing a composite dust of precisely the character of that which we have found. Of course, the same conditions obtain in other dwellings in this part of Dockhead, but the probability is in favour of the buildings. And that is all that we can say. It is no certainty. There may be some radical fallacy in our reasoning. But, on the face of it, the chances are a thousand to one that the door that that key will open is in some part of Dockhead, and most probably in Hanover Buildings. We must leave the verification to Miller."

"Wouldn't it be as well to look at the tram-ticket?" I asked.

"Dear me!" he exclaimed. "I had forgotten the ticket. Yes, by all means." He opened the envelope and, turning its contents out on the bench, picked up the dingy slip of paper. After a glance at it he

49

handed it to me. It was punched for the journey from Tooley Street to Dockhead.

"Another coincidence," he remarked; "and by yet another, I think I hear Miller knocking at our door."

It was the superintendent, and, as we let him into the room, the hum of a motor-car entering from Tudor Street announced the arrival of Mrs. Chater. We waited for her at the open door, and, as she entered, she held out her hands impulsively.

"Say, now, Dr. Thorndyke," she exclaimed, "have you gotten something to tell us?"

"I have a suggestion to make," replied Thorndyke. "I think that if the superintendent will take this key to Hanover Buildings, Dockhead, Bermondsey, he may possibly find a door that it will fit."

"The deuce!" exclaimed Miller. "I beg your pardon, madam; but I thought I had gone through that coat pretty completely. What was it that I had overlooked, sir? Was there a letter hidden in it, after all?"

"You overlooked the dust on it, Miller; that is all," said Thorndyke.

"Dust!" exclaimed the detective, staring round-eyed at my colleague. Then he chuckled softly. "Well," said he, "as I said before, I'm not a sorcerer; I'm only a policeman." He picked up the key and asked: "Are you coming to see the end of it, sir?"

"Of course he is coming," said Mrs. Chater, "and Dr. Jervis too, to identify the man. Now that we have gotten the villain we must leave him no loophole for escape."

Thorndyke smiled dryly. "We will come if you wish it, Mrs. Chater," he said, "but you mustn't look upon our quest as a certainty. We may have made an entire miscalculation, and I am, in fact, rather curious to see if the result works out correctly. But even if we run the man to earth, I don't see that you have much evidence against him. The most that you can prove is that he was at the house and that he left hurriedly."

Mrs. Chater regarded my colleague for a moment in scornful silence, and then, gathering up her skirts, stalked out of the room. If there is one thing that the average woman detests more than another, it is an entirely reasonable man.

The big car whirled us rapidly over Blackfriars Bridge into the region of the Borough, whence we presently turned down Tooley Street towards Bermondsey.

As soon as Dockhead came into view, the detective, Thorndyke and I, alighted and proceeded on foot, leaving our client, who was now closely veiled, to follow at a little distance in the car. Opposite the head of St. Saviour's Dock, Thorndyke halted and, looking over the wall, drew my attention to the snowy powder that had lodged on every projection on the backs of the tall buildings and on the decks of the barges that were loading with the flour and ground rice. Then, crossing the road, he pointed to the wooden lantern above the roof of the spice works, the louvres of which were covered with greyish-buff dust.

"Thus," he moralised, "does commerce subserve the ends of justice—at least, we hope it does," he added quickly, as Miller disappeared into the semi-basement of the buildings.

We met the detective returning from his quest as we entered the building.

"No go there," was his report. "We'll try the next floor."

This was the ground-floor, or it might be considered the first floor. At any rate, it yielded nothing of interest, and, after a glance at the doors that opened on the landing, he strode briskly up the stone stairs. The next floor was equally unrewarding, for our eager inspection disclosed nothing but the gaping keyhole associated with the common type of night-latch.

"What name was you wanting?" inquired a dusty knight of industry who emerged from one of the flats.

"Muggs," replied Miller, with admirable promptness.

"Don't know 'im," said the workman. "I expect it's farther up."

Farther up we accordingly went, but still from each door the artless grin of the invariable keyhole saluted us with depressing monotony. I began to grow uneasy, and when the fourth floor had been explored with no better result, my anxiety became acute. A mare's nest may be an interesting curiosity, but it brings no kudos to its discoverer.

"I suppose you haven't made any mistake, sir?" said Miller, stopping to wipe his brow.

"It's quite likely that I have." replied Thorndyke, with unmoved composure. "I only proposed this search as a tentative proceeding, you know."

The superintendent grunted. He was accustomed—as was I too, for that matter—to regard Thorndyke's "tentative suggestions" as equal to another man's certainties.

"It will be an awful suck-in for Mrs. Chater if we don't find him after all," he growled as we climbed up the last flight. "She's counted her chickens to a feather." He paused at the head of the stairs and stood for a few moments looking round the landing. Suddenly he turned eagerly, and, laying his hand on Thorndyke's arm, pointed to a door in the farthest corner.

"Yale lock!" he whispered impressively.

We followed him silently as he stole on tip-toe across the landing, and watched him as he stood for an instant with the key in his land looking gloatingly at the brass disc. We saw him softly apply the nose of the fluted key-blade to the crooked slit in the cylinder, and, as we watched, it slid noiselessly up to the shoulder. The detective looked round with a grin of triumph, and, silently withdrawing the key, stepped back to us.

"You've run him to earth, sir," he whispered, "but I don't think Mr. Fox is at home. He can't have got back yet."

"Why not?" asked Thorndyke.

Miller waved his hand towards the door. "Nothing has been disturbed," he replied. "There's not a mark on the paint. Now he hadn't got the key, and you can't pick a Yale lock. He'd have had to break in, and he hasn't broken in."

Thorndyke stepped up to the door and softly pushed in the flap of the letter-slit, through which he looked into the flat.

"There's no letterbox," said he. "My dear Miller, I would undertake to open that door in five minutes with a foot of wire and a bit of resined string."

Miller shook his head and grinned once more. "I am glad you're not on the lay, sir; you'd be one too many for us. Shall we signal to the lady?"

I went out onto the gallery and looked down at the waiting car. Mrs. Chater was staring intently up at the building, and the little crowd that the car had collected stared alternately at the lady and at the object of her regard. I wiped my face with my handkerchief—the signal agreed upon—and she instantly sprang out of the car, and in an incredibly short time she appeared on the landing, purple and gasping, but with the fire of battle flashing from her eyes.

"We've found his flat, madam," said Miller, "and we're going to enter. You're not intending to offer any violence, I hope," he added, noting with some uneasiness the lady's ferocious expression.

"Of course I'm not," replied Mrs. Chater. "In the States ladies don't have to avenge insults themselves. If you were American men you'd hang the ruffian from his own bedpost."

"We're not American men, madam," said the superintendent stiffly.

"We are law-abiding Englishmen, and, moreover, we are all officers of the law. These gentlemen are barristers and I am a police officer."

With this preliminary caution, he once more inserted the key, and as he turned it and pushed the door open, we all followed him into the sitting-room.

"I told you so, sir," said Miller, softly shutting the door; "he hasn't come back yet."

Apparently he was right. At any rate, there was no one in the flat, and we proceeded unopposed on our tour of inspection. It was a miserable spectacle, and, as we wandered from one squalid room to another, a feeling of pity for the starving wretch into whose lair we were intruding stole over me and began almost to mitigate the hideousness of his crime. On all sides poverty—utter, grinding poverty—stared us in the face. It looked at us hollow-eyed in the wretched sitting-room, with its bare floor, its solitary chair and tiny deal table; its unfurnished walls and windows destitute of blind or curtain.

A piece of Dutch cheese-rind on the table, scraped to the thinness of paper, whispered of starvation; and famine lurked in the gaping cupboard, in the empty bread-tin, in the tea-caddy with its pinch of dust at the bottom, in the jam-jar, wiped clean, as a few crumbs testified, with a crust of bread. There was not enough food in the place to furnish a meal for a healthy mouse.

The bedroom told the same tale, but with a curious variation. A miserable truckle-bed with a straw mattress and a cheap jute rug for bed-clothes, an orange-case, stood on end, for a dressing-table, and another, bearing a tin washing-bowl, formed the wretched furniture. But the suit that hung from a couple of nails was well-cut and even fashionable, though shabby; and another suit lay on the floor, neatly folded and covered with a newspaper; and, most incongruous of all, a silver cigarette-case reposed on the dressing-table.

"Why on earth does this fellow starve," I exclaimed, "when he has a silver case to pawn?"

"Wouldn't do," said Miller. "A man doesn't pawn the implements of his trade."

Mrs. Chater, who had been staring about her with the mute amazement of a wealthy woman confronted, for the first time, with abject poverty, turned suddenly to the superintendent. "This can't be the man!" she exclaimed. "You have made some mistake. This poor creature could never have made his way into a house like Willowdale."

Thorndyke lifted the newspaper. Beneath it was a dress suit

with the shirt, collar and tie all carefully smoothed out and folded. Thorndyke unfolded the shirt and pointed to the curiously crumpled front. Suddenly he brought it close to his eye and then, from the sham diamond stud, he drew a single hair—a woman's hair.

"That is rather significant," said he, holding it up between his finger and thumb; and Mrs. Chater evidently thought so too, for the pity and compunction suddenly faded from her face, and once more her eyes flashed with vindictive fire.

"I wish he would come," she exclaimed viciously. "Prison won't be much hardship to him after this, but I want to see him in the dock all the same."

"No," the detective agreed, "it won't hurt him much to swap this for Portland. Listen!"

A key was being inserted into the outer door, and as we all stood like statues, a man entered and closed the door after him. He passed the door of the bedroom without seeing us, and with the dragging steps of a weary, dispirited man. Almost immediately we heard him go to the kitchen and draw water into some vessel. Then he went back to the sitting-room.

"Come along," said Miller, stepping silently towards the door. We followed closely, and as he threw the door open, we looked in over his shoulder.

The man had seated himself at the table, on which now lay a hunk of household bread resting on the paper in which he had brought it, and a tumbler of water. He half rose as the door opened, and as if petrified remained staring at Miller with a dreadful expression of terror upon his livid face.

At this moment I felt a hand on my arm, and Mrs. Chater brusquely pushed past me into the room. But at the threshold she stopped short; and a singular change crept over the man's ghastly face, a change so remarkable that I looked involuntarily from him to our client. She had turned, in a moment, deadly pale, and her face had frozen into an expression of incredulous horror.

The dramatic silence was broken by the matter-of-fact voice of the detective.

"I am a police officer," said he, "and I arrest you for—?"

A peal of hysterical laughter from Mrs. Chater interrupted him, and he looked at her in astonishment. "Stop, stop!" she cried in a shaky voice. "I guess we've made a ridiculous mistake. This isn't the man. This gentleman is Captain Rowland, an old friend of mine."

"I'm sorry he's a friend of yours," said Miller, "because I shall have to ask you to appear against him."

"You can ask what you please," replied Mrs. Chater. "I tell you he's not the man."

The superintendent rubbed his nose and looked hungrily at his quarry. "Do I understand, madam," he asked stiffly, "that you refuse to prosecute?"

"Prosecute!" she exclaimed. "Prosecute my friends for offences that I know they have not committed? Certainly I refuse."

The superintendent looked at Thorndyke, but my colleague's countenance had congealed into a state of absolute immobility and was as devoid of expression as the face of a Dutch clock.

"Very well," said Miller, looking sourly at his watch. "Then we have had our trouble for nothing. I wish you good afternoon, madam."

"I am sorry I troubled you, now," said Mrs. Chater.

"I am sorry you did," was the curt reply; and the superintendent, flinging the key on the table, stalked out of the room.

As the outer door slammed the man sat down with an air of bewilderment; and then, suddenly flinging his arms on the table, he dropped his head on them and burst into a passion of sobbing.

It was very embarrassing. With one accord Thorndyke and I turned to go, but Mrs. Chater motioned us to stay. Stepping over to the man, she touched him lightly on the arm.

"Why did you do it?" she asked in a tone of gentle reproach.

The man sat up and flung out one arm in an eloquent gesture that comprehended the miserable room and the yawning cupboard.

"It was the temptation of a moment," he said. "I was penniless, and those accursed diamonds were thrust in my face; they were mine for the taking. I was mad, I suppose."

"But why didn't you take them?" she said. "Why didn't you?"

"I don't know. The madness passed; and then—when I saw you lying there—? Oh, God! Why don't you give me up to the police?" He laid his head down and sobbed afresh.

Mrs. Chater bent over him with tears standing in her pretty grey eyes. "But tell me," she said, "why didn't you take the diamonds? You could if you'd liked, I suppose?"

"What good were they to me?" he demanded passionately. "What did anything matter to me? I thought you were dead."

"Well, I'm not, you see," she said, with a rather tearful smile; "I'm just as well as an old woman like me can expect to be. And I want your address, so that I can write and give you some good advice."

The man sat up and produced a shabby card-case from his pocket, and, as he took out a number of cards and spread them out like the "hand" of a whist player, I caught a twinkle in Thorndyke's eye.

"My name is Augustus Bailey," said the man. He selected the appropriate card, and, having scribbled his address on it with a stump of lead pencil, relapsed into his former position.

"Thank you," said Mrs. Chater, lingering for a moment by the table. "Now we'll go. Goodbye, Mr. Bailey. I shall write tomorrow, and you must attend seriously to the advice of an old friend."

I held open the door for her to pass out and looked back before I turned to follow. Bailey still sat sobbing quietly, with his hand resting on his arms; and a little pile of gold stood on the corner of the table.

"I expect, doctor," said Mrs. Chater, as Thorndyke handed her into the car, "you've written me down a sentimental fool."

Thorndyke looked at her with an unwonted softening of his rather severe face and answered quietly, "It is written: *Blessed are the Merciful.*"

The Stolen Ingots

"In *medico*-legal practice," Thorndyke remarked, "one must be constantly on one's guard against the effects of suggestion, whether intentional or unconscious. When the facts of a case are set forth by an informant, they are nearly always presented, consciously or unconsciously, in terms of inference. Certain facts, which appear to the narrator to be the leading facts, are given with emphasis and in detail, while other facts, which appear to be subordinate or trivial, are partially suppressed. But this assessment of evidential value must never be accepted. The whole case must be considered and each fact weighed separately, and then it will commonly happen that the leading fact turns out to be the one that had been passed over as negligible."

The remark was made apropos of a case, the facts of which had just been stated to us by Mr. Halethorpe, of the Sphinx Assurance Company. I did not quite perceive its bearing at the time, but looking back when the case was concluded, I realised that I had fallen into the very error against which Thorndyke's warning should have guarded me.

"I trust," said Mr. Halethorpe, "that I have not come at an inconvenient time. You are so tolerant of unusual hours—"

"My practice," interrupted Thorndyke, "is my recreation, and I welcome you as one who comes to furnish entertainment. Draw your chair up to the fire, light a cigar and tell us your story."

Mr. Halethorpe laughed, but adopted the procedure suggested, and having settled his toes upon the kerb and selected a cigar from the box, he opened the subject of his call.

"I don't quite know what you can do for us," he began, "as it is hardly your business to trace lost property, but I thought I would come and let you know about our difficulty. The fact is that our company looks like dropping some four thousand pounds, which the directors won't like. What has happened is this:

"About two months ago the London House of the Akropong Gold Fields Company applied to us to insure a parcel of gold bars that were to be consigned to Minton and Borwell, the big manufacturing jewellers. The bars were to be shipped at Accra and landed at Bellhaven, which is the nearest port to Minton and Borwell's works. Well, we agreed to underwrite the risk—we have done business with the Akropong people before—and the matter was settled. The bars were put on board the *Labadi* at Accra, and in due course were landed at Belhaven, where they were delivered to Minton's agents. So far, so good. Then came the catastrophe. The case of bars was put on the train at Belhaven, consigned to Anchester, where Minton's have their factory. But the line doesn't go to Anchester direct.

"The junction is at Garbridge, a small country station close to the River Crouch, and here the case was put out and locked up in the station-master's office to wait for the Anchester train. It seems that the station-master was called away and detained longer than he had expected, and when the train was signalled he hurried back in a mighty twitter. However, the case was there all right, and he personally superintended its removal to the guard's van and put it in the guard's charge. All went well for the rest of the journey. A member of the firm was waiting at Anchester station with a closed van. The case was put into it and taken direct to the factory, where it was opened in the private office—and found to be full of lead pipe."

"I presume," said Thorndyke, "that it was not the original case."

"No," replied Halethorpe, "but it was a very fair imitation. The label and the marks were correct, but the seals were just plain wax. Evidently the exchange had been made in the station office, and it transpires that although the door was securely locked there was an unfastened window which opened on to the garden, and there were plain marks of feet on the flower-bed outside."

"What time did this happen?" asked Thorndyke.

"The Anchester train came in at a quarter past seven, by which time, of course, it was quite dark."

"And when did it happen?"

"The day before yesterday. We heard of it yesterday morning."

"Are you contesting the claim?"

"We don't want to. Of course, we could plead negligence, but in that case I think we should make a claim on the railway company. But, naturally, we should much rather recover the property. After all, it can't be so very far away."

"I wouldn't say that," said Thorndyke. "This was no impromptu theft. The dummy case was prepared in advance, and evidently by somebody who knew what the real case was like, and how and when it was to be despatched from Belhaven. We must assume that the disposal of the stolen case has been provided for with similar completeness. How far is Garbridge from the river?"

"Less than half a mile across the marshes. The detective-inspector—Badger, I think you know him—asked the same question."

"Naturally," said Thorndyke. "A heavy object like this case is much more easily and inconspicuously conveyed by water than on land. And then, see what facilities for concealment a navigable river offers. The case could be easily stowed away on a small craft, or even in a boat; or the bars could be taken out and stowed amongst the ballast, or even, at a pinch, dropped over board at a marked spot and left until the hue and cry was over."

"You are not very encouraging," Halethorpe remarked gloomily. "I take it that you don't much expect that we shall recover those bars."

"We needn't despair," was the reply, "but I want you to understand the difficulties. The thieves have got away with the booty, and that booty is an imperishable material which retains its value even if broken up into unrecognisable fragments. Melted down into small ingots, it would be impossible to identify."

"Well," said Halethorpe, "the police have the matter in hand—Inspector Badger, of the C.I.D., is in charge of the case—but our directors would be more satisfied if you would look into it. Of course we would give you any help we could. What do you say?"

"I am willing to look into the case," said Thorndyke, "though I don't hold out much hope. Could you give me a note to the shipping company and another to the consignees, Minton and Borwell?"

"Of course I will. I'll write them now. I have some of our stationery in my *attaché* case. But, if you will pardon my saying so, you seem to be starting your inquiry just where there is nothing to be learned. The case was stolen after it left the ship and before it reached the consignees—although their agent had received it from the ship."

"The point is," said Thorndyke, "that this was a preconcerted robbery, and that the thieves possessed special information. That information must have come either from the ship or from the factory. So, while we must try to pick up the track of the case itself, we must seek the beginning of the clue at the two ends—the ship and the factory one of which it must have started."

"Yes, that's true," said Halethorpe. "Well, I'll write those two notes and then I must run away; and we'll hope for the best."

He wrote the two letters asking for facilities from the respective parties, and then took his departure in a somewhat chastened frame of mind.

"Quite an interesting little problem," Thorndyke remarked, as Halethorpe footsteps died away on the stairs, "but not much in our line. It is really a police case—a case for patient and intelligent inquiry. And that is what we shall have to do—make some careful inquiries on the spot."

"Where do you propose to begin?" I asked.

"At the beginning," he replied. "Belhaven. I propose that we go down there tomorrow morning and pick up the thread at that end."

"What thread?" I demanded. "We know that the package started from there. What else do you expect to learn?"

"There are several curious possibilities in this case, as you must have noticed," he replied "The question is, whether any of them are probabilities. That is what I want to settle before we begin a detailed investigation."

"For my part," said I, "I should have supposed that the investigation would start from the scene of the robbery. But I presume that you have seen some possibilities that I have overlooked."

Which eventually turned out to be the case.

★★★★★★★★

"I think," said Thorndyke as we alighted at Belhaven on the following morning, "we had better go first to the Customs and make quite certain, if we can, that the bars were really in the case when it was delivered to the consignees' agents. It won't do to take it for granted that the substitution took place at Garbridge, although that is by far the most probable theory." Accordingly we made our way to the harbour, where an obliging mariner directed us to our destination.

At the Custom House we were received by a genial officer, who, when Thorndyke had explained his connection with the robbery, entered into the matter with complete sympathy and a quick grasp of the situation.

"I see," said he. "You want clear evidence that the bars were in the case when it left here. Well, I think we can satisfy you on that point. Bullion is not a customable commodity, but it has to be examined and reported. If it is consigned to the Bank of England or the Mint, the case is passed through with the seals unbroken, but as this was a private consignment, the seals will have been broken and the contents of the case examined. Jeffson, show these gentlemen the report on the case of gold bars from the *Labadi*."

"Would it be possible," Thorndyke asked, "for us to have a few words with the officer who opened the case? You know the legal partiality for personal testimony."

"Of course it would. Jeffson, when these gentlemen have seen the report, find the officer who signed it and let them have a talk with him."

We followed Mr. Jeffson into an adjoining office, where he produced the report and handed it to Thorndyke. The particulars that it gave were in effect those that would be furnished by the ship's manifest and the bill of lading. The case was thirteen inches long by twelve wide and nine inches deep, outside measurement; and its gross weight was one hundred and seventeen pounds three ounces, and it contained four bars of the aggregate weight of one hundred and thirteen pounds two ounces.

"Thank you," said Thorndyke, handing back the report. "And now can we see the officer—Mr. Byrne, I think—just to fill in the details?"

"If you will come with me," replied Mr. Jeffson, "I'll find him for you. I expect he is on the wharf."

We followed our conductor out on to the quay among a litter of cases, crates and barrels, and eventually, amidst a battalion of Madeira wine casks, found the officer deep in problems of "content and ullage," and other customs mysteries. As Jeffson introduced us, and then discreetly retired, Mr. Byrne confronted us, with a mahogany face and truculent blue eye.

"With reference to this bullion," said Thorndyke, "I understand that you weighed the bars separately from the case?"

"Oi did," replied Mr. Byrne.

"Did you weigh each bar separately?"

"Oi did not," was the concise reply.

"What was the appearance of the bars—I mean as to shape and size? Were they of the usual type?"

"Oi've not had a great deal to do with bullion," said Mr. Byrne, "but Oi should say that they were just ordinary gold bars, about nine inches long by four wide and about two inches deep."

"Was there much packing material in the case?"

"Very little. The bars were wrapped in thick canvas and jammed into the case. There wouldn't be more than about half an inch clearance all round to allow for the canvas. The case was inch and half stuff strengthened with iron bands."

"Did you seal the case after you had closed it up?"

"Oi did. 'Twas all shipshape when it was passed back to the mate. And oi saw him hand it over to the consignees' agent; so 'twas all in order when it left the wharf."

"That was what I wanted to make sure of," said Thorndyke; and, having pocketed his notebook and thanked the officer, he turned away among the wilderness of merchandise.

"So much for the Customs," said he. "I am glad we went there first. As you have no doubt observed, we have picked up some useful information."

"We have ascertained," I replied, "that the case was intact when it was handed over to the consignees' agents, so that our investigations at Garbridge will start from a solid basis. And that, I take it, is all you wanted to know."

"Not quite all," he rejoined. "There are one or two little details that I should like to fill in. I think we will look in on the shipping agents and present Halethorpe's note. We may as well learn all we can before we make our start from the scene of the robbery."

"Well," I said, "I don't see what more there is to learn here. But apparently you do. That seems to be the office, past those sheds."

The manager of the shipping agent's office looked us up and down as he sat at his littered desk with Halethorpe's letter in his hand.

"You've come about that bullion that was stolen," he said brusquely. "Well, it wasn't stolen here. Hadn't you better inquire at Garbridge, where it was?"

"Undoubtedly," replied Thorndyke. "But I am making certain preliminary inquiries. Now, first, as to the bill of lading, who has that—the original, I mean?

"The captain has it at present, but I have a copy."

"Could I see it?" Thorndyke asked.

The manager raised his eyebrows protestingly, but produced the document from a file and handed it to Thorndyke, watching him inquisitively as he copied the particulars of the package into his notebook.

"I suppose," said Thorndyke as he returned the document, "you have a copy of the ship's manifest?"

"Yes," replied the manager, "but the entry in the manifest is merely a copy of the particulars given in the bill of lading."

"I should like to see the manifest, if it is not troubling you too much."

"But," the other protested impatiently, "the manifest contains no information respecting this parcel of bullion excepting the one entry, which, as I have told you, has been copied from the bill of lading."

"I realise that," said Thorndyke; "but I should like to look over it, all the same."

Our friend bounced into an inner office and presently returned with a voluminous document, which he slapped down on a side-table.

"There, sir," he said. "That is the manifest. This is the entry relating to the bullion that you are inquiring about. The rest of the document is concerned with the cargo, in which I presume you are not interested."

In this, however, he was mistaken; for Thorndyke, having verified the bullion entry, turned the leaves over and began systematically, though rapidly, to run his eye over the long list from the beginning, a proceeding that the manager viewed with frenzied impatience.

"If you are going to read it right through, sir," the latter observed, "I shall ask you to excuse me. Art is long but life is short," he added with a sour smile.

Nevertheless he hovered about uneasily, and when Thorndyke proceeded to copy some of the entries into his notebook, he craned over and read them without the least disguise, though not without comment.

"Good God, sir!" he exclaimed. "What possible bearing on this robbery can that parcel of scrivelloes have? And do you realise that they are still in the ship's hold?"

"I inferred that they were, as they are consigned to London," Thorndyke replied, drawing his finger down the "description" column and rapidly scanning the entries in it. The manager watched that finger, and as it stopped successively at a bag of gum copal, a case of quartz specimens, a case of six-inch brass screw-bolts, a bag of beniseed and a package of kola nuts, he breathed hard and muttered like an angry parrot. But Thorndyke was quite unmoved. With calm deliberation he copied out each entry, conscientiously noting the marks, descriptions of packages and contents, gross and net weights, dimensions, names of consignors and consignees, ports of shipment and discharge, and, in fact, the entire particulars. It was certainly an amazing proceeding, and I could make no more of it than could our impatient friend.

At last Thorndyke closed and pocketed his notebook, and the

manager heaved a slightly obtrusive sigh. "Is there nothing more, sir?" he asked. "You don't want to examine the ship, for instance?"

The next moment, I think, he regretted his sarcasm, for Thorndyke inquired, with evident interest: "Is the ship still here?

"Yes," was the unwilling admission. "She finishes unloading here at midday today and will probably haul into the London Docks tomorrow morning."

"I don't think I need go on board," said Thorndyke, "but you might give me a card in case I find that I want to."

The card was somewhat grudgingly produced, and when Thorndyke had thanked our entertainer for his help, we took our leave and made our way towards the station.

"Well," I said, "you have collected a vast amount of curious information, but I am hanged if I can see that any of it has the slightest bearing on our inquiry."

Thorndyke cast on me a look of deep reproach. "Jervis!" he exclaimed, "you astonish me; you do, indeed. Why, my dear fellow, it stares you in the face!"

"When you say 'it,'" I said a little irritably, "you mean—?"

"I mean the leading fact from which we may deduce the *modus operandi* of this robbery. You shall look over my notes in the train and sort out the data that we have collected. I think you will find them extremely illuminating."

"I doubt it," said I. "But, meanwhile, aren't we wasting a good deal of time? Halethorpe wants to get the gold back; he doesn't want to know how the thieves contrived to steal it."

"That is a very just remark," answered Thorndyke. "My learned friend displays his customary robust common sense. Nevertheless, I think that a clear understanding of the mechanism of this robbery will prove very helpful to us, though I agree with you that we have spent enough time on securing our preliminary data. The important thing now is to pick up a trail from Garbridge. But I see our train is signalled. We had better hurry."

As the train rumbled into station, we looked out for an empty smoking compartment, and having been fortunate enough to secure one, we settled ourselves in opposite corners and lighted our pipes. Then Thorndyke handed me his notebook and as I studied, with wrinkled brows, the apparently disconnected entries, he sat and observed me thoughtfully and with the faintest suspicion of a smile. Again and again I read through those notes with ever-dwindling hopes of extracting the meaning that "stared me in the face." Vainly did I endeavour to connect gum copal, scrivelloes or beni-seed with the methods of the unknown robbers. The entries in the notebook persisted obstinately in remaining totally disconnected and hopelessly irrelevant. At last I shut the book with a savage snap and handed it back to its owner.

"It's no use, Thorndyke," I said. "I can't see the faintest glimmer of light."

"Well," said he, "it isn't of much consequence. The practical part of our task is before us, and it may turn out a pretty difficult part. But we have got to recover those bars if it is humanly possible. And here we are at our jumping-off place. This is Garbridge Station—and I see an old acquaintance of ours on the platform."

I looked out, as the train slowed down, and there, sure enough, was no less a person than Inspector Badger of the Criminal Investigation Department.

"We could have done very well without Badger," I remarked.

"Yes," Thorndyke agreed, "but we shall have to take him into partnership, I expect. After all, we are on his territory and on the same errand. How do you do, inspector?" he continued, as the officer, having observed our descent from the carriage, hurried forward with unwonted cordiality.

"I rather expected to see you here, sir," said he. "We heard that Mr. Halethorpe had consulted you. But this isn't the London train."

"No," said Thorndyke. "We've been to Belhaven, just to make sure that the bullion was in the case when it started."

"I could have told you that two days ago," said Badger. "We got on to the Customs people at once. That was all plain sailing; but the rest of it isn't."

"No clue as to how the case was taken away?"

"Oh, yes; that is pretty clear. It was hoisted out, and the dummy hoisted in, through the window of the stationmaster's office. And the same night, two men were seen carrying a heavy package, about the size of the bullion-case, towards the marshes. But there the clue ends. The stuff seems to have vanished into thin air. Of course our people are on the look-out for it in various likely directions, but I am staying here with a couple of plain-clothes men. I've a conviction that it is still somewhere in this neighbourhood, and I mean to stick here in the hope that I may spot somebody trying to move it."

As the inspector was speaking we had been walking slowly from the station towards the village, which was on the opposite side of the river. On the bridge Thorndyke halted and looked down the river and over the wide expanse of marshy country.

"This is an ideal place for a bullion robbery," he remarked. "A tidal river near to the sea and a network of creeks, in any one of which one could hide a boat or sink the booty below tide-marks. Have you heard of any strange craft having put in here?"

"Yes. There's a little ramshackle bawley from Leigh—but her crew of two ragamuffins are not Leigh men. And they've made a mess of their visit—got their craft on the mud on the top of the spring tide. There there she'll be till next spring tide. But I've been over her carefully and I'll swear the stuff isn't aboard her. I had all the ballast out and emptied the lazarette and the chain locker."

"And what about the barge?"

"She's a regular trader here. Her crew—the skipper and his son—are quite respectable men and they belong here. There they go in that boat; I expect they are off on this tide. But they seem to be making for the bawley."

As he spoke the inspector produced a pair of glasses, through which he watched the movement of the barge's jolly, and a couple of elderly fishermen, who were crossing the bridge, halted to look on. The barge's boat ran alongside the stranded bawley, and one of the rowers hailed; whereupon two men tumbled up from the cabin and dropped into the boat, which immediately pushed off and headed for the barge.

"Them bawley blokes seems to be taking a passage along of old Bill Somers," one of the fishermen remarked, levelling a small telescope at the barge as the boat drew alongside and the four men climbed on board. "Going to work their passage, too," he added as the two passengers proceeded immediately to man the windlass while the crew let go the brails and hooked the main block to the traveller.

"Rum go," commented Badger, glaring at the barge through his glasses; "but they haven't taken anything aboard with them. I could see that."

"You have overhauled the barge, I suppose?" said Thorndyke.

"Yes. Went right through her. Nothing there. She's light. There was no place aboard her where you could hide a split-pea."

"Did you get her anchor up?"

"No," replied Badger. "I didn't. I suppose I ought to have done so. However, they're getting it up themselves now." As he spoke, the rapid clink of a windlass-pawl was borne across the water, and through my prismatic glasses I could see the two passengers working for all they were worth at the cranks. Presently the clink of the pawl began to slow down somewhat and the two bargemen, having got the sails set, joined the toilers at the windlass, but even then there was no great increase of speed.

"Anchor seems to come up uncommon heavy," one of the fishermen remarked.

"Aye," the other agreed. "Got foul of an old mooring, maybe."

"Look out for the anchor, Badger," Thorndyke said in a low voice, gazing steadily through his binocular. "It is out of the ground. The cable is up and down and the barge is drifting off on the tide."

Even as he spoke the ring and stock of the anchor rose slowly out of the water, and now I could see that a second chain was shackled loosely to the cable, down which it had slid until it was stopped by the ring of the anchor. Badger had evidently seen it too, for he ejaculated, "Hallo!" and added a few verbal flourishes which I need not repeat. A few more turns of the windlass brought the flukes of the anchor clear of the water, and dangling against them was an undeniable wooden case, securely slung with lashings of stout chain. Badger cursed volubly, and, turning to the fishermen, exclaimed in a rather offensively peremptory tone:

"I want a boat. Now. This instant."

The elder piscator regarded him doggedly and replied. "All right. I ain't got no objection."

"Where can I get a boat?" the inspector demanded, nearly purple with excitement and anxiety.

"Where do you think?" the mariner responded, evidently nettled by the inspector's masterful tone. "Pastrycook's? Or livery stables?"

"Look here," said Badger. "I'm a police officer and I want to board that barge, and I am prepared to pay handsomely. Now where can I get a boat?"

"We'll put you aboard of her," replied the fisherman, "that is, if we can catch her. But I doubt it. She's off, that's what she is. And there's something queer a-going on aboard of her," he added in a somewhat different tone.

There was. I had been observing it. The case had been, with some difficulty, hoisted on board, and then suddenly there had broken out an altercation between the two bargees and their passengers, and this had now developed into what look like a free fight. It was difficult to see exactly what was happening, for the barge was drifting rapidly down the river, and her sails, blowing out first on one side and then on the other, rather obscured the view. Presently, however, the sails filled and a man appeared at the wheel; then the barge jibed round, and with a strong ebb tide and a fresh breeze, very soon began to grow small in the distance.

Meanwhile the fishermen had bustled off in search of a boat, and the inspector had raced to the bridge-head, where he stood gesticulating frantically and blowing his whistle, while Thorndyke continued placidly to watch the receding barge through his binocular.

"What are we going to do?" I asked, a little surprised at my colleague's inaction.

"What can we do?" he asked in reply. "Badger will follow the barge. He probably won't overtake her, but he will prevent her from making a landing until they get out into the estuary, and then he may possibly get assistance. The chase is in his hands."

"Are we going with him?"

"I am not. This looks like being an all-night expedition, and I must be at our chambers tomorrow morning. Besides, the chase is not our affair. But if you would like to join Badger there is no reason why you shouldn't. I can look after the practice."

"Well," I said, "I think I should rather like to be in at the death, if it won't inconvenience you. But it is possible that they may get away with the booty."

"Quite," he agreed; "and then it would be useful to know exactly how and where it disappears. Yes, go with them, by all means, and keep a sharp look-out."

At this moment Badger returned with the two plain clothes men whom his whistle had called from their posts, and simultaneously a boat was seen approaching the steps by the bridge, rowed by the two fishermen. The inspector looked at us inquiringly. "Are you coming to see the sport?" he asked.

"Doctor Jervis would like to come with you," Thorndyke replied. "I have to get back to London. But you will be a fair boat-load without me."

This appeared to be also the view of the two fishermen, as they brought up at the steps and observed the four passengers; but they made no demur beyond inquiring if there were not any more; and when we had taken our places in the stern sheets, they pushed off and pulled through the bridge and away down stream. Gradually, the village receded and the houses and the bridge grew small and more distant, though they remained visible for a long time over the marshy levels; and still, as I looked back through my glasses, I could see Thorndyke on the bridge, watching the pursuit with his binocular to his eyes.

Meanwhile the fugitive barge, having got some two miles start, seemed to be drawing ahead. But it was only at intervals that we could see her, for the tide was falling fast and we were mostly hemmed in by the high, muddy banks. Only when we entered a straight reach of the river could we see her sails over the land; and every time that she came into view, she appeared perceptibly smaller.

When the river grew wider, the mast was stepped and a good-sized lug-sail hoisted, though one of the fishermen continued to ply his oar on the weather side, while the other took the tiller. This improved our pace appreciably; but still, whenever we caught a glimpse of the barge, it was evident that she was still gaining.

On one of these occasions the man at the tiller, standing up to get a better view, surveyed our quarry intently for nearly a minute and then addressed the inspector.

"She's a-going to give us the go-by, mister," he observed with conviction.

"Still gaining?" asked Badger.

"Aye. She's a-going to slip across the tail of Foulness Sand into the deep channel. And that's the last we shall see of her."

"But can't we get into the channel the same way?" demanded Badger.

"Well, d'ye see," replied the fisherman, "'tis like this. Tide's a-running out, but there'll be enough for her. It'll just carry her out through the Whitaker Channel and across the spit. Then it'll turn, and up she'll go, London way, on the flood. But we shall catch the flood-tide in the Whitaker Channel, and a rare old job we'll have to get out; and when we do get out, that barge'll be miles away."

The inspector swore long and earnestly. He even alluded to himself as a "blithering idiot." But that helped matters not at all. The fisherman's dismal prophecy was fulfilled in every horrid detail. When we were approaching the Whitaker Channel the barge was just crossing the spit, and the last of the ebb-tide was trickling out. By the time we were fairly in the Channel the tide had turned and was already flowing in with a speed that increased every minute; while over the sand we could see the barge, already out in the open estuary, heading to the west on the flood-tide at a good six knots.

Poor Badger was frantic. With yearning eyes fixed on the dwindling barge, he cursed, entreated, encouraged and made extravagant offers. He even took an oar and pulled with such desperate energy that he caught a crab and turned a neat back somersault into the fisherman's lap. The two mariners pulled until their oars bent like canes; but still the sandy banks crept by, inch by inch, and ever the turbid water seemed to pour up the channel more and yet more swiftly. It was a fearful struggle and seemed to last for hours; and when, at last, the boat crawled out across the spit and the exhausted rowers rested on their oars, the sun was just setting and the barge had disappeared into the west.

I was really sorry for Badger. His oversight in respect of the anchor was a very natural one or a landsman, and he had evidently taken infinite pains over the case and shown excellent judgment in keeping a close watch on the neighbourhood of Garbridge; and now, after all his care, it looked as if both the robbers and their booty had slipped through his fingers. It was desperately bad luck.

"Well," said the elder fisherman, "they've give us a run for our money; but they've got clear away. What's to be done now, mister?"

Badger had nothing to suggest excepting that we should pull or sail up the river in the hope of getting some assistance on the way. He was in the lowest depths of despair and dejection. But now, when Fortune seemed to have deserted us utterly, and failure appeared to be an accomplished fact, Providence intervened.

A small steam vessel that had been approaching from the direction of the East Swin suddenly altered her course and bore down as if to speak us. The fisherman who had last spoken looked at her attentively for a few moments and then slapped his thigh. "Saved by gum!" he exclaimed. "This'll do your trick, mister. Here comes a Customs cruiser."

Instantly the two fishermen bent to their oars to meet the oncoming craft, and in a few minutes we were alongside, Badger hailing like a bull of Bashan. A brief explanation to the officer in charge secured a highly sympathetic promise of help. We all scrambled up on deck; the boat was dropped astern at the scope of her painter; the engine-room bell jangled merrily, and the smart, yacht-like vessel began to forge ahead.

"Now then," said the officer, as his craft gathered way, "give us a description of this barge. What is she like?

"She's a small stumpy," the senior fisherman explained, "flying

70

light; wants paint badly; steers with a wheel; green transom with *Bluebell, Maldon,* cut in and gilded. Seemed to be keeping along the north shore."

With these particulars in his mind, the officer explored the western horizon with a pair of night-glasses, although it was still broad daylight. Presently he reported: "There's a stumpy in a line with the Blacktail Spit buoy. Just take a look at her." He handed his glasses to the fisherman, who, after a careful inspection of the stranger, gave it as his opinion that she was our quarry. "Probably makin' for Southend or Leigh," said he, and added: "I'll bet she's bound for Benfleet Creek. Nice quiet place, that, to land the stuff."

Our recent painful experience was now reversed, for as our swift little vessel devoured the miles of water, the barge, which we were all watching eagerly, loomed up larger every minute. By the time we were abreast of the Mouse Lightship, she was but a few hundred yards ahead, and even through my glasses, the name *Bluebell* was clearly legible. Badger nearly wept with delight; the officer in charge smiled an anticipatory smile; the deck-hands girded up their loins for the coming capture and the plain-clothes men each furtively polished a pair of handcuffs.

At length the little cruiser came fairly abreast of the barge—not unobserved by the two men on her deck. Then she sheered in suddenly and swept alongside. One hand neatly hooked a shroud with a grappling iron and made fast while a couple of preventive officers, the plain men and the inspector jumped down simultaneously on to the barge's deck. For a moment, the two bawley men were inclined to show fight; but the odds were too great. After a perfunctory scuffle they both submitted to be handcuffed and were at once hauled up on board the cruiser and lodged in the fore-peak under guard. Then the chief officer, the two fishermen and I jumped on board the barge and followed Badger down the companion hatch to the cabin.

It was a curious scene that was revealed in that little cupboard-like apartment by the light of Badger's electric torch. On each of the two lockers was stretched a man, securely lashed with lead-line and having drawn over his face a knitted stocking cap, while on the little triangular fixed table rested an iron-bound box which I instantly identified by my recollection of the description of the bullion-case in the ship's manifest. It was but the work of a minute to liberate the skipper and his son and send them up, wrathful but substantially uninjured, to refresh on the cruiser; and then the ponderous treasure-chest was borne in triumph by two muscular deck-hands, up the narrow steps, to be hoisted to the Government vessel.

"Well, well," said the inspector, mopping his face with his handkerchief, "all's well that ends well, but I thought I had lost the men and the stuff that time. What are you going to do? I shall stay on board as this boat is going right up to the Custom House in London; but if you want to get home sooner, I dare say the chief officer will put you ashore at Southend."

I decided to adopt this course, and I was accordingly landed at Southend Pier with a telegram from Badger to his headquarters; and at Southend I was fortunate enough to catch an express train which brought me to Fenchurch Street while the night was still young.

When I reached our chambers, I found Thorndyke seated by the fire, serenely studying a brief. He stood up as I entered and, laying aside the brief, remarked: "You are back sooner than I expected. How sped the chase? Did you catch the barge?"

"Yes. We've got the men and we've got the bullion. But we very nearly lost both;" and here I gave him an account of the pursuit and the capture, to which he listened with the liveliest interest. "That Customs cruiser was a piece of sheer luck," said he, when I had concluded. "I am delighted. This capture simplifies the case for us enormously."

"It seems to me to dispose of the case altogether," said I. "The property is recovered and the thieves are in custody. But I think most of the credit belongs to Badger."

Thorndyke smiled enigmatically. "I should let him have it all, Jervis," he said; and then, after a reflective pause, he continued: "We will go round to Scotland Yard in the morning to verify the capture. If the package agrees with the description in the bill of lading, the case, as you say, is disposed of."

"It is hardly necessary," said I. "The marks were all correct and the Customs seals were unbroken—but still, I know you won't be satisfied until you have verified everything for yourself. And I suppose you are right."

It was past eleven in the following forenoon when we invaded Superintendent Miller's office at Scotland Yard. That genial officer looked up from his desk as we entered and laughed joyously. "I told you so, Badger," he chuckled, turning to the inspector, who had also looked up and was regarding us with a foxy smile. "I knew the doctor wouldn't be satisfied until he had seen it with his own eyes. I suppose that is what you have come for, sir?"

"Yes," was the reply. "It is a mere formality, of course, but, if you don't mind—"

"Not in the least," replied Miller. "Come along, Badger, and show the doctor your prize."

The two officers conducted us to a room, which the superintendent unlocked, and which contained a small table, a measuring standard, a weighing machine, a set of Snellen's test-types, and the now historic case of bullion. The latter Thorndyke inspected closely, checking the marks and dimensions by his notes.

"I see you haven't opened it," he remarked.

"No," replied Miller. "Why should we? The Customs seals are intact."

"I thought you might like to know what was inside," Thorndyke explained.

The two officers looked at him quickly and the inspector exclaimed:

"But we do know. It was opened and checked at the Customs."

"What do you suppose is inside?" Thorndyke asked.

"I don't suppose," Badger replied testily. "I know. There are four bars of gold inside."

"Well," said Thorndyke, "as the representative of the Insurance Company, I should like to see the contents of that case."

The two officers stared at him in amazement, as also, I must admit, did I. The implied doubt seemed utterly contrary to reason.

"This is scepticism with a vengeance!" said Miller. "How on earth is it possible—but there, I suppose if you are not satisfied, we should be justified—"

He glanced at his subordinate, who snorted impatiently: "Oh, open it and let him see the bars. And then, I suppose, he will want us to make an assay of the metal."

The superintendent retired with wrinkled brows and presently returned with a screwdriver, a hammer and a case-opener. Very deftly he broke the seals, extracted the screws and prised up the lid of the case, inside which were one or two folds of thick canvas. Lifting these with something of a flourish, he displayed the upper pair of dull, yellow bars.

"Are you satisfied now, sir?" demanded Badger. "Or do you want to see the other two?"

Thorndyke looked reflectively at the two bars, and the two officers looked inquiringly at him (but one might as profitably have watched the expression on the face of a ship's figure). Then he took from his pocket a folding foot-rule and quickly measured the three dimensions of one of the bars.

"Is that weighing machine reliable?" he asked.

"It is correct to an ounce," the superintendent replied, gazing at my colleague with a slightly uneasy expression. "Why?"

By way of reply Thorndyke lifted out the bar that he had measured and carrying it across to the machine, laid it on the platform and carefully adjusted the weights.

"Well?" the superintendent queried anxiously, as Thorndyke took the reading from the scale.

"Twenty-nine pounds, three ounces," replied Thorndyke.

"Well?" repeated the superintendent. "What about it?"

Thorndyke looked at him impassively for a moment, and then, in the same quiet tone, answered: "Lead."

"What!" the two officers shrieked in unison, darting across to the scale and glaring at the bar of metal. Then Badger recovered himself and expostulated, not without temper, "Nonsense, sir. Look at it. Can't you see that it is gold?"

"I can see that it is gilded," replied Thorndyke.

"But," protested Miller, "the thing is impossible! What makes you think it is lead?"

"It is just a question of specific gravity," was the reply. "This bar contains seventy-two cubic inches of metal and it weighs twenty pounds, three ounces. Therefore it is a bar of lead. But if you are still doubtful, it is quite easy to settle the matter. May I cut a small piece off the bar?"

The superintendent gasped and looked at his subordinate. "I suppose," said he, "under the circumstances, eh, Badger? Yes. Very well, doctor."

Thorndyke produced a strong pocket-knife and, having lifted the bar to the table, applied the knife to one corner and tapped it smartly with the hammer. The blade passed easily through the soft metal, and as the detached piece fell to the floor, the two officers and I craned forward eagerly. And then all possible doubts were set at rest. There was no mistaking the white, silvery lustre of the freshly-cut surface.

"Snakes!" exclaimed the superintendent. "This is a fair knock-out! Why, the blighters have got away with the stuff, after all! Unless," he added, with a quizzical look at Thorndyke, "you know where it is, doctor. I expect you do."

"I believe I do," said Thorndyke, "and if you care to come down with me to the London Docks, I think I can hand it over to you."

The superintendent's face brightened appreciably. Not so Badger's. That afflicted officer flung down the chip of metal that he had been examining, and turning to Thorndyke, demanded sourly: "Why didn't you tell us this before, sir? You let me go off chivvying that damn barge, and you knew all the time that the stuff wasn't on board."

"My dear Badger," Thorndyke expostulated, "don't you see that these lead bars are essential to our case? They prove that the gold bars were never landed and that they are consequently still on the ship. Which empowers us to detain any gold that we may find on her."

"There, now, Badger," said the superintendent, "it's no use for you to argue with the doctor. He's like a giraffe. He can see all round him at once. Let us get on to the Docks."

Having locked the room, we all sallied forth, and, taking a train at Charing Cross Station, made our way by Mark Lane and Fenchurch Street to Wapping, where, following Thorndyke, we entered the Docks and proceeded straight to a wharf near the Wapping entrance. Here Thorndyke exchanged a few words with a Customs official, who hurried away and presently returned, accompanied by an officer of higher rank. The latter, having saluted Thorndyke and cast a slightly amused glance at our little party, said: "They've landed that package that you spoke about. I've had it put in my office for the present. Will you come and have a look at it?"

We followed him to his office behind a long row of sheds, where, on a table, was a strong wooden case, somewhat larger than the "bullion"-case, while on the desk a large, many-leaved document lay open.

"This is your case, I think," said the official; "but you had better check it by the manifest. Here is the entry:

One case containing seventeen and three-quarter dozen brass six-inch by three-eighths screw-bolts with nuts. Dimensions, sixteen inches by thirteen by nine. Gross weight a hundred and nineteen pounds; net weight a hundred and thirteen pounds. Consigned to 'Jackson and Walker, 593 Great Alie Street, London, E.'

". . . . is that the one?"

"That is the one," Thorndyke replied.

"Then," said our friend, "we'll get it open and have a look at those brass screw-bolts."

With a dexterity surprising in an official of such high degree, he had the screws out in a twinkling, and prising up the lid, displayed a fold of coarse canvas. As he lifted this the two police officers peered eagerly into the case; and suddenly the eager expression on Badger's face changed to one of bitter disappointment.

"You've missed fire this time, sir," he snapped. "This is just a case of brass bolts."

"Gold bolts, inspector," Thorndyke corrected, placidly. He picked out one and handed it to the astonished detective. "Did you ever feel a brass bolt of that weight?" he asked.

"Well, it certainly is devilish heavy," the inspector admitted, weighing it in his hand and passing it on to Miller.

"Its weight, as stated on the manifest," said Thorndyke, "works out at well over eight and a half ounces, but we may as well check it." He produced from his pocket a little spring balance, to which he slung the bolt. "You see," he said, "it weighs eight ounces and two-thirds. But a brass bolt of the same size would weigh only three ounces and four-fifths. There is not the least doubt that these bolts are gold; and as you see that their aggregate weight is a hundred and thirteen while the weight of the four missing bars is a hundred and thirteen pounds, two ounces, it is a reasonable inference that these bolts represent those bars; and an uncommonly good job they made of the melting to lose only two ounces. Has the consignee's agent turned up yet?"

"He is waiting outside," replied the officer, with a pleased smile, "hopping about like a pea in a frying-pan. I'll call him in."

He did so, and a small, seedy man of strongly Semitic aspect approached the door with nervous caution and a rather pale face. But when his beady eye fell on the open case and the portentous assembly in the office, he turned about and fled along the wharf as if the hosts of the Philistines were at his heels.

"Of course it is all perfectly simple, as you say," I replied to Thorndyke as we strolled back up Nightingale Lane, "but I don't see where you got your start. What made you think that the stolen case was a dummy?"

"At first," Thorndyke replied, "it was just a matter of alternative hypotheses. It was purely speculative. The robbery described by Halethorpe was a very crude affair. It was planned in quite the wrong way. Noting this, I naturally asked myself: What is the right way to steal a case of gold ingots? Now, the outstanding difficulty in such a robbery arises from the ponderous nature of the thing stolen, and the way to overcome that difficulty is to get away with the booty at leisure before the robbery is discovered—the longer the better. It is also obvious that if you can delude someone into stealing your dummy you will have covered up your tracks most completely; for if that someone is caught, the issues are extremely confused, and if he is not caught, all the tracks lead away from you.

"Of course, he will discover the fraud when he tries to dispose of the swag, but his lips are sealed by the fact that he has, himself, committed a felony. So that is the proper strategical plan and, though it was wildly improbable, and there was nothing whatever to suggest it, still, the possibility that this crude robbery might cover a more subtle one had to be borne in mind. It was necessary to make absolutely certain that the gold bars were really in the case when it left Belhaven. I had practically no doubt that they were. Our visit to the Custom House was little more than a formality, just to give us an undeniable datum from which to make our start.

"We had to find somebody who had actually seen the case open and verified the contents, and when we found that man—Mr. Byrne—it instantly became obvious that the wildly improbable thing had really happened. The gold bars had already disappeared. I had calculated the approximate size of the real bars. They would contain forty-two cubic inches, and would be about seven inches by three by two. The dimensions given by Byrne—evidently correct, as shown by those of the case, which the bars fitted pretty closely—were impossible. If those bars had been gold, they would have weighed two hundred pounds, instead of the hundred and thirteen pounds shown on his report. The astonishing thing is that Byrne did not observe the discrepancy. There are not many Customs officers who would have let it pass."

"Isn't it rather odd," I asked, "that the thieves should have gambled on such a remote chance?"

"It is pretty certain," he replied, "that they were unaware of the risk they were taking. Probably they assumed—as most persons would have done—that a case of bullion would be merely inspected and passed. Few persons realise the rigorous methods of the Customs officers. But to resume: It was obvious that the 'gold' bars that Byrne had examined were dummies. The next question was, where were the real bars? Had they been made away with, or were they still on the ship? To settle this question I decided to go through the manifest and especially through the column of net weights. And there, presently, I came upon a package the net weight of which was within two ounces of the weight of stolen bars. And that package was a parcel of brass screw-bolts—on a homeward-bound ship!

"But who on earth sends brass bolts from Africa to London? The anomaly was so striking that I examined the entry more closely, and then I found—by dividing the net weight by the number of bolts—that each of these little bolts weighed over half a pound. But, if this were so, those bolts could be of no other metal than gold or platinum, and were almost certainly gold. Also, their aggregate weight was exactly that of the stolen bars, less two ounces, which probably represented loss in melting."

"And the scrivelloes," said I, "and the gum copal and the kola nuts; what was their bearing on the inquiry? I can't, even now, trace any connection."

Thorndyke cast an astonished glance at me, and then replied with a quiet chuckle: "There wasn't any. Those notes were for the benefit of the shipping gentleman. As he would look over my shoulder, I had to give him something to read and think about. If I had noted only the brass bolts, I should have virtually informed him of the nature of my suspicions."

"Then, really, you had the case complete when we left Belhaven?"

"Theoretically, yes. But we had to recover the stolen case, for without those lead ingots we could not prove that the gold bolts were stolen property, any more than one could prove a murder without evidence of the death of the victim."

"And how do you suppose the robbery was carried out? How was the gold got out of the ship's strong-room?"

"I should say it was never there. The robbers, I suspect, are the ship's mate, the chief engineer and possibly the purser. The mate controls the stowage of cargo, and the chief engineer controls the repair shop and has the necessary skill and knowledge to deal with the metal. On receiving the advice of the bullion consignment, I imagine they prepared the dummy case in agreement with the description. When the bullion arrived, the dummy case would be concealed on deck and the exchange made as soon as the bullion was put on board.

"The dummy would be sent to the strong-room and the real case carried to a prepared hiding place. Then the engineer would cut up the bars, melt them piecemeal and cast them into bolts in an ordinary casting flask, using an iron bolt as a model, and touching up the screw-threads with a die. The mate could enter the case on the manifest when he pleased, and send the bill of lading by post to the nominal consignee. That is what I imagine to have been the procedure."

Thorndyke's solution turned out to be literally correct. The consignee, pursued by Inspector Badger along the quay, was arrested at the dock gates and immediately volunteered king's evidence. Thereupon the mate, the chief engineer and the purser of the steamship *Labadi* were arrested and brought to trial; when they severally entered a plea of guilty and described the method of the robbery almost in Thorndyke's words.

The Echo of a Mutiny

Popular belief ascribes to infants and the lower animals certain occult powers of divining character denied to the reasoning faculties of the human adult; and is apt to accept their judgment as finally overriding the pronouncements of mere experience.

Whether this belief rests upon any foundation other than the universal love of paradox it is unnecessary to inquire. It is very generally entertained, especially by ladies of a certain social status; and by Mrs. Thomas Solly it was loyally maintained as an article of faith.

"Yes," she moralised, "it's surprisin' how they know, the little children and the dumb animals. But they do. There's no deceivin' them. They can tell the gold from the dross in a moment, they can, and they reads the human heart like a book. Wonderful, I call it. I suppose it's instinct."

Having delivered herself of this priceless gem of philosophic thought, she thrust her arms elbow-deep into the foaming wash-tub and glanced admiringly at her lodger as he sat in the doorway, supporting on one knee an obese infant of eighteen months and on the other a fine tabby cat.

James Brown was an elderly seafaring man, small and slight in build and in manner suave, insinuating and perhaps a trifle sly. But he had all the sailor's love of children and animals, and the sailor's knack of making himself acceptable to them, for, as he sat with an empty pipe wobbling in the grasp of his toothless gums, the baby beamed with humid smiles, and the cat, rolled into a fluffy ball and purring like a stocking-loom, worked its fingers ecstatically as if it were trying on a new pair of gloves.

"It must be mortal lonely out at the lighthouse," Mrs. Solly resumed. "Only three men and never a neighbour to speak to; and,

Lord! what a muddle they must be in with no woman to look after them and keep 'em tidy. But you won't be overworked, Mr. Brown, in these long days; daylight till past nine o'clock. I don't know what you'll do to pass the time."

"Oh, I shall find plenty to do, I expect," said Brown, "what with cleanin' the lamps and glasses and paintin' up the ironwork. And that reminds me," he added, looking round at the clock, "that time's getting on. High water at half-past ten, and here it's gone eight o'clock."

Mrs. Solly, acting on the hint, began rapidly to fish out the washed garments and wring them out into the form of short ropes. Then, having dried her hands on her apron, she relieved Brown of the protesting baby.

"Your room will be ready for you, Mr. Brown," said she, "when your turn comes for a spell ashore; and main glad me and Tom will be to see you back."

"Thank you, Mrs. Solly, ma'am," answered Brown, tenderly placing the cat on the floor; "you won't be more glad than what I will." He shook hands warmly with his landlady, kissed the baby, chucked the cat under the chin, and, picking up his little chest by its becket, swung it onto his shoulder and strode out of the cottage.

His way lay across the marshes, and, like the ships in the offing, he shaped his course by the twin towers of Reculver that stood up grotesquely on the rim of the land; and as he trod the springy turf, Tom Solly's fleecy charges looked up at him with vacant stares and valedictory bleatings. Once, at a dyke-gate, he paused to look back at the fair Kentish landscape: at the grey tower of St. Nicholas-at-Wade peeping above the trees and the faraway mill at Sarre, whirling slowly in the summer breeze; and, above all, at the solitary cottage where, for a brief spell in his stormy life, he had known the homely joys of domesticity and peace. Well, that was over for the present, and the lighthouse loomed ahead. With a half-sigh he passed through the gate and walked on towards Reculver.

Outside the whitewashed cottages with their official black chimneys a petty-officer of the coast-guard was adjusting the halyards of the flagstaff. He looked round as Brown approached, and hailed him cheerily.

"Here you are, then," said he, "all figged out in your new togs, too. But we're in a bit of a difficulty, d'ye see. We've got to pull up to Whitstable this morning, so I can't send a man out with you and I can't spare a boat."

"Have I got to swim out, then?" asked Brown.

The coast-guard grinned. "Not in them new clothes, mate," he answered. "No, but there's old Willett's boat; he isn't using her today; he's going over to Minster to see his daughter, and he'll let us have the loan of the boat. But there's no one to go with you, and I'm responsible to Willett."

"Well, what about it?" asked Brown, with the deep-sea sailor's (usually misplaced) confidence in his power to handle a sailing-boat. "D'ye think I can't manage a tub of a boat? Me what's used the sea since I was a kid of ten?"

"Yes," said the coast-guard; "but who's to bring her back?"

"Why, the man that I'm going to relieve," answered Brown. "He don't want to swim no more than what I do."

The coast-guard reflected with his telescope pointed at a passing barge. "Well, I suppose it'll be all right," he concluded; "but it's a pity they couldn't send the tender round. However, if you undertake to send the boat back, we'll get her afloat. It's time you were off."

He strolled away to the back of the cottages, whence he presently returned with two of his mates, and the four men proceeded along the shore to where Willett's boat lay just above high-water mark.

The *Emily* was a beamy craft of the type locally known as a "half-share skiff," solidly built of oak, with varnished planking and fitted with main and mizzen lugs. She was a good handful for four men, and, as she slid over the soft chalk rocks with a hollow rumble, the coast-guards debated the advisability of lifting out the bags of shingle with which she was ballasted. However, she was at length dragged down, ballast and all, to the water's edge, and then, while Brown stepped the mainmast, the petty-officer gave him his directions. "What you've got to do," said he, "is to make use of the flood-tide. Keep her nose nor'-east, and with this trickle of nor'-westerly breeze you ought to make the light-house in one board. Anyhow don't let her get east of the lighthouse, or, when the ebb sets in, you'll be in a fix."

To these admonitions Brown listened with jaunty indifference as he hoisted the sails and watched the incoming tide creep over the level shore. Then the boat lifted on the gentle swell. Putting out an oar, he gave a vigorous shove off that sent the boat, with a final scrape, clear of the beach, and then, having dropped the rudder onto its pintles, he seated himself and calmly belayed the main-sheet.

"There he goes," growled the coast-guard; "makin' fast his sheet. They will do it" (he invariably did it himself), "and that's how accidents happen. I hope old Willett'll see his boat back all right."

He stood for some time watching the dwindling boat as it sidled across the smooth water; then he turned and followed his mates towards the station.

Out on the south-western edge of the Girdler Sand, just inside the two-fathom line, the spindle-shanked lighthouse stood a-straddle on its long screw-piles like some uncouth red-bodied wading bird. It was now nearly half flood tide. The highest shoals were long since covered, and the lighthouse rose above the smooth sea as solitary as a slaver becalmed in the "middle passage."

On the gallery outside the lantern were two men, the entire staff of the building, of whom one sat huddled in a chair with his left leg propped up with pillows on another, while his companion rested a telescope on the rail and peered at the faint grey line of the distant land and the two tiny points that marked the twin spires of Reculver.

"I don't see any signs of the boat, Harry," said he.

The other man groaned. "I shall lose the tide," he complained, "and then there's another day gone."

"They can pull you down to Birchington and put you in the train," said the first man.

"I don't want no trains," growled the invalid. "The boat'll be bad enough. I suppose there's nothing coming our way, Tom?"

Tom turned his face eastward and shaded his eyes. "There's a brig coming across the tide from the north," he said. "Looks like a collier." He pointed his telescope at the approaching vessel, and added: "She's got two new cloths in her upper fore top-sail, one on each leech."

The other man sat up eagerly. "What's her trysail like, Tom?" he asked.

"Can't see it," replied Tom. "Yes, I can, now: it's tanned. Why, that'll be the old *Utopia*, Harry; she's the only brig I know that's got a tanned trysail."

"Look here, Tom," exclaimed the other, "If that's the *Utopia*, she's going to my home and I'm going aboard of her. Captain Mockett'll give me a passage, I know."

"You oughtn't to go until you're relieved, you know, Barnett," said Tom doubtfully; "it's against regulations to leave your station."

"Regulations be blowed!" exclaimed Barnett. "My leg's more to me than the regulations. I don't want to be a cripple all my life. Besides, I'm no good here, and this new chap, Brown, will be coming out presently. You run up the signal, Tom, like a good comrade, and hail the brig."

"Well, it's your look-out," said Tom, "and I don't mind saying that if I was in your place I should cut off home and see a doctor, if I got the chance." He sauntered off to the flag-locker, and, selecting the two code-flags, deliberately toggled them onto the halyards. Then, as the brig swept up within range, he hoisted the little balls of bunting to the flagstaff-head and jerked the halyards, when the two flags blew out making the signal "Need assistance."

Promptly a coal-soiled answering pennant soared to the brig's main-truck; less promptly the collier went about, and, turning her nose down stream, slowly drifted stern-forwards towards the lighthouse. Then a boat slid out through her gangway, and a couple of men plied the oars vigorously.

"Lighthouse ahoy!" roared one of them, as the boat came within hail. "What's amiss?"

"Harry Barnett has broke his leg," shouted the lighthouse keeper, "and he wants to know if Captain Mockett will give him a passage to Whitstable."

The boat turned back to the brig, and after a brief and bellowed consultation, once more pulled towards the lighthouse.

"Skipper says yus," roared the sailor, when he was within ear-shot, "and he says look alive, 'cause he don't want to miss his tide."

The injured man heaved a sigh of relief. "That's good news," said he, "though, how the blazes I'm going to get down the ladder is more than I can tell. What do you say, Jeffreys?"

"I say you'd better let me lower you with the tackle," replied Jeffreys. "You can sit in the bight of a rope and I'll give you a line to steady yourself with."

"Ah, that'll do, Tom," said Barnett; "but, for the Lord's sake, pay out the fall-rope gently."

The arrangements were made so quickly that by the time the boat was fast alongside everything was in readiness, and a minute later the injured man, dangling like a gigantic spider from the end of the tackle, slowly descended, cursing volubly to the accompaniment of the creaking of the blocks. His chest and kit-bag followed, and, as soon as these were unhooked from the tackle, the boat pulled off to the brig, which was now slowly creeping stern-foremost past the lighthouse. The sick man was hoisted up the side, his chest handed up after him, and then the brig was put on her course due south across the Kentish Flats.

Jeffreys stood on the gallery watching the receding vessel and listening to the voices of her crew as they grew small and weak in the increasing distance. Now that his gruff companion was gone, a strange loneliness had fallen on the lighthouse. The last of the homeward-bound ships had long since passed up the Princes Channel and left the calm sea desolate and blank. The distant buoys, showing as tiny black dots on the glassy surface, and the spindly shapes of the beacons which stood up from invisible shoals, but emphasized the solitude of the empty sea, and the tolling of the bell buoy on the Shivering Sand, stealing faintly down the wind, sounded weird and mournful.

The day's work was already done. The lenses were polished, the lamps had been trimmed, and the little motor that worked the fog-horn had been cleaned and oiled. There were several odd jobs, it is true, waiting to be done, as there always are in a lighthouse; but, just now, Jeffreys was not in a working humour. A new comrade was coming into his life today, a stranger with whom he was to be shut up alone, night and day, for a month on end, and whose temper and tastes and habits might mean for him pleasant companionship or jangling and discord without end. Who was this man Brown? What had he been? and what was he like? These were the questions that passed, naturally enough, through the lighthouse keeper's mind and distracted him from his usual thoughts and occupations.

Presently a speck on the landward horizon caught his eye. He snatched up the telescope eagerly to inspect it. Yes, it was a boat; but not the coast-guard's cutter, for which he was looking. Evidently a fisherman's boat and with only one man in it. He laid down the telescope with a sigh of disappointment, and, filling his pipe, leaned on the rail with a dreamy eye bent on the faint grey line of the land.

Three long years had he spent in this dreary solitude, so repugnant to his active, restless nature: three blank, interminable years, with nothing to look back on but the endless succession of summer calms, stormy nights and the chilly fogs of winter, when the unseen steamers hooted from the void and the fog-horn bellowed its hoarse warning.

Why had he come to this God-forsaken spot? and why did he stay, when the wide world called to him? And then memory painted him a picture on which his mind's eye had often looked before and which once again arose before him, shutting out the vision of the calm sea and the distant land. It was a brightly-coloured picture. It showed a cloudless sky brooding over the deep blue tropic sea: and in the middle of the picture, see-sawing gently on the quiet swell, a white-painted barque.

Her sails were clewed up untidily, her swinging yards jerked at the slack braces and her untended wheel revolved to and fro to the oscillations of the rudder.

She was not a derelict, for more than a dozen men were on her deck; but the men were all drunk and mostly asleep, and there was never an officer among them.

Then he saw the interior of one of her cabins. The chart-rack, the tell-tale compass and the chronometers marked it as the captain's cabin. In it were four men, and two of them lay dead on the deck. Of the other two, one was a small, cunning-faced man, who was, at the moment, kneeling beside one of the corpses to wipe a knife upon its coat. The fourth man was himself.

Again, he saw the two murderers stealing off in a quarter-boat, as the barque with her drunken crew drifted towards the spouting surf of a river-bar. He saw the ship melt away in the surf like an icicle in the sunshine; and, later, two shipwrecked mariners, picked up in an open boat and set ashore at an American port.

That was why he was here. Because he was a murderer. The other scoundrel, Amos Todd, had turned Queen's Evidence and denounced him, and he had barely managed to escape. Since then he had hidden himself from the great world, and here he must continue to hide, not from the law—for his person was unknown now that his shipmates were dead—but from the partner of his crime. It was the fear of Todd that had changed him from Jeffrey Rorke to Tom Jeffreys and had sent him to the Girdler, a prisoner for life. Todd might die—might even now be dead—but he would never hear of it: would never hear the news of his release.

He roused himself and once more pointed his telescope at the distant boat. She was considerably nearer now and seemed to be heading out towards the lighthouse. Perhaps the man in her was bringing a message; at any rate, there was no sign of the coast-guard's cutter.

He went in, and, betaking himself to the kitchen, busied himself with a few simple preparations for dinner. But there was nothing to cook, for there remained the cold meat from yesterday's cooking, which he would make sufficient, with some biscuit in place of potatoes. He felt restless and unstrung; the solitude irked him, and the everlasting wash of the water among the piles jarred on his nerves.

When he went out again into the gallery the ebb-tide had set in strongly and the boat was little more than a mile distant; and now, through the glass, he could see that the man in her wore the uniform cap of the Trinity House. Then the man must be his future comrade, Brown; but this was very extraordinary. What were they to do with the boat? There was no one to take her back.

The breeze was dying away. As he watched the boat, he saw the man lower the sail and take to his oars; and something of hurry in the way the man pulled over the gathering tide, caused Jeffreys to look round the horizon. And then, for the first time, he noticed a bank of fog creeping up from the east and already so near that the beacon on the East Girdler had faded out of sight. He hastened in to start the little motor that compressed the air for the fog-horn and waited awhile to see that the mechanism was running properly. Then, as the deck vibrated to the roar of the horn, he went out once more into the gallery.

The fog was now all round the lighthouse and the boat was hidden from view. He listened intently. The enclosing wall of vapour seemed to have shut out sound as well as vision. At intervals the horn bellowed its note of warning, and then all was still save the murmur of the water among the piles below, and, infinitely faint and far away, the mournful tolling of the bell on the Shivering Sand.

At length there came to his ear the muffled sound of oars working in the holes; then, at the very edge of the circle of grey water that was visible, the boat appeared through the fog, pale and spectral, with a shadowy figure pulling furiously. The horn emitted a hoarse growl; the man looked round, perceived the lighthouse and altered his course towards it.

Jeffreys descended the iron stairway, and, walking along the lower gallery, stood at the head of the ladder earnestly watching the approaching stranger. Already he was tired of being alone. The yearning for human companionship had been growing ever since Barnett left. But what sort of comrade was this stranger who was coming into his life? And coming to occupy so dominant a place in it.

The boat swept down swiftly athwart the hurrying tide. Nearer it came and yet nearer: and still Jeffreys could catch no glimpse of his new comrade's face. At length it came fairly alongside and bumped against the fender-posts; the stranger whisked in an oar and grabbed a rung of the ladder, and Jeffreys dropped a coil of rope into the boat. And still the man's face was hidden.

Jeffreys leaned out over the ladder and watched him anxiously, as he made fast the rope, unhooked the sail from the traveller and unstepped the mast. When he had set all in order, the stranger picked up a small chest, and, swinging it over his shoulder, stepped onto the ladder. Slowly, by reason of his encumbrance, he mounted, rung by rung, with never an upward glance, and Jeffreys gazed down at the top of his head with growing curiosity. At last he reached the top of the ladder and Jeffreys stooped to lend him a hand. Then, for the first time, he looked up, and Jeffreys started back with a blanched face.

"God Almighty!" he gasped. "It's Amos Todd!"

As the newcomer stepped on the gallery, the fog-horn emitted a roar like that of some hungry monster. Jeffreys turned abruptly without a word, and walked to the stairs, followed by Todd, and the two men ascended with never a sound but the hollow clank of their footsteps on the iron plates. Silently Jeffreys stalked into the living-room and, as his companion followed, he turned and motioned to the latter to set down his chest.

"You ain't much of a talker, mate," said Todd, looking round the room in some surprise; "ain't you going to say 'good-morning'? We're going to be good comrades, I hope. I'm Jim Brown, the new hand, I am; what might your name be?"

Jeffreys turned on him suddenly and led him to the window. "Look at me carefully, Amos Todd," he said sternly, "and then ask yourself what my name is."

At the sound of his voice Todd looked up with a start and turned pale as death. "It can't be," he whispered, "it can't be Jeff Rorke!"

The other man laughed harshly, and leaning forward, said in a low voice: "Hast thou found me, O mine enemy!"

"Don't say that!" exclaimed Todd. "Don't call me your enemy, Jeff. Lord knows but I'm glad to see you, though I'd never have known you without your beard and with that grey hair. I've been to blame, Jeff, and I know it; but it ain't no use raking up old grudges. Let bygones be bygones, Jeff, and let us be pals as we used to be." He wiped his face with his handkerchief and watched his companion apprehensively.

"Sit down," said Rorke, pointing to a shabby rep-covered armchair; "sit down and tell me what you've done with all that money. You've blued it all, I suppose, or you wouldn't be here."

"Robbed, Jeff," answered Todd; "robbed of every penny. Ah! that was an unfortunate affair, that job on board the old *Sea-flower*. But it's over and done with and we'd best forget it. They're all dead but us, Jeff, so we're safe enough so long as we keep our mouths shut; all at the bottom of the sea—and the best place for 'em too."

"Yes," Rorke replied fiercely, "that's the best place for your shipmates when they know too much; at the bottom of the sea or swinging at the end of a rope." He paced up and down the little room with rapid strides, and each time that he approached Todd's chair the latter shrank back with an expression of alarm.

"Don't sit there staring at me," said Rorke. "Why don't you smoke or do something?"

Todd hastily produced a pipe from his pocket, and having filled it from a moleskin pouch, stuck it in his mouth while he searched for a match. Apparently he carried his matches loose in his pocket, for he presently brought one forth—a red-headed match, which, when he struck it on the wall, lighted with a pale-blue flame. He applied it to his pipe, sucking in his cheeks while he kept his eyes fixed on his companion. Rorke, meanwhile, halted in his walk to cut some shavings from a cake of hard tobacco with a large clasp-knife; and, as he stood, he gazed with frowning abstraction at Todd.

"This pipe's stopped," said the latter, sucking ineffectually at the mouthpiece. "Have you got such a thing as a piece of wire, Jeff?"

"No, I haven't," replied Rorke; "not up here. I'll get a bit from the store presently. Here, take this pipe till you can clean your own: I've got another in the rack there." The sailor's natural hospitality overcoming for the moment his animosity, he thrust the pipe that he had just filled towards Todd, who took it with a mumbled "Thank you" and an anxious eye on the open knife. On the wall beside the chair was a roughly-carved pipe-rack containing several pipes, one of which Rorke lifted out; and, as he leaned over the chair to reach it, Todd's face went several shades paler.

"Well, Jeff," he said, after a pause, while Rorke cut a fresh "fill" of tobacco, "are we going to be pals same as what we used to be?"

Rorke's animosity lighted up afresh. "Am I going to be pals with the man that tried to swear away my life?" he said sternly; and after a pause he added: "That wants thinking about, that does; and meantime I must go and look at the engine."

When Rorke had gone the new hand sat, with the two pipes in his hands, reflecting deeply. Abstractedly he stuck the fresh pipe into his mouth, and, dropping the stopped one into the rack, felt for a match. Still with an air of abstraction he lit the pipe, and having smoked for a minute or two, rose from the chair and began softly to creep across the room, looking about him and listening intently. At the door he paused to look out into the fog, and then, having again listened attentively, he stepped on tip-toe out onto the gallery and along towards the stairway.

Of a sudden the voice of Rorke brought him up with a start.

"Hallo, Todd! where are you off to?"

"I'm just going down to make the boat secure," was the reply.

"Never you mind about the boat," said Rorke. "I'll see to her."

"Right-o, Jeff," said Todd, still edging towards the stairway. "But, I say, mate, where's the other man—the man that I'm to relieve?"

"There ain't any other man," replied Rorke; "he went off aboard a collier."

Todd's face suddenly became grey and haggard. "Then there's no one here but us two!" he gasped; and then, with an effort to conceal his fear, he asked: "But who's going to take the boat back?"

"We'll see about that presently," replied Rorke; "you get along in and unpack your chest."

He came out on the gallery as he spoke, with a lowering frown on his face. Todd cast a terrified glance at him, and then turned and ran for his life towards the stairway.

"Come back!" roared Rorke, springing forward along the gallery; but Todd's feet were already clattering down the iron steps. By the time Rorke reached the head of the stairs, the fugitive was near the bottom; but here, in his haste, he stumbled, barely saving himself by the handrail, and when he recovered his balance Rorke was upon him. Todd darted to the head of the ladder, but, as he grasped the stanchion, his pursuer seized him by the collar. In a moment he had turned with his hand under his coat. There was a quick blow, a loud curse from Rorke, an answering yell from Todd, and a knife fell spinning through the air and dropped into the fore-peak of the boat below.

"You murderous little devil!" said Rorke in an ominously quiet voice, with his bleeding hand gripping his captive by the throat. "Handy with your knife as ever, eh? So you were off to give information, were you?"

"No, I wasn't Jeff," replied Todd in a choking voice; "I wasn't, s'elp me, God. Let go, Jeff. I didn't mean no harm. I was only—" With a sudden wrench he freed one hand and struck out frantically at his captor's face. But Rorke warded off the blow, and, grasping the other wrist, gave a violent push and let go. Todd staggered backward a few paces along the staging, bringing up at the extreme edge; and here, for a sensible time, he stood with wide-open mouth and starting eye-balls, swaying and clutching wildly at the air. Then, with a shrill scream, he toppled backwards and fell, striking a pile in his descent and rebounding into the water.

91

In spite of the audible thump of his head on the pile, he was not stunned, for when he rose to the surface, he struck out vigorously, uttering short, stifled cries for help. Rorke watched him with set teeth and quickened breath, but made no move. Smaller and still smaller grew the head with its little circle of ripples, swept away on the swift ebb-tide, and fainter the bubbling cries that came across the smooth water. At length as the small black spot began to fade in the fog, the drowning man, with a final effort, raised his head clear of the surface and sent a last, despairing shriek towards the lighthouse. The fog-horn sent back an answering bellow; the head sank below the surface and was seen no more; and in the dreadful stillness that settled down upon the sea there sounded faint and far away the muffled tolling of a bell.

Rorke stood for some minutes immovable, wrapped in thought. Presently the distant hoot of a steamer's whistle aroused him. The ebb-tide shipping was beginning to come down and the fog might lift at any moment; and there was the boat still alongside. She must be disposed of at once. No one had seen her arrive and no one must see her made fast to the lighthouse. Once get rid of the boat and all traces of Todd's visit would be destroyed. He ran down the ladder and stepped into the boat. It was simple. She was heavily ballasted, and would go down if she filled.

He shifted some of the bags of shingle, and, lifting the bottom boards, pulled out the plug. Instantly a large jet of water spouted up into the bottom. Rorke looked at it critically, and, deciding that it would fill her in a few minutes, replaced the bottom boards; and having secured the mast and sail with a few turns of the sheet round a thwart, to prevent them from floating away, he cast off the mooring-rope and stepped on the ladder.

As the released boat began to move away on the tide, he ran up and mounted to the upper gallery to watch her disappearance. Suddenly he remembered Todd's chest. It was still in the room below. With a hurried glance around into the fog, he ran down to the room, and snatching up the chest, carried it out on the lower gallery. After another nervous glance around to assure himself that no craft was in sight, he heaved the chest over the handrail, and, when it fell with a loud splash into the sea, he waited to watch it float away after its owner and the sunken boat. But it never rose; and presently he returned to the upper gallery.

The fog was thinning perceptibly now, and the boat remained plainly visible as she drifted away. But she sank more slowly than he had expected, and presently as she drifted farther away, he fetched the telescope and peered at her with growing anxiety. It would be unfortunate if any one saw her; if she should be picked up here, with her plug out, it would be disastrous.

He was beginning to be really alarmed. Through the glass he could see that the boat was now rolling in a sluggish, water-logged fashion, but she still showed some inches of free-board, and the fog was thinning every moment.

Presently the blast of a steamer's whistle sounded close at hand. He looked round hurriedly and, seeing nothing, again pointed the telescope eagerly at the dwindling boat. Suddenly he gave a gasp of relief. The boat had rolled gunwale under; had staggered back for a moment and then rolled again, slowly, finally, with the water pouring in over the submerged gunwale.

In a few more seconds she had vanished. Rorke lowered the telescope and took a deep breath. Now he was safe. The boat had sunk unseen. But he was better than safe: he was free. His evil spirit, the standing menace of his life, was gone, and the wide world, the world of life, of action, of pleasure, called to him.

In a few minutes the fog lifted. The sun shone brightly on the red-funnelled cattle-boat whose whistle had startled him just now, the summer blue came back to sky and sea, and the land peeped once more over the edge of the horizon.

He went in, whistling cheerfully, and stopped the motor; returned to coil away the rope that he had thrown to Todd; and, when he had hoisted a signal for assistance, he went in once more to eat his solitary meal in peace and gladness.

PART 2. "THE SINGING BONE"
(Related by Christopher Jervis, M.D.)

In every kind of scientific work a certain amount of manual labour naturally appertains, labour that cannot be performed by the scientist himself, since art is long but life is short. A chemical analysis involves a laborious "clean up" of apparatus and laboratory, for which the chemist has no time; the preparation of a skeleton—the maceration, bleaching, "assembling," and riveting together of bones—must be carried out by someone whose time is not too precious. And so with other scientific activities. Behind the man of science with his outfit of knowledge is the indispensable mechanic with his outfit of manual skill.

Thorndyke's laboratory assistant, Polton, was a fine example of the latter type, deft, resourceful, ingenious and untiring. He was somewhat of an inventive genius, too; and it was one of his inventions that connected us with the singular case that I am about to record.

Though by trade a watchmaker, Polton was, by choice, an optician. Optical apparatus was the passion of his life; and when, one day, he produced for our inspection an improved prism for increasing the efficiency of gas-buoys, Thorndyke at once brought the invention to the notice of a friend at the Trinity House.

As a consequence, we three—Thorndyke, Polton and I—found ourselves early on a fine July morning making our way down Middle Temple Lane bound for the Temple Pier. A small oil-launch lay alongside the pontoon, and, as we made our appearance, a red-faced, white-whiskered gentleman stood up in the cockpit.

"Here's a delightful morning, doctor," he sang out in a fine, brassy, resonant, sea-faring voice; "sort of day for a trip to the lower river, hey? Hallo, Polton! Coming down to take the bread out of our mouths, are you? Ha, ha!" The cheery laugh rang out over the river and mingled with the throb of the engine as the launch moved off from the pier.

Captain Grumpass was one of the Elder Brethren of the Trinity House. Formerly a client of Thorndyke's he had subsided, as Thorndyke's clients were apt to do, into the position of a personal friend, and his hearty regard included our invaluable assistant.

"Nice state of things," continued the captain, with a chuckle, "when a body of nautical experts have got to be taught their business by a parcel of lawyers or doctors, what? I suppose trade's slack and 'Satan findeth mischief still,' hey, Polton?"

"There isn't much doing on the civil side, sir," replied Polton, with a quaint, crinkly smile, "but the criminals are still going strong."

"Ha! mystery department still flourishing, what? And, by Jove! talking of mysteries, doctor, our people have got a queer problem to work out; something quite in your line—quite. Yes, and, by the Lord Moses, since I've got you here, why shouldn't I suck your brains?"

"Exactly," said Thorndyke. "Why shouldn't you?"

"Well, then, I will," said the captain, "so here goes. All hands to the pump!" He lit a cigar, and, after a few preliminary puffs, began: "The mystery, shortly stated, is this: one of our lighthouse men has disappeared—vanished off the face of the earth and left no trace. He may have bolted, he may have been drowned accidentally or he may have been murdered. But I'd rather give you the particulars in order. At the end of last week a barge brought into Ramsgate a letter from the screw-pile lighthouse on the Girdler. There are only two men there, and it seems that one of them, a man named Barnett, had broken his leg, and he asked that the tender should be sent to bring him ashore.

"Well, it happened that the local tender, the warden, was up on the slip in Ramsgate Harbour, having a scrape down, and wouldn't be available for a day or two, so, as the case was urgent, the officer at Ramsgate sent a letter to the lighthouse by one of the pleasure steamers saying that the man should be relieved by boat on the following morning, which was Saturday. He also wrote to a new hand who had just been taken on, a man named James Brown, who was lodging near Reculver, waiting his turn, telling him to go out on Saturday morning in the coastguard's boat; and he sent a third letter to the coast-guard at Reculver asking him to take Brown out to the lighthouse and bring Barnett ashore.

"Well, between them, they made a fine muddle of it. The coast-guard couldn't spare either a boat or a man, so they borrowed a fisherman's boat, and in this the man Brown started off alone, like an idiot, on the chance that Barnett would be able to sail the boat back in spite of his broken leg.

"Meanwhile Barnett, who is a Whitstable man, had signalled a collier bound for his native town, and got taken off; so that the other keeper, Thomas Jeffreys, was left alone until Brown should turn up.

"But Brown never did turn up. The coast-guard helped him to put off and saw him well out to sea, and the keeper, Jeffreys, saw a sailing-boat with one man in her making for the lighthouse. Then a bank of fog came up and hid the boat, and when the fog cleared she was nowhere to be seen. Man and boat had vanished and left no sign."

"He may have been run down," Thorndyke suggested.

"He may," agreed the captain, "but no accident has been reported. The coast-guards think he may have capsized in a squall—they saw him make the sheet fast. But there weren't any squalls; the weather was quite calm."

"Was he all right and well when he put off?" inquired Thorndyke.

"Yes," replied the captain, "the coast-guards' report is highly circumstantial; in fact, it's full of silly details that have no bearing on anything. This is what they say." He pulled out an official letter and read: "'When last seen, the missing man was seated in the boat's stern to windward of the helm. He had belayed the sheet. He was holding a pipe and tobacco-pouch in his hands and steering with his elbow. He was filling the pipe from the tobacco-pouch.' There! 'He was holding the pipe in his hand,' mark you! not with his toes; and he was filling it from a tobacco-pouch, whereas you'd have expected him to fill it from a coalscuttle or a feeding-bottle. Bah!" The captain rammed the letter back in his pocket and puffed scornfully at his cigar.

"You are hardly fair to the coast-guard," said Thorndyke, laughing at the captain's vehemence. "The duty of a witness is to give all the facts, not a judicious selection."

"But, my dear sir," said Captain Grumpass, "what the deuce can it matter what the poor devil filled his pipe from?"

"Who can say?" answered Thorndyke. "It may turn out to be a highly material fact. One never knows beforehand. The value of a particular fact depends on its relation to the rest of the evidence."

"I suppose it does," grunted the captain; and he continued to smoke in reflective silence until we opened Black-wall Point, when he suddenly stood up.

"There's a steam trawler alongside our wharf," he announced. "Now what the deuce can she be doing there?" He scanned the little steamer attentively, and continued:

"They seem to be landing something, too. Just pass me those glasses, Polton. Why, hang me! it's a dead body! But why on earth are they landing it on our wharf? They must have known you were coming, doctor."

As the launch swept alongside the wharf, the captain sprang up lightly and approached the group gathered round the body. "What's this?" he asked. "Why have they brought this thing here?"

The master of the trawler, who had superintended the landing, proceeded to explain.

"It's one of your men, sir," said he. "We saw the body lying on the edge of the South Shingles Sand, close to the beacon, as we passed at low water, so we put off the boat and fetched it aboard. As there was nothing to identify the man by, I had a look in his pockets and found this letter."

He handed the captain an official envelope addressed to: "Mr. J. Brown, co Mr. Solly, Shepherd, Reculver, Kent."

"Why, this is the man we were speaking about, doctor," exclaimed Captain Grumpass. "What a very singular coincidence. But what are we to do with the body?"

"You will have to write to the coroner," replied Thorndyke. "By the way, did you turn out all the pockets?" he asked, turning to the skipper of the trawler.

"No, sir," was the reply. "I found the letter in the first pocket that I felt in, so I didn't examine any of the others. Is there anything more that you want to know, sir?"

"Nothing but your name and address, for the coroner," replied Thorndyke, and the skipper, having given this information and expressed the hope that the coroner would not keep him "hanging about," returned to his vessel and pursued his way to Billingsgate.

"I wonder if you would mind having a look at the body of this poor devil, while Polton is showing us his contraptions," said Captain Grumpass.

"I can't do much without a coroner's order," replied Thorndyke; "but if it will give you any satisfaction, Jervis and I will make a preliminary inspection with pleasure."

"I should be glad if you would," said the captain. "We should like to know that the poor beggar met his end fairly."

The body was accordingly moved to a shed, and, as Polton was led away, carrying the black bag that contained his precious model, we entered the shed and commenced our investigation.

The deceased was a small, elderly man, decently dressed in a somewhat nautical fashion. He appeared to have been dead only two or three days, and the body, unlike the majority of sea-borne corpses, was uninjured by fish or crabs. There were no fractured bones or other gross injuries, and no wounds, excepting a rugged tear in the scalp at the back of the head.

"The general appearance of the body," said Thorndyke, when he had noted these particulars, "suggests death by drowning, though, of course, we can't give a definite opinion until a post mortem has been made."

"You don't attach any significance to that scalp-wound, then?" I asked.

"As a cause of death? No. It was obviously inflicted during life, but it seems to have been an oblique blow that spent its force on the scalp, leaving the skull uninjured. But it is very significant in another way."

"In what way?" I asked.

Thorndyke took out his pocket-case and extracted a pair of forceps. "Consider the circumstances," said he. "This man put off from the shore to go to the lighthouse, but never arrived there. The question is, where did he arrive?" As he spoke he stooped over the corpse and turned back the hair round the wound with the beak of the forceps. "Look at those white objects among the hair, Jervis, and inside the wound. They tell us something, I think."

I examined, through my lens, the chalky fragments to which he pointed. "These seem to be bits of shells and the tubes of some marine worm," I said.

"Yes," he answered; "the broken shells are evidently those of the acorn barnacle, and the other fragments are mostly pieces of the tubes of the common *serpula*. The inference that these objects suggest is an important one. It is that this wound was produced by some body encrusted by acorn barnacles and *serpula*; that is to say, by a body that is periodically submerged. Now, what can that body be, and how can the deceased have knocked his head against it?"

"It might be the stem of a ship that ran him down," I suggested.

"I don't think you would find many *serpulae* on the stem of a ship," said Thorndyke. "The combination rather suggests some stationary object between tidemarks, such as a beacon. But one doesn't see how a man could knock his head against a beacon, while, on the other hand, there are no other stationary objects out in the estuary to knock against except buoys, and a buoy presents a flat surface that could hardly have produced this wound. By the way, we may as well see what there is in his pockets, though it is not likely that robbery had anything to do with his death."

"No," I agreed, "and I see his watch is in his pocket; quite a good silver one," I added, taking it out. "It has stopped at 12.13."

"That may be important," said Thorndyke, making a note of the fact; "but we had better examine the pockets one at a time, and put the things back when we have looked at them."

The first pocket that we turned out was the left hip-pocket of the monkey jacket. This was apparently the one that the skipper had rifled, for we found in it two letters, both bearing the crest of the Trinity House. These, of course, we returned without reading, and then passed on to the right pocket. The contents of this were common-place enough, consisting of a briar pipe, a moleskin pouch and a number of loose matches.

"Rather a casual proceeding, this," I remarked, "to carry matches loose in the pocket, and a pipe with them, too."

"Yes," agreed Thorndyke; "especially with these very inflammable matches. You notice that the sticks had been coated at the upper end with sulphur before the red phosphorous heads were put on. They would light with a touch, and would be very difficult to extinguish;

which, no doubt, is the reason that this type of match is so popular among seamen, who have to light their pipes in all sorts of weather." As he spoke he picked up the pipe and looked at it reflectively, turning it over in his hand and peering into the bowl. Suddenly he glanced from the pipe to the dead man's face and then, with the forceps, turned back the lips to look into the mouth.

"Let us see what tobacco he smokes," said he.

I opened the sodden pouch and displayed a mass of dark, fine-cut tobacco. "It looks like shag," I said.

"Yes, it is shag," he replied; "and now we will see what is in the pipe. It has been only half-smoked out." He dug out the "dottle" with his pocket-knife onto a sheet of paper, and we both inspected it. Clearly it was not shag, for it consisted of coarsely-cut shreds and was nearly black.

"Shavings from a cake of 'hard,'" was my verdict, and Thorndyke agreed as he shot the fragments back into the pipe.

The other pockets yielded nothing of interest, except a pocket-knife, which Thorndyke opened and examined closely. There was not much money, though as much as one would expect, and enough to exclude the idea of robbery.

"Is there a sheath-knife on that strap?" Thorndyke asked, pointing to a narrow leather belt. I turned back the jacket and looked.

"There is a sheath," I said, "but no knife. It must have dropped out."

"That is rather odd," said Thorndyke. "A sailor's sheath-knife takes a deal of shaking out as a rule. It is intended to be used in working on the rigging when the man is aloft, so that he can get it out with one hand while he is holding on with the other. It has to be and usually is very secure, for the sheath holds half the handle as well as the blade. What makes one notice the matter in this case is that the man, as you see, carried a pocket-knife; and, as this would serve all the ordinary purposes of a knife, it seems to suggest that the sheath-knife was carried for defensive purposes: as a weapon, in fact. However, we can't get much further in the case without a postmortem, and here comes the captain."

Captain Grumpass entered the shed and looked down commiseratingly at the dead seaman.

"Is there anything, doctor, that throws any light on the man's disappearance?" he asked.

"There are one or two curious features in the case," Thorndyke replied; "but, oddly enough, the only really important point arises out of that statement of the coastguard's, concerning which you were so scornful."

"You don't say so!" exclaimed the captain.

"Yes," said Thorndyke; "the coast-guard states that when last seen deceased was filling his pipe from his tobacco-pouch. Now his pouch contains shag; but the pipe in his pocket contains hard cut."

"Is there no cake tobacco in any of the pockets?"

"Not a fragment. Of course, it is possible that he might have had a piece and used it up to fill the pipe; but there is no trace of any on the blade of his pocket-knife, and you know how this juicy black cake stains a knife-blade. His sheath-knife is missing, but he would hardly have used that to shred tobacco when he had a pocket-knife."

"No," assented the captain; "but are you sure he hadn't a second pipe?"

"There was only one pipe," replied Thorndyke, "and that was not his own."

"Not his own!" exclaimed the captain, halting by a huge, chequered buoy, to stare at my colleague. "How do you know it was not his own?"

"By the appearance of the vulcanite mouthpiece," said Thorndyke. "It showed deep tooth-marks; in fact, it was nearly bitten through. Now a man who bites through his pipe usually presents certain definite physical peculiarities, among which is, necessarily, a fairly good set of teeth. But the dead man had not a tooth in his head."

The captain cogitated a while, and then remarked: "I don't quite see the bearing of this."

"Don't you?" said Thorndyke. "It seems to me highly suggestive. Here is a man who, when last seen, was filling his pipe with a particular kind of tobacco. He is picked up dead, and his pipe contains a totally different kind of tobacco. Where did that tobacco come from? The obvious suggestion is that he had met someone."

"Yes, it does look like it," agreed the captain.

"Then," continued Thorndyke, "there is the fact that his sheath-knife is missing. That may mean nothing, but we have to bear it in mind. And there is another curious circumstance: there is a wound on the back of the head caused by a heavy bump against some body that was covered with acorn barnacles and marine worms. Now there are no piers or stages out in the open estuary. The question is, what could he have struck?"

"Oh, there is nothing in that," said the captain. "When a body has been washing about in a tide-way for close on three days—"

"But this is not a question of a body," Thorndyke interrupted. "The wound was made during life."

"The deuce it was!" exclaimed the captain. "Well, all I can suggest is that he must have fouled one of the beacons in the fog, stove in his boat and bumped his head, though, I must admit, that's rather a lame explanation." He stood for a minute gazing at his toes with a cogitative frown and then looked up at Thorndyke.

"I have an idea," he said. "From what you say, this matter wants looking into pretty carefully. Now, I am going down on the tender today to make inquiries on the spot. What do you say to coming with me as adviser—as a matter of business, of course—you and Dr. Jervis? I shall start about eleven; we shall be at the lighthouse by three o'clock, and you can get back to town tonight, if you want to. What do you say?"

"There's nothing to hinder us," I put in eagerly, for even at Bugsby's Hole the river looked very alluring on this summer morning.

"Very well," said Thorndyke, "we will come. Jervis is evidently hankering for a sea-trip, and so am I, for that matter."

"It's a business engagement, you know," the captain stipulated.

"Nothing of the kind," said Thorndyke; "it's unmitigated pleasure; the pleasure of the voyage and your high well-born society."

"I didn't mean that," grumbled the captain, "but, if you are coming as guests, send your man for your night-gear and let us bring you back tomorrow evening."

"We won't disturb Polton," said my colleague; "we can take the train from Blackwall and fetch our things ourselves. Eleven o'clock, you said?"

"Thereabouts," said Captain Grumpass; "but don't put yourselves out."

The means of communication in London have reached an almost undesirable state of perfection. With the aid of the snorting train and the tinkling, two-wheeled "gondola," we crossed and re-crossed the town with such celerity that it was barely eleven when we re-appeared on Trinity Wharf with a joint Gladstone and Thorndyke's little green case.

The tender had hauled out of Bow Creek, and now lay alongside the wharf with a great striped can buoy dangling from her derrick, and Captain Grumpass stood at the gangway, his jolly, red face beaming with pleasure. The buoy was safely stowed forward, the derrick hauled up to the mast, the loose shrouds rehooked to the screw-lanyards, and the steamer, with four jubilant hoots, swung round and shoved her sharp nose against the incoming tide.

For near upon four hours the ever-widening stream of the "London River" unfolded its moving panorama. The smoke and smell of Woolwich Reach gave place to lucid air made soft by the summer haze; the grey huddle of factories fell away and green levels of cattle-spotted marsh stretched away to the high land bordering the river valley. Venerable training ships displayed their chequered hulls by the wooded shore, and whispered of the days of oak and hemp, when the tall three-decker, comely and majestic, with her soaring heights of canvas, like towers of ivory, had not yet given place to the mud-coloured saucepans that fly the white ensign now-a-days and devour the substance of the British taxpayer: when a sailor was a sailor and not a mere seafaring mechanic.

Sturdily breasting the flood tide, the tender threaded her way through the endless procession of shipping; barges, billy-boys, schooners, brigs; lumpish Black-seamen, blue-funnelled China tramps, rickety Baltic barques with twirling windmills, gigantic liners, staggering under a mountain of top-hamper. Erith, Purfleet, Greenhithe, Grays greeted us and passed astern. The chimneys of Northfleet, the clustering roofs of Gravesend, the populous anchorage and the lurking batteries, were left behind, and, as we swung out of the Lower Hope, the wide expanse of sea reach spread out before us like a great sheet of blue-shot satin.

About half-past twelve the ebb overtook us and helped us on our way, as we could see by the speed with which the distant land slid past, and the freshening of the air as we passed through it.

But sky and sea were hushed in a summer calm. Balls of fleecy cloud hung aloft, motionless in the soft blue; the barges drifted on the tide with drooping sails, and a big, striped bell buoy—surmounted by a staff and cage and labelled, "Shivering Sand"—sat dreaming in the sun above its motionless reflection, to rouse for a moment as it met our wash, nod its cage drowsily, utter a solemn ding-dong, and fall asleep again.

It was shortly after passing the buoy that the gaunt shape of a screw-pile lighthouse began to loom up ahead, its dull-red paint turned to vermilion by the early afternoon sun. As we drew nearer, the name Girdler, painted in huge, white letters, became visible, and two men could be seen in the gallery around the lantern, inspecting us through a telescope.

"Shall you be long at the lighthouse, sir?" the master of the tender inquired of Captain Grumpass; "because we're going down, to the North-East Pan Sand to fix this new buoy and take up the old one."

"Then you'd better put us off at the lighthouse and come back for us when you've finished the job," was the reply. "I don't know how long we shall be."

The tender was brought to, a boat lowered, and a couple of hands pulled us across the intervening space of water.

"It will be a dirty climb for you in your shore-going clothes," the captain remarked—he was as spruce as a new pin himself, "but the stuff will all wipe off." We looked up at the skeleton shape. The falling tide had exposed some fifteen feet of the piles, and piles and ladder alike were swathed in sea-grass and encrusted with barnacles and worm-tubes. But we were not such town-sparrows as the captain seemed to think, for we both followed his lead without difficulty up the slippery ladder, Thorndyke clinging tenaciously to his little green case, from which he refused to be separated even for an instant.

"These gentlemen and I," said the captain, as we stepped on the stage at the head of the ladder, "have come to make inquiries about the missing man, James Brown. Which of you is Jeffreys?"

"I am, sir," replied a tall, powerful, square-jawed, beetle-browed man, whose left hand was tied up in a rough bandage.

"What have you been doing to your hand?" asked the captain.

"I cut it while I was peeling some potatoes," was the reply. "It isn't much of a cut, sir."

"Well, Jeffreys," said the captain, "Brown's body has been picked up and I want particulars for the inquest. You'll be summoned as a witness, I suppose, so come in and tell us all you know."

We entered the living-room and seated ourselves at the table. The captain opened a massive pocket-book, while Thorndyke, in his attentive, inquisitive fashion, looked about the odd, cabin-like room as if making a mental inventory of its contents.

Jeffreys' statement added nothing to what we already knew. He had seen a boat with one man in it making for the lighthouse. Then the fog had drifted up and he had lost sight of the boat. He started the fog-horn and kept a bright look-out, but the boat never arrived. And that was all he knew. He supposed that the man must have missed the lighthouse and been carried away on the ebb-tide, which was running strongly at the time.

"What time was it when you last saw the boat?" Thorndyke asked.

"About half-past eleven," replied Jeffreys.

"What was the man like?" asked the captain.

"I don't know, sir; he was rowing, and his back was towards me."

"Had he any kit-bag or chest with him?" asked Thorndyke.

"He'd got his chest with him," said Jeffreys.

"What sort of chest was it?" inquired Thorndyke.

"A small chest, painted green, with rope beckets."

"Was it corded?"

"It had a single cord round, to hold the lid down."

"Where was it stowed?"

"In the stern-sheets, sir."

"How far off was the boat when you last saw it?"

"About half-a-mile."

"Half-a-mile!" exclaimed the captain. "Why, how the deuce could you see that chest half-a-mile away?"

The man reddened and cast a look of angry suspicion at Thorndyke. "I was watching the boat through the glass, sir," he replied sulkily.

"I see," said Captain Grumpass. "Well, that will do, Jeffreys. We shall have to arrange for you to attend the inquest. Tell Smith I want to see him."

The examination concluded, Thorndyke and I moved our chairs to the window, which looked out over the sea to the east. But it was not the sea or the passing ships that engaged my colleague's attention. On the wall, beside the window, hung a rudely-carved pipe-rack containing five pipes. Thorndyke had noted it when we entered the room, and now, as we talked, I observed him regarding it from time to time with speculative interest.

"You men seem to be inveterate smokers," he remarked to the keeper, Smith, when the captain had concluded the arrangements for the "shift."

"Well, we do like our bit of 'baccy, sir, and that's a fact," answered Smith. "You see, sir," he continued, "it's a lonely life, and tobacco's cheap out here."

"How is that?" asked Thorndyke.

"Why, we get it given to us. The small craft from foreign, especially the Dutchmen, generally heave us a cake or two when they pass close. We're not ashore, you see, so there's no duty to pay."

"So you don't trouble the tobacconists much? Don't go in for cut tobacco?"

"No, sir; we'd have to buy it, and then the cut stuff wouldn't keep. No, it's hard-tack to eat out here and hard tobacco to smoke."

"I see you've got a pipe-rack, too, quite a stylish affair."

"Yes," said Smith, "I made it in my off-time. Keeps the place tidy and looks more ship-shape than letting the pipes lay about anywhere."

"Someone seems to have neglected his pipe," said Thorndyke, pointing to one at the end of the rack which was coated with green mildew.

"Yes; that's Parsons, my mate. He must have left it when he went off near a month ago. Pipes do go mouldy in the damp air out here."

"How soon does a pipe go mouldy if it is left untouched?" Thorndyke asked.

"It's according to the weather," said Smith. "When it's warm and damp they'll begin to go in about a week. Now here's Barnett's pipe that he's left behind—the man that broke his leg, you know, sir—it's just beginning to spot a little. He couldn't have used it for a day or two before he went."

"And are all these other pipes yours?"

"No, sir. This here one is mine. The end one is Jeffreys', and I suppose the middle one is his too, but I don't know it."

"You're a demon for pipes, doctor," said the captain, strolling up at this moment; "you seem to make a special study of them."

"'The proper study of mankind is man,'" replied Thorndyke, as the keeper retired, "and 'man' includes those objects on which his personality is impressed. Now a pipe is a very personal thing. Look at that row in the rack. Each has its own physiognomy which, in a measure, reflects the peculiarities of the owner. There is Jeffreys' pipe at the end, for instance. The mouth-piece is nearly bitten through, the bowl scraped to a shell and scored inside and the brim battered and chipped. The whole thing speaks of rude strength and rough handling. He chews the stem as he smokes, he scrapes the bowl violently, and he bangs the ashes out with unnecessary force. And the man fits the pipe exactly: powerful, square-jawed and, I should say, violent on occasion."

"Yes, he looks a tough customer, does Jeffreys," agreed the captain.

"Then," continued Thorndyke, "there is Smith's pipe, next to it; 'coked' up until the cavity is nearly filled and burnt all round the edge; a talker's pipe, constantly going out and being relit. But the one that interests me most is the middle one."

"Didn't Smith say that was Jeffreys' too?" I said.

"Yes," replied Thorndyke, "but he must be mistaken. It is the very opposite of Jeffreys' pipe in every respect. To begin with, although it is an old pipe, there is not a sign of any tooth-mark on the mouth-piece. It is the only one in the rack that is quite unmarked. Then the brim is quite uninjured: it has been handled gently, and the silver band is jet-black, whereas the band on Jeffreys' pipe is quite bright."

"I hadn't noticed that it had a band," said the captain. "What has made it so black?"

Thorndyke lifted the pipe out of the rack and looked at it closely. "Silver sulphide," said he, "the sulphur no doubt derived from something carried in the pocket."

"I see," said Captain Grumpass, smothering a yawn and gazing out of the window at the distant tender. "Incidentally it's full of tobacco. What moral do you draw from that?"

Thorndyke turned the pipe over and looked closely at the mouth-piece. "The moral is," he replied, "that you should see that your pipe is clear before you fill it." He pointed to the mouth-piece, the bore of which was completely stopped up with fine fluff.

"An excellent moral too," said the captain, rising with another yawn. "If you'll excuse me a minute I'll just go and see what the tender is up to. She seems to be crossing to the East Girdler." He reached the telescope down from its brackets and went out onto the gallery.

As the captain retreated, Thorndyke opened his pocket-knife, and, sticking the blade into the bowl of the pipe, turned the tobacco out into his hand.

"Shag, by Jove!" I exclaimed.

"Yes," he answered, poking it back into the bowl. "Didn't you expect it to be shag?"

"I don't know that I expected anything," I admitted. "The silver band was occupying my attention."

"Yes, that is an interesting point," said Thorndyke, "but let us see what the obstruction consists of." He opened the green case, and, taking out a dissecting needle, neatly extracted a little ball of fluff from the bore of the pipe. Laying this on a glass slide, he teased it out in a drop of glycerine and put on a cover-glass while I set up the microscope.

"Better put the pipe back in the rack," he said, as he laid the slide on the stage of the instrument. I did so and then turned, with no little excitement, to watch him as he examined the specimen. After a brief inspection he rose and waved his hand towards the microscope.

"Take a look at it, Jervis," he said.

I applied my eye to the instrument, and, moving the slide about, identified the constituents of the little mass of fluff. The ubiquitous cotton fibre was, of course, in evidence, and a few fibres of wool, but the most remarkable objects were two or three hairs—very minute hairs of a definite zigzag shape and having a flat expansion near the free end like the blade of a paddle.

"These are the hairs of some small animal," I said; "not a mouse or rat or any rodent, I should say. Some small insectivorous animal, I fancy. Yes! Of course! They are the hairs of a mole." I stood up, and, as the importance of the discovery flashed on me, I looked at my colleague in silence.

"Yes," he said, "they are unmistakable; and they furnish the keystone of the argument."

"You think that this is really the dead man's pipe, then?" I said.

"According to the law of multiple evidence," he replied, "it is practically a certainty. Consider the facts in sequence. Since there is no sign of mildew on it, this pipe can have been here only a short time, and must belong either to Barnett, Smith, Jeffreys or Brown. It is an old pipe, but it has no tooth-marks on it. Therefore it has been used by a man who has no teeth. But Barnett, Smith and Jeffreys all have teeth and mark their pipes, whereas Brown has no teeth. The tobacco in it is shag.

"But these three men do not smoke shag, whereas Brown had shag in his pouch. The silver band is encrusted with sulphide; and Brown carried sulphur-tipped matches loose in his pocket with his pipe. We find hairs of a mole in the bore of the pipe; and Brown carried a moleskin pouch in the pocket in which he appears to have carried his pipe. Finally, Brown's pocket contained a pipe which was obviously not his and which closely resembled that of Jeffreys; it contained tobacco similar to that which Jeffreys smokes and different from that in Brown's pouch. It appears to me quite conclusive, especially when we add to this evidence the other items that are in our possession."

"What items are they?" I asked.

"First there is the fact that the dead man had knocked his head heavily against some periodically submerged body covered with acorn barnacles and *serpulae*. Now the piles of this lighthouse answer to the description exactly, and there are no other bodies in the neighbourhood that do: for even the beacons are too large to have produced that kind of wound. Then the dead man's sheath-knife is missing, and Jeffreys has a knife-wound on his hand. You must admit that the circumstantial evidence is overwhelming."

At this moment the captain bustled into the room with the telescope in his hand. "The tender is coming up towing a strange boat," he said. "I expect it's the missing one, and, if it is, we may learn something. You'd better pack up your traps and get ready to go on board."

We packed the green case and went out into the gallery, where the two keepers were watching the approaching tender; Smith frankly curious and interested, Jeffreys restless, fidgety and noticeably pale. As the steamer came opposite the lighthouse, three men dropped into the boat and pulled across, and one of them—the mate of the tender—came climbing up the ladder.

"Is that the missing boat?" the captain sang out.

"Yes, sir," answered the officer, stepping onto the staging and wiping his hands on the reverse aspect of his trousers, "we saw her lying on the dry patch of the East Girdler. There's been some hanky-panky in this job, sir."

"Foul play, you think, hey?"

"Not a doubt of it, sir. The plug was out and lying loose in the bottom, and we found a sheath-knife sticking into the kelson forward among the coils of the painter. It was stuck in hard as if it had dropped from a height."

"That's odd," said the captain. "As to the plug, it might have got out by accident."

"But it hadn't sir," said the mate. "The ballast-bags had been shifted along to get the bottom boards up. Besides, sir, a seaman wouldn't let the boat fill; he'd have put the plug back and baled out."

"That's true," replied Captain Grumpass; "and certainly the presence of the knife looks fishy. But where the deuce could it have dropped from, out in the open sea? Knives don't drop from the clouds—fortunately. What do you say, doctor?"

"I should say that it is Brown's own knife, and that it probably fell from this staging."

Jeffreys turned swiftly, crimson with wrath. "What d'ye mean?" he demanded. "Haven't I said that the boat never came here?"

"You have," replied Thorndyke; "but if that is so, how do you explain the fact that your pipe was found in the dead man's pocket and that the dead man's pipe is at this moment in your pipe-rack?"

The crimson flush on Jeffreys' face faded as quickly as it had come. "I don't know what you're talking about," he faltered.

"I'll tell you," said Thorndyke. "I will relate what happened and you shall check my statements. Brown brought his boat alongside and came up into the living-room, bringing his chest with him. He filled his pipe and tried to light it, but it was stopped and wouldn't draw. Then you lent him a pipe of yours and filled it for him. Soon afterwards you came out on this staging and quarrelled. Brown defended himself with his knife, which dropped from his hand into the boat. You pushed him off the staging and he fell, knocking his head on one of the piles. Then you took the plug out of the boat and sent her adrift to sink, and you flung the chest into the sea. This happened about ten minutes past twelve. Am I right?"

Jeffreys stood staring at Thorndyke, the picture of amazement and consternation; but he uttered no word in reply. "Am I right?" Thorndyke repeated.

"Strike me blind!" muttered Jeffreys. "Was you here, then? You talk as if you had been. Anyhow," he continued, recovering somewhat, "you seem to know all about it. But you're wrong about one thing. There was no quarrel. This chap, Brown, didn't take to me and he didn't mean to stay out here. He was going to put off and go ashore again and I wouldn't let him. Then he hit out at me with his knife and I knocked it out of his hand and he staggered backwards and went overboard."

"And did you try to pick him up?" asked the captain.

"How could I," demanded Jeffreys, "with the tide racing down and me alone on the station? I'd never have got back."

"But what about the boat, Jeffreys? Why did you scuttle her?"

"The fact is," replied Jeffreys, "I got in a funk, and I thought the simplest plan was to send her to the cellar and know nothing about it. But I never shoved him over. It was an accident, sir; I swear it!"

"Well, that sounds a reasonable explanation," said the captain. "What do you say, doctor?"

"Perfectly reasonable," replied Thorndyke, "and, as to its truth, that is no affair of ours."

"No. But I shall have to take you off, Jeffreys, and hand you over to the police. You understand that?"

"Yes, sir, I understand," answered Jeffreys.

"That was a queer case, that affair on the Girdler," remarked Captain Grumpass, when he was spending an evening with us some six months later. "A pretty easy let off for Jeffreys, too—eighteen months, wasn't it?"

"Yes, it was a very queer case indeed," said Thorndyke. "There was something behind that 'accident,' I should say. Those men had probably met before."

"So I thought," agreed the captain. "But the queerest part of it to me was the way you nosed it all out. I've had a deep respect for briar pipes since then. It was a remarkable case," he continued. "The way in which you made that pipe tell the story of the murder seems to me like sheer enchantment."

"Yes," said I, "it spoke like the magic pipe—only that wasn't a tobacco-pipe—in the German folk-story of the *Singing Bone*. Do you remember it? A peasant found the bone of a murdered man and fashioned it into a pipe. But when he tried to play on it, it burst into a song of its own—"

My brother slew me and buried my bones
Beneath the sand and under the stones.

"A pretty story," said Thorndyke, "and one with an excellent moral. The inanimate things around us have each of them a song to sing to us if we are but ready with attentive ears."

The Stalking Horse

As Thorndyke and I descended the stairs of the foot bridge at Densford Junction we became aware that something unusual had happened. The platform was nearly deserted save at one point, where a small but dense crowd had collected around the open door of a first-class compartment of the down train; heads were thrust out of the windows of the other coaches, and at intervals doors opened and inquisitive passengers ran along to join the crowd, from which an excited porter detached himself just as we reached the platform.

"You'd better go for Dr. Pooke first," the stationmaster called after him.

On this, Thorndyke stepped forward.

"My friend and I," said he, "are medical men. Can we be of any service until the local doctor arrives?"

"I'm very much afraid not, sir," was the reply, "but you'll see." He cleared a way for us and we approached the open door.

At the first glance there appeared to be nothing to account for the awe-stricken expression with which the bystanders peered into the carriage and gazed at its solitary occupant. For the motionless figure that sat huddled in the corner seat, chin on breast, might have been a sleeping man. But it was not. The waxen pallor of the face and the strange, image-like immobility forbade the hope of any awakening.

"It looks almost as if he had passed away in his sleep," said the station when we had concluded our brief examination and ascertained certainly that the man was dead. "Do you think it was a heart attack, sir?"

Thorndyke shook his head and touched with his finger a depressed spot on the dead man's waistcoat. When he withdrew his finger it was smeared with blood.

"Good God!" the official gasped, in a horrified whisper. "The man

111

has been murdered!" He stared incredulously at the corpse for a few moments and then turned and sprang out of the compartment, shutting the door behind him, and we heard him giving orders for the coach to be separated and shunted into the siding.

"This is a gruesome affair, Jervis," my colleague, said as he sat down on the seat opposite the dead man and cast a searching glance round the compartment. "I wonder who this poor fellow was and what was the object of the murder? It looks almost too determined, for a common robbery; and, in fact, the body does not appear to have been robbed." Here he stooped suddenly to pick up one or two minute fragments of glass which seemed to have been trodden into the carpet, and which he examined closely in the palm of his hand. I leaned over and looked at the fragments, and we agreed that they were portions of the bulb of an electric torch or flash-lamp.

"The significance of these—if they have any," said Thorndyke, "we can consider later. But if they are recent, it would appear that the metal part of the bulb has been picked up and taken away. That might be an important fact. But, on the other hand, the fragments may have been here some time and have no connection with the tragedy; though you notice that they were lying opposite the body and opposite the seat which the murderer must have occupied when the crime was committed."

As he was speaking, the uncoupled coach began slowly to move towards the siding, and we both stooped to make a further search for the remainder of the lamp-bulb, And then, almost at the same moment, we perceived two objects lying under the opposite seat—the seat occupied by the dead man. One was a small pocket-handkerchief, the other a sheet of notepaper.

"This," said I, as I picked up the former, "accounts for the strong smell of scent in the compartment."

"Possibly," Thorndyke agreed, "though you will notice that the odour does not come principally from the handkerchief, but from the back cushion of the corner seat. But here is something more distinctive—a most incriminating piece of evidence, unless it can be answered by an undeniable alibi." He held out to me a sheet of letter paper, both pages of which were covered with writing in bright blue ink, done with a Hectograph or some similar duplicator. It was evidently a circular letter, for it bore the printed heading, "Women's Emancipation League, 16 Barnabas Square, S.W.," and the contents appeared to refer to a "militant demonstration" planned for the near future.

"It is dated the day before yesterday," commented Thorndyke, "so that it might have been lying here for twenty-four hours, though that is obviously improbable; and as this is neither the first sheet nor the last, there are—or have been—at least two more sheets. The police will have something to start on, at any rate."

He laid the letter on the seat and explored both of the hat-racks, taking down the dead man's hat, gloves, and umbrella, and noting in the hat the initials "F. B." He had just replaced them when voices became audible outside, and the station-master climbed up on the foot-board and opened the door to admit two men, one of whom I assumed to be a doctor, the other being a police inspector.

"The station-master tells me that this is a case of homicide," said the former, addressing us jointly.

"That is what the appearances suggest," replied Thorndyke. "There is a bullet wound, inflicted apparently at quite short range—the waist-coat is perceptibly singed—and we have found no weapon in the compartment."

The doctor stepped past us and proceeded to make a rapid exami-nation of the body.

"Yes," he said, "I agree with you. The position of the wound and the posture of the body both suggest that death was practically in-stantaneous. If it had been suicide, the pistol would have been in the hand or on the floor. There is no clue to the identity of the murderer, I suppose?"

"We found these on the floor under the dead man's seat," replied Thorndyke, indicating the letter and the handkerchief; "and there is some glass trodden into the carpet—apparently the remains of an electric flash-lamp."

The inspector pounced on the handkerchief and the letter, and having scrutinised the former vainly in search of name or initials, turned to the letter.

"Why, this is a suffragist's letter!" he exclaimed. "But it can't have anything to do with this affair. They are mischievous beggars, but they don't do this sort of thing." Nevertheless, he carefully bestowed both articles in a massive wallet, and approaching the corpse, remarked: "We may as well see who he is while we are waiting for the stretcher."

With a matter-of-fact air, which seemed somewhat to shock the station-master, he unbuttoned the coat of the passive figure in the corner and thrust his hand into the breast pocket, drawing out a letter-case which he opened, and from which he extracted a visiting card. As he glanced at it, his face suddenly took on an expression of amazement.

"God!" he exclaimed in a startled tone. "Who do you think he is, doctor? He is Mr. Francis Burnham!"

The doctor looked at him with an interrogative frown. "Burnham—Burnham," he repeated. "Let me see, now—"

"Don't you know? The anti-suffrage man. Surely—"

"Yes, yes," interrupted the doctor. "Of course I remember him. The arch-enemy of the suffrage movement and—yes, of course." The doctor's brisk speech changed abruptly into a hesitating mumble. Like the inspector, he had suddenly "seen a great light;" and again, like the officer, his perception had begotten a sudden reticence.

Thorndyke glanced at his watch. "Our train is a minute overdue," said he. "We ought to get back to the platform." Taking a card from his case, he handed it to the inspector, who looked at it and slightly raised his eyebrows.

"I don't think my evidence will be of much value," said he; "but, of course, I am at your service if you want it." With this and a bow to the doctor and the station-master, he climbed down to the ground; and when I had given the inspector my card, I followed, and we made our way to the platform.

The case was not long in developing. That very evening, as Thorndyke and I were smoking our after-dinner pipes by the fire, a hurried step was heard on the stair and was followed by a peremptory knock on our door. The visitor was a man of about thirty, with a clean-shaved face, an intense and rather neurotic expression, and a restless, excited manner. He introduced himself by the name of Cadmus Bawley, and thereby, in effect, indicated the purpose of his visit.

"You know me by name, I expect," he said, speaking rapidly and with a sharp, emphatic manner, "and probably you can guess what I have come about. You have seen the evening paper, of course?"

"I have not," replied Thorndyke.

"Well," said Mr. Bawley, "you know about the murder of the man Burnham, because I see that you were present at the discovery; and you know that part of a circular letter from our League was found in the compartment. Perhaps you will not be surprised to learn that Miss Isabel Dalby has been arrested and charged with the murder."

"Indeed!" said Thorndyke.

"Yes. It's an infamous affair! A national disgrace!" exclaimed Bawley, banging the table with his fist. "A manifest plot of the enemies of social reform to get rid of a high-minded, noble-hearted lady whose championship of this Great Cause they are unable to combat by fair means in the open. And it is a wild absurdity, too. As to the fellow, Burnham, I can't pretend to feel any regret—"

"May I suggest"—Thorndyke interrupted somewhat stiffly—"that the expression of personal sentiments is neither helpful nor discreet? My methods of defence—if that is what you have come about—are based on demonstration rather than rhetoric. Could you give us the plain facts?"

Mr. Cadmus Bawley looked unmistakably sulky, but after a short pause, he began his recital in a somewhat lower key.

"The bald facts," he said, "are these: This afternoon, at half-past two, Miss Dalby took the train from King's Cross to Holmwood. This is the train that stops at Densford Junction and is the one in which Burnham travelled. She took a first-class ticket and occupied a compartment for ladies only, of which she was the only occupant. She got out at Holmwood and went straight to the house of our Vice-President, Miss Carleigh—who has been confined to her room for some days—and stayed there about an hour. She came back by the four-fifteen train, and I met her at the station—King's Cross—at a quarter to five. We had tea at a restaurant opposite the station, and over our tea we discussed the plans for the next demonstration, and arranged the rendezvous and the most convenient routes for retreat and dispersal when the police should arrive.

"This involved the making of sketch plans, and these Miss Dalby drew on a sheet of paper that she took from her pocket, and which happened to be part of the circular letter referring to the raid. After tea we walked together down Gray's Inn Road and parted at Theobald's Road, I going on to the headquarters and she to her rooms in Queen Square. On her arrival home, she found two detectives waiting outside her house, and then—and then, in short, she was arrested, like a common criminal, and taken to the police station, where she was searched and the remainder of the circular letter found in her pocket. Then she was formally charged with the murder of the man Burnham, and she was graciously permitted to send a telegram to headquarters. It arrived just after I got there, and, of course, I at once went to the police station. The police refused to accept bail, but they allowed me to see her to make arrangements for the defence."

"Does Miss Dalby offer any suggestion," asked Thorndyke, "as to how a sheet of her letter came to be in the compartment with the murdered man?"

"Oh, yes!" replied Mr. Bawley. "I had forgotten that. It wasn't her letter at all. She destroyed her copy of the letter as soon as she had read it."

"Then," inquired Thorndyke, "how came the letter to be in her pocket?"

"Ah," replied Bawley, "that is the mystery. She thinks someone must have slipped it into her pocket to throw suspicion on her."

"Did she seem surprised to find it in her pocket when you were having tea together?"

"No. She had forgotten having destroyed her copy. She only remembered it when I told her that the sheet had been found in Burnham's carriage."

"Can she produce the fragments of the destroyed letter?"

"No, she can't. Unfortunately she burned it."

"Do these circular letters bear any distinguishing mark? Are they addressed to members by name?"

"Only on the envelopes. The letters are all alike. They are run off a duplicator. Of course, if you don't believe the story—"

"I am not judging the case," interrupted Thorndyke; "I am simply collecting the facts. What do you want me to do?"

"If you feel that you could undertake the defence I should like you to do so. We shall employ the solicitors to the League, Bird & Marshall, but I know they will be willing and glad to act with you."

"Very well," said Thorndyke. "I will investigate the case and consult with your solicitors. By the way, do the police know about the sheet of the letter on which the plans were drawn?"

"No. I thought it best to say nothing about that, and I have told Miss Dalby not to mention it."

"That is just as well," said Thorndyke. "Have you the sheet with the plan on it?"

"I haven't it about me," was the reply. "It is in my desk at my chambers."

"You had better let me have it to look at," said Thorndyke.

"You can have it if you want it, of course," said Bawley, "but it won't help you. The letters are all alike, as I have told you."

"I should like to see it, nevertheless," said Thorndyke; "and perhaps you could give me some account of Mr. Burnham. What do you know about him?"

Mr. Bawley shut his lips tightly, and his face took on an expression of vindictiveness verging on malignity.

"All I know about Burnham," he said, "is that he was a fool and a ruffian. He was not only an enemy of the great reform that our League stands for; he was a treacherous enemy—violent, crafty, and indefatigably active. I can only regard his death as a blessing to mankind."

"May I ask," said Thorndyke, "if any members of your League have ever publicly threatened to take personal measures against him?"

"Yes," snapped Bawley. "Several of us—including myself—have threatened to give him the hiding that he deserved. But a hiding is a different thing from murder, you know."

"Yes," Thorndyke agreed somewhat dryly; then he asked: "Do you know anything about Mr. Burnham's occupation and habits?"

"He was a sort of manager of the London and Suburban Bank. His job was to supervise the suburban branches, and his habit was to visit them in rotation. He was probably going to the branch at Holmwood when he was killed. That is all I can tell you about him."

"Thank you," said Thorndyke; and as our visitor rose to depart he continued: "Then I will look into the case and arrange with your solicitors to have Miss Dalby properly represented at the inquest; and I shall be glad to have that sheet of the letter as soon as you can send or leave it."

"Very well," said Bawley, "though, as I have told you, it won't be of any use to you. It is only a duplicated circular."

"Possibly," Thorndyke assented. "But the other sheets will be produced in Court, so I may as well have an opportunity of examining it beforehand."

For some minutes after our client had gone Thorndyke remained silent and reflective, copying his rough notes into his pocket-book and apparently amplifying and arranging them. Presently he looked up at me with an unspoken question in his eyes.

"It is a queer case," said I. "The circumstantial evidence seems to be strongly against Miss Dalby, but it is manifestly improbable that she murdered the man."

"It seems so," he agreed. "But the case will be decided on the evidence; and the evidence will be considered by a judge, not by a Home Secretary. You notice the importance of Burnham's destination?"

"Yes. He was evidently dead when the train arrived at Holmwood. But it isn't clear how long he had been dead."

"The evidence," said Thorndyke, "points strongly to the tunnel between Cawden and Holmwood as the place where the murder was committed. You will remember that the up-express passed our train in the tunnel. If the adjoining compartments were empty, the sound of a pistol shot would be completely drowned by the noise of the express thundering past. Then you will remember the fragments of the electric bulb that we picked up, and that there was no light on in the carriage. That is rather significant. It not only suggests that the crime was committed in the dark, but there is a distinct suggestion of preparation—arrangement and premeditation. It suggests that the murderer knew what the circumstances would be and provided for them."

"Yes; and that is rather a point against our client. But I don't quite see what you expect to get out of that sheet of the letter. It is the presence of the letter, rather than its matter, that constitutes the evidence against Miss Dalby."

"I don't expect to learn anything from it," replied Thorndyke; "but the letter will be the prosecution's trump card, and it is always well to know in advance exactly what cards your opponent holds. It is a mere matter of routine to examine everything, relevant or irrelevant."

The inquest was to be held at Densford on the third day after the discovery of the body. But in the interval certain new facts had come to light. One was that the deceased was conveying to the Holmwood branch of the bank a sum of three thousand pounds, of which one thousand was in gold and the remainder in Bank of England notes, the whole being contained in a leather handbag. This bag had been found, empty, in a ditch by the side of the road which led from the station to the house of Miss Carleigh, the Vice-President of the Women's Emancipation League.

It was further stated that the ticket-collector at Holmwood had noticed that Miss Dalby—whom he knew by sight—was carrying a bag of the kind described when she passed the barrier, and that when she returned, about an hour later, she had no bag with her. On the other hand, Miss Carleigh had stated that the bag which Miss Dalby brought to her house was her (Miss Carleigh's) property, and she had produced it for the inspection of the police. So that already there was some conflict of evidence, with a balance distinctly against Miss Dalby.

"There is no denying," said Thorndyke, as we discussed the case at the breakfast table on the morning of the inquestthat the circumstantial evidence is formidably complete and consistent, while the rebutting evidence is of the feeblest. Miss Dalby's statement that the letter had been put into her pocket by some unknown person will hardly be taken seriously, and even Miss Carleigh's statement with reference to the bag will not carry much weight unless she can furnish corroboration."

"Nevertheless," said I, "the general probabilities are entirely in favour of the accused. It is grossly improbable that a lady like Miss Dalby would commit a robbery with murder of this cold-blooded, deliberate type."

"That may be," Thorndyke retorted, "but a jury has to find in accordance with the evidence."

"By the way," said I, "did Bawley ever send you that sheet of the letter that you asked for?"

"No, confound him! But I have sent Polton round to get it from him, so that I can look it over carefully in the train. Which reminds me that I can't get down in time for the opening of the inquest. You had better travel with the solicitors and see the shorthand writers started. I shall have to come down by a later train."

Half an hour later, just as I was about to start, a familiar step was heard on the stair, and then our laboratory assistant, Polton, let himself in with his key.

"Just caught him, sir, as he was starting for the station," he said, with a satisfied, crinkly smile, laying an envelope on the table, and added, "Lord! how he did swear!"

Thorndyke chuckled, and having thanked his assistant, opened the envelope and handed it to me. It contained a single sheet of letter-paper, exactly similar to the one that we had found in the railway carriage, excepting that the writing filled one side and a quarter only, and, since it concluded with the signature "Letitia Humboe, President," it was evidently the last sheet. There was no water-mark nor anything, so far as I could see, to distinguish it from the dozens of other impressions that had been run off on the duplicator with it, excepting the roughly-pencilled plan on the blank side of the sheet.

"Well," I said as I put on my hat and walked towards the door, "I suspect that Bawley was right. You won't get much help from this to support Miss Dalby's rather improbable statement." And Thorndyke agreed that appearances were not very promising.

The scene in the coffee-room of "The Plough" Inn at Densford was one with which I was familiar enough. The quiet, business-like coroner, the half-embarrassed jurors, the local police and witnesses and the spectators, penned up at one end of the room, were all well-known characters. The unusual feature was the handsome, distinguished-looking young lady who sat on a plain Windsor chair between two inscrutable policemen, watched intently by Mr. Cadmus Bawley. Miss Dalby was pale and obviously agitated, but quiet, resolute, and somewhat defiant in manner. She greeted me with a pleasant smile when I introduced myself, and hoped that I and my colleague would have no difficulty in disposing of "this grotesque and horrible accusation."

I need not describe the proceedings in detail. Evidence of the identity of the deceased having been taken, Dr. Pooke deposed that death was due to a wound of the heart produced by a spherical bullet, apparently fired from a small, smooth-bore pistol at very short range. The wound was in his opinion not self-inflicted. The coroner then produced the sheet of the circular letter found in the carriage, and I was called to testify to the finding of it. The next witness was Superintendent Miller of the Criminal Investigation Department, who produced the two sheets of the letter which were taken from Miss Dalby's pocket when she was arrested. These he handed to the coroner for comparison with the one found in the carriage with the body of deceased.

"There appear," said the coroner, after placing the three sheets together, "to be one or more sheets missing. The two you have handed me are sheets one and three, and the one found in the railway carriage is sheet two."

"Yes," the witness agreed, "sheet four is missing, but I have a photograph of it. Here is a set of the complete letter," and he laid four unmounted prints on the table.

The coroner examined them with a puzzled frown. "May I ask," he said, "how you obtained these photographs?"

"They are not photographs of the copy that you have," the witness explained, "but of another copy of the same letter which we intercepted in the post. That letter was addressed to a stationer's shop to be called for. We have considered it necessary to keep ourselves informed of the contents of these circulars, so that we can take the necessary precautions; and as the envelopes are marked with the badge and are invariably addressed in blue ink, it is not difficult to identify them."

"I see," said the coroner, glaring stonily at Mr. Bawley, who had accompanied the superintendent's statement with audible and unfavourable comments. "Is that the whole of your evidence? Thank you. Then, if there is no cross-examination, I will call the next witness. Mr. Bernard Parsons."

Mr. Parsons was the general manager of the London and Suburban Bank, and he deposed that deceased was, on the day when be met his death, travelling to Holmwood to visit and inspect the new local branch of the bank, and that he was taking thither the sum of three thousand pounds, of which one thousand was in gold and the remainder in Bank of England notes—mostly five-pound notes. He carried the notes and specie in a strong leather handbag.

"Can you say if either of these is the bag that he carried?" the coroner asked, indicating two largish, black leather bags that his officer had placed on the table.

Mr. Parsons promptly pointed to the larger of the two, which was smeared externally with mud. The coroner noted the answer and then asked: "Did anyone besides yourself know that deceased was making this visit?"

"Many persons must have known," was the reply. "Deceased visited the various branches in a fixed order. He came to Holmwood on the second Tuesday in the month."

"And would it be known that he had this great sum of money with him?"

"The actual amount would not be generally known, but he usually took with him supplies of specie and notes—sometimes very large sums—and this would be known to many of the bank staff, and probably to a good many persons outside. The Holmwood Branch consumes a good deal of specie, as most of the customers pay in cheques and draw out cash for local use."

This was the substance of Mr. Parsons' evidence, and when he sat down the ticket-collector was called. That official identified Miss Dalby as one of the passengers by the train in which the body of deceased was found. She was carrying a bag when she passed the barrier. He could not identify either of the bags, but both were similar to the one that she was carrying. She returned about an hour later and caught an up-train, and he noticed that she was then not carrying a bag. He could not say whether any of the other passengers was carrying a bag.

There were very few first-class passengers by that train, but a large number of third-class—mostly fruit-pickers—and they made a dense crowd at the barrier so that he did not notice individual passengers particularly. He noticed Miss Dalby because he knew her by sight, as she often came to Holmwood with other suffragist ladies. He did not see which carriage Miss Dalby came from, and he did not see any first-class compartment with an open door.

The coroner noted down this evidence with thoughtful deliberation, and I was considering whether there were any questions that it
would be advisable to ask the witness when I felt a light touch on my
shoulder, and looking up perceived a constable holding out a telegram.
Observing that it was addressed to "Dr. Jervis, Plough Inn, Densford,"
I nodded to the constable, and taking the envelope from him, opened
it and unfolded the paper. The telegram was from Thorndyke, in the
simple code that he had devised for our private use. I was able to de-
code it without referring to the key—which each of us always carried
in his pocket—and it then read:

"I am starting for Folkestone in re Burnham deceased. Follow immediately and bring Miller if you can for possible arrest. Meet me on
pier near Ostend boat. Thorndyke."

Accustomed as I was to my colleague's inveterate habit of acting
in the least expected manner, I must confess that I gazed at the decoded message in absolute stupefaction. I had been totally unaware of
the faintest clue beyond the obvious evidence to which I had been
listening, and behold! here was Thorndyke with an entirely fresh case,
apparently cut-and-dried, and the unsuspected criminal in the hollow
of his hand. It was astounding.

Unconsciously I raised my eyes—and met those of Superintendent
Miller, fixed on me with devouring curiosity. I held up the telegram
and beckoned, and immediately he tip-toed across and took a seat by
my side. I laid the decoded telegram before him, and when he had
glanced through it, I asked in a whisper: "Well, what do you say?"

By way of reply, he whisked out a time-table, conned it eagerly for
a few minutes, and then held it towards me with his thumb-nail on
the words "Densford Junction."

"There's a fast train up in seven minutes," he whispered hoarsely.
"Get the coroner to excuse us and let your solicitors carry on for you."

A brief, and rather vague, explanation secured the assent of the
coroner—since we had both given our evidence—and the less willing
agreement of my clients. In another minute the superintendent and I
were heading for the station, which we reached just as the train swept
up alongside the platform.

"This is a queer start," said Miller, as the train moved out of the station; "but, Lord! there is never any calculating Dr. Thorndyke's moves.
Did you know that he had anything up his sleeve?"

"No; but then one never does know. He is as close as an oyster. He
never shows his hand until he can play a trump card. But it is possible

that he has struck a fresh clue since I left."

"Well," rejoined Miller, "we shall know when we get to the other end And I don't mind telling you that it will be a great relief to me if we can drop this charge against Miss Dalby."

From time to time during the journey to London, and from thence to Folkestone, the superintendent reverted to Thorndyke's mysterious proceedings. But it was useless to speculate. We had not a single fact to guide us; and when, at last, the train ran into Folkestone Central Station we were as much in the dark as when we started.

Assuming that Thorndyke would have made any necessary arrangements for assistance from the local police, we chartered a cab and proceeded direct to the end of Rendez-vous Street—a curiously appropriate destination, by the way. Here we alighted in order that we might make our appearance at the meeting-place as inconspicuously as possible, and, walking towards the harbour, perceived Thorndyke waiting on the quay, ostensibly watching the loading of a barge, and putting in their case a pair of prismatic binoculars with which he had apparently observed our arrival.

"I am glad you have come, Miller," he said, shaking the superintendent's hand. "I can't make any promises, but I have no doubt that it is a case for you even if it doesn't turn out all that I hope and expect. The *Cornflower* is our ship, and we had better go on board separately in case our friends are keeping a look-out. I have arranged matters with the captain, and the local superintendent has got some plain-clothes men on the pier."

With this we separated. Thorndyke went on in advance, and Miller and I followed at a discreet interval.

As I descended the gangway a minute or so after Miller, a steward approached me, and having asked my name requested me to follow him, when he conducted me to the purser's office, in which I found Thorndyke and Miller in conversation with the purser.

"The gentlemen you are inquiring for," said the latter, "are in the smoking-room playing cards with another passenger. I have put a tarpaulin over one of the ports, in case you want to have a look at them without being seen."

"Perhaps you had better make a preliminary inspection, Miller," said Thorndyke. "You may know some of them."

To this suggestion the superintendent agreed, and forthwith went off with the purser, leaving me and Thorndyke alone. I at once took the opportunity to demand an explanation. "I take it that you struck some new evidence after I left you?"

"Yes," Thorndyke replied. "And none too soon, as you see. I don't quite know what it will amount to, but I think we have secured the defence, at any rate and that is really all that we are concerned with. The positive aspects of the case are the business of the police. But here comes Miller, looking very pleased with himself, and with the purser."

The superintendent, however, was not only pleased; he was also not a little puzzled.

"Well!" he exclaimed, "this is a quaint affair. We have got two of the leading lights of the suffrage movement in there. One is Jameson, the secretary of the Women's Emancipation League, the other is Pinder, their chief bobbery-monger. Then there are two men named Dorman and Spiller, both of them swell crooks, I am certain, though we have never been able to fix anything on them. The fifth man I don't know."

"Neither do I," said Thorndyke. "My repertoire includes only four. And now we will proceed to sort them out. Could we have a few words with Mr. Thorpe—in here, if you don't mind."

"Certainly," replied the purser "I'll go and fetch him." He bustled away in the direction of the smoking-room, whence he presently re-appeared, accompanied by a tall, lean man who wore large bi-focal spectacles of the old-fashioned, split-lens type, and was smoking a cigar. As the newcomer approached down the alley-way, it was evident that he was nervous and uneasy, though he maintained a certain jaunty swagger that accorded ill with a pronounced, habitual stoop. As he en-tered the cabin, however, and became aware of the portentous group of strangers, the swagger broke down completely; suddenly his face became ashen and haggard, and he peered through his great spectacles from one to the others, with an expression of undisguisable terror.

"Mr. Thorpe?" queried Thorndyke; and the superintendent mur-mured: "Alias Pinder."

"Yes," was the reply, in a husky undertone. "What can I do for you?"

Thorndyke turned to the superintendent. "I charge this man," said he, "with having murdered Francis Burnham in the train between London and Holmwood."

The superintendent was visibly astonished, but not more so than the accused, on whom Thorndyke's statement produced the most sin-gular effect. In a moment, his terror seemed to drop from him; the colour returned to his face, the haggard expression of which gave place to one of obvious relief.

Miller stood up, and addressing the accused, began "It is my duty to caution you—" but the other interrupted: "Caution your grandmother! You are talking a parcel of dam' nonsense. I was in Birmingham when the murder was committed. I can prove it, easily."

The superintendent was somewhat taken aback, for the accused spoke with a confidence that carried conviction.

"In that case," said Thorndyke, "you can probably explain how a letter belonging to you came to be found in the carriage with the murdered man."

"Belonging to me!" exclaimed Thorpe. "What the deuce do you mean? That letter belonged to Miss Dalby. The rest of it was found in her pocket."

"Precisely," said Thorndyke. "One sheet had been placed in the railway carriage and the remainder in Miss Dalby's pocket to fix suspicion on her. But it was your letter, and the inference is that you disposed of it in that manner for the purpose that I have stated."

"But," persisted Thorpe, with visibly-growing uneasiness, "this was a duplicated circular. You couldn't tell one copy from another."

"Mr. Pinder," said Thorndyke, in an impressively quiet tone, "if I tell you that I ascertained from that letter that you had taken a passage on this ship in the name of Thorpe, you will probably understand what I mean."

Apparently he did understand, for, once more, the colour faded from his face and he sat down heavily on a locker, fixing on Thorndyke a look of undisguised dismay. Thus he sat for some moments, motionless and silent, apparently thinking hard.

Suddenly he started up. "My God!" he exclaimed, "I see now what has happened. The infernal scoundrel! First he put it on to Miss Dalby, and now he has put it on to me. Now I understand why he looked so startled when I ran against him."

"What do you mean?" asked Thorndyke.

"I'll tell you," replied Pinder. "As I move about a good deal—and for other reasons—I used to have my suffrage letters sent to a stationer's shop in Barlow Street—"

"I know," interrupted the superintendent; "Bedall's. I used to look them over and take photographs of them." He grinned craftily as he made this statement, and, rather to my surprise, the accused grinned too. A little later I understood that grin.

"Well," continued Pinder, "I used to collect these letters pretty regularly. But this last letter was delivered while I was away at Birmingham. Before I came back I met a man who gave me certain—er—instructions—you know what they were," he added, addressing Thorndyke—"so I did not need the letter. But, of course, I couldn't leave it there uncollected, so when I got back to London, I called for it. That was two days ago. To my astonishment Miss Bedall declared that I had collected it three days previously. I assured her that I was not in London on that day, but she was positive that I had called. 'I remember clearly,' she said, 'giving you the letter myself.' Well, there was no arguing. Evidently she had given the letter to the wrong person—she is very near-sighted, I should say, judging by the way she holds things against her nose—but how it happened I couldn't understand.

"But I think I understand now. There is one person only in the world who knew that I had my letters addressed there: a sort of pal of mine named Payne. He happened to be with me one evening when I called to collect my letters. Now, Payne chanced to be a good deal like me—at least he is tall and thin and stoops a bit; but he does not wear spectacles. He tried on my spectacles once for a joke, and then he really looked extremely like me. He looked in a mirror and remarked on the resemblance himself. Now, Payne did not belong to the Women's League, and I suggest that he took advantage of this resemblance to get possession of this letter. He got a pair of spectacles like mine and personated me at the shop."

"Why should he want to get possession of that letter?" Miller demanded.

"To plant it as he has planted it," replied Pinder, "and set the police on a false trail."

"This sounds pretty thin," said Miller. "You are accusing this man of having murdered Mr. Burnham. What grounds have you for this accusation?"

"My grounds," replied Pinder, "are, first, that he stole this letter which has been found, obviously planted; and, second, that he had a grudge against Burnham and knew all about his movements."

"Indeed!" said Miller, with suddenly increased interest. "Then who and what is this man Payne?"

"Why," replied Pinder, "until a month ago, he was assistant cashier at the Streatham branch of the bank. Then Burnham came down and hoofed him out without an hour's notice. I don't know what for, but I can guess."

"Do you happen to know where Payne is at this moment?"

"Yes, I do. He is on this ship, in the smoking-room—only he is

Mr. Shenstone now. And mighty sick he was when he found me on board."

The superintendent looked at Thorndyke. "What do you think about it, doctor?" he asked.

"I think," said Thorndyke, "that we had better have Mr. Shenstone in here and ask him a few questions. Would you see if you can get him to come here?" he added, addressing the purser, who had been listening with ecstatic enjoyment.

"I'll get him to come along all right," replied the purser, evidently scenting a new act in this enthralling drama; and away he bustled, all agog. In less than a minute we saw him returning down the alley-way, with a tall, thin man, who, at a distance, was certainly a good deal like Pinder, though the resemblance diminished as he approached. He, too, was obviously agitated, and seemed to be plying the purser with questions. But when he came opposite the door of the cabin he stopped dead and seemed disposed to shrink back.

"Is that the man?" Thorndyke demanded sharply and rather loudly, springing to his feet as he spoke.

The effect of the question was electrical. As Thorndyke rose, the new-comer turned, and, violently thrusting the purser aside, raced madly down the alley-way and out on to the deck.

"Stop that man!" roared Miller, darting out in pursuit; and at the shout a couple of loitering deck-hands headed the fugitive off from the gangway. Following, I saw the terrified man swerving this way and that across the littered deck to avoid the seamen, who joined in the pursuit; I saw him make a sudden frantic burst for a baggage-slide springing from a bollard up to the bulwark-rail. Then his foot must have tripped on a lashing, for he staggered for a moment, flung out his arms with a wild shriek, and plunged headlong into the space between the ship's side and the quay wall.

In an instant the whole ship was in an uproar. An officer and two hands sprang to the rail with ropes and a boathook, while others manned the cargo derrick and lowered a rope with a running bowline between the ship and the quay.

"He's gone under," a hoarse voice proclaimed from below; "but I can see him jammed against the side."

There were a couple of minutes of sickening suspense. Then the voice from below was heard again. "Heave up!"

The derrick-engine rattled, the taut rope came up slowly, and at length out of that horrid gulf arose a limp and dripping shape that, as it cleared the bulwark, was swung inboard and let down gently on the deck. Thorndyke and I stooped over him. But it was a dead man's face that we looked into; and a tinge of blood on the lips told the rest of the tale.

"Cover him up," said the superintendent. "He's out of our jurisdiction now. But what's going on there?"

Following his look, I perceived a small scattered crowd of men all running furiously along the quay towards the town. Some of them I judged to be the late inmates of the smoking-room and some plain-clothes men. The only figure that I recognised was that of Mr. Pinder, and he was already growing small in the distance.

"The local police will have to deal with them," said Miller. Then turning to the purser, he asked: "What baggage had this man?"

"Only two cabin trunks," was the reply. "They are both in his state-room."

To the state-room we followed the purser, when Miller had possessed himself of the dead man's keys, and the two trunks were hoisted on to the bunk and opened. Each trunk contained a large cash-box, and each cash-box contained five hundred pounds in gold and a big bundle of notes. The latter Miller examined closely, checking their numbers by a column of entries in his pocket-book.

"Yes," he reported at length; "it's a true bill. These are the notes that were stolen from Mr. Burnham. And now I will have a look at the baggage of those other four sportsmen."

This being no affair of ours, Thorndyke and I went ashore and slowly made our way towards the town. But presently the superintendent overtook us in high glee, with the news that he had discovered what appeared to be the accumulated "swag" of a gang of swell burglars for whom he had been for some months vainly on the look-out.

"How was it done?" repeated Thorndyke in reply to Miller's question, as we sat at a retired table in the "Lord Warden" Hotel. "Well, it was really very simple. I am afraid I shall disappoint you if you expect anything ingenious and recondite. Of course, it was obvious that Miss Dalby had not committed this atrocious murder and robbery; and it was profoundly improbable that this extremely incriminating letter had been dropped accidentally. That being so, it was almost certain that the letter had been 'planted,' as Pinder expressed it. But that was a mere opinion that helped us not at all.

"The actual solution turned upon a simple chemical fact with which I happened to be acquainted; which is this: that all the basic coal-tar dyes, and especially methylene blue, dye *oxycellulose* without requiring a mordant, but do not react in this way on cellulose. Now, good paper is practically pure cellulose; and if you dip a sheet of such paper into certain oxidising liquids, such as a solution of potassium chlorate with a slight excess of hydrochloric acid, the paper is converted into *oxycellulose*. But if instead of immersing the paper, you write on it with a quill or glass pen dipped in the solution, only the part which has been touched by the pen is changed into *oxycellulose*. No change is visible to the eye: but if a sheet of paper written on with this colourless fluid is dipped in a solution of, say, methylene blue, the invisible writing immediately becomes visible. The *oxycellulose* takes up the blue dye.

"Now, when I picked up that sheet of the letter in the railway carriage and noted that the ink used appeared to be methylene blue, this fact was recalled to my mind. Then, on looking at it closely, I seemed to detect a certain slight spottiness in the writing. There were points on some of the letters that were a little deeper in colour than the rest; and it occurred to me that it was possible that these circulars might be used to transmit secret messages of a less innocent kind than those that met the unaided eye, just as these political societies might form an excellent cover for the operations of criminal associations.

"But if the circulars had been so used, it is evident that the secret writing would not be on all the circulars. The prepared sheets would be used only for the circulars that were to be sent to particular persons, and in those cases the secret writing would probably be in the nature of a personal communication, either to a particular individual or to a small group. The possible presence of a secret message thus became of vital evidential importance; for if it could be shown that this letter was addressed to some person other than Miss Dalby, that would dispose of the only evidence connecting her with the crime.

"It happened, most fortunately, that I was able to get possession of the final sheet of this letter—"

"Of course it did," growled Miller, with a sour smile.

"It reached me," continued Thorndyke, "only after Dr. Jervis had started for Densford. The greater part of one side was blank, excepting for a rough plan drawn in pencil, and this blank side I laid down on a sheet of glass and wetted the written side with a small wad of cotton-wool dipped in distilled water. Of course, the blue writing began to run and dissolve out; and then, very faintly, some other writing began to show through in reverse. I turned the paper over, and now the new writing, though faint, was quite legible, and became more so when I wiped the blue-stained cotton-wool over it a few times. A solution of methylene blue would have made it still plainer, but I used water only, as I judged that the blue writing was intended to furnish the dye for development. Here is the final result."

He drew from his pocket a letter-case, from which he extracted a folded paper which he opened and laid on the table. It was stained a faint blue, through which the original writing could be seen, dim and blurred, while the secret message, though very pale, was quite sharp and clear. And this was the message:

". . . so although we are not actually blown on, the position is getting risky and it's time for us to hop. I have booked passages for the four of us to Ostend by the *Cornflower*, which sails on Friday evening next (20th). The names of the four illustrious passengers are, Walsh (that's me), Grubb (Dorman), Jenkins (Spiller) and Thorpe (that's you). Get those names well into your canister—better make a note of them—and turn up in good time on Friday."

"Well," said Miller, as he handed back the letter, "we can't know everything—unless we are Dr. Thorndyke. But there's one thing I do know."

"What is that?" I asked.

"I know why that fellow Pinder grinned when I told him that I had photographed his confounded letters."

The Pathologist to the Rescue

"I hope," said I, as I looked anxiously out of our window up King's Bench Walk, "that our friend, Foxley, will turn up to time, or I shall lose the chance of hearing his story. I must be in court by half-past eleven. The telegram said that he was a parson, didn't it?"

"Yes," replied Thorndyke. "The Reverend Arthur Foxley."

"Then perhaps this may be he. There is a parson crossing from the Row in this direction, only he has a girl with him. He didn't say anything about a girl, did he?"

"No. He merely asked for the appointment. However," he added, as he joined me at the window and watched the couple approaching with their eyes apparently fixed on the number above our portico, "this is evidently our client, and punctual to the minute."

In response to the old-fashioned flourish on our little knocker, he opened the inner door and invited the clergyman and his companion to enter; and while the mutual introductions were in progress, I looked critically at our new clients. Mr. Foxley was a typical and favourable specimen of his class: a handsome, refined, elderly gentleman, prim as to his speech, suave and courteous in bearing, with a certain engaging simplicity of manner which impressed me very favourably.

His companion I judged to be a parishioner for she was what ladies are apt to describe as "not quite;" that is to say, her social level appeared to appertain to the lower *strata* of the middle-class. But she was a fine, strapping girl, very sweet-faced and winsome, quiet and gentle in manner and obviously in deep trouble, for her clear grey eyes—fixed earnestly, almost devouringly, on Thorndyke—were reddened and swimming with unshed tears.

"We have sought your aid, Dr. Thorndyke," the clergyman began, "on the advice of my friend, Mr. Brodribb, who happened to call on me on some business. He assured me that you would be able to solve our difficulties if it were humanly possible, so I have come to lay those difficulties before you. I pray to God that you may be able to help us, for my poor young friend here, Miss Markham, is in a most terrible position, as you will understand when I tell you that her future husband, a most admirable young man named Robert Fletcher, is in the custody of the police, charged with robbery and murder."

Thorndyke nodded gravely, and the clergyman continued: "I had better tell you exactly what has happened. The dead man is one Joseph Riggs, a maternal uncle of Fletcher's, a strange, eccentric man, solitary, miserly, and of a violent, implacable temper. He was quite well-to-do, though penurious and haunted constantly by an absurd fear of poverty. His nephew, Robert, was apparently his only known relative, and, under his will, was his sole heir. Recently, however, Robert has become engaged to my friend, Miss Lilian, and this engagement was violently opposed by his uncle, who had repeatedly urged him to make what he called a profitable marriage.

"For Miss Lilian is a dowerless maiden—dowerless save for those endowments with which God has been pleased to enrich her, and which her future husband has properly prized above mere material wealth. However, Riggs declared, in his brutal way, that he was not going to leave his property to the husband of a shop-woman, and that Robert might look out for a wife with money or be struck out of his will.

"The climax was reached yesterday when Robert, in response to a peremptory summons, went to see his uncle. Mr. Riggs was in a very intractable mood. He demanded that Robert should break off his engagement unconditionally and at once, and when Robert bluntly insisted on his right to choose his own wife the old man worked himself up into a furious rage, shouting, cursing, using the most offensive language and even uttering threats of personal violence. Finally, he drew his gold watch from his pocket and laid it with its chain on the table then, opening a drawer, he took out a bundle of bearer bonds and threw them down by the watch.

"'There, my friend,' said he, 'that is your inheritance. That is all you will get from me, living or dead. Take it and go, and don't let me ever set eyes on you again.'

"At first Robert refused to accept the gift, but his uncle became so violent that eventually, for peace's sake, he took the watch and the bonds, intending to return them later, and went away. He left at half-past five, leaving his uncle alone in the house."

"How was that?" Thorndyke asked. "Was there no servant?"

"Mr. Riggs kept no resident servant. The young woman who did his housework came at half-past eight in the morning and left at half-past four. Yesterday she waited until five to get tea ready, but then, as the uproar in the sitting-room was still unabated, she thought it best to go. She was afraid to go in to lay the tea-things.

"This morning, when she arrived at the house, she found the front door unlocked, as it always was during the day. On entering, her attention was at once attracted by two or three little pools of blood on the floor of the hall, or passage. Somewhat alarmed by this, she looked into the sitting-room, and finding no one there, and being impressed by the silence in the house, she went along the passage to a back room—a sort of study or office, which was usually kept locked when Mr. Riggs was not in. Now, however, it was unlocked and the door was ajar; so having first knocked and receiving no answer, she pushed open the door and looked in; and there, to her horror, she saw her employer lying on the floor, apparently dead, with a wound on the side of his head and a pistol on the floor by his side.

"Instantly she turned and rushed out of the house, and she was running up the street in search of a policeman when she encountered me at a corner and burst out with her dreadful tidings. I walked with her to the police station, and as we went she told me what had happened on the previous afternoon. Naturally, I was profoundly shocked and also alarmed, for I saw that—rightly or wrongly—suspicion must immediately fall on Robert Fletcher. The servant, Rose Turnmill, took it for granted that he had murdered her master; and when we found the station inspector, and Rose had repeated her statement to him, it was evident that he took the same view.

"With him and a sergeant, we went back to the house; but on the way we met Mr. Brodribb, who was staying at the 'White Lion' and had just come out for a walk. I told him, rapidly, what had occurred and begged him to come with us, which, with the inspector's consent, he did; and as we walked I explained to him the awful position that Robert Fletcher might be placed in, and asked him to advise me what to do. But, of course, there was nothing to be said or done until we had seen the body and knew whether any suspicion rested on Robert.

"We found the man Riggs lying as Rose had said. He was quite dead, cold and stiff. There was a pistol wound on the right temple, and a pistol lay on the floor at his right side. A little blood—but not much—had trickled from the wound and lay in a small pool on the oilcloth. The door of an iron safe was open and a bunch of keys hung from the lock; and on a desk one or two share certificates were spread out. On searching the dead man's pockets it was found that the gold watch which the servant told us he usually carried was missing, and when Rose went to the bedroom to see if it was there, it was nowhere to be found.

"Apart from the watch, however, the appearances suggested that the man had taken his own life. But against this view was the blood on the hall floor. The dead man appeared to have fallen at once from the effects of the shot, and there had been very little bleeding. Then how came the blood in the hall? The inspector decided that it could not have been the blood of the deceased; and when we examined it and saw that there were several little pools and that they seemed to form a track towards the street door, he was convinced that the blood had fallen from some person who had been wounded and was escaping from the house. And, under the circumstances, he was bound to assume that that person was Robert Fletcher; and on that assumption, he dispatched the sergeant forthwith to arrest Robert.

"On this I held a consultation with Mr. Brodribb, who pointed out that the case turned principally on the blood in the hall. If it was the blood of deceased, and the absence of the watch could be explained, a verdict of suicide could be accepted. But if it was the blood of some other person, that fact would point to murder. The question, he said, would have to be settled, if possible, and his advice to me, if I believed Robert to be innocent—which, from my knowledge of him, I certainly did—was this: Get a couple of small, clean, labelled bottles from a chemist and—with the inspector's consent—put in one a little of the blood from the hall and in the other some of the blood of the deceased. Seal them both in the inspector's presence and mine and take them up to Dr. Thorndyke. If it is possible to answer the question, Are they or are they not from the same person? he will answer it.

"Well, the inspector made no objection, so I did what he advised. And here are the specimens. I trust they may tell us what we want to know."

Here Mr. Foxley took from his *attaché*-case a small cardboard box, and opening it, displayed two little wide-mouthed bottles carefully packed in cotton wool. Lifting them out tenderly, he placed them on the table before Thorndyke. They were both neatly corked, sealed—with Brodribb's seal, as I noticed—and labelled; the one inscribed "Blood of Joseph Riggs," and the other "Blood of unknown origin," and both signed "Arthur Foxley" and dated. At the bottom of each was a small mass of gelatinous blood-clot.

Thorndyke looked a little dubiously at the two bottles, and addressing the clergyman, said: "I am afraid Mr. Brodribb has rather over-estimated our resources. There is no known method by which the blood of one person can be distinguished with certainty from that of another."

"Dear, dear!" exclaimed Mr. Foxley. "How disappointing! Then these specimens are useless, after all?"

"I won't say that; but it is in the highest degree improbable that they will yield any information. You must build no expectations on them."

"But you will examine them and see if anything is to be gleaned," the parson urged, persuasively.

"Yes, I will examine them. But you realise that if they should yield any evidence, that evidence might be unfavourable?"

"Yes; Mr. Brodribb pointed that out, but we are willing to take the risk, and so, I may say, is Robert Fletcher, to whom I put the question."

"Then you have seen Mr. Fletcher since the discovery?"

"Yes, I saw him at the police station after his arrest. It was then that he gave me—and also the police—the particulars that I have repeated to you. He had to make a statement, as the dead man's watch and the bonds were found in his possession."

"With regard to the pistol. Has it been identified?"

"No. It is an old-fashioned derringer which no one has ever seen before, so there is no evidence as to whose property it was."

"And as to those share certificates which you spoke of as lying on the desk. Do you happen to remember what they were?"

"Yes, they were West African mining shares; Abusum Pa-pa was the name, I think."

"Then," said Thorndyke, "Mr. Riggs had been losing money. The Abusum Pa-pa Company has just gone into liquidation. Do you know if anything had been taken from the safe?"

"It is impossible to say, but apparently not, as there was a good deal of money in the cashbox, which we unlocked and inspected. But we shall hear more tomorrow at the inquest, and I trust we shall hear something there from you. But in any case I hope you will attend to watch the proceedings on behalf of poor Fletcher. And if possible, to be present at the autopsy at eleven o'clock. Can you manage that?"

"Yes. And I shall come down early enough to make an inspection of the premises if the police will give the necessary facilities."

Mr. Foxley thanked him effusively, and when the details as to the trains had been arranged, our clients rose to depart. Thorndyke shook their hands cordially, and as he bade farewell to Miss Markham he murmured a few words of encouragement. She looked up at him gratefully and appealingly as she *naïvely* held his hand.

"You will try to help us, Dr. Thorndyke, won't you?" she urged. "And you will examine that blood very, very carefully. Promise that you will. Remember that poor Robert's life may hang upon what you can tell about it."

"I realise that, Miss Markham," he replied gently, "and I promise you that the specimens shall be most thoroughly examined; and further, that no stone shall be left unturned in my endeavours to bring the truth to light."

At his answer, spoken with infinite kindliness and sympathy, her eyes filled and she turned away with a few broken words of thanks, and the good clergyman—himself not unmoved by the little episode—took her arm and led her to the door.

"Well," I remarked as their retreating footsteps died away, "old Brodribb's enthusiasm seems to have let you in for a queer sort of task; and I notice that you appear to have accepted Fletcher's statement."

"Without prejudice," he replied. "I don't know Fletcher, but the balance of probabilities is in his favour. Still, that blood-track in the hall is a curious feature. It certainly requires explanation."

"It does, indeed!" I exclaimed, "and you have got to find the explanation! Well, I wish you joy of the job. I suppose you will carry out the farce to the bitter end as you have promised?"

"Certainly," he replied. "But it is hardly a farce. I should have looked the specimens over in any case. One never knows what illuminating fact a chance observation may bring into view."

I smiled sceptically.

"The fact that you are asked to ascertain is that these two samples of blood came from the same person. If there are any means of proving that, they are unknown to me. I should have said it was an impossibility."

"Of course," he rejoined, "you are quite right, speaking academically and in general terms. No method of identifying the blood of individual persons has hitherto been discovered. But yet I can imagine the possibility, in particular and exceptional cases, of an actual, personal identification by means of blood. What does my learned friend think?"

"He thinks that his imagination is not equal to the required effort," I answered; and with that I picked up my brief-bag and went forth to my duties at the courts.

That Thorndyke would keep his promise to poor Lilian Markham was a foregone conclusion, preposterous as the examination seemed. But even my long experience of my colleague's scrupulous conscientiousness had not prepared me for the spectacle which met my eyes when I returned to our chambers. On the table stood the microscope, flanked by three slide-boxes. Each box held six trays, and each tray held six slides—a hundred and eight slides in all!

But why three boxes? I opened one. The slides—carefully mounted blood-films—were labelled "Joseph Riggs." Those in the second box were labelled, "Blood from hall floor." But when I opened the third box, I beheld a collection of empty slides labelled "Robert Fletcher"!

I chuckled aloud. Prodigious! Thorndyke was going even one better than his promise. He was not only going to examine—probably had examined—the two samples produced; he was actually going to collect a third sample for himself!

I picked out one of Mr. Riggs's slides and laid it on the stage of the microscope. Thorndyke seemed to have been using a low-power objective—the inch-and-a-half. After a glance through this, I swung round the nose-piece to the high power. And then I got a further surprise. The brightly-coloured "white" corpuscles showed that Thorndyke had actually been to the trouble of staining the films with eosin! Again I murmured, "Prodigious!" and put the slide back in its box. For, of course, it showed just what one expected: blood—or rather, broken-up blood-clot. From its appearance I could not even have sworn that it was human blood.

I had just closed the box when Thorndyke entered the room. His quick eye at once noted the changed objective and he remarked: "I see you have been having a look at the specimens."

"A specimen." I corrected. "Enough is as good as a feast."

"Blessed are they who are easily satisfied," he retorted; and then he added: "I have altered my arrangements, though I needn't interfere with yours. I shall go down to Southaven tonight; in fact, I am starting in a few minutes."

"Why?" I asked.

"For several reasons. I want to make sure of the post-mortem tomorrow morning, I want to pick up any further facts that are available, and finally, I want to prepare a set of blood-films from Robert

Fletcher. We may as well make the series complete," he added with a smile, to which I replied by a broad grin.

"Really, Thorndyke," I protested. "I'm surprised at you, at your age, too. She is a nice girl, but she isn't so beautiful as to justify a hundred and eight blood-films."

I accompanied him to the taxi, followed by Polton, who carried his modest luggage, and then returned to speculate on his probable plan of campaign. For, of course, he had one. His purposive, resolute manner told me that he had seen farther into this case than I had. I accepted that as natural and inevitable. Indeed, I may admit that my disrespectful badinage covered a belief in his powers hardly second even to old Brodribb's. I was, in fact, almost prepared to discover that those preposterous blood-films had, after all, yielded some "illuminating fact" which had sent him hurrying down to Southaven in search of corroboration.

When I alighted from the train on the following day at a little past noon, I found him waiting on the platform, ready to conduct me to his hotel for an early lunch.

"All goes well, so far," he reported. "I attended the post-mortem, and examined the wound thoroughly. The pistol was held in the right hand not more than two inches from the head; probably quite close, for the skin is scorched and heavily tattooed with black powder grains. I find that Riggs was right-handed. So the *prima facie* probabilities are in favour of suicide; and the recent loss of money suggests a reasonable motive."

"But what about that blood in the hall?"

"Oh, we have disposed of that. I completed the blood-film series last night."

I looked at him quickly to see if he was serious or only playing a facetious return-shot. But his face was as a face of wood.

"You are an exasperating old devil, Thorndyke!" I exclaimed with conviction. Then, knowing that cross-examination would be futile, I asked: "What are we going to do after lunch?"

"The inspector is going to show us over 'the scene of the tragedy,' as the newspapers would express it."

I noted gratefully that he had reserved this item for me, and dismissed professional topics for the time being, concentrating my attention on the old-world, amphibious streets through which we were walking. There is always something interesting in the aspect of a seaport town, even if it is only a small one like Southaven.

The inspector arrived with such punctuality that he found us still at the table and was easily induced to join us with a cup of coffee and to accept a cigar—administered by Thorndyke, as I suspected, with the object of hindering conversation. I could see that his interest in my colleague was intense and not unmingled with awe, a fact which, in conjunction with the cigar, restrained him from any undue manifestations of curiosity, but not from continuous, though furtive, observation of my friend. Indeed, when we arrived at the late Mr. Riggs's house, I was secretly amused by the close watch that he kept on Thorndyke's movements, unsensational as the inspection turned out to be.

The house, itself, presented very little of interest excepting its picturesque old-world exterior, which fronted on a quiet by-street and was furnished with a deep bay which, as Thorndyke ascertained, commanded a clear view of the street from end to end. It was a rather shabby, neglected little house, as might have been expected, and our examination of it yielded, so far as I could see, only a single fact of any significance: which was that there appeared to be no connection whatever between the blood-stain on the study floor and the train of large spots from the middle of the hall to the street door. And on this piece of evidence—definitely unfavourable from our point of view—Thorndyke concentrated his attention when he had made a preliminary survey.

Closely followed by the watchful inspector, he browsed round the little room, studying every inch of the floor between the bloodstain and the door. The latter he examined minutely from top to bottom, especially as to the handle, the jambs, and the lintel. Then he went out into the hall, scrutinising the floor inch by inch, poring over the walls, and even looking behind the framed prints that hung on them. A reflector lamp suspended by a nail on the wall received minute and prolonged attention, as did also a massive lamp-hook screwed into one of the beams of the low ceiling, of which Thorndyke remarked as he stooped to pass under it, that it must have been fixed there by a dwarf.

"Yes," the inspector agreed, "and a fool. A swinging lamp hung on that hook would have blocked the whole fairway. There isn't too much room as it is. What a pity we weren't a bit more careful about footprints in this place. There are plenty of tracks of wet feet here on this oil-cloth; faint, but you could have made them out all right if they hadn't been all on top of one another. There's Mr. Foxley's, the girl's, mine, and the men who carried out the body, but I'm hanged if I can tell which is which. It's a regular mix up."

"Yes," I agreed, "it is all very confused. But I notice one rather odd thing. There are several faint traces of a large right foot, but I can't see any sign of the corresponding left foot. Can you?"

"Perhaps this is it," said Thorndyke, pointing to a large, vague oval mark. "I have noticed that it seems to occur in some sort of connection with the big right foot; but I must admit that it is not a very obvious foot-print."

"I shouldn't have taken it for a footprint at all, or at any rate, not a human footprint. It is more like the spoor of some big animal."

"It is," Thorndyke agreed; "but whatever it is, it seems to have been here before any of the others arrived. You notice that wherever it occurs, it seems to have been trodden on by some of the others."

"Yes, I had noticed that, and the same is true of the big right foot, so it seems probable that they are connected, as you say. But I am hanged if I can make anything of it. Can you, inspector?"

The inspector shook his head. He could not recognise the mark as a footprint, but he could see very plainly that he had been a fool not to have taken more care to protect the floor.

When the examination of the hall was finished, Thorndyke opened the door and looked at the big, flat doorstep. "What was the weather like here on Wednesday evening?" he asked.

"Showery," the inspector replied; "and there were one or two heavy showers during the night. You were noticing that there are no blood-tracks on the doorstep. But there wouldn't be in any case; for if a man had come out of this door dropping blood, the blood would have dropped on wet stone and got washed away at once."

Thorndyke admitted the truth of this; and so another item of favourable evidence was extinguished. The probability that the blood in the hall was that of some person other than the deceased remained undisturbed; and I could not see that a single fact had been elicited by our inspection of the house that was in any way helpful to our client. Indeed, it appeared to me that there was absolutely no case for the defence, and I even asked myself whether we were not, in fact, merely trying to fudge up a defence for an obviously guilty man. It was not like Thorndyke to do that. But how did the case stand?

There was a suggestion of suicide, but a clear possibility of homicide. There was strong evidence that a second person had been in the house, and that person appeared to have received a wound. But a wound suggested a struggle; and the servant's evidence was to the effect that when she left the house a violent altercation was in progress. The deceased was never again seen alive; and the other party to the quarrel bad been found with property of the dead man in his possession. Moreover, there was a clear motive for the crime, stupid as that crime was. For the dead man had threatened to revoke his will but as he had presumably not done so, his death left the will still operative. In short, everything pointed to the guilt of our client, Robert Fletcher.

I had just reached this not very gratifying conclusion when a statement of Thorndyke's shattered my elaborate summing up into impalpable fragments.

"I suppose, sir," said the inspector, "there isn't anything that you would care to tell us, as you are for the defence. But we are not hostile to Fletcher. In fact, he hasn't been charged. He is only being detained in custody until we have heard what turns up at the inquest. I know you have examined that blood that Mr. Foxley took, and Fletcher's blood, too, and you've seen the premises. We have given all the facilities that we could, and if you could give us any sort of hint that might be useful, I should be very much obliged."

Thorndyke reflected for a few moments. Then he replied: "There is no reason for secrecy in regard to you, inspector, who have been so helpful and friendly, so I will be quite frank. I have examined both samples of blood and Fletcher's, and I have inspected the premises; and what I am able to say definitely is this: the blood in the hall is not the blood of the deceased—"

"Ah!" exclaimed the inspector, "I was afraid it wasn't."

"And it is not the blood of Robert Fletcher."

"Isn't it now! Well, I am glad to hear that."

"Moreover," continued Thorndyke, "it was shed well after nine o'clock at night, probably not earlier than midnight."

"There, now!" the inspector exclaimed, with an admiring glance at Thorndyke, "just think of that. See what it is to be a man of science! I suppose, sir, you couldn't give us any sort of description of the person who dropped that blood in the hall?"

Staggered as I had been by Thorndyke's astonishing statements, I could not repress a grin at the inspector's artless question. But the grin faded rather abruptly as Thorndyke replied in matter-of-fact tones: "A detailed description is, of course, impossible. I can only sketch out the probabilities. But if you should happen to meet with a man—a tall negro with a bandaged head or a contused wound of the scalp and a swollen leg—you had better keep your eye on him. The leg which is swollen is probably the left."

The inspector was thrilled; and so was I, for that matter. The thing was incredible; but yet I knew that Thorndyke's amazing deductions were the products of perfectly orthodox scientific methods. Only I could form no sort of guess as to how they had been arrived at. A negro's blood is no different from any other person's, and certainly affords no clue to his height or the condition of his legs. I could make nothing of it: and as the dialogue and the inspector's note-takings brought us to the little town hall in which the inquest was to be held, I dismissed the puzzle until such time as Thorndyke chose to solve it.

When we entered the town hall we found everything in readiness for the opening of the proceedings. The jury were already in their places and the coroner was just about to take his seat at the head of the long table. We accordingly slipped on to the two chairs that were found for us by the inspector, and the latter took his place behind the jury and facing us. Near to him Mr. Foxley and Miss Markham were seated, and evidently hailed our arrival with profound relief, each of them smiling us a silent greeting. A professional-looking man sitting next to Thorndyke I assumed to be the medical witness, and a rather good young man who sat apart with a police constable I identified as Robert Fletcher.

The evidence of the "common" witnesses, who deposed to the general facts, told us nothing that we did not already know, excepting that it was made clear that Fletcher had left his uncle's house not later than seven o'clock and that thereafter until the following morning his whereabouts were known. The medical witness was cautious, and kept an uneasy eye on Thorndyke. The wound which caused the death of deceased might have been inflicted by himself or by some other person. He had originally given the probable time of death as six or seven o'clock on Wednesday evening. He now admitted in reply to a question from Thorndyke that he had not taken the temperature of the body, and that the rigidity and other conditions were not absolutely inconsistent with a considerable later time of death. Death might even have occurred after midnight.

In spite of this admission, however, the sum of the evidence tended strongly to implicate Fletcher, and one or two questions from jury-men suggested a growing belief in his guilt. I had no doubt whatever that if the case had been put to the jury at this stage, a unanimous verdict of "wilful murder" would have been the result. But, as the medical witness returned to his seat, the coroner fixed an inquisitive eye on Thorndyke.

"You have not been summoned as a witness, Dr. Thorndyke," said he, "but I understand that you have made certain investigations in this case. Are you able to throw any fresh light on the circumstances of the death of the deceased, Joseph Riggs?"

"Yes," Thorndyke replied. "I am in a position to give important and material evidence."

Thereupon he was sworn, and the coroner, still watching him curiously, said: "I am informed that you have examined samples of the blood of deceased and the blood which was found in the hall of deceased's house. Did you examine them, and if so, what was the object of the examination?"

"I examined both samples and also samples of the blood of Robert Fletcher. The object was to ascertain whether the blood on the hall floor was the blood of the deceased or of Robert Fletcher."

The coroner glanced at the medical witness, and a faint smile appeared on the face of each.

"And did you," the former asked in a slightly ironical tone, "form any opinion on the subject?"

"I ascertained definitely that the blood in the hall was neither that of the deceased nor that of Robert Fletcher."

The coroner's eyebrows went up, and once more he glanced significantly at the doctor.

"But," he demanded incredulously, "is it possible to distinguish the blood of one person from that of another?"

"Usually it is not, but in certain exceptional cases it is. This happened to be an exceptional case."

"In what respect?"

"It happened," Thorndyke replied, "that the person whose blood was found in the hall suffered from the parasitic disease known as *filariasis*. His blood was infested with swarms of a minute worm named *Filaria nocturna*. I have here," he continued, taking out of his research-case the two bottles and the three boxes, "thirty-six mounted specimens of this blood, and in every one of them one or more of the parasites is to be seen. I have also thirty-six mounted specimens each of the blood of the deceased and the blood of Robert Fletcher. In not one of these specimens is a single parasite to be found. Moreover, I have examined Robert Fletcher and the body of the deceased, and can testify that no sign of *filarial* disease was to be discovered in either. Hence it is certain, that the blood found in the hall was not the blood of either of these two persons."

The ironic smile had faded from the coroner's face. He was evidently deeply impressed, and his manner was quite deferential as he asked: "Do these very remarkable observations of yours lead to any further inferences?"

"Yes," replied Thorndyke. "They render it certain that this blood was shed no earlier than nine o'clock and probably nearer midnight."

"Really!" the astonished coroner exclaimed. "Now, how is it possible to fix the time in that exact manner?"

"By inference from the habits of the parasite," Thorndyke explained. "This particular *filaria* is distributed by the mosquito, and its habits are adapted to the habits of the mosquito. During the day, the worms are not found in the blood; they remain hidden in the tissues of the body. But about nine o'clock at night they begin to migrate from the tissues into the blood, and remain in the blood during the hours when the mosquitoes are active. Then about six o'clock in the morning, they leave the blood and migrate back into the tissues.

"There is another very similar species—*Filaria diurna*—which has exactly opposite habits, adapted to day-flying suctorial insects. It appears in the blood about eleven in the forenoon and goes back into the tissues at about six o'clock in the evening."

"Astonishing!" exclaimed the coroner. "Wonderful! By the way, the parasites that you found could not, I suppose, have been *Filaria diurna?*"

"No," Thorndyke replied. "The time excludes that possibility. The blood was certainly shed after six. They were undoubtedly *nocturna*, and the large numbers found suggest a late hour. The parasites come out of the tissues very gradually, and it is only about midnight that they appear in the blood in really large numbers."

"That is very important," said the coroner. "But does this disease affect any particular class of persons?"

"Yes," Thorndyke replied. "As the disease is confined to tropical countries, the sufferers are naturally residents of the tropics, and nearly always natives. In West Africa, for instance, it is common among the negroes but practically unknown among the white residents."

"Should you say that there is a distinct probability that this unknown person was a negro?"

"Yes. But apart from the *filaria* there is direct evidence that he was. Searching for some cause of the bleeding, I noticed a lamp-hook screwed into the ceiling, and low enough to strike a tall man's head.

I examined it closely, and observed on it a dark, shiny mark, like a blood-smear, and one or two short coiled hairs which I recognised as the scalp-hairs of a negro. I have no doubt who this unknown man is, and that he has a wound of the scalp."

"Does *filarial* disease produce any effects that can be recognised?"

"Frequently it does. One of the commonest effects produced by *Filaria nocturna*, especially among negroes, is the condition known as elephantiasis. This consists of an enormous swelling of the extremities, most usually of one leg, including the foot; whence the name. The leg and foot look like those of an elephant. As a matter of fact, the negro who was in the hall suffered from elephantiasis of the left leg. I observed prints of the characteristically deformed foot on the oil-cloth covering the floor."

Thorndyke's evidence was listened to with intense interest by everyone present, including myself. Indeed, so spell-bound was his audience that one could have heard a pin drop; and the breathless silence continued for some seconds after he had ceased speaking. Then, in the midst of the stillness, I heard the door creak softly behind me.

There was nothing particularly significant in the sound. But its effects were amazing. Glancing at the inspector, who faced the door, I saw his eyes open and his jaw drop until his face was a very mask of astonishment. And as this expression was reflected on the faces of the jurymen, the coroner and everyone present, excepting Thorndyke, whose back was towards the door, I turned to see what had happened. And then I was as astonished as the others.

The door had been pushed open a few inches and a head thrust in—a negro's head, covered with a soiled and blood rag forming a rough bandage. As I gazed at the black, shiny, inquisitive face, the man pushed the door farther open and shuffled into the room; and instantly there arose on all sides a soft rustle and an inarticulate murmur followed by breathless silence, while every eye was riveted on the man's left leg.

It certainly was a strange, repulsive-looking member, its monstrous bulk exposed to view through the slit trouser and its great shapeless foot—shoeless, since no shoe could have contained it—rough and horny like the foot of an elephant. But it was tragic and pitiable too, for the man, apart from this horrible excrescence, was a fine, big, athletic-looking fellow.

The coroner was the first to recover. Addressing Thorndyke, but keeping an eye on the man, he said: "Your evidence, then, amounts to this: On the night of Joseph Riggs' death, there was a stranger in the house. That stranger was a negro, who seems to have wounded his head and who, you say, had a swelled left leg."

"Yes," Thorndyke admitted, "that is the substance of my evidence."

Once more a hush fell on the room. The negro stood near the door, rolling his eyes to and fro over the assembly as if uneasily conscious that everyone was looking at him. Suddenly, he shuffled up to the foot of the table and addressed the coroner in deep, buzzing, resonant tones. "You tink I kill dat ole man! I no kill um. He kill himself. I look um."

Having made this statement, he rolled his eyes defiantly round the court, and then turned his face expectantly towards the coroner, who said: "You say you know that Mr. Riggs killed himself?"

"Yas. I look um. He shoot himself. You tink I shoot um. I tell you I no shoot um. Why I fit kill this man? I no sabby um."

"Then," said the coroner, "if you know that he killed himself, you must tell us all that you know; and you must swear to tell us the truth."

"Yas," he agreed, "I tell you eberyting one time. I tell you de troof. Dat ole man kill himself."

When the coroner had explained to him that he was not bound to make any statement that would incriminate him, as he still elected to give evidence, he was sworn and proceeded to make his statement with curious fluency and self-possession.

"My name Robert Bruce. Dat my English name. My country name Kwaku Mensah. I live for Winnebah on de Gold Coast. Dis time I cook's mate for dat steamer *Leckie*. On Wednesday night I lay in my bunk. I no fit sleep. My leg he chook me. I look out of de porthole. Plenty moon live. In my country when de moon big, peoples walk about. So I get up. I go ashore to walk about de town. Den de rain come. Plenty rain. Rain no good for my sickness. So I try for open house doors. No fit. All doors locked. Den I come to dis ole man's house. I turn de handle. De door open. I go in. I look in one room. All dark. Nobody live. Den I look annudder room. De door open a little. Light live inside. I no like dat I tink, spose somebody come out and see me, be tink I come for teef someting. So I tink I go away.

"Den someting make 'Ping!' same like gun. I hear someting fall down in dat room. I go to de door and I sing out, 'Who live in dere?' Nobody say nutting. So I open de door and look in. De room full ob smoke. I look dat ole man on de floor. I look dat pistol. I sabby dat ole man kill himself. Den I frighten too much. I run out. De place all dark. Someting knock my head. He make blood come plenty. I go back for ship. I no say nutting to nobody. Dis day I hear peoples talk 'bout dis inquess to find out who kill dat ole man. So I come to hear what peoples say. I hear dat gentleman say I kill dat ole man. So I tell you eberyting. I tell you de troof. Finish."

"Do you know what time it was when you came ashore?" the coroner asked.

"Yas. When I come down de ladder I hear eight bells ring. I get back to de ship jus' before dey ring two bells in de middle watch."

"Then you came ashore at midnight and got back just before one o'clock?"

"Yas. Dat is what I say."

A few more questions put by the coroner having elicited nothing fresh, the case was put briefly to the jury.

"You have heard the evidence, gentlemen, and most remarkable evidence it was. Like myself, you must have been deeply impressed by the amazing skill with which Dr. Thorndyke reconstructed the personality of the unknown visitor to that house, and even indicated correctly the very time of the visit, from an examination of a mere chance bloodstain. As to the statement of Kwaku Mensab, I can only say that I see no reason to doubt its truth. You will note that it is in complete agreement with Dr. Thorndyke's evidence, and it presents no inconsistencies or improbabilities. Possibly the police may wish to make some further inquiries, but for our purposes it is the evidence of an eyewitness, and as such must be given full weight. With these remarks, I leave you to consider your verdict."

The jury took but a minute or two to deliberate. Indeed, only one verdict was possible if the evidence was to be accepted, and that was agreed on unanimously—suicide whilst temporarily insane. As soon as it was announced, the inspector, formally and with congratulations, released Fletcher from custody, and presently retired in company with the negro to make a few inquiries on board the ship.

The rising of the court was the signal for a wild demonstration of enthusiasm and gratitude to Thorndyke. To play his part efficiently in that scene he would have needed to be furnished, like certain repulsive Indian deities, with an unlimited outfit of arms. For everyone wanted to shake his hand, and two of them—Mr. Foxley and Miss Markham—did so with such pertinacity as entirely to exclude the other candidates.

"I can never thank you enough," Miss Markham exclaimed, with swimming eyes, "if I should live to be a hundred. But I shall think of you with gratitude every day of my life. Whenever I look at Robert, I shall remember that his liberty, and even his life, are your gifts."

Here she was so overcome by grateful emotion that she again seized and pressed his hand. I think she was within an ace of kissing him; but being, perhaps, doubtful how he would take it, compromised by kissing Robert instead. And, no doubt, it was just as well.

The Puzzle Lock

I do not remember what was the occasion of my dining with Thorndyke at Giamborini's on the particular evening that is now in my mind. Doubtless, some piece of work completed had seemed to justify the modest festival. At any rate, there we were, seated at a somewhat retired table, selected by Thorndyke, with our backs to the large window through which the late June sunlight streamed. We had made our preliminary arrangements, including a bottle of Barsac, and were inspecting dubiously a collection of semi-edible *hors d'oeuvres*, when a man entered and took possession of a table just in front of ours, which had apparently been reserved for him, since he walked directly to it and drew away the single chair that had been set aslant against it.

I watched with amused interest his methodical procedure, for he was clearly a man who took his dinner seriously. A regular customer, too, I judged by the waiter's manner and the reserved table with its single chair. But the man himself interested me. He was out of the common and there was a suggestion of character, with perhaps a spice of oddity, in his appearance. He appeared to be about sixty years of age, small and spare, with a much-wrinkled, mobile and rather whimsical face, surmounted by a crop of white, upstanding hair. From his waistcoat pocket protruded the ends of a fountain-pen, a pencil and a miniature electric torch such as surgeons use; a silver-mounted Coddington lens hung from his watch-guard and the middle finger of his left hand bore the largest seal ring that I have ever seen.

"Well," said Thorndyke, who had been following my glance, "what do you make of him?"

"I don't quite know," I replied. "The Coddington suggests a naturalist or a scientist of some kind, but that blatant ring doesn't. Perhaps he is an antiquary or a numismatist or even a philatelist. He deals with small objects of some kind."

At this moment a man who had just entered strode up to our friend's table and held out his hand, which the other shook, with no great enthusiasm, as I thought. Then the newcomer fetched a chair, and setting it by the table, seated himself and picked up the menu card, while the other observed him with a shade of disapproval. I judged that he would rather have dined alone, and that the personality of the new arrival—a flashy, bustling, obtrusive type of man—did not commend him.

From this couple my eye was attracted to a tall man who had halted near the door and stood looking about the room as if seeking someone. Suddenly he spied an empty, single table, and, bearing down on it, seated himself and began anxiously to study the menu under the supervision of a waiter. I glanced at him with slight disfavour. One makes allowances for the exuberance of youth, but when a middle-aged man presents the combination of heavily-greased hair parted in the middle, a waxed moustache of a suspiciously intense black, a pointed imperial and a single eye-glass, evidently ornamental in function, one views him with less tolerance. However, his get-up was not my concern, whereas my dinner was, and I had given this my undivided attention for some minutes when I heard Thorndyke emit a soft chuckle.

"Not bad," he remarked, setting down his glass.

"Not at all," I agreed, "for a restaurant wine."

"I was not alluding to the wine," said he "but to our friend Badger."

"The inspector!" I exclaimed. "He isn't here, is he? I don't see him."

"I am glad to hear you say that, Jervis," said he. "It is a better effort than I thought. Still, he might manage his properties a little better. That is the second time his eye-glass has been in the soup."

Following, the direction of his glance, I observed the man with the waxed moustache furtively wiping his eye-glass; and the temporary absence of the monocular grimace enabled me to note a resemblance to the familiar features of the detective officer.

"If you say that is Badger, I suppose it is," said I. "He is certainly a little like our friend. But I shouldn't have recognised him."

"I don't know that I should," said Thorndyke, "but for the little unconscious tricks of movement. You know the habit he has of stroking the back of his head, and of opening his mouth and scratching the side of his chin. I saw him do it just now. He had forgotten his imperial until he touched it, and then the sudden arrest of movement was very striking. It doesn't do to forget a false beard."

"I wonder what his game is," said I. "The disguise suggests that he is on the look-out for somebody who might know him; but apparently that somebody has not turned up yet. At any rate, he doesn't seem to be watching anybody in particular."

"No," said Thorndyke. "But there is somebody whom he seems rather to avoid watching. Those two men at the table in front of ours are in his direct line of vision, but he hasn't looked at them once since he sat down, though I noticed that he gave them one quick glance before he selected his table. I wonder if he has observed us. Probably not, as we have the strong light of the window behind us and his attention is otherwise occupied."

I looked at the two men and from them to the detective, and I judged that my friend was right. On the inspector's table was a good-sized fern in an ornamental pot, and this he had moved so that it was directly between him and the two strangers, to whom he must have been practically invisible; and now I could see that he did, in fact, steal an occasional glance at them over the edge of the menu card. Moreover, as their meal drew to an end, he hastily finished his own and beckoned to the waiter to bring the bill.

"We may as well wait and see them off," said Thorndyke, who had already settled our account. "Badger always interests me. He is so ingenious and he has such shockingly bad luck."

We had not long to wait. The two men rose from the table and walked slowly to the door, where they paused to light their cigars before going out. Then Badger rose, with his back towards them and his eyes on the mirror opposite; and as they went out, he snatched up his hat and stick and followed. Thorndyke looked at me inquiringly.

"Do we indulge in the pleasures of the chase?" he asked, and as I replied in the affirmative, we, too, made our way out and started in the wake of the inspector.

As we followed Badger at a discreet distance, we caught an occasional glimpse of the quarry ahead, whose proceedings evidently caused the inspector some embarrassment, for they had a way of stopping suddenly to elaborate some point that they were discussing, whereby it became necessary for the detective to drop farther in the rear than was quite safe, in view of the rather crowded state of the pavement. On one of these occasions, when the older man was apparently delivering himself of some excruciating joke, they both turned suddenly and looked back, the joker pointing to some object on the opposite side of the road. Several people turned to see what was being pointed at, and, of course, the inspector had to turn, too, to avoid being recognised. At this moment the two men popped into an entry, and when the inspector once more turned they were gone.

As soon as he missed them, Badger started forward almost at a run, and presently halted at the large entry of the Celestial Bank Chambers, into which he peered eagerly. Then, apparently sighting his quarry, he darted in, and we quickened our pace and followed. Halfway down the long hall we saw him standing at the door of a lift, frantically pressing the call-button.

"Poor Badger!" chuckled Thorndyke, as we walked past him unobserved. "His usual luck! He will hardly run them to earth now in this enormous building. We may as well go through to the Blenheim Street entrance."

We pursued our way along the winding corridor and were close to the entrance when I noticed two men coming down the staircase that led to the ball.

"By Jingo! Here they are!" I exclaimed. "Shall we run back and give Badger the tip?"

Thorndyke hesitated. But it was too late. A taxi had just driven up and was discharging its fare. The younger man, catching the driver's eye, ran out and seized the door-handle; and when his companion had entered the cab, he gave an address to the driver, and, stepping in quickly, slammed the door. As the cab moved off, Thorndyke pulled out his notebook and pencil and jotted down the number of the vehicle. Then we turned and retraced our steps; but when we reached the lift-door, the inspector had disappeared. Presumably, like the incomparable Tom Bowling, he had gone aloft.

"We must give it up, Jervis," said Thorndyke. "I will send him anonymously the number of the cab, and that is all we can do. But I am sorry for Badger."

With this we dismissed the incident from our minds—at least, I did; assuming that I had seen the last of the two strangers. Little did I suspect how soon and under what strange and tragic circumstances I should meet with them again!

It was about a week later that we received a visit from our old friend, Superintendent Miller of the Criminal Investigation Department. The passing years had put us on a footing of mutual trust and esteem, and the capable, straightforward detective officer was always a welcome visitor.

"I've just dropped in," said Miller, cutting off the end of the inevitable cigar, "to tell you about a rather queer case that we've got in hand. I know you are always interested in queer cases."

Thorndyke smiled blandly. He had heard that kind of preamble before, and he knew, as did I, that when Miller became communicative we could safely infer that the Millerian bark was in shoal water.

"It is a case," the superintendent continued, "of a very special brand of crook. Actually there is a gang, but it is the managing director that we have particularly got our eye on."

"Is he a regular 'habitual,' then?" asked Thorndyke.

"Well," replied Miller, "as to that, I can't positively say. The fact is that we haven't actually seen the man to be sure of him."

"I see," said Thorndyke, with a grim smile. "You mean to say that you have got your eye on the place where he isn't."

"At the present moment," Miller admitted, "that is the literal fact. We have lost sight of the man we suspected, but we hope to pick him up again presently. We want him badly, and his pals too. It is probably quite a small gang, but they are mighty fly; a lot too smart to be at large. And they'll take some catching, for there is someone running the concern with a good deal more brains than crooks usually have."

"What is their lay?" I asked.

"Burglary," he replied. "Jewels and plate, but principally jewels; and the special feature of their work is that the swag disappears completely every time. None of the stuff has ever been traced. That is what drew our attention to them. After each robbery we made a round of all the fences, but there was not a sign. The stuff seemed to have vanished into smoke. Now that is very awkward. If you never see the men and you can't trace the stuff, where are you? You've got nothing to go on."

"But you seem to have got a clue of some kind." I said.

"Yes. There isn't a lot in it; but it seemed worth following up. One of our men happened to travel down to Colchester with a certain man, and when he came back two days later, he noticed this same man on the platform at Colchester and saw him get out at Liverpool Street. In the interval there had been a jewel robbery at Colchester. Then there was a robbery at Southampton, and our man went at once to Waterloo and saw all the trains in. On the second day, behold! the Colchester sportsman turns up at the barrier, so our man, who had a special taxi waiting, managed to track him home and afterwards got some particulars about him. He is a chap named Shemmonds; belongs to a firm of outside brokers. But nobody seems to know much about him and he doesn't put in much time at the office.

"Well, then, Badger took him over and shadowed him for a day or two, but just as things were looking interesting, he slipped off the hook. Badger followed him to a restaurant, and, through the glass door, saw him go up to an elderly man at a table and shake hands with him. Then he took a chair at the table himself, so Badger popped in and took a seat near them where he could keep them in view. They went out together and Badger followed them, but he lost them in the Celestial Bank Chambers. They went up in the lift just before he could get to the door and that was the last he saw of them. But we have ascertained that they left the building in a taxi and that the taxi set them down at Great Turnstile."

"It was rather smart of you to trace the cab," Thorndyke remarked.

"You've got to keep your eyes skinned in our line of business," said Miller. "But now we come to the real twister. From the time those two men went down Great Turnstile, nobody has set eyes on either of them. They seem to have vanished into thin air."

"You found out who the other man was, then?" said I.

"Yes. The restaurant manager knew him; an old chap named Luttrell. And we knew him, too, because he has a thumping burglary insurance, and when he goes out of town he notifies his company, and they make arrangements with us to have the premises watched."

"What is Luttrell?" I asked.

"Well, he is a bit of a mug, I should say, at least that's his character in the trade. Goes in for being a dealer in jewels and antiques, but he'll buy anything—furniture, pictures, plate, any blooming thing. Does it for a hobby, the regular dealers say. Likes the sport of bidding at the sales. But the knock-out men hate him; never know what he's going to do.

"Must have private means, for though he doesn't often drop money, he can't make much. He's no salesman. It is the buying that he seems to like. But he is a regular character, full of cranks and oddities. His rooms in Thavies Inn look like the British Museum gone mad. He has got electric alarms from all the doors up to his bedroom and the strong-room in his office is fitted with a puzzle lock instead of keys."

"That doesn't seem very safe," I remarked.

"It is," said Miller. "This one has fifteen alphabets. One of our men has calculated that it has about forty billion changes. No one is going to work that out, and there are no keys to get lost. But it is that strong-room that is worrying us, as well as the old joker himself. The Lord knows how much valuable stuff there is in it. What we are afraid of is that Shemmonds may have made away with the old chap and be lying low, waiting to swoop down on that strong-room."

"But you said that Luttrell goes away sometimes," said I.

"Yes; but then he always notifies his insurance company and he seals up his strong-room with a tape round the door-handle and a great seal on the door-post. This time he hasn't notified the company and the door isn't sealed. There's a seal on the door-post—left from last time, I expect—but only the cut ends of tape. I got the caretaker to let me see the place this morning; and, by the way, doctor, I have taken a leaf out of your book. I always carry a bit of squeezing wax in my pocket now and a little box of French chalk. Very handy they are, too. As I had 'em with me this morning, I took a squeeze of the seal. May want it presently for identification."

He brought out of his pocket a small tin box from which he carefully extracted an object wrapped in tissue paper. When the paper had been tenderly removed there was revealed a lump of moulding wax, one side of which was flattened and bore a sunk design.

"It's quite a good squeeze," said Miller, handing it to Thorndyke. "I dusted the seal with French chalk so that the wax shouldn't stick to it."

My colleague examined the "squeeze" through his lens, and passing it and the lens to me, asked: "Has this been photographed, Miller?"

"No," was the reply, "but it ought to be before it gets damaged."

"It ought, certainly," said Thorndyke, "if you value it. Shall I get Polton to do it now?"

The superintendent accepted the offer gratefully and Thorndyke accordingly took the squeeze up to the laboratory, where he left it for our assistant to deal with. When he returned, Miller remarked: "It is a baffling case, this. Now that Shemmonds has dropped out of sight, there is nothing to go on and nothing to do but wait for something else to happen; another burglary or an attempt on the strong-room."

"Is it clear that the strong-room has not been opened?" asked Thorndyke.

"No, it isn't," replied Miller. "That's part of the trouble. Luttrell has disappeared and he may be dead. If he is, Shemmonds will probably have been through his pockets. Of course there is no strong-room key. That is one of the advantages of a puzzle lock. But it is quite possible that Luttrell may have kept a note of the combination and carried it about him. It would have been risky to trust entirely to memory. And he would have had the keys of the office about him. Any one who had those could have slipped in during business hours without much difficulty. Luttrell's premises are empty, but there are people in and out all day going to the other offices. Our man can't follow them all in. I suppose you can't make any suggestion, doctor?"

"I am afraid I can't," answered Thorndyke. "The case is so very much in the air. There is nothing against Shemmonds but bare suspicion. He has disappeared only in the sense that you have lost sight of him, and the same is true of Luttrell—though there is an abnormal element in his case. Still, you could hardly get a search-warrant on the facts that are known at present."

"No," Miller agreed, "they certainly would not authorise us to break open the strong-room, and nothing short of that would be much use."

Here Polton made his appearance with the wax squeeze in a neat little box such as jewellers use.

"I've got two enlarged negatives," said he; "nice clear ones. How many prints shall I make for Mr. Miller?"

"Oh, one will do, Mr. Polton," said the superintendent. "If I want any more I'll ask you." He took up the little box, and, slipping it in his pocket, rose to depart. "I'll let you know, doctor, how the case goes on, and perhaps you wouldn't mind turning it over a bit in the interval. Something might occur to you."

Thorndyke promised to think over the case, and when we had seen the superintendent launched down the stairs, we followed Polton up to the laboratory, where we each picked up one of the negatives and examined it against the light. I had already identified the seal by its shape—a *vesica piscis* or boat-shape—with the one that I had seen on Mr. Luttrell's finger. Now, in the photograph, enlarged three diameters, I could clearly make out the details. The design was distinctive and curious rather than elegant. The two triangular spaces at the ends were occupied respectively by a *memento mori* and a winged hour-glass and the central portion was filled by a long inscription in Roman capitals, of which I could at first make nothing.

"Do you suppose this is some kind of cryptogram?" I asked.

"No," Thorndyke replied. "I imagine the words were run together merely to economise space. This is what I make of it."

He held the negative in his left hand, and with his right wrote down in pencil on a slip of paper the following four lines of doggerel verse:

Eheu alas how fast the dam fugaces
Labuntur anni especially in the cases
Of poor old blokes like you and me Posthumus
Who only wait for vermes to consume us.

"Well," I exclaimed, "it is a choice specimen; one of old Luttrell's merry conceited jests, I take it. But the joke was hardly worth the labour of engraving on a seal."

"It is certainly a rather mild jest," Thorndyke admitted. "But there may be something more in it than meets the eye."

He looked at the inscription reflectively and appeared to read it through once or twice. Then he replaced the negative in the drying rack, and, picking up the paper, slipped it into his pocket-book.

"I don't quite see," said I, "why Miller brought this case to us or what he wants you to think over. In fact, I don't see that there is a case at all."

"It is a very shadowy case," Thorndyke admitted. "Miller has done a good deal of guessing, and so has Badger; and it may easily turn out that they have found a mare's nest. Nevertheless there is something to think about."

"As, for instance—?"

"Well, Jervis, you saw the men; you saw how they behaved; you have heard Miller's story and you have seen Mr. Luttrell's seal. Put all those data together and you have the material for some very interesting speculation, to say the least. You might even carry it beyond speculation."

I did not pursue the subject, for I knew that when Thorndyke used the word "speculation," nothing would induce him to commit himself to an opinion. But later, bearing in mind the attention that he had seemed to bestow on Mr. Luttrell's schoolboy verses, I got a print from the negative and studied the foolish lines exhaustively. But if it had any hidden meaning—and I could imagine no reason for supposing that it had—that meaning remained hidden; and the only conclusion at which I could arrive was that a man of Luttrell's age might have known better than to write such nonsense.

The superintendent did not leave the matter long in suspense. Three days later he paid us another visit. and half-apologetically reopened the subject.

"I am ashamed to come badgering you like this," he said, "but I can't get this case out of my head. I've a feeling that we ought to get a move of some kind on. And, by the way—though that is nothing to do with it—I've copied out the stuff on that seal and I can't make any sense of it. What the deuce are *fugaces*? I suppose '*vermes*' are worms, though I don't see why he spelt it that way."

"The verses," said Thorndyke, "are apparently a travesty of a Latin poem; one of the odes of Horace which begins:

Eheu fugaces, Postume, Postume, Labuntur anni,

"which means, in effect, 'Alas! *Postume*, the flying years slip by.'"

"Well," said Miller, "any fool knows that—any middle-aged fool, at any rate. No need to put it into Latin. However, it's of no consequence. To return to this case; I've got an authority to look over Luttrell's premises—not to pull anything about, you know, just to look round. I called in on my way here to let the caretaker know that I should be coming in later. I thought that perhaps you might like to come with me. I wish you would, doctor. You've got such a knack of spotting things that other people overlook."

He looked wistfully at Thorndyke, and as the latter was considering the proposal, he added: "The caretaker mentioned a rather odd circumstance. It seems that he keeps an eye on the electric meters in the building and that he has noticed a leakage of current in Mr. Luttrell's. It is only a small leak; about thirty watts an hour. But he can't account for it in any way. He has been right through the premises to see if any lamp has been left on in any of the rooms. But all the switches are off everywhere, and it can't be a short circuit. Funny, isn't it?"

It was certainly odd, but there seemed to me nothing in it to account for the expression of suddenly awakened interest that I detected in Thorndyke's face. However, it evidently had some special significance for him, for he asked almost eagerly "When are you making your inspection?"

"I am going there now," replied Miller, and he added coaxingly, "Couldn't you manage to run round with me?"

Thorndyke stood up. "Very well," said he. "Let us go together. You may as well come, too, Jervis, if you can spare an hour."

I agreed readily, for my colleague's hardly disguised interest in the inspection suggested a definite problem in his mind; and we at once issued forth and made our way by Mitre Court and Fetter Lane to the abode of the missing dealer, an old-fashioned house near the end of Thavies Inn.

"I've been over the premises once," said Miller, as the caretaker appeared with the keys, "and I think we had better begin the regular inspection with the offices. We can examine the stores and living-rooms afterwards."

We accordingly entered the outer office, and as this was little more than a waiting-room, we passed through into the private office, which had the appearance of having been used also as a sitting-room or study. It was furnished with an easy-chair, a range of book-shelves and a handsome bureau book-case, while in the end wall was the massive iron door of the strong-room. On this, as the chief object of interest, we all bore down, and the superintendent expounded its peculiarities.

"It is quite a good idea," said he, "this letter-lock. There's no key-hole—though a safe-lock is pretty hopeless to pick even if there was a keyhole—and no keys to get lost. As to guessing what the 'open sesame' may be—well, just look at it. You could spend a lifetime on it and be no forrader."

The puzzle lock was contained in the solid iron door post, through a slot in which a row of fifteen A's seemed to grin defiance on the would-be safe-robber. I put my finger on the milled edges of one or two of the letters and rotated the discs, noticing how easily and smoothly they turned.

"Well," said Miller, "it's no use fumbling with that. I'm just going to have a look through his ledger and see who his customers were. The book-case is unlocked. I tried it last time. And we'd better leave this as we found it."

He put back the letters that I had moved, and turned away to ex-plore the book-case; and as the letter-lock appeared to present noth-ing but an insoluble riddle, I followed him, leaving Thorndyke ear-nestly gazing at the meaningless row of letters.

The superintendent glanced back at him with an indulgent smile.

"The doctor is going to work out the combination," he chuckled. "Well, well. There are only forty billion changes and he's a young man for his age."

With this encouraging comment, he opened the glass door of the book-case, and reaching down the ledger, laid it on the desk-like slope of the bureau.

"It is a poor chance," said he, opening the ledger at the index, "but some of these people may be able to give us a hint where to look for Mr. Luttrell, and it is worth while to know what sort of business he did."

He ran his finger down the list of names and had just turned to the account of one of the customers when we were startled by a loud click from the direction of the strong-room. We both turned sharply and beheld Thorndyke grasping the handle of the strong-room door, and I saw with amazement that the door was now slightly ajar.

"God!" exclaimed Miller, shutting the ledger and starting forward, "he's got it open!" He strode over to the door, and directing an eager look at the indicator of the lock, burst into a laugh. "Well, I'm hanged!" he exclaimed. "Why, it was unlocked all the time! To think that none of us had the sense to tug the handle! But isn't it just like old Luttrell to have a fool's answer like that to the blessed puzzle!"

I looked at the indicator, not a little astonished to observe the row of fifteen A's, which apparently formed the key combination. It may have been a very amusing joke on Mr. Luttrell's part, but it did not look very secure. Thorndyke regarded us with an inscrutable glance and still grasped the handle, holding the door a bare half-inch open.

"There is something pushing against the door," said he. "Shall I open it?

"May as well have a look at the inside," replied Miller. Thereupon Thorndyke released the handle and quickly stepped aside. The door swung slowly open and the dead body of a man fell out into the room and rolled over on to its back.

"Mercy on us!" gasped Miller, springing back hastily and staring with horror and amazement at the grim apparition. "That is not Luttrell." Then, suddenly starting forward and stooping over the dead man, he exclaimed "Why, it is Shemmonds. So that is where he disappeared to. I wonder what became of Luttrell?"

"There is somebody else in the strong-room," said Thorndyke; and now, peering in through the doorway, I perceived a dim light, which seemed to come from a hidden recess, and by which I could see a pair of feet projecting round the corner. In a moment Miller had sprung in, and I followed. The strong-room was L shaped in plan, the arm of the L formed by a narrow passage at right angles to the main room. At the end of this a single small electric bulb was burning, the light of which showed the body of an elderly man stretched on the floor of the passage. I recognised him instantly in spite of the dimness of the light and the disfigurement caused by a ragged wound on the forehead.

"We had better get him out of this," said Miller, speaking in a flurried tone, partly due to the shock of the horrible discovery and partly to the accompanying physical unpleasantness, "and then we will have a look round, This wasn't just a mere robbery. We are going to find things out."

With my help he lifted Luttrell's corpse and together we carried it out, laying it on the floor of the room at the farther end, to which we also dragged the body of Shemmonds.

"There is no mystery as to how it happened," I said, after a brief inspection of the two corpses. "Shemmonds evidently shot the old man from behind with the pistol close to the back of the head. The hair is all scorched round the wound of entry and the bullet came out at the forehead."

"Yes," agreed Miller, "that is all clear enough. But the mystery is why on earth Shemmonds didn't let himself out. He must have known that the door was unlocked. Yet instead of turning the handle, he must have stood there like a fool, battering at the door with his fists. Just look at his hands."

"The further mystery," said Thorndyke who, all this time, had been making a minute examination of the lock both front without and within, "is how the door came to be shut. That is quite a curious problem."

"Quite," agreed Miller. "But it will keep. And there is a still more curious problem inside there. There is nearly all the swag from that Colchester robbery. Looks as if Luttrell was in it."

Half reluctantly he re-entered the strong-room and Thorndyke and I followed. Near the angle of the passage he stooped to pick up an automatic pistol and a small, leather book, which he opened and looked into by the light of the lamp. At the first glance he uttered an exclamation and shut the book with a snap.

"Do you know what this is?" he asked, holding it out to us. "It is the nominal roll, address book and journal of the gang. We've got them in the hollow of our hand; and it is dawning upon me that old Luttrell was the managing director whom I have been looking for so long. Just run your eyes along those shelves. That's loot; every bit of it. I can identify the articles from the lists that I made out."

He stood looking gloatingly along the shelves with their burden of jewellery, plate and other valuables. Then his eye lighted on a drawer in the end wall just under the lamp; an iron drawer with a dispro-portionately large handle and bearing a very legible label inscribed "unmounted stones."

"We'll have a look at his stock of unmounted gems," said Miller; and with that he bore down on the drawer, and seizing the handle, gave a vigorous pull. "Funny," said he. "It isn't locked, but something seems to be holding it back."

He planted his foot on the wall and took a fresh purchase on the handle. "Wait a moment, Miller," said Thorndyke; but even as he spoke, the superintendent gave a mighty heave; the drawer came out a full two feet; there was a loud click, and a moment later the strong-room door slammed.

"Good God!" exclaimed Miller, letting go the drawer, which immediately slid in with another click. "What was that?"

"That was the door shutting," replied Thorndyke. "Quite a clever arrangement; like the mechanism of a repeater watch. Pulling out the drawer wound up and released a spring that shut the door. Very ingenious."

"But," gasped Miller, turning an ashen face to my colleague, "we're shut in."

"You are forgetting," said I—a little nervously, I must admit—"that the lock is as we left it."

The superintendent laughed, somewhat hysterically. "What a fool I am!" said he. "As bad as Shemmonds. Still we may as well—" Here he started along the passage and I heard him groping his way to the door, and later heard the handle turn. Suddenly the deep silence of the tomb-like chamber was rent by a yell of terror.

"The door won't move! It's locked fast!"

On this I rushed along the passage with a sickening fear at my heart. And even as I ran, there rose before my eyes the horrible vision of the corpse with the battered hands that had fallen out when we opened the door of this awful trap. He had been caught as we were caught. How soon might it not be that some stranger would be looking in on our corpses.

In the dim twilight by the door I found Miller clutching the handle and shaking it like a madman. His self-possession was completely shattered. Nor was my own condition much better. I flung my whole weight on the door in the faint hope that the lock was not really closed, but the massive iron structure was as immovable as a stone wall. I was nevertheless, gathering myself up for a second charge when I heard Thorndyke's voice close behind me.

"That is no use, Jervis. The door is locked. But there is nothing to worry about."

As he spoke, there suddenly appeared a bright circle of light from the little electric lamp that he always carried in his pocket. Within the circle, and now clearly visible, was a second indicator of the puzzle lock on the inside of the door-post. Its appearance was vaguely reassuring, especially in conjunction with Thorndyke's calm voice; and it evidently appeared so to Miller, for he remarked, almost in his natural tones:

"But it seems to be unlocked still. There is the same AAAAAA that it showed when we came in."

It was perfectly true. The slot of the letter-lock still showed the range of fifteen A's, just as it had when the door was open. Could it be that the lock was a dummy and that there was some other means of opening the door? I was about to put this question to Thorndyke when he put the lamp into my hand, and, gently pushing me aside, stepped up to the indicator.

"Keep the light steady, Jervis," said he, and forthwith he began to manipulate the milled edges of the letter discs, beginnings as I noticed, at the right or reverse end of the slot and working backwards. I watched him with feverish interest and curiosity, as also did Miller, looking to see some word of fifteen letters develop in the slot. Instead of which, I saw, to my amazement and bewilderment my colleague's finger transforming the row of A's into a succession of M's, which, however, were presently followed by an L and some X's. When the row was completed it looked like some remote, antediluvian date set down in Roman numerals.

"Try the handle now, Miller," said Thorndyke.

The superintendent needed no second bidding. Snatching at the handle, he turned it and bore heavily on the door. Almost instantly a thin line of light appeared at the edge; there was a sharp click, and the door swung right open. We fell out immediately—at least the superintendent and I did—thankful to find ourselves outside and alive. But, as we emerged, we both became aware of a man, white-faced and horror-stricken of aspect, stooping over the two corpses at the other end of the room. Our appearance was so sudden and unexpected—for the massive solidity of the safe-door had rendered our movements inaudible outside—that, for a moment or two, he stood immovable, staring at us, wild-eyed and open-mouthed. Then, suddenly, he sprang up erect, and, darting to the door, opened it and rushed out with Miller close on his heels.

He did not get very far. Following the superintendent, I saw the fugitive wriggling in the embrace of a tall man on the pavement, who, with Miller's assistance, soon had a pair of handcuffs snapped on the man's wrists and then departed with his captive in search of a cab.

"That's one of 'em, I expect," said Miller, as we returned to the office; then, as his glance fell on the open strong-room door, he mopped his face with his handkerchief. "That door gives me the creeps to look at it," said he. "Lord! what a shake-up that was! I've never had such a scare in my life. When I heard that door shut and I remembered how that poor devil, Shemmonds, came tumbling out—phoo!" He wiped his brow again, and, walking towards the strong-room door, asked: "By the way, what was the magic word after all?" He stepped up to the indicator, and, after a quick glance, looked round at me in surprise. "Why!" he exclaimed, "blow me if it isn't AAAA still! But the doctor altered it, didn't he?"

At this moment Thorndyke appeared from the strong-room, where he had apparently been conducting some explorations, and to him the superintendent turned for an explanation.

"It is an ingenious device," said he; "in fact, the whole strong-room is a monument of ingenuity, somewhat misapplied, but perfectly effective, as Mr. Shemmonds's corpse testifies. The key-combination is a number expressed in Roman numerals, but the lock has a fly-back mechanism which acts as soon as the door begins to open. That was how Shemmonds was caught. He, no doubt purposely, avoided watching Luttrell set the lock—or else Luttrell didn't let him—but as he went in with his intended victim, he looked at the indicator and saw the row of A's, which he naturally assumed to be the key. Then, when he tried to let himself out, of course, the lock wouldn't open."

"It is rather odd that he didn't try some other combinations," said I.

"He probably did," replied Thorndyke, "but when they failed he would naturally come back to the A's, which he had seen when the door was open. This is how it works."

He shut the door, and then, closely watched by the superintendent and me, turned the milled rims of the letter-discs until the indicator showed a row of numerals thus: MMMMMMMCCCLXXXV. Grasping the handle, he turned it and gave a gentle pull, when the door began to open. But the instant it started from its bed, there was a loud click and all the letters of the indicator flew back to A.

"Well, I'm jiggered!" exclaimed Miller. "It must have been an awful suck-in for that poor blighter, Shemmonds. Took me in, too. I saw those A's and the door open, and I thought I knew all about it. But what beats me, doctor, is how you managed to work it out. I can't see what you had to go on. Would it be allowable to ask how it was done?"

"Certainly," replied Thorndyke "but we had better defer the explanation. You have got those two bodies to dispose of and some other matters, and we must get back to our chambers. I will write down the key-combination, in case you want it, and then you must come and see us and let us know what luck you have had."

He wrote the numerals on a slip of paper, and when he had handed it to the superintendent, we took our leave.

"I find myself," said I, as we walked home, "in much the same position as Miller. I don't see what you had to go on. It is clear to me that you not only worked out the lock-combination—from the seal inscription, as I assume—but that you identified Luttrell as the director of the gang. I don't, in the least, understand how you did it."

"And yet, Jervis," said he, "it was an essentially simple case. If you review it and cast up the items of evidence, you will see that we really had all the facts. The problem was merely to co-ordinate them and extract their significance. Take first the character of Luttrell. We saw the man in company with another, evidently a fairly intimate acquaintance. They were being shadowed by a detective, and it is pretty clear that they detected the sleuth, for they shook him off quite neatly. Later, we learn from Miller that one of these men is suspected to be a member of a firm of swell burglars and that the other is a well-to-do, rather eccentric and very miscellaneous dealer, who has a strong-room fitted with a puzzle lock.

"I am astonished that the usually acute Miller did not notice how well Luttrell fitted the part of the managing director whom he was looking for. Here was a dealer who bought and sold all sorts of queer but valuable things, who must have had unlimited facilities for getting rid of stones, bullion and silver, and who used a puzzle lock. Now, who uses a puzzle lock? No one, certainly, who can conveniently use a key. But to the manager of a gang of thieves it would be a valuable safeguard, for he might at any moment be robbed of his keys, and perhaps made away with. But he could not be robbed of the secret passwords and his possession of it would be a security against murder. So you see that the simple probabilities pointed to Luttrell as the head of the gang.

"And now consider the problem of the lock. First, we saw that Luttrell wore on his left hand a huge, cumbrous seal ring, that he carried a Coddington lens on his watch-guard, and a small electric lamp in his pocket. That told us very, little. But when Miller told us about the lock and showed us the squeeze of the seal, and when we saw that the seal bore a long inscription in minute lettering, a connection began to appear. As Miller justly observed, no man—especially no elderly man—could trust the key combination exclusively to his memory. He would carry about him some record to which he could refer in case his memory failed him. But that record would hardly be one that anybody could read, or the secrecy and safety of the lock would be gone. It would probably be some kind of cryptogram; and when we saw this inscription and considered it in conjunction with the lens and the lamp, it seemed highly probable that the key-combination was contained in the inscription; and that probability was further increased when we saw the nonsensical doggerel of which the inscription was made up. The suggestion was that the verses bad been made for some purpose independent of their sense. Accordingly I gave the inscription very careful consideration.

"Now we learned from Miller that the puzzle lock had fifteen letters. The key might be one long word, such as 'superlativeness', a number of short words, or some chemical or other formula. Or it was possible that it might be of the nature of a chronogram. I have never heard of chronograms being used for secret records or messages, but it has often occurred to me that they would be extremely suitable. And this was an exceptionally suitable case."

"Chronogram," said I. "Isn't that something connected with med-als?"

"They have often been used on medals," he replied. "In effect, a chronogram is an inscription some of the letters of which form a date connected with the subject of the inscription. Usually the date letters are or cut larger than the others for convenience in reading, but, of course, this is not essential. The principle of a chronogram is this. The letters of the Roman alphabet are of two kinds: those that are simply letters and nothing else, and those that are numerals as well as letters. The numeral letters are M = a thousand, D = five hundred, C = one hundred, L = fifty, X = ten, V = five, and I = one. Now, in deciphering a chronogram, you pick out all the numeral letters and add them up without regard to their order. The total gives you the date.

"Well, as I said, it occurred to me that this might be of the nature of a chronogram; but as the lock had letters and not figures, the num-ber, if there was one, would have to be expressed in Roman numerals, and it would have to form a number of fifteen numeral letters. As it was thus quite easy to put my hypothesis to the test, I proceeded to treat the inscription as a chronogram and decipher it; and behold! it yielded a number of fifteen letters, which, of course, was as near certainty as was possible, short of actual experiment."

"Let us see how you did the decipherment," I said, as we entered our chambers and shut the door. I procured a large note-block and pencil, and, laying them on the table, drew up two chairs.

"Now," said I, "fire away."

"Very well," he said. "We will begin by writing the inscription in proper chronogram form with the numeral letters double size and treating the U's as V's and the W's as double V's according to the rules."

Here he wrote out the inscription in Roman capitals thus:

eheV aLas hoVV fast the DaM fVgaCes LabVntVr annI espe-CIaLLy In the Cases of poor oLD bLokes LIke yoV anD Me posthVMVs VVho onLy VVaIt for VerMes to ConsVMe Vs.

"Now," said he, "let us make a column of each line and add them up, thus:

1. V=5, L=50, VV=10, D=500, M=1000, V=5, C=100—Total 1670

2. L=50, V=5, V=5, I=1, C=100, I=1, L=50, L=50, I=1, C=100—Total 363

3. L=50, D=500, L=50, L=50, I=1, V=5, D=500, M=1000, V=5, M=1000, V=5—Total 3166

4. VV=10, L=50, VV=10, I=1, V=5, M=1000, C=100, V=5, M=1000, V=5—Total 2186

"Now," he continued "we take the four totals and add them together, thus:

$$1670+363+3166+2186 = 7385$$

"—and we get the grand total of seven thousand three hundred and eighty-five and this, expressed in Roman numerals, is MMMMMMMCCCLXXXV. Here, then, is a number consisting of fifteen letters, the exact number of spaces in the indicator of the puzzle lock; and I repeat that this striking coincidence, added to, or rather multiplied into, the other probabilities, made it practically certain that this was the key-combination. It remained only to test it by actual experiment."

"By the way," said I, "I noticed that you perked up rather suddenly when Miller mentioned the electric meter."

"Naturally," he replied. "It seemed that there must be a small lamp switched on somewhere in the building, and the only place that had not been examined was the strong-room. But if there was a lamp alight there, someone had been in the strong-room. And, as, the only person who was known to be able to get in was missing, it seemed probable that he was in there still. But if he was, he was pretty certainly dead; and there was quite a considerable probability that some one else was in there with him, since his companion was missing, too, and both had disappeared at the same time. But I must confess that that spring drawer was beyond my expectations, though I suspected it as soon as I saw Miller pulling at it. Luttrell was an ingenious old rascal; he almost deserved a better fate. However, I expect his death will have delivered the gang into the hands of the police."

Events fell out as Thorndyke surmised. Mr. Luttrell's little journal, in conjunction with the confession of the spy who had been captured on the premises, enabled the police to swoop down on the disconcerted gang before any breath of suspicion had reached them; with the result that they are now secured in strong-rooms of another kind whereof the doors are fitted with appliances as effective as, though less ingenious than, Mr. Luttrell's puzzle lock.

The Green Check Jacket

The visits of our old friend, Mr. Brodribb, even when strictly professional, usually took the outward form of a friendly call. On the present occasion there was no such pretence. The old solicitor entered our chambers carrying a small suit-case (the stamped initials on which, "R.M.," I noticed, instantly attracted an inquisitive glance from Thorndyke, being obviously not Mr. Brodribb's own) which he placed on the table and then shook hands with an evident air of business.

"I have come, Thorndyke," he said, with unusual directness, "to ask your advice on a matter which is causing me some uneasiness. Do you know Reginald Merrill?"

"Slightly," was the reply. "I meet him occasionally in court; and, of course, I know him as the author of that interesting book on Prehistoric Flint-mines."

"Well," said Brodribb, "he has disappeared. He is missing. I don't like to use the expression; but when a responsible man is absent from his usual places of resort, when he apparently had no expectation of being so absent, and when he has made no provision for such absence, I think we may regard him as having disappeared in a legal sense. His absence calls for active inquiry."

"Undoubtedly," agreed Thorndyke; "and I take it that you are the person on whom the duty devolves?"

"I think so. I am his solicitor and the executor of his will—at least I believe so; and the only near relative of his whom I know is his nephew and heir, Ethelbert Crick, his sister's son. But Crick seems to have disappeared, too; and about the same time as Merrill. It is an extraordinary affair."

"You say that you believe you are Merrill's executor. Haven't you seen the will?"

"I have seen a will. I have it in my safe. But Merrill said he was going to draw up another, and he may have done so. But if he has, he will almost certainly have appointed me his executor, and I shall assume that he has and act accordingly."

"Was there any special reason for making a new will?" Thorndyke asked.

"Yes," replied Brodribb. "He has just come into quite a considerable fortune, and he was pretty well off before. Under the old will, practically the whole of his property went to Crick. There was a small bequest to a man named Samuel Horder, his cousin's son; and Horder was the alternative legatee if Crick should die before Merrill. Now, I understood Merrill to say that, in view of this extra fortune, he wished to do rather more for Horder, and I gathered that he proposed to divide the estate more or less equally between the two men. The whole estate was more than he thought necessary for Crick. And now, as we have cleared up the preliminaries, I will give you the circum stances of the disappearance.

"Last Wednesday, the 5th, I had a note from him saying that he would have some reports ready for me on the following day, but that he would be away from his office from 10.30 a.m. to about 6.30, and suggesting that I should send round in the evening if I wanted the papers particularly. Now it happened that my clerk, Page, had to go to a place near London Bridge on Thursday morning, and, oddly enough, he saw Mr. Merrill come out of Edginton's, the ship-fitters, with a man who was carrying a largish hand-bag. There was nothing in it, of course, but Page is an observant man and he noticed Merrill's companion so far as to observe that he was wearing a Norfolk jacket of a greenish shepherd's plaid and a grey tweed hat.

"He also noted the time by the big clock in the street near to Edginton's—11.46—and that Merrill looked up at it, and that the two men then walked off rather quickly in the direction of the station. Well, in the evening, I sent Page round to Merrill's chambers in Fig-tree Court to get the papers. He arrived there just after 6.30, but he found the oak shut, and though he rapped at the door on the chance that Merrill might have come in—he lives in the chambers adjoining the office—there was no answer. So he went for a walk round the Temple, deciding to return a little later.

"Well, he had gone as far as the cloisters and was loitering there to look in the window of the wig shop when he saw a man in a greenish shepherd's plaid jacket and a tweed hat coming up Pump Court. As the man approached Page thought he recognised him; in fact, he felt so sure that he stopped him and asked him if he knew what time Mr. Merrill would be home. But the man looked at him in astonishment. 'Merrill?' said he. 'I don't know anyone of that name.' Thereupon Page apologised and explained how he had been misled by the pattern and colour of the jacket.

"After walking about for nearly half an hour, Page went back to Merrill's chambers; but the oak was shut and he could get no answer by rapping with his stick, so he scribbled a note and dropped it into the letter-box and came away. The next morning I sent him round again, but the chambers were still shut up, and they have been shut up ever since; and nothing what ever has been seen or heard of Merrill.

"On Saturday, thinking it possible that Crick might be able to give me some news of his uncle, I called at his lodgings; and then, to my astonishment, I learned that he also was missing. He had gone away early on Thursday morning, saying that he had to go on business to Rochester, and that he might not be home to dinner. But he never came home at all. I called again on Sunday evening, and, as he had still not returned, I decided to take more active measures.

"This afternoon, immediately after lunch, I called at the Porter's Lodge, and, having briefly explained the circumstances and who I was, asked the porter to bring the duplicate key—which he had for the laundress—and accompany me to Mr. Merrill's chambers to see if, by chance, the tenant might be lying in them dead or insensible. He assured me that this could not be the case, since he had given the key every morning to the laundress, who had, in fact, returned it to him only a couple of hours previously. Nevertheless, he took the key and looked up the laundress, who had rooms near the lodge, who was fortunately at home and who turned out to be a most respectable and intelligent elderly woman; and we went together to Merrill's chambers. The porter admitted us, and when we had been right through the set and ascertained definitely that Merrill was not there, he handed the key to the laundress, Mrs. Butler, and went away.

"When he was gone, I had a talk with Mrs. Butler, from which some rather startling facts transpired. It seemed that on Thursday, as Merrill was going to be out all day, she took the opportunity to have a grand clean-up of the chambers, to tidy up the lobby, and to look over the chests of drawers and the wardrobe and shake out and brush the clothes and see that no moths had got in. 'When I had finished,' she said, 'the place was like the inside of a band-box; just as he liked to see it.'

"'And, after all, Mrs. Butler,' said I, 'he never did see it.'

"'Oh, yes, he did,' says she. 'I don't know when he came in, but when I let myself in the next morning, I could see that he had been in since I left.'

"'How did you know that?' I asked.

"'Well,' says she, 'I left the carpet-sweeper standing against the wardrobe door. I remembered it after I left and would have gone back and moved it, but I had already handed the key in at the Porter's Lodge. But when I went in next morning it wasn't there. It had been moved into the corner by the fireplace. Then the looking-glass had been moved. I could see that, because, before I went away, I had tidied my hair by it, and being short, I had to tilt it to see my face in it. Now it was tilted to suit a tall person and I could not see myself in it. Then I saw that the shaving had been moved, and when I put it back in its place, I found it was damp. It wouldn't have kept damp for twenty-four hours at this time of year.' That was perfectly true, you know, Thorndyke."

"Perfectly," agreed Thorndyke, "that woman is an excellent observer."

"Well," continued Brodribb, "on this she examined the shaving soap and the sponge and found them both perceptibly damp. It appeared practically certain that Merrill had been in on the preceding evening and had shaved; but by way of confirmation, I suggested that she should look over his clothes and see whether he had changed any of his garments. She did so, beginning with those that were hanging in the wardrobe, which she took down one at a time. Suddenly she gave a cry of surprise, and I got a bit of a start myself when she handed out a greenish shepherd's plaid Norfolk jacket.

"'That,' she said, 'was not here when I brushed these clothes,' and it was obvious from its dusty condition that it could not have been; 'and,' she added, 'I have never seen it before to my knowledge, and I think I should have remembered it.' I asked her if there was any coat missing and she answered that she had brushed a grey tweed jacket that seemed to have disappeared.

"Well, it was a queer affair. The first thing to be done was to ascertain, if possible whether that jacket was or was not Merrill's. That, I thought, you would be able to judge better than I; so I borrowed his suit-case and popped the jacket into it, together with another jacket that was undoubtedly his, for comparison. Here is the suit-case and the two jackets are inside."

"It is really a question that could be better decided by a tailor," said Thorndyke. "The differences of measurement can't be great if they could both be worn by the same person. But we shall see." He rose, and having spread some sheets of newspaper over the table, opened the suit-case and took out the two jackets, which he laid out side by side. Then, with his spring-tape, he proceeded systematically to measure the two garments, entering each pair of measurements on a slip of paper divided into two columns. Mr. Brodribb and I watched him expectantly and compared the two sets of figures as they were written down; and very soon it became evident that they were, at least, not identical. At length Thorndyke laid down the tape, and picking up the paper, studied it closely.

"I think," he said, "we may conclude that these two jackets were not made for the same person. The differences are not great, but they are consistent. The elbow creases, for instance, agree with the total length of the sleeves. The owner of the green jacket has longer arms and a bigger span than Merrill, but his chest measurement is nearly two inches greater and he has much more sloping shoulders. He could hardly have buttoned Merrill's jacket."

"Then," said Brodribb, "the next question is, did Merrill come home in some other man's coat or did some other man enter his chambers? From what Page has told us it seems pretty evident that a stranger must have got into those chambers. But if that is so, the questions arise: What the deuce was the fellow's object in changing into Merrill's clothes and shaving? How did he get into Merrill's chambers? What was he doing there? What has become of Merrill? And what is the meaning of the whole affair?"

"To some of those questions," said Thorndyke, "the answers are fairly obvious. If we assume, as I do, that the owner of the green jacket is the man whom Page saw at London Bridge and afterwards in the cloisters, the reason for the change of garments becomes plain enough. Page told the man that he had identified him by this very distinctive jacket as the person with whom Merrill was last seen alive. Evidently that man's safety demanded hat he should get rid of the incriminating jacket without delay. Then, as to his having shaved: did Page give you any description of the man?"

"Yes; he was a tallish man, about thirty-five, with a large dark moustache and a torpedo beard."

"Very well," said Thorndyke; "then we may say that the man who went into Merrill's chambers was a moustached bearded man in a green jacket and that he man who came out was a clean-shaved man in a grey jacket, whom Page himself would probably have passed without a second glance. That is clear enough. And as to how he got into the chambers, evidently he let himself in with Merrill's key; and if he did, I am afraid we can make a pretty shrewd guess as to what has become of Merrill, and only hope that we are guessing wrong.

"As to what this man was doing in those chambers and what is the meaning of the whole affair, that is a more difficult question. If the man had Merrill's latchkey, we may assume that he had the rest of Merrill's keys; that he had, in fact, free access to any locked receptacles in those chambers. The circumstances suggest that he entered the chambers for the purpose of getting possession of some valuable objects contained in them. Do you happen to know whether Merrill had any property of considerable value on the premises?"

"I don't," replied Brodribb. "He had a safe, but I don't know what he kept in it. Principally documents, I should think. Certainly not money, in any considerable amounts. The only thing of value that I actually know of is the new will; and that would only be valuable in certain circumstances."

The abrupt and rather ambiguous conclusion of Mr. Brodribb's statement was not lost either on Thorndyke or on me. Apparently the cautious old lawyer had suddenly realised, as I had, that if anything had happened to Merrill, those "certain circumstances" had already come into being. From what he had told us it appeared that, under the new will, Crick stood to inherit a half of Mr. Merrill's fortune, whereas under the old will he stood to inherit nearly the whole. And it was a great fortune. The loss or destruction of the new will would be worth a good many thousand pounds to Mr. Crick.

"Well," said Brodribb, after a pause, "what is to be done? I suppose I ought to communicate with the police."

"You will have to, sooner or later," said Thorndyke; "but meanwhile, leave these two jackets—or, at least, the green one—with me for the present and let me see if I can extract any further information from it."

"You won't find anything in the pockets but dirt. I've tried them."

"I hope you left the dirt," said Thorndyke.

"I did," replied Brodribb, "excepting what came out on my fingers. Very well; I'll leave the coats with you for today, and I will see if I can get any further news of Crick from his landlady."

With this the old solicitor shook hands and went off with such an evident air of purpose that I remarked: "Brodribb is off to find out whether Mr. Crick was the proprietor of a green plaid Norfolk jacket."

Thorndyke smiled. "It was rather quaint," said he, "to see the sudden way in which he drew in his horns when the inwardness of the affair dawned on him. But we mustn't start with a preconceived theory. Our business is to get hold of some more facts. There is little enough to go on at present. Let us begin by having a good look at this green jacket."

He picked it up and carried it to the window, where we both looked it over critically.

"It is rather dusty," I remarked, "especially on the front, and there is a white mark on the middle button."

"Yes. Chalk, apparently; and if you look closely, there are white traces on the other buttons and on the front of the coat. The back is much less dusty."

As he spoke, Thorndyke turned the garment round, and then, from the side of the skirt, picked a small, hair-like object which he felt between his finger and thumb, looked at closely and handed to me.

"A bit of barley beard," said I, "and there are two more on the other side. He must have walked along a narrow path through a barley field—the state of the front of his coat almost suggests that he had crawled."

"Yes; it is earthy dust; but Polton's extractor will give us more information about that. We had better hand it over to him; but first we will go through the pockets in spite of Brodribb's discouragement."

"By Jove!" I exclaimed, as I thrust my hand into one of the side pockets, "he was right about the dirt. Look at this." I drew out my hand with a quite considerable pinch of dry earth and one or two little fragments of chalk. "It looks as if he had been crawling in loose earth."

"It does," Thorndyke agreed, inspecting his own "catch"—a pinch of reddish earth and a fragment of chalk of the size of a large pea. "The earth is very characteristic, this red-brown loam that you find overlying the chalk. All his outside pockets seem to have caught more or less of it. However, we can leave Polton to collect it and prepare it for examination. I'll take the coat up to him now, and while he is working at it I think I will walk round to Edginton's and see if I can pick up any further particulars."

He went up to the laboratory floor, where our assistant, Polton, carried on his curious and varied activities, and when he returned we sallied forth together. In Fleet Street we picked up a disengaged taxi-cab, by which we were whisked across Blackfriars Bridge and a few minutes later set down at the corner of Tooley Street. We made our way to the ship-chandler's shop, where Thorndyke proceeded to put a few discreet questions to the manager, who listened politely and with sympathetic interest.

"The difficulty is," said he, "that there were a good many gentlemen in here last Thursday. You say they came about 11.45. If you could tell me what they bought, we could look at the bill-duplicate book and that might help us."

"I don't actually know what they bought," said Thorndyke. "It might have been a length of rope; a rope, perhaps, say twelve or fourteen fathoms or perhaps more. But I may be wrong."

I stared at Thorndyke in amazement. Long as I known him, this extraordinary faculty of instantaneous induction always came on me as a fresh surprise. I had supposed that in this case we had absolutely nothing to go on; and yet here he was with at least a tentative suggestion before the inquiry appeared to have begun. And that suggestion was clear evidence that he had already arrived at a hypothetical solution of the mystery. I was still pondering on this astonishing fact when the manager approached with an open book and accompanied by an assistant.

"I see," said he, "that there is an entry, apparently about mid-day on Thursday, of the sale of a fifteen-fathom length of deep-sea lead-line, and my friend, here, remembers selling it."

"Yes," the assistant confirmed, "I remember it because he wanted to get it into his hand-bag, and it took the three of us to stuff it in. Thick lead-line is pretty stiff when it's new."

"Do you remember what these gentlemen were like and how they were dressed?"

"One was a rather elderly gentleman, clean-shaved, I think. The other I remember better because he had rather queer-looking eyes—very pale grey. He had a pointed beard and he wore a greenish check coat and a cloth hat. That's all I remember about him."

"It is more than most people would have remembered," said Thorndyke. "I am very much obliged to you; and I think I will ask you to let me have a fifteen-fathom length of that same lead-line."

By this time my capacity for astonishment was exhausted. What on earth could my colleague want with a deep-sea lead-line? But, after all, why not? If he had then and there purchased a Trotman's anchor, a shark-hook and a set of International code signals, I should have been prepared to accept the proceeding with out comment. Thorndyke was a law unto himself.

Nevertheless, as I walked homeward by his side, carrying the coil of rope, I continued to speculate on this singular case. Thorndyke had arrived at a hypothetical solution of Mr. Brodribb's problem; and it was evidently correct, so far, as the entry in the bill-book proved. But what was the connection between a dusty jacket and a length of thin rope? And why this particular length? I could make nothing of it. But I determined, as soon as we got home, to see what new facts Polton's activities had brought to light.

The results were disappointing. Polton's dust extractor had been busy, and the products in the form of tiny heaps of dust, were methodically set out on a sheet of white paper, each little heap covered with a watch-glass and accompanied by its written particulars as to the part of the garment from which it had come. I examined a few samples under the microscope, but though curious and interesting, as all dust is, they showed nothing very distinctive. The dust might have come from anyone's coat. There was, of course, a good deal of yellowish sandy loam, a few particles of chalk, a quantity of fine ash, clinker and particles of coal—railway dust from a locomotive—ordinary town and house dust and some oddments such as pollen grains, including those of the sow-thistle, mallow, poppy and valerian, and in one sample I found two scales from the wing of the common blue butterfly. That was all; and it told me nothing but that the owner of the coat had recently been in a chalk district and that he had taken a railway journey.

While I was working with the microscope, Polton was busy with an occupation that I did not understand. He had cemented the little pieces of chalk that we had found in the pockets to a plate of glass by means of pitch, and he was now brushing them under water with a soft brush and from time to time decanting the milky water into a tall sediment glass. Now, as most people know, chalk is largely composed of microscopic shells—*foraminifera*—which can be detached by gently brushing the chalk under water. But what was the object? There was no doubt that the material was chalk, and we knew that *foraminifera* were there. Why trouble to prove what is common knowledge?

I questioned Polton, but he knew nothing of the purpose of the investigation. He merely beamed on me like a crinkly old graven image and went on brushing. I dipped up a sample of the white sediment and examined it under the microscope. Of course there were *foraminifera*, and very beautiful they were. But what about it? The whole proceeding looked purposeless. And yet I knew that it was not. Thorndyke was the last man in the world to expend his energies in flogging a dead horse.

Presently he came up to the laboratory, and, when he had looked at the dust specimens and confirmed my opinion of them, he fell to work on the chalk sediment. Having prepared a number of slides, he sat down at the microscope with a sharp pencil and a block of smooth paper with the apparent purpose of cataloguing and making drawings of the *foraminifera*. And at this task I left him while I went forth to collect some books that I had ordered from a bookseller in the Charing Cross Road.

When I returned with my purchases about an hour later I found him putting back in a press a portfolio of large-scale Ordnance maps of Kent which he had apparently been consulting, and I noticed on the table his sheet of drawings and a monograph of the fossil *foraminifera*.

"Well, Thorndyke," I said cheerfully, "I suppose this time, you know exactly what has become of Merrill."

"I can guess," he replied, "and so can you. But the actual data are distressingly vague. We have certain indications, as you will have noticed. The trouble will be to bring them to a focus. It is a case for constructive imagination on the one hand and the method of exclusion on the other. I shall make a preliminary circle-round tomorrow."

"Meaning by that?"

"I have a hypothesis. It is probably wrong. If it is, we must try another, and yet another. Every time we fail we shall narrow the field of inquiry until by eliminating one possibility after another, we may hope to arrive at the solution. My first essay will take me down into Kent."

"You are not going into those wild regions alone, Thorndyke," said I. "You will need my protection and support to say nothing of my invaluable advice. I presume you realise that?"

"Undoubtedly." he replied gravely. "I was reckoning on a two-man expedition. Besides, you are as much interested in the case as I am. And now, let us go forth and dine and fortify ourselves for the perils of tomorrow."

In the course of dinner I led the conversation to the products of Polton's labours and remarked upon their very indefinite significance; but Thorndyke was more indefinite still, as he usually was in cases of a highly speculative character.

"You are expecting too much from Polton," he said with a smile. "This is not a matter of *foraminifera* or pollen or butterfly-scales; they are only items of circumstantial evidence. What we have to do is to consider the whole body of facts in our possession; what Brodribb has told us, what we know for ourselves and what we have ascertained by investigation. The case is still very much in the air, but it is not so vague as you seem to imply."

This was all I could get out of him; and as the "whole body of facts" yielded no suggestion at all to me, I could only possess my soul in patience and hope for some enlightenment on the morrow.

About a quarter to eleven on the following morning, while Thorndyke was giving final instructions to Polton and I was speculating on the contents of the suit-case that was going to accompany us, footsteps became audible on our stairs. Their *crescendo* terminated in a flourish on our little brass knocker which I recognised as Brodribb's knock. I accordingly opened the door, and in walked our old friend. His keen blue eye took in at once our informal raiment and the suit-case and lighted up with something like curiosity.

"Off on an expedition?" he asked.

"Yes," replied Thorndyke. "A little trip down into Kent. Gravesend, in fact."

"Gravesend," repeated Brodribb with further awakened interest. "That was rather a favourite resort of poor Merrill's. By the way, your expedition is not connected with his disappearance, I suppose?"

"As a matter of fact it is," replied Thorndyke. "Just a tentative exploration, you know."

"I know," said Brodribb, all agog now, "and I'm coming with you. I've got a clear day and I'm not going to take a refusal."

"No refusal was contemplated," rejoined Thorndyke. "You'll probably waste a day, but we shall benefit by your society. Polton will let your clerk know that you haven't absconded, or you can look in at the office yourself. We have plenty of time."

Brodribb chose the latter plan, which enabled him to exchange his tall hat and morning coat for a soft hat and jacket, and we accordingly made our way to Charing Cross *via* Lincoln's Inn, where Brodribb's office was situated. I noticed that Brodribb, with his customary discretion, asked no questions, though he must have observed, as I had, the striking fact that Thorndyke had in some way connected Merrill with Gravesend; and in fact with the exception of Brodribb's account of his failure to get any news of Mr. Crick, no reference was made to the nature of our expedition until we alighted at our destination.

On emerging from the station, Thorndyke turned to the left and led the way out of the approach into a street, on the opposite side of which a rather grimy statue of Queen Victoria greeted us with a supercilious stare. Here we turned to the south along a prosperous thoroughfare, and presently crossing a main road, followed its rather sordid continuation until the urban squalor began to be tempered by traces of rusticity, and the suburb became a village. Passing a pleasant looking inn and a smithy, which seemed to have an out-patient department for invalid carts, we came into a quiet lane offering a leafy vista with glimpses of thatched and tiled cottages whose gardens were gay with summer flowers.

Opposite these, some rough stone steps led up to a stile by the side of an open gate which gave access to a wide cart-track. Here Thorndyke halted, and producing his pocket map-case, compared the surroundings with the map. At length he pocketed the case, and turning towards the cart-track, said: "This is our way, for better or worse. In a few minutes we shall probably know whether we have found a clue or a mare's nest."

We followed the track up a rise until, reaching the crest of the hill, we saw stretching away below us a wide, fertile valley with wooded heights beyond, over the brow of which peeped the square tower of some village church.

"Well," said Brodribb, taking off his hat to enjoy the light breeze, "clue or no clue, this is perfectly delightful and well worth the journey. Just look at those charming little blue butterflies fluttering round that mallow. What a magnificent prospect And where, but in Kent, will you see such a barley field as that?"

It was, indeed, a beautiful landscape. But as my eye travelled over the enormous barley field, its tawny surface rippling, in golden waves before the summer breeze, it was not the beauty of the scene that occupied my mind. I was thinking of those three ends of barley beard that we had picked from the skirts of the green jacket. The cart-track had now contracted to a foot path; but it was a broader path than I should have looked for, running straight across the great field to a far-away stile; and half way along it on the left hand side I could see, rising above the barley, the top of a rough fence around a small, square enclosure that looked like a pound—though it was in an unlikely situation.

We pursued the broad path across the field until we were nearly abreast of the pound, and I was about to draw Thorndyke's attention to it, when I perceived a narrow lane through the barley—hardly a path, but rather a track, trodden through the crop by some persons who had gone to the enclosure. Into this track Thorndyke turned as if he had been looking for it, and walked towards the enclosure, closely scrutinising the ground as he went. Brodribb and I, of course, followed in single file, brushing through the barley as we went; and as we drew nearer we could see that there was an opening in the enclosing fence and that inside was a deep hollow the edges of which were fringed with clumps of pink valerian. At the opening of the fence Thorndyke halted and looked back.

"Well," said Brodribb, "is it going to be a mare's nest?"

"No," replied Thorndyke. "It is a clue, and something more!"

As he spoke, he pointed to the foot of one of the principal posts of the fence, to which was secured a short length of rope, the frayed ends of which suggested that it had broken under a heavy strain. And now I could see what the enclosure was. Inside it was a deep pit, and at the bottom of the pit, to one side, was a circular hole, black as night, and apparently leading down into the bowels of the earth.

"That must be a dene hole," said I, looking at the yawning cavity.

"It is," Thorndyke replied.

"Ha," said Brodribb, "so that is a dene hole, is it? Damned unpleasant looking place. Dene holes were one of poor Merrill's hobbies. He used to go down to explore them. I hope you are not suggesting that he went down this one."

"I am afraid that is what has happened, Brodribb," was the reply. "That end of rope looks like his. It is deep-sea lead-line. I have a length of it here, bought at the same place as he bought his, and probably cut from the same sample." He opened the suit-case, and taking out the coil of line that we had bought, flung it down by the foot of the post. Obviously it was identical with the broken end. "However," he added, "we shall see."

"We are going down, are we?" asked Brodribb.

"We?" repeated Thorndyke. "I am going down if it is practicable. Not otherwise. If it is an ordinary seventy-foot shaft with perpendicular sides, we shall have to get proper appliances. But you had better stay above, in any case."

"Nonsense!" exclaimed Brodribb. "I am not such a back number as you think. I have been a mountain-climber in my time and I'm not a bit nervous. I can get down all right if there is any foothold, and I've got a rope to hang on to. And you can see for yourself that somebody has been down with a rope only."

"Yes," replied Thorndyke, "but I don't see that that somebody has come up again."

"No," Brodribb admitted; "that's true. The rope seems to have broken; and you say your rope is the same stuff?"

Thorndyke looked at me inquiringly as I stooped and examined the frayed end of the strange rope.

"What do you say, Jervis?" he asked.

"That rope didn't break," I replied. "It has been, chafed or sawn through. It is quite different in appearance from a broken end."

"That was what I decided as soon as I saw it," said Thorndyke. "Besides, a new rope of this size and quality couldn't possibly break under the weight of a man."

Brodribb gazed at the frayed end with an expression of horror.

"What a diabolical thing!" he exclaimed. "You mean that some wretch deliberately cut the rope and let another man drop down the shaft! But it can't be. I really think you must be mistaken. It must have been a defective rope."

"Well, that is what it looks like," replied Thorndyke. He made a 'running bowline' at the end of our rope and slipped the loop over his shoulders, drawing it tight under his arms. Then he turned towards the pit. "You had better take a couple of turns round the foot of the post, Jervis," said he, "and pay out just enough to keep the rope taut."

He took an electric inspection-lamp from the suit case, slipped the battery in his pocket and hooked the bull's-eye to a button-hole, and when all was ready, he climbed down into the pit, crossed the sloping floor, and crouching down, peered into the forbidding hole, throwing down it a beam of light from his bull's-eye. Then he stood up and grasped the rope.

"It is quite practicable," said he; "only about twenty feet deep, and good foothold all the way." With this he crouched once more, backed into the hole and disappeared from view. He evidently descended pretty quickly, to judge by the rate at which I had to pay out the rope, and in quite a short time I felt the tension slacken and began to haul up the line. As the loop came out of the hole, Mr. Brodribb took possession of it, and regardless of my protests, proceeded to secure it under his arms.

"But how the deuce am I going to get down?" I demanded.

"That's all right, Jervis," he replied persuasively. "I'll just have a look round and then come up and let you down."

It being obviously useless to argue, I adjusted the rope and made ready to pay out. He climbed down into the pit with astonishing agility, backed into the hole and disappeared; and the tension of the rope informed me that he was making quite a rapid descent. He had nearly reached the bottom when there were borne to my ears the hollow reverberations of what sounded like a cry of alarm. But all was apparently well, for the rope continued to draw out steadily, and when at last its tension relaxed, I felt an unmistakable signal shake, and at once drew it up.

As my curiosity made me unwilling to remain passively waiting for Brodribb's return, I secured the end of the rope to the post with a "fisherman's bend" and let myself down into the pit. Advancing to the hole, I lay down and put my head over the edge. A dim light from Thorndyke's lamp came up the shaft and showed me that we were by no means the first explorers, for there were foot-holes cut in the chalk all the way down, apparently of some considerable age. With the aid of these and the rope, it appeared quite easy to descend and I decided to go down forthwith.

Accordingly I backed towards the shaft, found the first of the foot-holes, and grasping the rope with one hand and using the other to hang on to the upper cavities, easily let myself down the well-like shaft. As I neared the bottom the light of the lamp was thrown full on the shaft-wall; a pair of hands grasped me and I heard Thorndyke's voice saying: "Look where you are treading, Jervis;" on which I looked down and saw immediately below me a man lying on his face by an irregular coil of rope.

I stepped down carefully on to the chalk floor and looked round. We were in a small chamber in one side of which was the black opening of a low tunnel. Thorndyke and Brodribb were standing at the feet of the prostrate figure examining a revolver which the solicitor held.

"It has certainly been fired," said the latter. "One chamber is empty and the barrel is foul."

"That may be," replied Thorndyke; "but there is no bullet wound. This man died from a knife wound in the chest." He threw the light of his lamp on the corpse and as I turned it partly over to verify his statement, he added: "This is poor Mr. Merrill. We found the revolver lying by his side."

"The cause of death is clear enough," said I, "and it certainly wasn't suicide. The question is—" At this moment Thorndyke stooped and threw a beam of light down the tunnel, and Brodribb and I simultaneously uttered an exclamation. At the extreme end, about forty feet away, the body of another man lay. Instantly Brodribb started forward, and stooping to clear the low roof—it was about four feet six inches high—hurried along the tunnel. Thorndyke and I followed close behind. As we reached the body, which was lying supine with a small electric torch by its side, and the light of Thorndyke's lamp fell on the upturned face, Brodribb gasped: "God save us! it's Crick! And here is the knife." He was about to pick up the weapon when Thorndyke put out his hand.

"That knife," said he, "must be touched by no hand but the one that dealt the blow. It may be crucial evidence."

"Evidence of what?" demanded Brodribb. "There is Merrill with a knife wound in his chest and a pistol by his side. Here is Crick with a bullet wound in his breast, a knife by his side and the empty sheath secured round his waist. What more evidence do you want?"

"That depends on what you seek to prove," said Thorndyke. "What is your interpretation of the facts that you have stated?

"Why, it is as plain as daylight," answered Brodribb, "incredible as the affair seems, having regard to the characters of the two men. Crick stabbed Merrill and Merrill shot him dead. Then Merrill tried to escape, but the rope broke, he was trapped and he bled to death at the foot of the shaft."

"And who do you say died first?" Thorndyke asked.

It was a curious question and it caused me to look inquisitively at my colleague. But Brodribb answered promptly: "Why, Crick, of course. Here he lies where he fell. There is a track of blood along the floor of the tunnel, as you can see, and there is Merrill at the entrance, dead in the act of trying to escape."

Thorndyke nodded in a rather mysterious way and there was a brief silence. Then I ventured to remark: "You seem to be losing sight of the man with the green jacket."

Brodribb started and looked at me with a frown of surprise.

"Bless my soul!" he exclaimed, "so I am. I had clean forgotten him in these horrors. But what is your point? Is there any evidence that he has been here?"

"I don't know," said I. "He bought the rope and he was seen with

Merrill apparently going towards London Bridge Station. And I gather that it was the green jacket that piloted Thorndyke to this place."

"In a sense," Thorndyke admitted, "that is so. But we will talk about that later. Meanwhile there are one or two facts that I will draw your attention to. First as to the wounds; they are almost identical in position. Each is on the left side, just below the nipple; a vital spot, which would be fully exposed by a man who was climbing down holding on to a rope. Then, if you look along the floor where I am throwing the light, you can see a distinct trace of something having been dragged along, although there seems to have been an effort to obliterate it; and the blood marks are more in the nature of smears than drops." He gently turned the body over and pointed to the back, which was thickly covered with chalk.

"This corpse has obviously been dragged along the floor," he continued. "It wouldn't have been marked in that way by merely falling. Further, the rope, when last seen, was being stuffed into a hand-bag. The rope is here, but where is the hand-bag? Finally, the rope was cut by some one outside, and evidently after the murders had been committed."

As he concluded, he spread his handkerchief over the knife, and wrapping it up carefully without touching it with his fingers, placed it in his outside breast-pocket. Then we went back towards the shaft, where Thorndyke knelt down by the body of Merrill and systematically emptied the pockets.

"What are you searching for?" asked Brodribb.

"Keys," was the reply; "and there aren't any. It is a vital point, seeing that the man with the green jacket evidently let himself into Merrill's chambers that same day."

"Yes," Brodribb agreed with a reflective frown; "it is. But tell us, Thorndyke, how you reconstruct this horrible crime."

"My theory," said Thorndyke, "is that the three men came here together. They made the rope fast to the post. The stranger in the green jacket came down first and waited at the foot of the shaft. Merrill came down next, and the stranger stabbed him just as he reached the bottom, while his arms were still up hanging on to the rope. Crick followed and was shot in the same place and the same manner. Then the stranger dragged Crick's body along the tunnel, swept away the marks as well as he could, put the knife and the lamp by the body, dropped the revolver by Merrill's corpse, took the keys and went up, sawed through the rope—probably with a pocket saw—and threw the end down the shaft. Then he took the next train to London and went straight to Merrill's chambers, where he opened the safe or other receptacles and took possession of what he wanted."

Brodribb nodded. "It was a diabolically clever scheme," said he.

"The scheme was ingenious enough," Thorndyke agreed, "but the execution was contemptible. He has left traces at every turn. Otherwise we shouldn't be here. He has acted on the assumption that the world contains no one but fools. But that is a fool's assumption."

When we had ascended, in the reverse order of our descent, Thorndyke detached our rope and also the frayed end, which we took with us, and we then took our way back towards the town; and I noted that as we stood by the dene hole, there was not a human creature in sight; nor did we meet a single person until we were close to the village. It was an ideal spot for a murder.

"I suppose you will notify the police?" said Brodribb.

"Yes," replied Thorndyke. "I shall call on the Chief Constable and give him the facts and advise him to keep some of them to himself for the present, and also to arrange for an adjournment of the inquest. Our friend with the green jacket must be made to think that he has played a trump card."

Apparently the Chief Constable was a man who knew all the moves of criminal investigation, for at the inquest the discovery was attributed to the local police acting on information received from somebody who had "noticed the broken rope."

None of us was summoned to give evidence nor were our names mentioned, but the inquest was adjourned for three weeks, for further inquiries.

But in those three weeks there were some singular developments, of which the scene was the clerks' office at Mr. Brodribb's premises in Lincoln's Inn. There late on a certain forenoon, Thorndyke and I arrived, each provided with a bag and a sheaf of documents, and were duly admitted by Mr. Page.

"Now," said Thorndyke, "are you quite confident, Mr. Page, that you would recognise this man, even if he had shaved off his beard and moustache?"

"Quite confident," replied Page. "I should know him by his eyes. Very queer eyes they were; light, greenish grey. And I should know his voice, too."

"Good," said Thorndyke; and as Page disappeared into the private office, we sat down and examined our documents, eyed furtively by the junior clerk. Some ten minutes later the door opened and a man entered; and the first glance at him brought my nerves to concert pitch. He was a thick-set, muscular man, clean-shaved and rather dark. But my attention was instantly arrested by his eyes—singularly pale eyes which gave an almost unhuman character to his face. He reminded me of a certain species of lemur that I once saw.

"I have got an appointment with Mr. Brodribb," he said, addressing the clerk. "My name is Horder."

The clerk slipped off his stool and moved towards the door of the private office, but at that moment Page came out. As his eyes met Horder's, he stopped dead; and instantly the two men seemed to stiffen like a couple of dogs that have suddenly met at a street corner. I watched Horder narrowly. He had been rather pale when he came in. Now he was ghastly, and his whole aspect indicated extreme nervous tension.

"Did you wish to see Mr. Brodribb?" asked Page, still gazing intently at the other.

"Yes," was the irritable reply; "I have given my name once— Horder."

Mr. Page turned and re-entered the private office, leaving the door ajar.

"Mr. Horder to see you, sir," I heard him say. He came out and shut the door. "If you will sit down, Mr. Brodribb will see you in a minute or two," he said, offering a chair; he then took his hat from a peg, glanced at his watch and went out.

A couple of minutes passed. Once, I thought I heard stealthy footsteps out in the entry; but no one came in or knocked. Presently the door of the private office opened and a tall gentleman came out. And then, once more, my nerves sprang to attention. The tall gentleman was Detective-Superintendent Miller.

The superintendent walked across the office, opened the door, looked out, and then, leaving it ajar, came back to where Horder was sitting.

"You are Mr. Samuel Horder, I think," said he.

"Yes, I am," was the reply. "What about it?"

"I am a police officer, and I arrest you on a charge of having unlawfully entered the premises of the late Reginald Merrill; and it is my duty to caution you—"

Here Horder, who had risen to his feet, and slipped his right hand under the skirt of his coat, made a sudden spring at the officer. But in that instant Thorndyke had gripped his right arm at the elbow and wrist and swung him round; the superintendent seized his left arm while I pounced upon the revolver in his right hand and kept its muzzle pointed to the floor. But it was an uncomfortable affair. Our prisoner was a strong man and he fought like a wild beast; and he had his finger hooked round the trigger of the revolver.

The four of us, locked together, gyrated round the office, knocking over chairs and bumping against the walls, the junior clerk skipped round the room with his eyes glued on the pistol and old Brodribb charged out of his sanctum, flourishing a long ruler. However, it did not last long. In the midst of the uproar, two massive constables stole in and joined the fray. There was a yell from the prisoner, the revolver rattled to the floor and then I heard two successive metallic clicks.

"He'll be all right now," murmured the constable who had fixed on the handcuffs, with the manner of one who has administered a soothing remedy.

"I notice," said Thorndyke, when the prisoner had been removed, "that you charged him only with unlawful entry."

"Yes," replied Miller, "until we have taken his finger-prints. Mr. Singleton has developed up three fingers and a thumb, beautifully clear, on that knife that you gave us. If they prove to be Horder's finger prints, of course, it is a true bill for the murder."

The finger-prints on the knife proved undoubtedly to be Horder's. But the case did not rest on them alone. When his rooms were searched, there were found not only Mr. Merrill's keys but also Mr. Merrill's second will, which had been missed from the safe when it was opened by the maker's locksmith; thus illustrating afresh the perverse stupidity of the criminal mind.

"A satisfactory case," remarked Thorndyke, "in respect of the result; but there was too much luck for us to take much credit from it. On Brodribb's opening statement, it was pretty clear that a crime had been committed. Merrill was missing and someone had possession of his keys and had entered his premises. It also appeared nearly certain that the thing stolen must be the second will, since there was nothing else of value to steal; and the will was of very great value to two persons, Crick and Horder, to each of whom its destruction was worth many thousands of pounds.

"To both of them its value was conditional on the immediate death of Merrill, before another will could be made; and to Horder it was further conditional on the death of Crick and that he should die before Merrill—for otherwise the estate would go to Crick's heirs or next of kin. The prima facie suspicion therefore fell on these two men. But Crick was missing; and the question was, had he absconded or was he dead?

"And now as to the investigation. The green jacket showed earthy dust and chalk on the front and chalk-marks on the buttons. The indication was that the wearer had either crawled on chalky ground or climbed up a chalky face. But the marks on the buttons suggested climbing; for a horizontal surface is usually covered by soil, whereas on a vertical surface the chalk is exposed. But the time factor showed us that this man could not have travelled far from London. He was seen going towards London Bridge Station about the time when a train was due to go down to Kent.

"That train went to Maidstone and Gillingham, calling at Gravesend, Strood, Snodland, Rochester, Chatham and other places abounding in chalk and connected with the cement industry. In that district there were no true cliffs, but there were numerous chalk-pits, railway embankments and other excavations. The evidence pointed to one of these excavations. Then Crick was known to have gone to Rochester—earlier in the day—which further suggested the district, though Rochester is the least chalky part of it.

"The question was, what kind of excavation had been climbed into? And for what purpose had the climbing been performed? But here the personality of the missing man gave us a hint. Merrill had written a book to prove that dene holes were simply prehistoric flint-mines. He had explored a number of dene holes and described them in his book. Now the district through which this train had passed was peculiarly rich in dene holes; and then there was the suggestive fact that Merrill had been last seen coming out of a rope-seller's shop. This latter fact was so important that I followed it up at once by calling at Edginton's.

"There I ascertained that Merrill or his companion had bought a fifteen-fathom length of deep-sea lead-line. Now this was profoundly significant. The maximum depth of a dene hole is about seventy feet. Fifteen fathoms—ninety feet—is therefore the exact length required, allowing for loops and fastenings. This new fact converted the dene-hole hypothesis into what was virtually a certainty, especially when one considered how readily these dangerous pits lent themselves either to fatal accidents or to murder. I accordingly adopted the dene-hole suggestion as a working hypothesis.

"The next question was, 'Where was this dene-hole?' And an uncommonly difficult question it was. I began to fear that the inquiry would fail from the impossibility of solving it. But at this point I got some help from a new quarter. I had given the coat to Polton to extract the dust and I had told him to wash the little lumps of chalk for *foraminifera*."

"What are *foraminifera*?" asked Brodribb.

"They are minute sea shells. Chalk is largely composed of them; and although chalk is in no sense a local rock, there is nevertheless a good deal of variation in the species of *foraminifera* found in different localities. So I had the chalk washed out as a matter of routine. Well, the dust was confirmatory but not illuminating. There was railway dust, of the South Eastern type—I expect you know it—chalk, loam dust, pollen-grains of the mallow and valerian (which grows in chalk-pits and railway cuttings) and some wing scales of the common blue butterfly, which haunts the chalk—I expect he had touched a dead butterfly.

"But all this would have answered for a good part of Kent. Then I examined the *foraminifera* and identified the species by the plates in *Warnford's Monograph*. The result was most encouraging. There were nine species in all, and of these five were marked as 'found in the Gravesend chalk,' two more 'from the Kentish chalk' and the other two 'from the English chalk.' This was a very striking result. More than half the contained *foraminifera* were from the Gravesend chalk.

"The problem now was to determine the geologic meaning of the term Gravesend. I ruled out Rochester, as I had heard of no dene holes in that neighbourhood, and I consulted Merrill's book and the large-scale Ordnance map. Merrill had worked in the Gravesend district and the adjacent part of Essex and he gave a list of the dene holes that he had explored, including the Clapper Napper Hole in Swanscombe Wood. But, checking his list by the Ordnance map, I found that there was one dene hole marked on the map which was not in his list. As it was evidently necessary to search all the dene holes in the district, I determined to begin with the one that he seemed to have missed. And there luck favoured us. It turned out to be the right one."

"I don't see that there was much luck in it," said Brodribb. "You calculated the probabilities and adopted the greatest."

"At any rate," said Thorndyke, "there was Merrill and there was Crick; and as soon as I saw them I knew that Horder was the murderer. For the whole tableau had obviously been arranged to demonstrate that Crick died before Merrill and establish Horder as Merrill's heir."

"A diabolical plot," commented Brodribb. "Horribly ingenious, too. By the way—which of them did die first in your opinion?"

"Merrill, I should say, undoubtedly," replied Thorndyke.

"That will be good hearing for Crick's next of kin," said Brodribb. "And you haven't done with this case yet, Thorndyke. I shall retain you on the question of survivorship."

The New Jersey Sphinx

"A rather curious neighbourhood this, Jervis," my friend Thorndyke remarked as we turned into Upper Bedford Place; "a sort of aviary for cosmopolitan birds of passage, especially those of the Oriental variety. The Asiatic and African faces that one sees at the windows of these Bloomsbury boarding houses almost suggest an overflow from the ethnographical galleries of the adjacent British Museum."

"Yes," I agreed, "there must be quite a considerable population of Africans, Japanese and Hindus in Bloomsbury; particularly Hindus."

As I spoke, and as if in illustration of my statement, a dark-skinned man rushed out of one of the houses farther down the street and began to advance towards us in a rapid, bewildered fashion, stopping to look at each street door as he came to it. His hatless condition—though he was exceedingly well dressed—and his agitated manner immediately attracted my attention, and Thorndyke's too, for the latter remarked, "Our friend seems to be in trouble. An accident, perhaps, or a case of sudden illness."

Here the stranger, observing our approach, ran forward to meet us and asked in an agitated tone, "Can you tell me, please, where I can find a doctor?"

"I am a medical man," replied Thorndyke, "and so is my friend."

Our acquaintance grasped Thorndyke's sleeve and exclaimed eagerly, "Come with me, then, quickly, if you please. A most dreadful thing has happened."

He hurried us along at something between a trot and a quick walk, and as we proceeded he continued excitedly, "I am quite confused and terrified; it is all so strange and sudden and terrible."

"Try," said Thorndyke, "to calm yourself a little and tell us what has happened."

"I will," was the agitated reply. "It is my cousin, Dinanath Byramji—his surname is the same as mine. Just now I went to his room and was horrified to find him lying on the floor, staring at the ceiling and blowing—like this," and he puffed out his cheeks with a soft blowing noise. "I spoke to him and shook his hand, but he was like a dead man. This is the house."

He darted up the steps to an open door at which a rather scared page-boy was on guard, and running along the hall, rapidly ascended the stairs. Following him closely, we reached a rather dark first-floor landing where, at a half-open door, a servant-maid stood listening with an expression of awe to a rhythmical snoring sound that issued from the room.

The unconscious man lay as Mr. Byramji had said staring fixedly at the ceiling with wide-open, glazy eyes, puffing out his cheeks slightly at each breath. But the breathing was shallow and slow, and it grew perceptibly slower, with lengthening pauses. And even as I was timing it with my watch while Thorndyke examined the pupils with the aid of a wax match, it stopped. I laid my finger on the wrist and caught one or two slow, flickering beats. Then the pulse stopped too.

"He is gone," said I. "He must have burst one of the large arteries."

"Apparently," said Thorndyke, "though one would not have expected it at his age. But wait! What is this?"

He pointed to the right ear, in the hollow of which a few drops of blood had collected, and as he spoke he drew his hand gently over the dead man's head and moved it slightly from side to side.

"There is a fracture of the base of the skull," said he, "and quite distinct signs of contusion of the scalp." He turned to Mr. Byramji, who stood wringing his hand and gazing incredulously at the dead man, and asked: "Can you throw any light on this?"

The Indian looked at him vacantly. The sudden tragedy seemed to have paralysed his brain. "I don't understand," said he. "What does it mean?"

"It means," replied Thorndyke, "that he has received a heavy blow on the head."

For a few moments Mr. Byramji continued to stare vacantly at my colleague. Then he seemed suddenly to realise the import of Thorndyke's remark, for he started up excitedly and turned to the door, outside which the two servants were hovering.

"Where is the person gone who came in with my cousin?" he demanded.

"You saw him go out, Albert," said the maid. "Tell Mr. Byramji where he went to."

The page tiptoed into the room with a fearful eye fixed on the corpse, and replied falteringly, "I only see the back of him as he went out, and all I know is that he turned to the left. P'raps he's gone for a doctor."

"Can you give us any description of him?" asked Thorndyke.

"I only see the back of him," repeated the page. "He was a shortish gentleman and he had on a dark suit of clothes and a hard felt hat. That's all I know."

"Thank you," said Thorndyke. "We may want to ask you some more questions presently," and having conducted the page to the door, he shut it and turned to Mr. Byramji.

"Have you any idea who it was that was with your cousin?" he asked.

"None at all," was the reply. "I was sitting in my room opposite, writing, when I heard my cousin come up the stairs with another person, to whom he was talking. I could not hear what he was saying. They went into his room—this room—and I could occasionally catch the sound of their voices. In about a quarter of an hour I heard the door open and shut, and then someone went downstairs, softly and rather quickly. I finished the letter that I was writing, and when I had addressed it I came in here to ask my cousin who the visitor was. I thought it might be someone who had come to negotiate for the ruby."

"The ruby!" exclaimed Thorndyke. "What ruby do you refer to?"

"The great ruby," replied Byramji. "But of course you have not—" He broke off suddenly and stood for a few moments staring at Thorndyke with parted lips and wide-open eyes; then abruptly he turned, and kneeling beside the dead man he began, in a curious, caressing, half-apologetic manner, first to pass his hands gently over the body at the waist and then to unfasten the clothes. This brought into view a handsome, soft leather belt, evidently of native workmanship, worn next to the skin and furnished with three pockets. Mr. Byramji unbuttoned and explored them in quick succession, and it was evident that they were all empty.

"It is gone!" he exclaimed in low, intense tones, "Gone! Ah! But how little would it signify! But thou, dear Dinanath, my brother, my friend, thou art gone, too!"

He lifted the dead man's hand and pressed it to his cheek, murmuring endearments in his own tongue. Presently he laid it down reverently, and sprang up, and I was startled at the change in his aspect. The delicate, gentle, refined face had suddenly become the face of a Fury—fierce, sinister, vindictive.

"This wretch must die!" he exclaimed huskily. "This sordid brute who, without compunction, has crushed out a precious life as one would carelessly crush a fly, for the sake of a paltry crystal—he must die, if I have to follow him and strangle him with my own hands!"

Thorndyke laid his hand on Byramji's shoulder. "I sympathise with you most cordially," said he. "If it is as you think, and appearances suggest, that your cousin has been murdered as a mere incident of robbery, the murderer's life is forfeit, and Justice cries aloud for retribution. The fact of murder will be determined, for or against, by a proper inquiry. Meanwhile we have to ascertain who this unknown man is and what happened while he was with your cousin."

Byramji made a gesture of despair. "But the man has disappeared, and nobody has seen him! What can we do?"

"Let us look around us," plied Thorndyke, "and see if we can judge what has happened in this room. What, for instance, is this?"

He picked up from a corner near the door a small leather object, which he handed to Mr. Byramji. The Indian seized it eagerly, exclaiming: "Ah! It is the little bag in which my cousin used to carry the ruby. So he had taken it from his belt."

"It hasn't been dropped, by any chance?" I suggested.

In an instant Mr. Byramji was down on his knees, peering and groping about the floor, and Thorndyke and I joined in the search. But, as might have been expected there was no sign of the ruby, nor, indeed, of anything else, excepting a hat which I picked up from under the table.

"No," said Mr. Byramji, rising with a dejected air. "It is gone—of course it is gone, and the murderous villain—"

Here his glance fell on the hat, which I had laid on the table, and he bent forward to look at it.

"Whose hat is this?" he demanded, glancing at the chair on which Thorndyke's hat and mine had been placed.

"Is it not your cousin's?" asked Thorndyke.

"No, certainly not. His hat was like mine—we bought them both together. It had a white silk lining with his initials, D. B., in gold. This has no lining and is a much older hat. It must be the murderer's hat."

"If it is," said Thorndyke, "that is a most important fact—important in two respects. Could you let us see your hat?"

"Certainly," replied Byramji, walking quickly, but with a soft tread, to the door. As he went out, shutting the door silently behind him, Thorndyke picked up the derelict hat and swiftly tried it on the head of the dead man. As far as I could judge, it appeared to fit, and this Thorndyke confirmed as he replaced it on the table.

"As you see," said he, "it is at least a practical fit, which is a fact of some significance."

Here Mr. Byramji returned with his own hat, which he placed on the table by the side of the other, and thus placed, crown uppermost, the two hats were closely similar. Both were black, hard felts of the prevalent "bowler" shape, and of good quality, and the difference in their age and state of preservation was not striking; but when Byramji turned them over and exhibited their interiors it was seen that whereas the strange hat was unlined save for the leather head-band, Byramji's had a white silk lining and bore the owner's initials in embossed gilt letters.

"What happened," said Thorndyke, when he had carefully compared the two hats, "seems fairly obvious. The two men, on entering, placed their hats crown upwards on the table. In some way—perhaps during a struggle—the visitor's hat was knocked down and rolled under the table. Then the stranger, on leaving, picked up the only visible hat—almost identically similar to his own—and put it on."

"Is it not rather singular," I asked, "that he should not have noticed the different feel of a strange hat?"

"I think not," Thorndyke replied. "If he noticed anything unusual he would probably assume that he had put it on the wrong way round. Remember that he would be extremely hurried and agitated. And when once he had left the house he would not dare to take the risk of returning, though he would doubtless realise the gravity of the mistake. And now," he continued, "would you mind giving us a few particulars? You have spoken of a great ruby, which your cousin had, and which seems to be missing."

"Yes. You shall come to my room and I will tell you about it; but first let us lay my poor cousin decently on his bed."

"I think," said Thorndyke, "the body ought not to be moved until the police have seen it."

"Perhaps you are right," Byramji agreed reluctantly, "though it seems callous to leave him lying there." With a sigh he turned to the door, and Thorndyke followed, carrying the two hats.

"My cousin and I," said our host, when we were seated in his own large bed-sitting-room, "were both interested in gem-stones. I deal in all kinds of stones that are found in the East, but Dinanath dealt almost exclusively in rubies. He was a very fine judge of those beautiful gems, and he used to make periodical tours in Burma in search of uncut rubies of unusual size or quality. About four months ago he acquired at Mogok, in Upper Burma, a magnificent specimen over twenty-eight carats in weight, perfectly flawless and of the most gorgeous colour. It had been roughly cut, but my cousin was intending to have it recut unless he should receive an advantageous offer for it in the meantime."

"What would be the value of such a stone?" I asked.

"It is impossible to say. A really fine large ruby of perfect colour is far, far more valuable than the finest diamond of the same size. It is the most precious of all gems, with the possible exception of the emerald. A fine ruby of five carats is worth about three thousand pounds, but of course, the value rises out of all proportion with increasing size. Fifty thousand pounds would be a moderate price for Dinanath's ruby."

During this recital I noticed that Thorndyke, while listening attentively, was turning the stranger's hat over in his hands, narrowly scrutinising it both inside and outside. As Byramji concluded, he remarked:

"We shall have to let the police know what has happened, but, as my friend and I will be called as witnesses, I should like to examine this hat a little more closely before you hand it over to them. Could you let me have a small, hard brush? A dry nail-brush would do." Our host complied readily—in fact eagerly. Thorndyke's authoritative, purposeful manner had clearly impressed him, for he said as he handed my colleague a new nail-brush: "I thank you for your help and value it. We must not depend on the police only."

Accustomed as I was to Thorndyke's methods, his procedure was not unexpected, but Mr. Byramji watched him with breathless interest and no little surprise as, laying a sheet of notepaper on the table, he brought the hat close to it and brushed firmly but slowly, so that the dust dislodged should fall on it. As it was not a very well-kept hat, the yield was considerable, especially when the brush was drawn under the curl of the brim, and very soon the paper held quite a little heap. Then Thorndyke folded the paper into a small packet and having written "outside" on it, put it in his pocketbook.

"Why do you do that?" Mr. Byramji asked. "What will the dust tell you?"

"Probably nothing," Thorndyke replied. "But this hat is our only direct clue to the identity of the man who was with your cousin, and we must make the most of it. Dust, you know, is only a mass of fragments detached from surrounding objects. If the objects are unusual the dust may be quite distinctive. You could easily identify the hat of a miller or a cement worker." As he was speaking he reversed the hat and turned down the leather head-lining, whereupon a number of strips of folded paper fell down into the crown.

"Ah!" exclaimed Byramji, "perhaps we shall learn something now."

He picked out the folded slips and began eagerly to open them out, and we examined them systematically—one by one. But they were singularly disappointing and uninforming. Mostly they consisted of strips of newspaper, with one or two circulars, a leaf from a price list of gas stoves, a portion of a large envelope on which were the remains of an address which read "—n—don, W.C.," and a piece of paper evidently cut down vertically and bearing the right-hand half of some kind of list. This read:

$$—\text{el 3 oz. 5 dwts.}$$
$$—\text{eep 9½ oz.}$$

"Can you make anything of this?" I asked, handing the paper to Thorndyke.

He looked at it reflectively, and answered, as he copied it into his notebook: "It has, at least, some character. If we consider it with the other data we should get some sort of hint from it. But these scraps of paper don't tell us much. Perhaps their most suggestive feature is their quantity and the way in which, as you have no doubt noticed, they were arranged at the sides of the hat. We had better replace them as we found them for the benefit of the police."

The nature of the suggestion to which he referred was not very obvious to me, but the presence of Mr. Byramji rendered discussion inadvisable; nor was there any opportunity, for we had hardly reconstituted the hat when we became aware of a number of persons ascending the stairs, and then we heard the sound of rather peremptory rapping at the door of the dead man's room.

Mr. Byramji opened the door and went out on to the landing, where several persons had collected, including the two servants and a constable.

"I understand," said the policeman, "that there is something wrong here. Is that so?"

"A very terrible thing has happened," replied Byramji. "But the doctors can tell you better than I can." Here he looked appealingly at

Thorndyke, and we both went out and joined him.

"A gentleman—Mr. Dinanath Byramji—has met with his death under somewhat suspicious circumstances," said Thorndyke, and, glancing at the knot of naturally curious persons on the landing, he continued: "If you will come into the room where the death occurred, I will give you the facts so far as they are known to us."

With this he opened the door and entered the room with Mr. Byramji, the constable, and me. As the door opened, the bystanders craned forward and a middle-aged woman uttered a cry of horror and followed us into the room.

"This is dreadful!" she exclaimed, with a shuddering glance at the corpse. "The servants told me about it when I came in just now and I sent Albert for the police at once. But what does it mean? You don't think poor Mr. Dinanath has been murdered?"

"We had better get the facts, ma'am," said the constable, drawing out a large black notebook and laying his helmet on the table. He turned to Mr. Byramji, who had sunk into a chair and sat, the picture of grief, gazing at his dead cousin. "Would you kindly tell me what you know about how it happened?"

Byramji repeated the substance of what he had told us, and when the constable had taken down his statement, Thorndyke and I gave the few medical particulars that we could furnish and handed the constable our cards. Then, having helped to lay the corpse on the bed and cover it with a sheet, we turned to take our leave.

"You have been very kind," Mr. Byramji said as he shook our hands warmly. "I am more than grateful. Perhaps I may be permitted to call on you and hear if—if you have learned anything fresh," he concluded discreetly.

"We shall be pleased to see you," Thorndyke replied, "and to give you any help that we can;" and with this we took our departure, watched inquisitively down the stairs by the boarders and the servants who still lurked in the vicinity of the chamber of death.

"If the police have no more information than we have," I remarked as we walked homeward, "they won't have much to go on."

"No," said Thorndyke. "But you must remember that this crime—as we are justified in assuming it to be—is not an isolated one. It is the fourth of practically the same kind within the last six months. I understand that the police have some kind of information respecting the presumed criminal, though it can't be worth much, seeing that no arrest has been made. But there is some new evidence this time. The exchange of hats may help the police considerably."

"In what way? What evidence does it furnish?"

"In the first place it suggests a hurried departure, which seems to connect the missing man with the crime. Then, he is wearing the dead man's hat, and though he is not likely to continue wearing it, it may be seen and furnish a clue. We know that that hat fits him fairly well and we know its size, so that we know the size of his head. Finally, we have the man's own hat."

"I don't fancy the police will get much information from that," said I.

"Probably not," he agreed. "Yet it offered one or two interesting suggestions, as you probably observed."

"It made no suggestions whatever to me," said I.

"Then," said Thorndyke, "I can only recommend you to recall our simple inspection and consider the significance of what we found."

This I had to accept as closing the discussion for the time being, and as I had to make a call at my bookseller's concerning some reports that I had left to be bound, I parted from Thorndyke at the corner of Chichester Rents and left him to pursue his way alone. My business with the bookseller took me longer than I had expected, for I had to wait while the lettering on the backs was completed, and when I arrived at our chambers in King's Bench Walk, I found Thorndyke apparently at the final stage of some experiment evidently connected with our late adventure. The microscope stood on the table with one slide on the stage and a second one beside it; but Thorndyke had apparently finished his microscopical researches, for as I entered he held in his hand a test-tube filled with a smoky-coloured fluid.

"I see that you have been examining the dust from the hat," said I. "Does it throw any fresh light on the case?"

"Very little," he replied. "It is just common dust—assorted fibres and miscellaneous organic and mineral particles. But there are a couple of hairs from the inside of the hat—both lightish brown, and one of the atrophic, note-of-exclamation type that one finds at the margin of bald patches; and the outside dust shows minute traces of lead, apparently in the form of oxide. What do you make of that?"

"Perhaps the man is a plumber or a painter," I suggested.

"Either is possible and worth considering," he replied; but his tone made clear to me that this was not his own inference; and a row of five consecutive Post Office Directories, which I had already noticed ranged along the end of the table, told me that he had not only formed a hypothesis on the subject, but had probably either confirmed or disproved it. For the Post Office Directory was one of Thorndyke's favourite books of reference; and the amount of curious and recondite information that he succeeded in extracting from its matter-of-fact pages would have surprised no one more than it would the compilers of the work.

At this moment the sound of footsteps ascending our stairs became audible. It was late for business callers, but we were not unaccustomed to late visitors; and a familiar rat-tat of our little brass knocker seemed to explain the untimely visit.

"That sounds like Superintendent Miller's knock," said Thorndyke, as he strode across the room to open the door. And the superintendent it turned out to be. But not alone.

As the door opened the officer entered with two gentlemen, both natives of India, and one of whom was our friend Mr. Byramji.

"Perhaps," said Miller, "I had better look in a little later."

"Not on my account," said Byramji. "I have only a few words to say and there is nothing secret about my business. May I introduce my kinsman, Mr. Khambata, a student of the Inner Temple?"

Byramji's companion bowed ceremoniously. "Byramji came to my chambers just now," he explained, "to consult me about this dreadful affair, and he chanced to show me your card. He had not heard of you, but supposed you to be an ordinary medical practitioner. He did not realise that he had entertained an angel unawares. But I, who knew of your great reputation, advised him to put his affairs in your hands—without prejudice to the official investigations," Mr. Khambata added hastily, bowing to the superintendent.

"And I," said Mr. Byramji, "instantly decided to act on my kinsman's advice. I have come to beg you to leave no stone unturned to secure the punishment of my cousin's murderer. Spare no expense. I am a rich man and my poor cousin's property will come to me. As to the ruby, recover it if you can, but it is of no consequence. Vengeance—justice is what I seek. Deliver the wretch into my hands, or into the hands of justice, and I give you the ruby or its value, freely—gladly."

"There is no need," said Thorndyke, "of such extraordinary inducement. If you wish me to investigate this case, I will do so and will use every means at my disposal, without prejudice, as your friend says, to the proper claims of the officers of the law. But you understand that I can make no promises. I cannot guarantee success."

"We understand that," said Mr. Khambata. "But we know that if you undertake the case, everything that is possible will be done. And now we must leave you to your consultation."

As soon as our clients had gone, Miller rose from his chair with his hand in his breast pocket. "I dare say, doctor," said he, "you can guess what I have come about. I was sent for to look into this Byramji case and I heard from Mr. Byramji that you had been there and that you had made a minute examination of the missing man's hat. So have I; and I don't mind telling you that I could learn nothing from it."

"I haven't learnt much myself," said Thorndyke.

"But you've picked up something," urged Miller, "if it is only a hint; and we have just a little clue. There is very small doubt that this is the same man—'The New Jersey Sphinx,' as the papers call him—that committed those other robberies; and a very difficult type of criminal he is to get hold of. He is bold, he is wary, he plays a lone hand, and he sticks at nothing. He has no confederates, and he kills every time. The American police never got near him but once; and that once gives us the only clues we have."

"Fingerprints?" inquired Thorndyke.

"Yes, and very poor ones, too. So rough that you can hardly make out the pattern. And even those are not absolutely guaranteed to be his; but in any case, fingerprints are not much use until you've got the man. And there is a photograph of the fellow himself, But it is only a snapshot, and a poor one at that. All it shows is that he has a mop of hair and a pointed beard—or at least he had when the photograph was taken. But for identification purposes it is practically worthless. Still, there it is; and what I propose is this: we want this man and so do you; we've worked together before and can trust one another. I am going to lay my cards on the table and ask you to do the same."

"But, my dear Miller," said Thorndyke, "I haven't any cards. I haven't a single solid fact."

The detective was visibly disappointed. Nevertheless, he laid two photographs on the table and pushed them towards Thorndyke, who inspected them through his lens and passed them to me.

"The pattern is very indistinct and broken up," he remarked.

"Yes," said Miller; "the prints must have been made on a very rough surface, though you get prints something like those from fitters or other men who use files and handle rough metal. And now, doctor, can't you give us a lead of any kind?"

Thorndyke reflected a few moments. "I really have not a single real fact," said he, "and I am unwilling to make merely speculative suggestions."

"Oh, that's all right," Miller replied cheerfully. "Give us a start. I shan't complain if it comes to nothing."

"Well," Thorndyke said reluctantly, "I was thinking of getting a few particulars as to the various tenants of No. 51 Clifford's Inn. Perhaps you could do it more easily and it might be worth your while."

"Good!" Miller exclaimed gleefully. "He 'gives to airy nothing a local habitation and a name.'"

"It is probably the wrong name," Thorndyke reminded him.

"I don't care," said Miller. "But why shouldn't we go together? It's too late tonight, and I can't manage tomorrow morning. But say tomorrow afternoon. Two heads are better than one, you know, especially when the second one is yours. Or perhaps," he added, with a glance at me, "three would be better still."

Thorndyke considered for a moment or two and then looked at me.

"What do you say, Jervis?" he asked.

As my afternoon was unoccupied, I agreed with enthusiasm, being as curious as the superintendent to know how Thorndyke had connected this particular locality with the vanished criminal, and Miller departed in high spirits with an appointment for the morrow three o'clock in the afternoon.

For some time after the superintendent's depart I sat wrapped in profound meditation. In some mysterious way the address, 51 Clifford's Inn, had emerged from the formless data yielded by the derelict hat. But what had been the connection? Apparently the fragment of the addressed envelope had furnished the clue. But how had Thorndyke extended "—n" into "51, Clifford's Inn"? It was to me a complete mystery.

Meanwhile, Thorndyke had seated himself at writing-table, and I noticed that of the two letters which he wrote, one was written on our headed paper and other on ordinary plain notepaper. I was speculating on the reason for this when he rose, and as he stuck on the stamps, said to me, "I am just going out to post these two letters. Do you care for a short stroll through the leafy shades of Fleet Street? The evening is still young."

"The rural solitudes of Fleet Street attract me at all hours," I replied, fetching my hat from the adjoining office, and we accordingly sallied forth together, strolling up King's Bench Walk and emerging into Fleet Street by way of Mitre Court. When Thorndyke had dropped his letters into the post office box he stood awhile gazing up at the tower of St. Dunstan's Church.

"Have you ever been in Clifford's Inn, Jervis?" he inquired.

"Never," I replied (we passed through it together on an average a dozen times a week), "but it is not too late for an exploratory visit."

We crossed the road, and entering Clifford's Inn Passage, passed through the still half-open gate, crossed the outer court and threaded the tunnel-like entry by the hall to the inner court, in the middle of which Thorndyke halted, and looked up at one of the ancient houses, remarked, "No. 51."

"So that is where our friend hangs out his flag," said I.

"Oh come, Jervis," he protested, "I am surprised at you; you are as bad as Miller. I have merely suggested a possible connection between these premises and the hat that was left at Bedford Place. As to the nature of that connection I have no idea, and there may be no connection at all. I assure you, Jervis, that I am on the thinnest possible ice. I am working on a hypothesis which is in the highest degree speculative, and I should not have given Miller a hint but that he was so eager and so willing to help—and also that I wanted his finger-prints. But we are really only at the beginning, and may never get any farther."

I looked up at the old house. It was all in darkness excepting the top floor, where a couple of lighted windows showed the shadow of a man moving rapidly about the room. We crossed to the entry and inspected the names painted on the door-posts. The ground floor was occupied by a firm of photo-engravers, the first floor by a Mr. Carrington, whose name stood out conspicuously on its oblong of comparatively fresh white paint, while the tenants of the second floor—old residents, to judge by the faded and discoloured paint in which their names were announced—were Messrs. Burt & Highley, metallurgists.

"Burt has departed," said Thorndyke, as I read out the names; and he pointed to two red lines of erasure which I had not noticed in the dim light, "so the active gentleman above is presumably Mr. Highley, and we may take it that he has residential as well as business premises. I wonder who and what Mr. Carrington is—but I dare say we shall find out tomorrow."

With this he dismissed the professional aspects of Clifford's Inn, and, changing the subject to its history and associations, chatted in his inimitable, picturesque manner until our leisurely perambulations brought us at length to the Inner Temple Gate.

On the following morning we bustled through our work in order to leave the afternoon free, making several joint visits to solicitors from whom we were taking instructions. Returning from the last of these—a City lawyer—Thorndyke turned into St. Helen's Place and halted at a doorway bearing the brass plate of a firm of assayists and refiners. I followed him into the outer office, where, on his mentioning his name, an elderly man came to the counter.

"Mr. Grayson has put out some specimens for you, sir," said he. "They are about thirty grains to the ton—you said that the content was of no importance—I am to tell you that you need not return them. They are not worth treating." He went to a large safe from which he took a canvas bag, and returning to the counter, turned out on it the contents of the bag, consisting of about a dozen good-sized lumps of quartz and a glittering yellow fragment, which Thorndyke picked out and dropped in his pocket.

"Will that collection do?" our friend inquired.

"It will answer my purpose perfectly," Thorndyke replied, and when the specimens had been replaced the bag, and the latter deposited in Thorndyke's hand-bag, my colleague thanked the assistant and we went on our way.

"We extend our activities into the domain of mineralogy," I remarked.

Thorndyke smiled an inscrutable smile. "We also employ the suction pump as an instrument of research," he observed. "However, the strategic uses of chunks of quartz—otherwise than as missiles—will develop themselves in due course, and the interval may be used for reflection."

It was. But my reflection brought no solution. I noticed, however, that when at three o'clock we set forth in company with the superintendent, the bag went with us; and having offered to carry it and having had my offer accepted with a sly twinkle, its weight assured me that the quartz was still inside.

"Chambers and Offices to let," Thorndyke read aloud as we approached the porter's lodge. "That lets us in, I think. And the porter knows Dr. Jervis and me by sight, so he will talk more freely."

"He doesn't know me," said the superintendent, "but I'll keep in the background, all the same."

A pull at the bell brought out a clerical-looking man in a tall hat and a frock coat, who regarded Thorndyke and me through his spectacles with an amiable air of recognition.

"Good afternoon, Mr. Larkin," said Thorndyke. "I am asked to get particulars of vacant chambers. What have you got to let?"

Mr. Larkin reflected. "Let me see. There's a ground floor at No. 5—rather dark—and a small second-pair set at No. 12. And then there is—oh, yes, there is a good first-floor set at No. 51. They wouldn't have been vacant until Michaelmas, but Mr. Carrington, the tenant, has had to go abroad suddenly. I had a letter from him this morning, enclosing the key. Funny letter, too." He dived into his pocket, and hauling out a bundle of letters, selected one and handed it to Thorndyke with a broad smile.

Thorndyke glanced at the postmark ("London, E."), and having taken out the key, extracted the letter, which he opened and held so that Miller and I could see it. The paper bore the printed heading, "Baltic Shipping Company, Wapping," and the further written heading, "S.S. Gothenburg," and the letter was brief and to the point:

Dear Sir,

I am giving up my chambers at No. 51, as I have been suddenly called abroad. I enclose the key, but am not troubling you with the rent. The sale of my costly furniture will more than cover it, and the surplus can be expended on painting the garden railings,

Yours sincerely,

A. Carrington.

Thorndyke smilingly replaced the letter and the key in the envelope and asked: "What is the furniture like?"

"You'll see," chuckled the porter, "if you care to look at the rooms. And I think they might suit, They're a good set."

"Quiet?"

"Yes, pretty quiet. There's a metallurgist overhead—Highley—used to be Burt & Highley, but Burt has gone to the City, and I don't think Highley does much business now."

"Let me see," said Thorndyke, "I think I used to meet Highley sometimes—a tall, dark man, isn't he?"

"No, that would be Burt. Highley is a little, fairish man, rather bald, with a pretty rich complexion"—here Mr. Larkin tapped his nose knowingly and raised his little finger—"which may account for the falling off of business."

"Hadn't we better have a look at the rooms?" Miller interrupted a little impatiently.

"Can we see them, Mr. Larkin?" asked Thorndyke.

"Certainly," was the reply. "You've got the key. Let me have it when you've seen the rooms; and whatever ever you do," he added with a broad grin, "be careful of the furniture."

"It looks," the superintendent remarked as we crossed the inner court, "as if Mr. Carrington had done a mizzle. That's hopeful. And I see," he continued, glancing at the fresh paint on the door-post as we passed through the entry, "that he hasn't been here long. That's hopeful, too."

We ascended to the first floor, and as Thorndyke unlocked and threw open the door, Miller laughed aloud. The "costly furniture" consisted of a small kitchen table, a Windsor chair and a dilapidated deck-chair. The kitchen contained a gas ring, a small saucepan and a frying-pan, and the bedroom was furnished with a camp-bed devoid of bed-clothes, a wash-hand basin on a packing-case, and a water can.

"Hallo!" exclaimed the superintendent. "He's left a hat behind. Quite a good hat, too." He took it down from the peg, glanced at its exterior and then, turning it over, looked inside. And then his mouth opened with a jerk.

"Great Solomon Eagle!" he gasped. "Do you see, doctor? It's *the* hat."

He held it out to us, and sure enough on the white silk lining of the crown were the embossed, gilt letters, D.B., just as Mr. Byramji had described them.

"Yes," Thorndyke agreed, as the superintendent snatched up a greengrocer's paper bag from the kitchen floor and persuaded the hat into it, "it is undoubtedly the missing link. But what are you going to do now?"

"Do!" exclaimed Miller. "Why, I am going to collar the man. These Baltic boats put in at Hull and Newcastle—perhaps he didn't know that—and they are pretty slow boats, too. I shall wire to Newcastle to have the ship detained and take Inspector Badger down to make the arrest. I'll leave you to explain to the porter, and I owe you a thousand thanks for your valuable tip."

With this he bustled away, clasping the precious hat and from the window we saw him hurry across the court and dart out through the postern into Fetter Lane.

"I think Miller was rather precipitate," said Thorndyke. "He should have got a description of the man and some further particulars."

"Yes," said I. "Miller had much better have waited until you had finished with Mr. Larkin. But you can get some more particulars when we take back the key."

"We shall get more information from the gentleman who lives on the floor above, and I think we will go up and interview him now. I wrote to him last night and made a metallurgical appointment, signing myself W. Polton. Your name, if he should ask, is Stevenson."

As we ascended the stairs to the next floor, I meditated on the rather tortuous proceedings of my usually straightforward colleague. The use of the lumps of quartz was now obvious; but why these mysterious tactics? And why, before knocking at the door, did Thorndyke carefully take the reading of the gas meter on the landing?

The door was opened in response to our knock—a shortish, alert-looking, clean-shaved man in a white overall, who looked at us keenly and rather forbiddingly. But Thorndyke was geniality personified.

"How do you do, Mr. Highley?" said he, holding out his hand, which the metallurgist shook coolly. "You got my letter, I suppose?"

"Yes. But I am not Mr. Highley. He's away and I am carrying on. I think of taking over his business if there is any to take over. My name is Sherwood. Have you got the samples?"

Thorndyke produced the canvas bag, which Mr. Sherwood took from him and emptied out on a bench, picking up the lumps of quartz one by one and examining them closely. Meanwhile Thorndyke took a rapid survey of the premises. Against the wall were two cupel furnaces and a third larger furnace like a small pottery kiln. On a set of narrow shelves were several rows of bone-ash cupels, looking like little white flower-pots, and near them was the cupel-press—an appliance into which powdered bone-ash was fed and compressed by a plunger to form the cupels—while by the side of the press was a tub of bone-ash—a good deal coarser, I noticed, than the usual fine powder. This coarseness was also observed by Thorndyke, who edged up to the tub and dipped his hand into the ash and then wiped his fingers on his handkerchief.

"This stuff doesn't seem to contain much gold," said Mr. Sherwood. "But we shall see when we make the assay."

"What do you think of this?" asked Thorndyke, taking from his pocket the small lump of glittering, golden-looking mineral that he had picked out at the assayist's. Mr. Sherwood took it from him and examined it closely. "This looks more hopeful," said he; "rather rich, in fact."

Thorndyke received this statement with an unmoved countenance; but as for me, I stared at Mr. Sherwood in amazement. For this lump of glittering mineral was simply a fragment of common iron pyrites! It would not have deceived a schoolboy, much less a metallurgist.

Still holding the specimen, and taking a watchmaker's lens from a shelf, Mr. Sherwood moved over to the window. Simultaneously, Thorndyke stepped softly to the cupel shelves and quickly ran his eye along the rows of cupels. Presently he paused at one, examined it more closely, and then, taking it from the shelf, began to pick at it with his finger-nail.

At this moment Mr. Sherwood turned and observed him; and instantly there flashed into the metallurgist's face an expression of mingled anger and alarm.

"Put that down!" he commanded peremptorily, and then, as Thorndyke continued to scrape with his finger nail, he shouted furiously, "Do you hear? Drop it!"

Thorndyke took him literally at his word and let the cupel fall on the floor, when it shattered into innumerable fragments, of which one of the largest separated itself from the rest. Thorndyke pounced upon it, and in an instantaneous glance, as he picked it up, I recognised it as a calcined tooth.

Then followed a few moments of weird, dramatic silence. Thorndyke, holding the tooth between his finger and thumb, looked steadily into the eyes of the metallurgist; and the latter, pallid as a corpse, glared at Thorndyke and furtively unbuttoned his overall.

Suddenly the silence broke into a tumult as bewildering as the crash of a railway collision. Sherwood's right hand darted under his overall. Instantly, Thorndyke snatched up another cupel and hurled it with such truth of aim that it shattered on the metallurgist's forehead. And as he flung the missile, he sprang forward, and delivered a swift upper-cut. There was a thunderous crash, a cloud of white dust, and an automatic pistol clattered along the floor.

I snatched up the pistol and rushed to my friend's assistance. But there was no need. With his great strength and his uncanny skill—to say nothing of the effects of the knock-out blow—Thorndyke had the man pinned down immovably.

"See if you can find some cord, Jervis," he said in a calm, quiet tone that seemed almost ridiculously out of character with the circumstances.

There was no difficulty about this, for several corded boxes stood in a corner of the laboratory. I cut off two lengths, with one of which I secured the prostrate man's arms, and with the other fastened his knees and ankles.

"Now," said Thorndyke, "if you will take charge of his hands, we will make a preliminary inspection. Let us first see if he wears a belt."

Unbuttoning the man's waistcoat, he drew up the shirt, disclosing a broad, webbing belt furnished with several leather pockets, the buttoned flaps of which he felt carefully, regardless of the stream of threats and imprecations that poured from our victim's swollen lips. From the front pockets he proceeded to the back, passing an exploratory hand under the writhing body.

"Ah!" he exclaimed suddenly, "just turn him over, and look out for his heels."

We rolled our captive over, and as Thorndyke "skinned the rabbit," a central pocket came into view, into which, when he had unbuttoned it, he inserted his fingers. "Yes," he continued, "I think this is what we are looking for." He withdrew his fingers, between which he held a small packet of Japanese paper, and with feverish excitement I watched him open out layer after layer of the soft wrapping. As he turned back the last fold a wonderful crimson sparkle told me that the "great ruby" was found.

"There, Jervis," said Thorndyke, holding the magnificent gem towards me in the palm of his hand, "look on this beautiful, sinister thing, charged with untold potentialities of evil—and thank the gods that it is not yours."

He wrapped it up again carefully and, having bestowed it in an inner pocket, said, "And now give me the pistol and run down to the telegraph office and see if you can stop Miller. I should like him to have the credit for this."

I handed him the pistol and made my way out into Fetter Lane and so down to Fleet Street, where at the post office my urgent message was sent off to Scotland Yard immediately. In a few minutes the reply came that Superintendent Miller had not yet left and that he was starting immediately for Clifford's Inn. A quarter of an hour later he drove up in a hansom to the Fetters Lane gate and I conducted him up to the second floor, where Thorndyke introduced him to his prisoner and witnessed the official arrest.

"You don't see how I arrived at it," said Thorndyke as we walked homeward after returning the key. "Well, I am not surprised. The initial evidence was of the weakest; it acquired significance only by cumulative effect. Let us reconstruct it as it developed.

"The derelict hat was, of course, the starting-point. Now, the first thing one noticed was that it appeared to have had more than one owner. No man would buy a new hat that fitted so badly as to need all that packing; and the arrangement of the packing suggested a long-headed man wearing a hat that had belonged to a man with a short head. Then there were the suggestions offered by the slips of paper. The fragmentary address referred to a place the name of which ended in 'n' and the remainder was evidently 'London, W.C.' Now what West Central place names end in 'n'? It was not a street, a square or a court, and Barbican is not in the W.C. district. It was almost certainly one of the half-dozen surviving Inns of Court or Chancery. But, of course, it was not necessarily the address of the owner of the hat.

"The other slip of paper bore the end of a word ending in 'el,' and another word ending in 'eep,' and connected with these were quantities stated in ounces and pennyweights troy weight. But the only persons who use troy weight are those who deal in precious metals. I inferred therefore that the 'el' was part of 'lemel,' and that the 'eep' was part of 'floor-sweep,' an inference that was supported by the respective quantities, three ounces five pennyweights of lemel and nine and a half ounces of floor-sweep."

"What is lemel?" I asked.

"It is the trade name for the gold or silver filings that collect in the 'skin' of a jeweller's bench. Floor-sweep is, of course, the dust swept up on the floor of a jeweller's or goldsmith's workshop. The lemel is actual metal, though not of uniform fineness, but the sweep is a mixture of dirt and metal. Both are saved and sent to the refiners to have the gold and silver extracted.

"This paper, then, was connected either with a gold smith or a gold refiner—who might call himself an assayist or a metallurgist. The connection was supported by the leaf of a price list of gas stoves. A metallurgist would be kept well supplied with lists of gas stoves and furnaces. The traces of lead in the dust from the hat gave us another straw blowing the same direction, for gold assayed by the dry process is fused in the cupel furnace with lead; and as the lead oxidises and the oxide is volatile, traces of lead would tend to appear in the dust deposited in the laboratory.

"The next thing to do was to consult the directory; and when I did so, I found that there were no goldsmiths in any of the Inns and only one assayist—Mr. Highley, of Clifford's Inn. The probabilities therefore, slender as they were, pointed to some connection between this stray hat and Mr. Highley. And this was positively all the information that we had when we came out this afternoon.

"As soon as we got to Clifford's Inn, however, the evidence began to grow like a rolling snowball. First there was Larkin's contribution; and then there was the discovery of the missing hat. Now, as soon as I saw that hat my suspicions fell upon the man upstairs. I felt a conviction that the hat had been left there purposely and that the letter to Larkin was just a red herring to create a false trail. Nevertheless, the presence of that hat completely confirmed the other evidence. It showed that the apparent connection was a real connection."

"But," I asked, "what made you suspect the man upstairs?"

"My dear Jervis!" he exclaimed, "consider the facts. That hat was enough to hang the man who left it there. Can you imagine this astute, wary villain making such an idiot's mistake—going away and leaving the means of his conviction for anyone to find? But you are forgetting that whereas the missing hat was found on the first floor, the murderer's hat was connected with the second floor. The evidence suggested that it was Highley's hat. And now, before we go on to the next stage, let me remind you of those finger-prints. Miller thought that their rough appearance was due to the surface on which they had been made, But it was not. They were the prints of a person who was suffering from *ichthyosis, palmar psoriasis* or sonic dry dermatitis.

"There is one other point. The man we were looking for was a murderer. His life was already forfeit. To such a man another murder more or less is of no consequence. If this man, having laid the false trail, had determined to take sanctuary in Highley's rooms, it was probable that he had already got rid of Highley. And remember that a metallurgist has unrivalled means disposing of a body; for not only is each of his muffle furnaces a miniature crematorium, but the very residue of a cremated body—bone-ash—is one of the materials of his trade.

"When we went upstairs, I first took the reading of the gas meter and ascertained that a large amount of gas had been used recently. Then, when we entered I took the opportunity to shake hands with Mr. Sherwood, and immediately I became aware that he suffered from a rather extreme form of *ichthyosis*. That was the first point of verification. Then we discovered that he actually could not distinguish between iron pyrites and auriferous quartz. He was not a metallurgist at all. He was a masquerader. Then the bone-ash in the tub was mixed with fragments of calcined bone, and the cupels all showed similar fragments. In one of them I could see part of the crown of a tooth. That was pure luck. But observe that by that time I had enough evidence to justify an arrest. The tooth served only to bring the affair to a crisis; and his response to my unspoken accusation saved us the trouble of further search for confirmatory evidence."

"What is not quite clear to me," said I, "is when and why he made away with Highley. As the body has been completely reduced to bone-ash, Highley must have been dead at least some days."

"Undoubtedly," Thorndyke agreed. "I take it that the course of events was like this: The police have been searching eagerly for this man, and every new crime must have made his position more unsafe—for a criminal can never be sure that he has not dropped some clue. It began to be necessary for him to make some arrangements for leaving the country and meanwhile to have a retreat in case his whereabouts should chance to be discovered. Highley's chambers were admirable for both purposes. Here was a solitary man who seldom had a visitor, and who would probably not be missed for some considerable time; and in those chambers were the means of rapidly and completely disposing of the body. The mere murder would be a negligible detail to this ruffian.

"I imagine that Highley was done to death at least a week ago, and that the murderer did not take up his new tenancy until the body was reduced to ash. With that large furnace in addition to the small ones, this would not take long. When the new premises were ready, he could make a sham disappearance to cover his actual flight later; and you must see how perfectly misleading that sham disappearance was. If the police had discovered that hat in the empty room only a week later, they would have been certain that he had escaped to one of the Baltic ports; and while they were following his supposed tracks, he could have gone off comfortably via Folkestone or Southampton."

"Then you think he had only just moved into Highley's rooms?"

"I should say he moved in last night. The murder of Byramji was probably planned on some information that the murderer had picked up, and as soon as it was accomplished he began forthwith to lay down the false tracks. When he reached his rooms yesterday afternoon, he must have written the letter to Larkin and gone off at once to the East End to post it.

"Then he probably had his bushy hair cut short and shaved off his beard and moustache—which would render him quite unrecognisable by Larkin—and moved into Highley's chambers, from which he would have quietly sallied forth in a few days' time to take his passage to the Continent. It was quite a good plan, and but for the accident of taking the wrong hat, would almost certainly have succeeded."

Once every year, on the second of August, there is delivered with unfailing regularity at No. 5A King's Bench Walk a large box of carved sandal-wood filled with the choicest Trichinopoly cheroots and accompanied by an affectionate letter from our late client, Mr. Byramji. For the second of August is the anniversary of the death (in the execution shed at Newgate) of Cornelius Barnett, otherwise known as the "New Jersey Sphinx."

The Old Lag

Among the minor and purely physical pleasures of life, I am disposed to rank very highly that feeling of bodily comfort that one experiences on passing from the outer darkness of a wet winter's night to a cheerful interior made glad by mellow lamplight and blazing hearth. And so I thought when, on a dreary November night, I let myself into our chambers in the Temple and found my friend smoking his pipe in slippered ease, by a roaring fire, and facing an empty arm-chair evidently placed in readiness for me.

As I shed my damp overcoat, I glanced inquisitively at my colleague, for he held in his hand an open letter, and I seemed to perceive in his aspect something meditative and self-communing—something, in short, suggestive of a new case.

"I was just considering," he said, in answer to my inquiring look, "whether I am about to become an accessory after the fact. Read that and give me your opinion."

He handed me the letter, which I read aloud.

"Dear sir,—I am in great danger and distress. A warrant has been issued for my arrest on a charge of which I am entirely innocent. Can I come and see you, and will you let me leave in safety? The bearer will wait for a reply."

"I said 'Yes,' of course; there was nothing else to do," said Thorndyke. "But if I let him go, as I have promised to do, I shall be virtually conniving at his escape."

"Yes, you are taking a risk," I answered. "When is he coming?"

"He was due five minutes ago—and I rather think—yes, here he is."

A stealthy tread on the landing was followed by a soft tapping on the outer door.

217

Thorndyke rose and, flinging open the inner door, unfastened the massive "oak."

"Dr. Thorndyke?" inquired a breathless, quavering voice.

"Yes, come in. You sent me a letter by hand?"

"I did, sir," was the reply; and the speaker entered, but at the sight of me he stopped short.

"This is my colleague, Dr. Jervis," Thorndyke explained. "You need have no—?"

"Oh, I remember him," our visitor interrupted in a tone of relief. "I have seen you both before, you know, and you have seen me too—though I don't suppose you recognise me," he added, with: a sickly smile.

"Frank Belfield?" asked Thorndyke, smiling also.

Our visitor's jaw fell and he gazed at my colleague in sudden dismay.

"And I may remark," pursued Thorndyke, "that for a man in your perilous position, you are running most unnecessary risks. That wig, that false beard and those spectacles—through which you obviously cannot see—are enough to bring the entire police force at your heels. It is not wise for a man who is wanted by the police to make up as though he had just escaped from a comic opera."

Mr. Belfield seated himself with a groan, and, taking off his spectacles, stared stupidly from one of us to the other.

"And now tell us about your little affair," said Thorndyke. "You say that you are innocent?"

"I swear it, doctor," replied Belfield; adding, with great earnestness, "And you may take it from me, sir, that if I was not, I shouldn't be here. It was you that convicted me last time, when I thought myself quite safe, so I know your ways too well to try to gammon you."

"If you are innocent," rejoined Thorndyke, "I will do what I can for you; and if you are not—well, you would have been wiser to stay away."

"I know that well enough," said Belfield, "and I am only afraid that you won't believe what I am going to tell you."

"I shall keep an open mind, at any rate," replied Thorndyke.

"If you only will," groaned Belfield, "I shall have a look in, in spite of them all. You know, sir, that I have been on the crook, but I have paid in full. That job when you tripped me up was the last of it—it was, sir, so help me. It was a woman that changed me—the best and truest woman on God's earth. She said she would marry me when I came out if I promised her to go straight and live an honest life. And she kept her promise—and I have kept mine. She found me work as clerk in a warehouse and I have stuck to it ever since, earning fair wages and building up a good character as an honest, industrious man. I thought all was going well, and that I was settled for life, when only this very morning the whole thing comes tumbling about my ears like a house of cards."

"What happened this morning, then?" asked Thorndyke.

"Why, I was on my way to work when, as I passed the police station, I noticed a bill with the heading 'Wanted' and a photograph. I stopped for a moment to look at it, and you may imagine my feelings when I recognised my own portrait—taken at Holloway—and read my own name and description. I did not stop to read the bill through, but ran back home and told my wife, and she ran down to the station and read the bill carefully. Good God, sir! What do you think I am wanted for?" He paused for a moment, and then replied in breathless tones to his own question: "The Camberwell murder!"

Thorndyke gave a low whistle.

"My wife knows I didn't do it," continued Belfield, "because I was at home all the evening and night; but what use is a man's wife to prove an alibi?"

"Not much, I fear," Thorndyke admitted; "and you have no other witness?"

"Not a soul. We were alone all the evening."

"However," said Thorndyke, "if you are innocent—as I am assuming—the evidence against you must be entirely circumstantial and your alibi may be quite sufficient. Have you any idea of the grounds of suspicion against you?"

"Not the faintest. The papers said that the police had an excellent clue, but they did not say what it was. Probably someone has given false information for the—?"

A sharp rapping at the outer door cut short the explanation, and our visitor rose, trembling and aghast, with beads of sweat standing upon his livid face.

"You had better go into the office, Belfield, while we see who it is," said Thorndyke. "The key is on the inside."

The fugitive wanted no second bidding, but hurried into the empty apartment, and, as the door closed, we heard the key turn in the lock.

As Thorndyke threw open the outer door, he cast a meaning

glance at me over his shoulder which I understood when the new-comer entered the room; for it was none other than Superintendent Miller of Scotland Yard.

"I have just dropped in," said the superintendent, in his brisk, cheerful way, "to ask you to do me a favour. Good-evening, Dr. Jervis. I hear you are reading for the bar; learned counsel soon, sir, hey? Med-ico-legal expert. Dr. Thorndyke's mantle going to fall on you, sir?"

"I hope Dr. Thorndyke's mantle will continue to drape his own majestic form for many a long year yet," I answered; "though he is good enough to spare me a corner—but what on earth have you got there?" For during this dialogue the superintendent had been deftly unfastening a brown-paper parcel, from which he now drew a linen shirt, once white, but now of an unsavoury grey.

"I want to know what this is," said Miller, exhibiting a brownish-red stain on one sleeve. "Just look at that, sir, and tell me if it is blood, and, if so, is it human blood?"

"Really, Miller," said Thorndyke, with a smile, "you flatter me; but I am not like the wise woman of Bagdad who could tell you how many stairs the patient had tumbled down by merely looking at his tongue. I must examine this very thoroughly. When do you want to know?"

"I should like to know tonight," replied the detective.

"Can I cut a piece out to put under the microscope?"

"I would rather you did not," was the reply.

"Very well; you shall have the information in about an hour."

"It's very good of you, doctor," said the detective; and he was tak-ing up his hat preparatory to departing, when Thorndyke said sud-denly—"By the way, there is a little matter that I was going to speak to you about. It refers to this Camberwell murder case. I understand you have a clue to the identity of the murderer?"

"Clue!" exclaimed the superintendent contemptuously. "We have spotted our man all right, if we could only lay hands on him; but he has given us the slip for the moment."

"Who is the man?" asked Thorndyke.

The detective looked doubtfully at Thorndyke for some seconds and then said, with evident reluctance: "I suppose there is no harm in telling you—especially as you probably know already"—this with a sly grin; "it's an old crook named Belfield."

"And what is the evidence against him?"

Again the superintendent looked doubtful and again relented.

"Why, the case is as clear as—as cold Scotch," he said (here Thorndyke in illustration of this figure of speech produced a decanter, a syphon and a tumbler, which he pushed towards the officer). "You see, sir, the silly fool went and stuck his sweaty hand on the window; and there we found the marks—four fingers and a thumb, as beautiful prints as you could wish to see. Of course we cut out the piece of glass and took it up to the Fingerprint Department; they turned up their files and out came Mr. Belfield's record, with his fingerprints and photograph all complete."

"And the fingerprints on the window-pane were identical with those on the prison form?"

"Identical."

"H'm!" Thorndyke reflected for a while, and the superintendent watched him foxily over the edge of his tumbler.

"I guess you are retained to defend Belfield," the latter observed presently.

"To look into the case generally," replied Thorndyke.

"And I expect you know where the beggar is hiding," continued the detective.

"Belfield's address has not yet been communicated to me," said Thorndyke. "I am merely to investigate the case—and there is no reason, Miller, why you and I should be at cross purposes. We are both working at the case; you want to get a conviction and you want to convict the right man."

"That's so—and Belfield's the right man—but what do you want of us, doctor?"

"I should like to see the piece of glass with the fingerprints on it, and the prison form, and take a photograph of each. And I should like to examine the room in which the murder took place—you have it locked up, I suppose?"

"Yes, we have the keys. Well, it's all rather irregular, letting you see the things. Still, you've always played the game fairly with us, so we might stretch a point. Yes, I will. I'll come back in an hour for your report and bring the glass and the form. I can't let them go out of my custody, you know. I'll be off now—no, thank you, not another drop."

The superintendent caught up his hat and strode away, the personification of mental alertness and bodily vigour.

No sooner had the door closed behind him than Thorndyke's stolid calm changed instantaneously into feverish energy. Darting to the electric bell that rang into the laboratories above, he pressed the button while he gave me my directions.

"Have a look at that bloodstain, Jervis, while I am finishing with Belfield. Don't wet it; scrape it into a drop of warm normal saline solution."

I hastened to reach down the microscope and set out on the table the necessary apparatus and reagents, and, as I was thus occupied, a latch-key turned in the outer door and our invaluable helpmate, Polton, entered the room in his habitual silent, unobtrusive fashion.

"Let me have the fingerprint apparatus, please, Polton," said Thorndyke; "and have the copying camera ready by nine o'clock. I am expecting Mr. Miller with some documents."

As his laboratory assistant departed, Thorndyke rapped at the office door.

"It's all clear, Belfield," he called; "you can come out."

The key turned and the prisoner emerged, looking ludicrously woebegone in his ridiculous wig and beard.

"I am going to take your fingerprints, to compare with some that the police found on the window."

"Fingerprints!" exclaimed Belfield, in a tone of dismay. "They don't say they're my fingerprints, do they, sir?"

"They do indeed," replied Thorndyke, eyeing the man narrowly. "They have compared them with those taken when you were at Holloway, and they say that they are identical."

"Good God!" murmured Belfield, collapsing into a chair, faint and trembling. "They must have made some awful mistake. But are mistakes possible with fingerprints?"

"Now look here, Belfield," said Thorndyke. "Were you in that house that night, or were you not? It is of no use for you to tell me any lies."

"I was not there, sir; I swear to God I was not."

"Then they cannot be your fingerprints, that is obvious." Here he stepped to the door to intercept Polton, from whom he received a substantial box, which he brought in and placed on the table.

"Tell me all you know about this case," he continued, as he set out the contents of the box on the table.

"I know nothing about it whatever," replied Belfield; "nothing, at least, except—?"

"Except what?" demanded Thorndyke, looking up sharply as he squeezed a drop from a tube of fingerprint ink onto a smooth copper plate.

"Except that the murdered man, Caldwell, was a retired fence."

"A fence, was he?" said Thorndyke in a tone of interest.

"Yes; and I suspect he was a 'nark' too. He knew more than was wholesome for a good many."

"Did he know anything about you?"

"Yes; but nothing that the police don't know."

With a small roller Thorndyke spread the ink upon the plate into a thin film. Then he laid on the edge of the table a smooth white card and, taking Belfield's right hand, pressed the forefinger firmly but quickly, first on the inked plate and then on the card, leaving on the latter a clear print of the fingertip. This process he repeated with the other fingers and thumb, and then took several additional prints of each.

"That was a nasty injury to your forefinger, Belfield," said Thorndyke, holding the finger to the light and examining the tip carefully. "How did you do it?"

"Stuck a tin-opener into it—a dirty one, too. It was bad for weeks; in fact, Dr. Sampson thought at one time that he would have to amputate the finger."

"How long ago was that?"

"Oh, nearly a year ago, sir."

Thorndyke wrote the date of the injury by the side of the finger-print and then, having rolled up the inking plate afresh, laid on the table several larger cards. "I am now going to take the prints of the four fingers and the thumb all at once," he said.

"They only took the four fingers at once at the prison," said Belfield. "They took the thumb separately."

"I know," replied Thorndyke; "but I am going to take the impression just as it would appear on the window glass."

He took several impressions thus, and then, having looked at his watch, he began to repack the apparatus in its box. While doing this, he glanced, from time to time, in meditative fashion, at the suspected man who sat, the living picture of misery and terror, wiping the greasy ink from his trembling fingers with his handkerchief.

"Belfield," he said at length, "you have sworn to me that you are an innocent man and are trying to live an honest life. I believe you; but in a few minutes I shall know for certain."

"Thank God for that, sir," exclaimed Belfield, brightening up wonderfully.

"And now," said Thorndyke, "you had better go back into the office, for I am expecting Superintendent Miller, and he may be here at any moment."

Belfield hastily slunk back into the office, locking the door after him, and Thorndyke, having returned the box to the laboratory and deposited the cards bearing the fingerprints in a drawer, came round to inspect my work. I had managed to detach a tiny fragment of dried clot from the blood-stained garment, and this, in a drop of normal saline solution, I now had under the microscope.

"What do you make out, Jervis?" my colleague asked.

"Oval corpuscles with distinct *nuclei*," I answered.

"Ah," said Thorndyke, "that will be good hearing for some poor devil. Have you measured them?"

"Yes. Long diameter one twenty-one hundredth of an inch; short diameter about one thirty-four hundredth of an inch."

Thorndyke reached down an indexed note-book from a shelf of reference volumes and consulted a table of histological measurements.

"That would seem to be the blood of a pheasant, then, or it might, more probably, be that of a common fowl." He applied his eye to the microscope and, fitting in the eyepiece micrometer, verified my measurements. He was thus employed when a sharp tap was heard on the outer door, and rising to open it he admitted the superintendent.

"I see you are at work on my little problem, doctor," said the latter, glancing at the microscope. "What do you make of that stain?"

"It is the blood of a bird—probably a pheasant, or perhaps a common fowl."

The superintendent slapped his thigh. "Well, I'm hanged!" he exclaimed. "You're a regular wizard, doctor, that's what you are. The fellow said he got that stain through handling a wounded pheasant and here are you able to tell us yes or no without a hint from us to help you. Well, you've done my little job for me, sir, and I'm much obliged to you; now I'll carry out my part of the bargain." He opened a handbag and drew forth a wooden frame and a blue foolscap envelope and laid them with extreme care on the table.

"There you are, sir," said he, pointing to the frame; "you will find Mr. Belfield's trademark very neatly executed, and in the envelope is the fingerprint sheet for comparison."

Thorndyke took up the frame and examined it. It enclosed two sheets of glass, one being the portion of the window-pane and the other a cover-glass to protect the fingerprints. Laying a sheet of white paper on the table, where the light was strongest, Thorndyke held the frame over it and gazed at the glass in silence, but with that faint lighting up of his impassive face which I knew so well and which meant so much to me. I walked round, and looking over his shoulder saw upon the glass the beautifully distinct imprints of four fingers and a thumb—the fingertips, in fact, of an open hand.

After regarding the frame attentively for some time, Thorndyke produced from his pocket a little wash-leather bag, from which he extracted a powerful doublet lens, and with the aid of this he again explored the fingerprints, dwelling especially upon the print of the forefinger.

"I don't think you will find much amiss with those fingerprints, doctor," said the superintendent, "they are as clear as if he made them on purpose."

"They are indeed," replied Thorndyke, with an inscrutable smile, "exactly as if he had made them on purpose. And how beautifully clean the glass is—as if he had polished it before making the impression."

The superintendent glanced at Thorndyke with quick suspicion; but the smile had faded and given place to a wooden immobility from which nothing could be gleaned.

When he had examined the glass exhaustively, Thorndyke drew the fingerprint form from its envelope and scanned it quickly, glancing repeatedly from the paper to the glass and from the glass to the paper. At length he laid them both on the table, and turning to the detective looked him steadily in the face.

"I think, Miller," said he, "that I can give you a hint."

"Indeed, sir? And what might that be?"

"It is this: you are after the wrong man."

The superintendent snorted—not a loud snort, for that would have been rude, and no officer could be more polite than Superintendent Miller. But it conveyed a protest which he speedily followed up in words.

"You don't mean to say that the prints on that glass are not the fingerprints of Frank Belfield?"

"I say that those prints were not made by Frank Belfield," Thorndyke replied firmly.

"Do you admit, sir, that the fingerprints on the official form were made by him?"

"I have no doubt that they were."

"Well, sir, Mr. Singleton, of the Fingerprint Department, has compared the prints on the glass with those on the form and he says they are identical; and I have examined them and I say they are identical."

"Exactly," said Thorndyke; "and I have examined them and I say they are identical—and that therefore those on the glass cannot have been made by Belfield."

The superintendent snorted again—somewhat louder this time—and gazed at Thorndyke with wrinkled brows.

"You are not pulling my leg, I suppose, sir?" he asked, a little sourly.

"I should as soon think of tickling a porcupine," Thorndyke answered, with a suave smile.

"Well," rejoined the bewildered detective, "if I didn't know you, sir, I should say you were talking confounded nonsense. Perhaps you wouldn't mind explaining what you mean."

"Supposing," said Thorndyke, "I make it clear to you that those prints on the windowpane were not made by Belfield. Would you still execute the warrant?"

"What do you think?" exclaimed Miller. "Do you suppose we should go into court to have you come and knock the bottom out of our case, like you did in that Hornby affair? By the way, that was a fingerprint case too, now I come to think of it," and the superintendent suddenly became thoughtful.

"You have often complained," pursued Thorndyke, "that I have withheld information from you and sprung unexpected evidence on you at the trial. Now I am going to take you into my confidence, and when I have proved to you that this clue of yours is a false one, I shall expect you to let this poor devil Belfield go his way in peace."

The superintendent grunted—a form of utterance that committed him to nothing.

"These prints," continued Thorndyke, taking up the frame once more, "present several features of interest, one of which, at least, ought not to have escaped you and Mr. Singleton, as it seems to have done. Just look at that thumb."

The superintendent did so, and then pored over the official paper.

"Well," he said, "I don't see anything the matter with it. It's exactly like the print on the paper."

"Of course it is," rejoined Thorndyke, "and that is just the point. It ought not to be. The print of the thumb on the paper was taken separately from the fingers. And why? Because it was impossible to take it at the same time. The thumb is in a different plane from the fingers; when the hand is laid flat on any surface—as this windowpane, for instance—the palmar surfaces of the fingers touch it, whereas it is the side of the thumb which comes in contact and not the palmar surface. But in this"—he tapped the framed glass with his finger—"the prints show the palmar surfaces of all the five digits in contact at once, which is an impossibility. Just try to put your own thumb in that position and you will see that it is so."

The detective spread out his hand on the table and immediately perceived the truth of my colleague's statement.

"And what does that prove?" he asked.

"It proves that the thumbprint on the window-pane was not made at the same time as the fingerprints—that it was added separately; and that fact seems to prove that the prints were not made accidentally, but—as you ingeniously suggested just now—were put there for a purpose."

"I don't quite see the drift of all this," said the superintendent, rubbing the back of his head perplexedly; "and you said a while back that the prints on the glass can't be Belfield's because they are identical with the prints on the form. Now that seems to me sheer nonsense, if you will excuse my saying so."

"And yet," replied Thorndyke, "it is the actual fact. Listen: these prints"—here he took up the official sheet—"were taken at Holloway six years ago. These"—pointing to the framed glass—"were made within the present week. The one is, as regards the ridge-pattern, a perfect duplicate of the other. Is that not so?"

"That is so, doctor," agreed the superintendent.

"Very well. Now suppose I were to tell you that within the last twelve months something had happened to Belfield that made an appreciable change in the ridge-pattern on one of his fingers?"

"But is such a thing possible?"

"It is not only possible but it has happened. I will show you."

He brought forth from the drawer the cards on which Belfield had made his fingerprints, and laid them before the detective.

"Observe the prints of the forefinger," he said, indicating them; "there are a dozen, in all, and you will notice in each a white line crossing the ridges and dividing them. That line is caused by a scar, which has destroyed a portion of the ridges, and is now an integral part of Belfield's fingerprint. And since no such blank line is to be seen in this print on the glass—in which the ridges appear perfect, as they were before the injury—it follows that that print could not have been made by Belfield's finger."

"There is no doubt about the injury, I suppose?"

"None whatever. There is the scar to prove it, and I can produce the surgeon who attended Belfield at the time."

The officer rubbed his head harder than before, and regarded Thorndyke with puckered brows.

"This is a teaser," he growled, "it is indeed. What you say, sir, seems perfectly sound, and yet—there are those fingerprints on the window-glass. Now you can't get fingerprints without fingers, can you?"

"Undoubtedly you can," said Thorndyke.

"I should want to see that done before I could believe even you, sir," said Miller.

"You shall see it done now," was the calm rejoinder. "You have evidently forgotten the Hornby case—the case of the Red Thumb-mark, as the newspapers called it."

"I only heard part of it," replied Miller, "and I didn't really follow the evidence in that."

"Well, I will show you a relic of that case," said Thorndyke. He unlocked a cabinet and took from one of the shelves a small box labelled "Hornby," which, being opened, was seen to contain a folded paper, a little red-covered oblong book and what looked like a large boxwood pawn.

"This little book," Thorndyke continued, "is a 'thumbograph'—a sort of fingerprint album—I dare say you know the kind of thing."

The superintendent nodded contemptuously at the little volume.

"Now while Dr. Jervis is finding us the print we want, I will run up to the laboratory for an inked slab."

He handed me the little book and, as he left the room, I began to turn over the leaves—not without emotion, for it was this very "thumbograph" that first introduced me to my wife, as is related elsewhere—glancing at the various prints above the familiar names and marvelling afresh at the endless variations of pattern that they displayed. At length I came upon two thumbprints of which one—the left—was marked by a longitudinal white line—evidently the trace of a scar; and underneath them was written the signature "Reuben Hornby."

At this moment Thorndyke re-entered the room carrying the inked slab, which he laid on the table, and seating himself between the superintendent and me, addressed the former.

"Now, Miller, here are two thumb-prints made by a gentleman named Reuben Hornby. Just glance at the left one; it is a highly characteristic print."

"Yes," agreed Miller, "one could swear to that from memory, I should think."

"Then look at this." Thorndyke took the paper from the box and, unfolding it, handed it to the detective. It bore a pencilled inscription, and on it were two blood-smears and a very distinct thumb-print in blood. "What do you say to that thumb-print?"

"Why," answered Miller, "it's this one, of course; Reuben Hornby's left thumb."

"Wrong, my friend," said Thorndyke. "It was made by an ingenious gentleman named Walter Hornby (whom you followed from the Old Bailey and lost on Ludgate Hill); but not with his thumb."

"How, then?" demanded the superintendent incredulously.

"In this way." Thorndyke took the boxwood "pawn" from its receptacle and pressed its flat base onto the inked slab; then lifted it and pressed it onto the back of a visiting-card, and again raised it; and now the card was marked by a very distinct thumbprint.

"My God!" exclaimed the detective, picking up the card and viewing it with a stare of dismay, "this is the very devil, sir. This fairly knocks the bottom out of fingerprint identification. May I ask, sir, how you made that stamp—for I suppose you did make it?"

"Yes, we made it here, and the process we used was practically that used by photo-engravers in making line blocks; that is to say, we photographed one of Mr. Hornby's thumbprints, printed it on a plate of chrome-gelatine, developed the plate with hot water and this"—here he touched the embossed surface of the stamp—"is what remained. But we could have done it in various other ways; for instance, with common transfer paper and lithographic stone; indeed, I assure you, Miller, that there is nothing easier to forge than a fingerprint, and it can be done with such perfection that the forger himself cannot tell his own forgery from a genuine original, even when they are placed side by side."

"Well, I'm hanged," grunted the superintendent, "you've fairly knocked me, this time, doctor." He rose gloomily and prepared to depart. "I suppose," he added, "your interest in this case has lapsed, now Belfield's out of it?"

"Professionally, yes; but I am disposed to finish the case for my own satisfaction. I am quite curious as to who our too-ingenious friend may be."

Miller's face brightened. "We shall give you every facility, you know—and that reminds me that Singleton gave me these two photographs for you, one of the official paper and one of the prints on the glass. Is there anything more that we can do for you?"

"I should like to have a look at the room in which the murder took place."

"You shall, doctor; tomorrow, if you like; I'll meet you there in the morning at ten, if that will do."

It would do excellently, Thorndyke assured him, and with this the superintendent took his departure in renewed spirits.

We had only just closed the door when there came a hurried and urgent tapping upon it, whereupon I once more threw it open, and a quietly-dressed woman in a thick veil, who was standing on the threshold, stepped quickly past me into the room.

"Where is my husband?" she demanded, as I closed the door; and then, catching sight of Thorndyke, she strode up to him with a threatening air and a terrified but angry face.

"What have you done with my husband, sir?" she repeated. "Have you betrayed him, after giving your word? I met a man who looked like a police officer on the stairs."

"Your husband, Mrs. Belfield, is here and quite safe," replied Thorndyke. "He has locked himself in that room," indicating the office.

Mrs. Belfield darted across and rapped smartly at the door. "Are you there, Frank?" she called.

In immediate response the key turned, the door opened and Belfield emerged looking very pale and worn.

"You have kept me a long time in there, sir," he said.

"It took me a long time to prove to Superintendent Miller that he was after the wrong man. But I succeeded, and now, Belfield, you are free. The charge against you is withdrawn."

Belfield stood for a while as one stupefied, while his wife, after a moment of silent amazement, flung her arms round his neck and burst into tears. "But how did you know I was innocent, sir?" demanded the bewildered Belfield.

"Ah! how did I? Every man to his trade, you know. Well, I congratulate you, and now go home and have a square meal and get a good night's rest."

He shook hands with his clients—vainly endeavouring to prevent Mrs. Belfield from kissing his hand—and stood at the open door listening until the sound of their retreating footsteps died away.

"A noble little woman, Jervis," said he, as he closed the door. "In another moment she would have scratched my face—and I mean to find out the scoundrel who tried to wreck her happiness."

PART 2. THE SHIP OF THE DESERT

The case which I am now about to describe has always appeared to me a singularly instructive one, as illustrating the value and importance of that fundamental rule in the carrying out of investigations which Thorndyke had laid down so emphatically—the rule that all facts, in any way relating to a case, should be collected impartially and without reference to any theory, and each fact, no matter how trivial or apparently irrelevant, carefully studied. But I must not anticipate the remarks of my learned and talented friend on this subject which I have to chronicle anon; rather let me proceed to the case itself.

I had slept at our chambers in King's Bench Walk—as I commonly did two or three nights a week—and on coming down to the sitting-room, found Thorndyke's man, Polton, putting the last touches to the breakfast-table, while Thorndyke himself was poring over two photographs of fingerprints, of which he seemed to be taking elaborate measurements with a pair of hair-dividers. He greeted me with his quiet, genial smile and, laying down the dividers, took his seat at the breakfast-table.

"You are coming with me this morning, I suppose," said he; "the Camberwell murder case, you know."

"Of course I am if you will have me, but I know practically nothing of the case. Could you give me an outline of the facts that are known?"

Thorndyke looked at me solemnly, but with a mischievous twinkle. "This," he said, "is the old story of the fox and the crow; you '*bid me discourse*,' and while I '*enchant thine ear*,' you claw to windward with the broiled ham. A deep-laid plot, my learned brother."

"And such," I exclaimed, "is the result of contact with the criminal classes!"

"I am sorry that you regard yourself in that light," he retorted, with a malicious smile. "However, with regard to this case. The facts are briefly these: The murdered man, Caldwell, who seems to have been formerly a receiver of stolen goods and probably a police spy as well, lived a solitary life in a small house with only an elderly woman to attend him.

"A week ago this woman went to visit a married daughter and

stayed the night with her, leaving Caldwell alone in the house. When she returned on the following morning she found her master lying dead on the floor of his office, or study, in a small pool of blood.

"The police surgeon found that he had been dead about twelve hours. He had been killed by a single blow, struck from behind, with some heavy implement, and a jemmy which lay on the floor beside him fitted the wound exactly. The deceased wore a dressing-gown and no collar, and a bedroom candlestick lay upside down on the floor, although gas was laid on in the room; and as the window of the office appears to have been forced with the jemmy that was found, and there were distinct footprints on the flowerbed outside the window, the police think that the deceased was undressing to go to bed when he was disturbed by the noise of the opening window; that he went down to the office and, as he entered, was struck down by the burglar who was lurking behind the door.

"On the window-glass the police found the greasy impression of an open right hand, and, as you know, the fingerprints were identified by the experts as those of an old convict named Belfield. As you also know, I proved that those fingerprints were, in reality, forgeries, executed with rubber or gelatine stamps. That is an outline of the case."

The close of this recital brought our meal to an end, and we prepared for our visit to the scene of the crime. Thorndyke slipped into his pocket his queer outfit—somewhat like that of a field geologist—locked up the photographs, and we set forth by way of the Embankment.

"The police have no clue, I suppose, to the identity of the murderer, now that the fingerprints have failed?" I asked, as we strode along together.

"I expect not," he replied, "though they might have if they examined their material. I made out a rather interesting point this morning, which is this: the man who made those sham fingerprints used two stamps, one for the thumb and the other for the four fingers; and the original from which those stamps were made was the official fingerprint form."

"How did you discover that?" I inquired.

"It was very simple. You remember that Mr. Singleton of the Fingerprint Department sent me, by Superintendent Miller, two photographs, one of the prints on the window and one of the official form with Belfield's fingerprints on it. Well, I have compared them and made the most minute measurements of each, and they are obviously duplicates. Not only are all the little imperfections on the form—due to defective inking—reproduced faithfully on the window-pane, but the relative positions of the four fingers on both cases agree to the hundredth of an inch. Of course the thumb stamp was made by taking an oval out of the rolled impression on the form."

"Then do you suggest that this murder was committed by some-one connected with the Fingerprint Department at Scotland Yard?"

"Hardly. But someone has had access to the forms. There has been leakage somewhere."

When we arrived at the little detached house in which the mur-dered man had lived, the door was opened by an elderly woman, and our friend, Superintendent Miller, greeted us in the hall.

"We are all ready for you, doctor," said he. "Of course, the things have all been gone over once, but we are turning them out more thor-oughly now." He led the way into the small, barely-furnished office in which the tragedy had occurred. A dark stain on the carpet and a square hole in one of the window-panes furnished memorials of the crime, which were supplemented by an odd assortment of objects laid out on the newspaper-covered table. These included silver teaspoons, watches, various articles of jewellery, from which the stones had been removed—none of them of any considerable value—and a roughly-made jemmy.

"I don't know why Caldwell should have kept all these odds and ends," said the detective superintendent. "There is stuff here, that I can identify, from six different burglaries—and not a conviction among the six."

Thorndyke looked over the collection with languid interest; he was evidently disappointed at finding the room so completely turned out.

"Have you any idea what has been taken?" he asked.

"Not the least. We don't even know if the safe was opened. The keys were on the writing-table, so I suppose he went through every-thing, though I don't see why he left these things if he did. We found them all in the safe."

"Have you powdered the jemmy?"

The superintendent turned very red. "Yes," he growled, "but some half-dozen blithering idiots had handled the thing before I saw it—been trying it on the window, the blighters—so, of course, it showed nothing but the marks of their beastly paws."

"The window had not really been forced, I suppose?" said

Thorndyke.

"No," replied Miller, with a glance of surprise at my colleague, "that was a plant; so were the footprints. He must have put on a pair of Caldwell's boots and gone out and made them—unless Caldwell made them himself, which isn't likely."

"Have you found any letter or telegram?"

"A letter making an appointment for nine o'clock on the night of the murder. No signature or address, and the handwriting evidently disguised."

"Is there anything that furnishes any sort of clue?"

"Yes, sir, there is. There's this, which we found in the safe." He produced a small parcel which he proceeded to unfasten, looking somewhat queerly at Thorndyke the while. It contained various odds and ends of jewellery, and a smaller parcel formed of a pocket-handkerchief tied with tape. This the detective also unfastened, revealing half-a-dozen silver teaspoons, all engraved with the same crest, two salt-cellars and a gold locket bearing a monogram. There was also a half-sheet of note-paper on which was written, in a manifestly disguised hand:

"These are the goods I told you about. F. B."

But what riveted Thorndyke's attention and mine was the handkerchief itself (which was not a very clean one and was sullied by one or two small bloodstains), for it was marked in one corner with the name "F. Belfield," legibly printed in marking-ink with a rubber stamp.

Thorndyke and the superintendent looked at one another and both smiled.

"I know what you are thinking, sir," said the latter.

"I am sure you do," was the reply, "and it is useless to pretend that you don't agree with me."

"Well, sir," said Miller doggedly, "if that handkerchief has been put there as a plant, it's Belfield's business to prove it. You see, doctor," he added persuasively, "it isn't this job only that's affected. Those spoons, those salt-cellars and that locket are part of the proceeds of the Winchmore Hill burglary, and we want the gentleman who did that crack—we want him very badly."

"No doubt you do," replied Thorndyke, "but this handkerchief won't help you. A sharp counsel—Mr. Anstey, for instance—would demolish it in five minutes. I assure you, Miller, that handkerchief has no evidential value whatever, whereas it might prove an invaluable instrument of research. The best thing you can do is to hand it over to me and let me see what I can learn from it."

The superintendent was obviously dissatisfied, but he eventually agreed, with manifest reluctance, to Thorndyke's suggestion.

"Very well, doctor," he said; "you shall have it for a day or two. Do you want the spoons and things as well?"

"No. Only the handkerchief and the paper that was in it."

The two articles were accordingly handed to him and deposited in a tin box which he usually carried in his pocket, and, after a few more words with the disconsolate detective, we took our departure.

"A very disappointing morning," was Thorndyke's comment as we walked away. "Of course the room ought to have been examined by an expert before anything was moved."

"Have you picked up anything in the way of information?" I asked.

"Very little excepting confirmation of my original theory. You see, this man Caldwell was a receiver and evidently a police spy. He gave useful information to the police, and they, in return, refrained from inconvenient inquiries. But a spy, or 'nark,' is nearly always a black-mailer too, and the probabilities in this case are that some crook, on whom Caldwell was putting the screw rather too tightly, made an appointment for a meeting when the house was empty, and just knocked Caldwell on the head.

"The crime was evidently planned beforehand, and the murderer came prepared to kill several birds with one stone. Thus he brought with him the stamps to make the sham fingerprints on the window, and I have no doubt that he also brought this handkerchief and the various oddments of plate and jewellery from those burglaries that Miller is so keen about, and planted them in the safe. You noticed, I suppose, that none of the things were of any value, but all were capable of easy identification?"

"Yes, I noticed that. His object, evidently, was to put those burglaries as well as the murder onto poor Belfield."

"Exactly. And you see what Miller's attitude is; Belfield is the bird in the hand, whereas the other man—if there is another—is still in the bush; so Belfield is to be followed up and a conviction obtained if possible. If he is innocent, that is his affair, and it is for him to prove it."

"And what shall you do next?" I asked.

"I shall telegraph to Belfield to come and see us this evening. He may be able to tell us something about this handkerchief that, with the clue we already have, may put us on the right track. What time is your consultation?"

"Twelve-thirty—and here comes my 'bus. I shall be in to lunch." I sprang onto the footboard, and as I took my seat on the roof and looked back at my friend striding along with an easy swing, I knew that he was deep in thought, though automatically attentive to all that was happening. My consultation—it was a lunacy case of some importance—was over in time to allow of my return to our chambers punctually at the luncheon hour; and as I entered, I was at once struck by something new in Thorndyke's manner—a certain elation and gaiety which I had learned to associate with a point scored successfully in some intricate and puzzling case. He made no confidences, however, and seemed, in fact, inclined to put away, for a time, all his professional cares and business.

"Shall we have an afternoon off, Jervis?" he said gaily. "It is a fine day and work is slack just now. What say you to the Zoo? They have a splendid chimpanzee and several specimens of that remarkable fish *Periophthalmos Kolreuteri*. Shall we go?"

"By all means," I replied; "and we will mount the elephant, if you like, and throw buns to the grizzly bear and generally renew our youth like the eagle."

But when, an hour later, we found ourselves in the gardens, I began to suspect my friend of some ulterior purpose in this holiday jaunt; for it was not the chimpanzee or even the wonderful fish that attracted his attention. On the contrary, he hung about the vicinity of the lamas and camels in a way that I could not fail to notice; and even there it appeared to be the sheds and houses rather than the animals themselves that interested him.

"Behold, Jervis," he said presently, as a saddled camel of seedy aspect was led towards its house, "behold the ship of the desert, with raised saloon-deck amidships, fitted internally with watertight compartments and displaying the effects of rheumatoid arthritis in his starboard hip-joint. Let us go and examine him before he hauls into dock." We took a cross-path to intercept the camel on its way to its residence, and Thorndyke moralized as we went.

"It is interesting," he remarked, "to note the way in which these specialized animals, such as the horse, the reindeer and the camel, have been appropriated by man, and their special character made to subserve human needs. Think, for instance, of the part the camel has played in history, in ancient commerce—and modern too, for that matter—and in the diffusion of culture; and of the role he has enacted in war and conquest from the Egyptian campaign of Cambyses down to that of Kitchener. Yes, the camel is a very remarkable animal, though it must be admitted that this particular specimen is a scurvy-looking beast."

The camel seemed to be sensible of these disparaging remarks, for as it approached it saluted Thorndyke with a supercilious grin and then turned away its head.

"Your charge is not as young as he used to be," Thorndyke observed to the man who was leading the animal.

"No, sir, he isn't; he's getting old, and that's the fact. He shows it too."

"I suppose," said Thorndyke, strolling towards the house by the man's side, "these beasts require a deal of attention?"

"You're right, sir; and nasty-tempered brutes they are."

"So I have heard; but they are interesting creatures, the camels and lamas. Do you happen to know if complete sets of photographs of them are to be had here?"

"You can get a good many at the lodge, sir," the man replied, "but not all, I think. If you want a complete set, there's one of our men in the camel-house that could let you have them; he takes the photos himself, and very clever he is at it, too. But he isn't here just now."

"Perhaps you could give me his name so that I could write to him," said Thorndyke.

"Yes, sir. His name is Woodthorpe—Joseph Woodthorpe. He'll do anything for you to order. Thank you, sir; good-afternoon, sir;" and pocketing an unexpected tip, the man led his charge towards its lair.

Thorndyke's absorbing interest in the camels seemed now suddenly to become extinct, and he suffered me to lead him to any part of the gardens that attracted me, showing an imperial interest in all the inmates from the insects to the elephants, and enjoying his holiday—if it was one—with the gaiety and high spirits of a schoolboy. Yet he never let slip a chance of picking up a stray hair or feather, but gathered up each with care, wrapped it in its separate paper, on which was written its description, and deposited it in his tin collecting-box.

"You never know," he remarked, as we turned away from the ostrich enclosure, "when a specimen for comparison may be of vital importance. Here, for instance, is a small feather of a cassowary, and here the hair of a wapiti deer; now the recognition of either of those might, in certain circumstances, lead to the detection of a criminal or save the life of an innocent man. The thing has happened repeatedly, and may happen again tomorrow."

"You must have an enormous collection of hairs in your cabinet," I remarked, as we walked home.

"I have," he replied, "probably the largest in the world. And as to other microscopical objects of medico-legal interest, such as dust and mud from different localities and from special industries and manufactures, fibres, food-products and drugs, my collection is certainly unique."

"And you have found your collection useful in your work?" I asked.

"Constantly. Over and over again I have obtained, by reference to my specimens, the most unexpected evidence, and the longer I practise, the more I become convinced that the microscope is the sheet-anchor of the medical jurist."

"By the way," I said, "you spoke of sending a telegram to Belfield. Did you send it?"

"Yes. I asked him to come to see me tonight at half-past eight, and, if possible, bring his wife with him. I want to get to the bottom of that handkerchief mystery."

"But do you think he will tell you the truth about it?"

"That is impossible to judge; he will be a fool if he does not. But I think he will; he has a godly fear of me and my methods."

As soon as our dinner was finished and cleared away, Thorndyke produced the "collecting-box" from his pocket, and began to sort out the day's "catch," giving explicit directions to Polton for the disposal of each specimen. The hairs and small feathers were to be mounted as microscopic objects, while the larger feathers were to be placed, each in its separate labelled envelope, in its appropriate box.

While these directions were being given, I stood by the window absently gazing out as I listened, gathering many a useful hint in the technique of preparation and preservation, and filled with admiration alike at my colleague's exhaustive knowledge of practical detail and the perfect manner in which he had trained his assistant. Suddenly I started, for a well-known figure was crossing from Crown Office Row and evidently bearing down on our chambers.

"My word, Thorndyke," I exclaimed, "here's a pretty mess!"

"What is the matter?" he asked, looking up anxiously.

"Superintendent Miller heading straight for our doorway. And it is now twenty minutes past eight."

Thorndyke laughed. "It will be a quaint position," he remarked, "and somewhat of a shock for Belfield. But it really doesn't matter;

in fact, I think, on the whole, I am rather pleased that he should have come."

The superintendent's brisk knock was heard a few moments later, and when he was admitted by Polton, he entered and looked round the room a little, sheepishly.

"I am ashamed to come worrying you like this, sir," he began apologetically.

"Not at all," replied Thorndyke, serenely slipping the cassowary's feather into an envelope, and writing the name, date and locality on the outside. "I am your servant in this case, you know. Polton, whisky and soda for the superintendent."

"You see, sir," continued Miller, "our people are beginning to fuss about this case, and they don't approve of my having handed that handkerchief and the paper over to you as they will have to be put in evidence."

"I thought they might object," remarked Thorndyke.

"So did I, sir; and they do. And, in short, they say that I have got to get them back at once. I hope it won't put you out, sir."

"Not in the least," said Thorndyke. "I have asked Belfield to come here tonight—I expect him in a few minutes—and when I have heard what he has to say I shall have no further use for the handkerchief."

"You're not going to show it to him!" exclaimed the detective, aghast.

"Certainly I am."

"You mustn't do that, sir. I can't sanction it; I can't indeed."

"Now, look you here, Miller," said Thorndyke, shaking his fore-finger at the officer; "I am working for you in this case, as I have told you. Leave the matter in my hands. Don't raise silly objections; and when you leave here tonight you will take with you not only the handkerchief and the paper, but probably also the name and address of the man who committed this murder and those various burglaries that you are so keen about."

"Is that really so, sir?" exclaimed the astonished detective. "Well, you haven't let the grass grow under your feet. Ah!" as a gentle rap at the door was heard, "here's Belfield, I suppose."

It was Belfield—accompanied by his wife—and mightily disturbed they were when their eyes lighted on our visitor.

"You needn't be afraid of me, Belfield," said Miller, with fero-cious geniality; "I am not here after you." Which was not literally true, though it served to reassure the affrighted ex-convict.

239

"The superintendent dropped in by chance," said Thorndyke; "but it is just as well that he should hear what passes. I want you to look at this handkerchief and tell me if it is yours. Don't be afraid, but just tell us the simple truth."

He took the handkerchief out of a drawer and spread it on the table; and I now observed that a small square had been cut out of one of the bloodstains.

Belfield took the handkerchief in his trembling hands, and as his eye fell on the stamped name in the corner he turned deadly pale.

"It looks like mine," he said huskily. "What do you say, Liz?" he added, passing it to his wife.

Mrs. Belfield examined first the name and then the hem. "It's yours, right enough, Frank," said she. "It's the one that got changed in the wash. You see, sir," she continued, addressing Thorndyke, "I bought him half-a-dozen new ones about six months ago, and I got a rubber stamp made and marked them all. Well, one day when I was looking over his things I noticed that one of his handkerchiefs had got no mark on it. I spoke to the laundress about it, but she couldn't explain it, so as the right one never came back, I marked the one that we got in exchange."

"How long ago was that?" asked Thorndyke.

"About two months ago I noticed it."

"And you know nothing more about it."

"Nothing whatever, sir. Nor you, Frank, do you?"

Her husband shook his head gloomily, and Thorndyke replaced the handkerchief in the drawer.

"And now," said he, "I am going to ask you a question on another subject. When you were at Holloway there was a warder—or assistant warder—there, named Woodthorpe. Do you remember him?"

"Yes, sir, very well indeed; in fact, it was him that—?"

"I know," interrupted Thorndyke. "Have you seen him since you left Holloway?"

"Yes, sir, once. It was last Easter Monday. I met him at the Zoo; he is a keeper there now in the camel-house" (here a sudden light dawned upon me and I chuckled aloud, to Belfield's great astonishment). "He gave my little boy a ride on one of the camels and made himself very pleasant."

"Do you remember anything else happening?" Thorndyke inquired.

"Yes, sir. The camel had a little accident; he kicked out—he was

240

an ill-tempered beast—and his leg hit a post; there happened to be a nail sticking out from that post, and it tore up a little flap of skin. Then Woodthorpe got out his handkerchief to tie up the wound, but as it was none of the cleanest, I said to him: 'Don't use that, Woodthorpe; have mine,' which was quite a clean one. So he took it and bound up the camel's leg, and he said to me: 'I'll have it washed and send it to you if you give me your address.' But I told him there was no need for that; I should be passing the camel-house on my way out and I would look in for the handkerchief. And I did: I looked in about an hour later, and Woodthorpe gave me my handkerchief, folded up but not washed."

"Did you examine it to see if it was yours?" asked Thorndyke.

"No, sir. I just slipped it in my pocket as it was."

"And what became of it afterwards?"

"When I got home I dropped it into the dirty-linen basket."

"Is that all you know about it?"

"Yes, sir; that is all I know."

"Very well, Belfield, that will do. Now you have no reason to be uneasy. You will soon know all about the Camberwell murder—that is, if you read the papers."

The ex-convict and his wife were obviously relieved by this assurance and departed in quite good spirits. When they were gone, Thorndyke produced the handkerchief and the half-sheet of paper and handed them to the superintendent, remarking—"This is highly satisfactory, Miller; the whole case seems to join up very neatly indeed. Two months ago the wife first noticed the substituted handkerchief, and last Easter Monday—a little over two months ago—this very significant incident took place in the Zoological Gardens."

"That is all very well, sir," objected the superintendent, "but we've only their word for it, you know."

"Not so," replied Thorndyke. "We have excellent corroborative evidence. You noticed that I had cut a small piece out of the bloodstained portion of the handkerchief?"

"Yes; and I was sorry you had done it. Our people won't like that."

"Well, here it is, and we will ask Dr. Jervis to give us his opinion of it."

From the drawer in which the handkerchief had been hidden he brought forth a microscope slide, and setting the microscope on the table, laid the slide on the stage.

"Now, Jervis," he said, "tell us what you see there."

I examined the edge of the little square of fabric (which had been mounted in a fluid reagent) with a high-power objective, and was, for a time, a little puzzled by the appearance of the blood that adhered to it.

"It looks like bird's blood," I said presently, with some hesitation, "but yet I can make out no *nuclei*." I looked again, and then, suddenly, "By Jove!" I exclaimed, "I have it; of course! It's the blood of a camel!"

"Is that so, doctor?" demanded the detective, leaning forward in his excitement.

"That is so," replied Thorndyke. "I discovered it after I came home this morning. You see," he explained, "it is quite unmistakable. The rule is that the blood corpuscles of mammals are circular; the one exception is the camel family, in which the corpuscles are elliptical."

"Why," exclaimed Miller, "that seems to connect Woodthorpe with this Camberwell job."

"It connects him with it very conclusively," said Thorndyke. "You are forgetting the fingerprints."

The detective looked puzzled. "What about them?" he asked.

"They were made with stamps—two stamps, as a matter of fact—and those stamps were made by photographic process from the official fingerprint form. I can prove that beyond all doubt."

"Well, suppose they were. What then?"

Thorndyke opened a drawer and took out a photograph, which he handed to Miller. "Here," he said, "is the photograph of the official fingerprint form which you were kind enough to bring me. What does it say at the bottom there?" and he pointed with his finger.

The superintendent read aloud:

Impressions taken by Joseph Woodthorpe. Rank, Warder; Prison, Holloway."

He stared at the photograph for a moment, and then exclaimed—"Well, I'm hanged! You have worked this out neatly, doctor! and so quick too. We'll have Mr. Woodthorpe under lock and key the first thing tomorrow morning. But how did he do it, do you think?"

"He might have taken duplicate fingerprints and kept one form; the prisoners would not know there was anything wrong; but he did not in this case. He must have contrived to take a photograph of the form before sending it in—it would take a skilful photographer only a minute or two with a suitable hand-camera placed on a table at the proper distance from the wall; and I have ascertained that he is a skilful photographer. You will probably find the apparatus, and the stamps too, when you search his rooms."

"Well, well. You do give us some surprises, doctor. But I must be off now to see about this warrant. Good-night, sir, and many thanks for your help."

When the superintendent had gone we sat for a while looking at one another in silence. At length Thorndyke spoke. "Here is a case, Jervis," he said, "which, simple as it is, teaches a most invaluable lesson—a lesson which you should take well to heart. It is this: The evidential value of any fact is an unknown quantity until the fact has been examined. That seems a self-evident truth, but like many other self-evident truths, it is constantly overlooked in practice. Take this present case. When I left Caldwell's house this morning the facts in my possession were these:

(1) The man who murdered Caldwell was directly or indirectly connected with the Fingerprint Department.

(2) He was almost certainly a skilled photographer.

(3) He probably committed the Winchmore Hill and the other burglaries.

(4) He was known to Caldwell, had had professional dealings with him and was probably being blackmailed.

"This was all; a very vague clue, as you see.

"There was the handkerchief, planted, as I had no doubt; but could not prove; the name stamped on it was Belfield's, but any one can get a rubber stamp made. Then it was stained with blood, as handkerchiefs often are; that blood might or might not be human blood; it did not seem to matter a straw whether it was or not. Nevertheless, I said to myself: If it is human, or at least mammalian blood, that is a fact; and if it is not human blood, that is also a fact. I will have that fact, and then I shall know what its value is. I examined the stain when I reached home, and behold! it was camel's blood; and immediately this insignificant fact swelled up into evidence of primary importance.

"The rest was obvious. I had seen Woodthorpe's name on the form, and I knew several other officials. My business was to visit all places in London where there were camels, to get the names of all persons connected with them and to ascertain if any among them was a photographer. Naturally I went first to the Zoo, and at the very first cast hooked Joseph Woodthorpe. Wherefore I say again: Never call any fact irrelevant until you have examined it."

The remarkable evidence given above was not heard at the trial, nor did Thorndyke's name appear among the witnesses; for when the police searched Woodthorpe's rooms, so many incriminating articles were found (including a pair of fingerprint stamps which exactly answered to Thorndyke's description of them, and a number of photographs of fingerprint forms) that his guilt was put beyond all doubt; and society was shortly after relieved of a very undesirable member.

The Moabite Cipher

A large and motley crowd lined the pavements of Oxford Street as Thorndyke and I made our way leisurely eastward. Floral decorations and drooping bunting announced one of those functions inaugurated from time to time by a benevolent government for the entertainment of fashionable loungers and the relief of distressed pickpockets. For a Russian grand duke, who had torn himself away, amidst valedictory explosions, from a loving if too demonstrative people, was to pass anon on his way to the Guildhall; and a British prince, heroically indiscreet, was expected to occupy a seat in the ducal carriage.

Near Rathbone Place Thorndyke halted and drew my attention to a smart-looking man who stood lounging in a doorway, cigarette in hand.

"Our old friend Inspector Badger," said Thorndyke. "He seems mightily interested in that gentleman in the light overcoat. How d'ye do, Badger?" for at this moment the detective caught his eye and bowed. "Who is your friend?"

"That's what I want to know, sir," replied the inspector. "I've been shadowing him for the last half-hour, but I can't make him out, though I believe I've seen him somewhere. He don't look like a foreigner, but he has got something bulky in his pocket, so I must keep him in sight until the duke is safely past. I wish," he added gloomily, "these beastly Russians would stop at home. They give us no end of trouble."

"Are you expecting any—occurrences, then?" asked Thorndyke.

"Bless you, sir," exclaimed Badger, "the whole route is lined with plain-clothes men. You see, it is known that several desperate characters followed the duke to England, and there are a good many exiles living here who would like to have a rap at him. Hallo! What's he up to now?"

The man in the light overcoat had suddenly caught the inspector's too inquiring eye, and forthwith dived into the crowd at the edge of the pavement. In his haste he trod heavily on the foot of a big, rough-looking man, by whom he was in a moment hustled out into the road with such violence that he fell sprawling face downwards. It was an unlucky moment. A mounted constable was just then backing in upon the crowd, and before he could gather the meaning of the shout that arose from the bystanders, his horse had set down one hind-hoof firmly on the prostrate man's back.

The inspector signalled to a constable, who forthwith made a way for us through the crowd; but even as we approached the injured man, he rose stiffly and looked round with a pale, vacant face.

"Are you hurt?" Thorndyke asked gently, with an earnest look into the frightened, wondering eyes.

"No, sir," was the reply; "only I feel queer—sinking—just here."

He laid a trembling hand on his chest, and Thorndyke, still eyeing him anxiously, said in a low voice to the inspector: "Cab or ambulance, as quickly as you can."

A cab was led round from Newman Street, and the injured man put into it. Thorndyke, Badger, and I entered, and we drove off up Rathbone Place. As we proceeded, our patient's face grew more and more ashen, drawn, and anxious; his breathing was shallow and uneven, and his teeth chattered slightly. The cab swung round into Goodge Street, and then—suddenly, in the twinkling of an eye—there came a change. The eyelids and jaw relaxed, the eyes became filmy, and the whole form subsided into the corner in a shrunken heap, with the strange gelatinous limpness of a body that is dead as a whole, while its tissues are still alive.

"God save us! The man's dead!" exclaimed the inspector in a shocked voice—for even policemen have their feelings. He sat staring at the corpse, as it nodded gently with the jolting of the cab, until we drew up inside the courtyard of the Middlesex Hospital, when he got out briskly, with suddenly renewed cheerfulness, to help the porter to place the body on the wheeled couch.

"We shall know who he is now, at any rate," said he, as we followed the couch to the casualty-room. Thorndyke nodded unsympathetically. The medical instinct in him was for the moment stronger than the legal.

The house-surgeon leaned over the couch, and made a rapid examination as he listened to our account of the accident. Then he straightened himself up and looked at Thorndyke.

"Internal haemorrhage, I expect," said he. "At any rate, he's dead, poor beggar!—as dead as Nebuchadnezzar. Ah! here comes a bobby; it's his affair now."

A sergeant came into the room, breathing quickly, and looked in surprise from the corpse to the inspector. But the latter, without loss of time, proceeded to turn out the dead man's pockets, commencing with the bulky object that had first attracted his attention; which proved to be a brown-paper parcel tied up with red tape.

"Pork-pie, begad!" he exclaimed with a crestfallen air as he cut the tape and opened the package. "You had better go through his other pockets, sergeant."

The small heap of odds and ends that resulted from this process tended, with a single exception, to throw little light on the man's identity; the exception being a letter, sealed, but not stamped, addressed in an exceedingly illiterate hand to Mr. Adolf Schoenberg, 213, Greek Street, Soho.

"He was going to leave it by hand, I expect," observed the inspector, with a wistful glance at the sealed envelope. "I think I'll take it round myself, and you had better come with me, sergeant."

He slipped the letter into his pocket, and, leaving the sergeant to take possession of the other effects, made his way out of the building.

"I suppose, doctor," said he, as we crossed into Berners Street, "you are not coming our way! Don't want to see Mr. Schoenberg, h'm?"

Thorndyke reflected for a moment. "Well, it isn't very far, and we may as well see the end of the incident. Yes; let us go together."

No. 213, Greek Street, was one of those houses that irresistibly suggest to the observer the idea of a church organ, either jamb of the doorway being adorned with a row of brass bell-handles corresponding to the stop-knobs.

These the sergeant examined with the air of an expert musician, and having, as it were, gauged the capacity of the instrument, selected the middle knob on the right-hand side and pulled it briskly; whereupon a first-floor window was thrown up and a head protruded. But it afforded us a momentary glimpse only, for, having caught the sergeant's upturned eye, it retired with surprising precipitancy, and before we had time to speculate on the apparition, the street-door was opened and a man emerged. He was about to close the door after him when the inspector interposed.

"Does Mr. Adolf Schoenberg live here?"

The newcomer, a very typical Jew of the red-haired type, surveyed us thoughtfully through his gold-rimmed spectacles as he repeated the name.

"Schoenberg—Schoenberg? Ah, yes! I know. He lives on the third-floor. I saw him go up a short time ago. Third-floor back;" and indicating the open door with a wave of the hand, he raised his hat and passed into the street.

"I suppose we had better go up," said the inspector, with a dubious glance at the row of bell-pulls. He accordingly started up the stairs, and we all followed in his wake.

There were two doors at the back on the third-floor, but as the one was open, displaying an unoccupied bedroom, the inspector rapped smartly on the other. It flew open almost immediately, and a fierce-looking little man confronted us with a hostile stare.

"Well?" said he.

"Mr. Adolf Schoenberg?" inquired the inspector.

"Well? What about him?" snapped our new acquaintance.

"I wished to have a few words with him," said Badger.

"Then what the deuce do you come banging at my door for?" demanded the other.

"Why, doesn't he live here?"

"No. First-floor front," replied our friend, preparing to close the door.

"Pardon me," said Thorndyke, "but what is Mr. Schoenberg like? I mean—"

"Like?" interrupted the resident. "He's like a blooming Sheeny, with a carroty beard and gold gig-lamps!" and, having presented this impressionist sketch, he brought the interview to a definite close by slamming the door and turning the key.

With a wrathful exclamation, the inspector turned towards the stairs, down which the sergeant was already clattering in hot haste, and made his way back to the ground-floor, followed, as before, by Thorndyke and me. On the doorstep we found the sergeant breathlessly interrogating a smartly-dressed youth, whom I had seen alight from a hansom as we entered the house, and who now stood with a notebook tucked under his arm, sharpening a pencil with deliberate care.

"Mr. James saw him come out, sir," said the sergeant. "He turned up towards the Square."

"Did he seem to hurry?" asked the inspector.

"Rather," replied the reporter. "As soon as you were inside, he went off like a lamplighter. You won't catch him now."

"We don't want to catch him," the detective rejoined gruffly; then, backing out of earshot of the eager pressman, he said in a lower tone: "That was Mr. Schoenberg, beyond a doubt, and it is clear that he has some reason for making himself scarce; so I shall consider myself justified in opening that note."

He suited the action to the word, and, having cut the envelope open with official neatness, drew out the enclosure.

"My hat!" he exclaimed, as his eye fell upon the contents. "What in creation is this? It isn't shorthand, but what the deuce is it?"

He handed the document to Thorndyke, who, having held it up to the light and felt the paper critically, proceeded to examine it with keen interest. It consisted of a single half-sheet of thin notepaper, both sides of which were covered with strange, crabbed characters, written with a brownish-black ink in continuous lines, without any spaces to indicate the divisions into words; and, but for the modern material which bore the writing, it might have been a portion of some ancient manuscript or forgotten codex.

"What do you make of it, doctor?" inquired the inspector anxiously, after a pause, during which Thorndyke had scrutinized the strange writing with knitted brows.

"Not a great deal," replied Thorndyke. "The character is the Moabite or Phoenician—primitive Semitic, in fact—and reads from right to left. The language I take to be Hebrew. At any rate, I can find no Greek words, and I see here a group of letters which may form one of the few Hebrew words that I know—the word *badim*, 'lies.' But you had better get it deciphered by an expert."

"If it is Hebrew," said Badger, "we can manage it all right. There are plenty of Jews at our disposal."

"You had much better take the paper to the British Museum," said Thorndyke, "and submit it to the keeper of the Phoenician antiquities for decipherment."

Inspector Badger smiled a foxy smile as he deposited the paper in his pocket-book. "We'll see what we can make of it ourselves first," he said; "but many thanks for your advice, all the same, doctor. No, Mr. James, I can't give you any information just at present; you had better apply at the hospital."

"I suspect," said Thorndyke, as we took our way homewards, "that Mr. James has collected enough material for his purpose already. He must have followed us from the hospital, and I have no doubt that he has his report, with 'full details,' mentally arranged at this moment. And I am not sure that he didn't get a peep at the mysterious paper, in spite of the inspector's precautions."

"By the way," I said, "what do you make of the document?"

"A cipher, most probably," he replied. "It is written in the primitive Semitic alphabet, which, as you know, is practically identical with primitive Greek. It is written from right to left, like the Phoenician, Hebrew, and Moabite, as well as the earliest Greek, inscriptions. The paper is common cream-laid notepaper, and the ink is ordinary indelible Chinese ink, such as is used by draughtsmen. Those are the facts, and without further study of the document itself, they don't carry us very far."

"Why do you think it is a cipher rather than a document in straightforward Hebrew?"

"Because it is obviously a secret message of some kind. Now, every educated Jew knows more or less Hebrew, and, although he is able to read and write only the modern square Hebrew character, it is so easy to transpose one alphabet into another that the mere language would afford no security. Therefore, I expect that, when the experts translate this document, the translation or transliteration will be a mere farrago of unintelligible nonsense. But we shall see, and meanwhile the facts that we have offer several interesting suggestions which are well worth consideration."

"As, for instance—?"

"Now, my dear Jervis," said Thorndyke, shaking an admonitory forefinger at me, "don't, I pray you, give way to mental indolence. You have these few facts that I have mentioned. Consider them separately and collectively, and in their relation to the circumstances. Don't attempt to suck my brain when you have an excellent brain of your own to suck."

On the following morning the papers fully justified my colleague's opinion of Mr. James. All the events which had occurred, as well as a number that had not, were given in the fullest and most vivid detail, a lengthy reference being made to the paper "found on the person of the dead anarchist," and "written in a private shorthand or cryptogram."

The report concluded with the gratifying—though untrue—statement that "in this intricate and important case, the police have wisely secured the assistance of Dr. John Thorndyke, to whose acute intellect and vast experience the portentous cryptogram will doubtless soon deliver up its secret."

"Very flattering," laughed Thorndyke, to whom I read the extract on his return from the hospital, "but a little awkward if it should induce our friends to deposit a few trifling mementoes in the form of nitro-compounds on our main staircase or in the cellars. By the way, I met Superintendent Miller on London Bridge. The 'cryptogram,' as Mr. James calls it, has set Scotland Yard in a mighty ferment."

"Naturally. What have they done in the matter?"

"They adopted my suggestion, after all, finding that they could make nothing of it themselves, and took it to the British Museum. The Museum people referred them to Professor Poppelbaum, the great palaeographer, to whom they accordingly submitted it."

"Did he express any opinion about it?"

"Yes, provisionally. After a brief examination, he found it to consist of a number of Hebrew words sandwiched between apparently meaningless groups of letters. He furnished the superintendent off-hand with a translation of the words, and Miller forthwith struck off a number of hectograph copies of it, which he has distributed among the senior officials of his department; so that at present"—here Thorndyke gave vent to a soft chuckle—"Scotland Yard is engaged in a sort of missing word—or, rather, missing sense—competition. Miller invited me to join in the sport, and to that end presented me with one of the hectograph copies on which to exercise my wits, together with a photograph of the document."

"And shall you?" I asked.

"Not I," he replied, laughing. "In the first place, I have not been formally consulted, and consequently am a passive, though interested, spectator. In the second place, I have a theory of my own which I shall test if the occasion arises. But if you would like to take part in the competition, I am authorised to show you the photograph and the translation. I will pass them on to you, and I wish you joy of them."

He handed me the photograph and a sheet of paper that he had just taken from his pocket-book, and watched me with grim amusement as I read out the first few lines.

"Woe, city, lies, robbery, prey, noise, whip, rattling, wheel, horse, chariot, day, darkness, gloominess, clouds, darkness, morning, mountain, people, strong, fire, them, flame."

"It doesn't look very promising at first sight," I remarked. "What is the professor's theory?"

"His theory—provisionally, of course—is that the words form the message, and the groups of letters represent mere filled-up spaces between the words."

"But surely," I protested, "that would be a very transparent device."

Thorndyke laughed. "There is a childlike simplicity about it," said he, "that is highly attractive—but discouraging. It is much more probable that the words are dummies, and that the letters contain the message. Or, again, the solution may lie in an entirely different direction. But listen! Is that cab coming here?"

It was. It drew up opposite our chambers, and a few moments later a brisk step ascending the stairs heralded a smart rat-tat at our door. Flinging open the latter, I found myself confronted by a well-dressed stranger, who, after a quick glance at me, peered inquisitively over my shoulder into the room.

"I am relieved, Dr. Jervis," said he, "to find you and Dr. Thorndyke at home, as I have come on somewhat urgent professional business. My name," he continued, entering in response to my invitation, "is Barton, but you don't know me, though I know you both by sight. I have come to ask you if one of you—or, better still, both—could come tonight and see my brother."

"That," said Thorndyke, "depends on the circumstances and on the whereabouts of your brother."

"The circumstances," said Mr. Barton, "are, in my opinion, highly suspicious, and I will place them before you—of course, in strict confidence."

Thorndyke nodded and indicated a chair.

"My brother," continued Mr. Barton, taking the proffered seat, "has recently married for the second time. His age is fifty-five, and that of his wife twenty-six, and I may say that the marriage has been—well, by no means a success. Now, within the last fortnight, my brother has been attacked by a mysterious and extremely painful affliction of the stomach, to which his doctor seems unable to give a name. It has resisted all treatment hitherto. Day by day the pain and distress increase, and I feel that, unless something decisive is done, the end cannot be far off."

"Is the pain worse after taking food?" inquired Thorndyke.

"That's just it!" exclaimed our visitor. "I see what is in your mind, and it has been in mine, too; so much so that I have tried repeatedly to obtain samples of the food that he is taking. And this morning I succeeded." Here he took from his pocket a wide-mouthed bottle, which, disengaging from its paper wrappings, he laid on the table. "When I called, he was taking his breakfast of arrowroot, which he complained had a gritty taste, supposed by his wife to be due to the sugar. Now I had provided myself with this bottle, and, during the absence of his wife, I managed unobserved to convey a portion of the arrowroot that he had left into it, and I should be greatly obliged if you would examine it and tell me if this arrowroot contains anything that it should not."

He pushed the bottle across to Thorndyke, who carried it to the window, and, extracting a small quantity of the contents with a glass rod, examined the pasty mass with the aid of a lens; then, lifting the bell-glass cover from the microscope, which stood on its table by the window, he smeared a small quantity of the suspected matter on to a glass slip, and placed it on the stage of the instrument.

"I observe a number of crystalline particles in this," he said, after a brief inspection, "which have the appearance of *arsenious* acid."

"Ah!" ejaculated Mr. Barton, "just what I feared. But are you certain?"

"No," replied Thorndyke; "but the matter is easily tested."

He pressed the button of the bell that communicated with the laboratory, a summons that brought the laboratory assistant from his lair with characteristic promptitude.

"Will you please prepare a Marsh's apparatus, Polton," said Thorndyke.

"I have a couple ready, sir," replied Polton.

"Then pour the acid into one and bring it to me, with a tile."

As his familiar vanished silently, Thorndyke turned to Mr. Barton.

"Supposing we find arsenic in this arrowroot, as we probably shall, what do you want us to do?"

"I want you to come and see my brother," replied our client.

"Why not take a note from me to his doctor?"

"No, no; I want you to come—I should like you both to come—and put a stop at once to this dreadful business. Consider! It's a matter of life and death. You won't refuse! I beg you not to refuse me your help in these terrible circumstances."

"Well," said Thorndyke, as his assistant reappeared, "let us first see what the test has to tell us."

Polton advanced to the table, on which he deposited a small flask, the contents of which were in a state of brisk effervescence, a bottle labelled "calcium *hypochlorite*," and a white porcelain tile. The flask was fitted with a safety-funnel and a glass tube drawn out to a fine jet, to which Polton cautiously applied a lighted match. Instantly there sprang from the jet a tiny, pale violet flame. Thorndyke now took the tile, and held it in the flame for a few seconds, when the appearance of the surface remained unchanged save for a small circle of condensed moisture.

His next proceeding was to thin the arrowroot with distilled water until it was quite fluid, and then pour a small quantity into the funnel. It ran slowly down the tube into the flask, with the bubbling contents of which it became speedily mixed. Almost immediately a change began to appear in the character of the flame, which from a pale violet turned gradually to a sickly blue, while above it hung a faint cloud of white smoke. Once more Thorndyke held the tile above the jet, but this time, no sooner had the pallid flame touched the cold surface of the porcelain, than there appeared on the latter a glistening black stain.

"That is pretty conclusive," observed Thorndyke, lifting the stopper out of the reagent bottle, "but we will apply the final test." He dropped a few drops of the *hypochlorite* solution on to the tile, and immediately the black stain faded away and vanished. "We can now answer your question, Mr. Barton," said he, replacing the stopper as he turned to our client. "The specimen that you brought us certainly contains arsenic, and in very considerable quantities."

"Then," exclaimed Mr. Barton, starting from his chair, "you will come and help me to rescue my brother from this dreadful peril. Don't refuse me, Dr. Thorndyke, for mercy's sake, don't refuse."

Thorndyke reflected for a moment.

"Before we decide," said he, "we must see what engagements we have."

With a quick, significant glance at me, he walked into the office, whither I followed in some bewilderment, for I knew that we had no engagements for the evening.

"Now, Jervis," said Thorndyke, as he closed the office door, "what are we to do?"

"We must go, I suppose," I replied. "It seems a pretty urgent case."

"It does," he agreed. "Of course, the man may be telling the truth, after all."

"You don't think he is, then?"

"No. It is a plausible tale, but there is too much arsenic in that arrowroot. Still, I think I ought to go. It is an ordinary professional risk. But there is no reason why you should put your head into the noose."

"Thank you," said I, somewhat huffily. "I don't see what risk there is, but if any exists I claim the right to share it."

"Very well," he answered with a smile, "we will both go. I think we can take care of ourselves."

He re-entered the sitting-room, and announced his decision to Mr. Barton, whose relief and gratitude were quite pathetic.

"But," said Thorndyke, "you have not yet told us where your brother lives."

"Rexford," was the reply—"Rexford, in Essex. It is an out-of-the-way place, but if we catch the seven-fifteen train from Liverpool Street, we shall be there in an hour and a half."

"And as to the return? You know the trains, I suppose?"

"Oh yes," replied our client; "I will see that you don't miss your train back."

"Then I will be with you in a minute," said Thorndyke; and, taking the still-bubbling flask, he retired to the laboratory, whence he returned in a few minutes carrying his hat and overcoat.

The cab which had brought our client was still waiting, and we were soon rattling through the streets towards the station, where we arrived in time to furnish ourselves with dinner-baskets and select our compartment at leisure.

During the early part of the journey our companion was in excellent spirits. He despatched the cold fowl from the basket and quaffed the rather indifferent claret with as much relish as if he had not had a single relation in the world, and after dinner he became genial to the verge of hilarity. But, as time went on, there crept into his manner a certain anxious restlessness. He became silent and preoccupied, and several times furtively consulted his watch.

"The train is confoundedly late!" he exclaimed irritably. "Seven minutes behind time already!"

"A few minutes more or less are not of much consequence," said Thorndyke.

"No, of course not; but still—Ah, thank Heaven, here we are!"

He thrust his head out of the off-side window, and gazed eagerly down the line; then, leaping to his feet, he bustled out on to the platform while the train was still moving.

Even as we alighted a warning bell rang furiously on the up-platform, and as Mr. Barton hurried us through the empty booking-office to the outside of the station, the rumble of the approaching train could be heard above the noise made by our own train moving off.

"My carriage doesn't seem to have arrived yet," exclaimed Mr. Barton, looking anxiously up the station approach. "If you will wait here a moment, I will go and make inquiries."

He darted back into the booking-office and through it on to the platform, just as the up-train roared into the station. Thorndyke followed him with quick but stealthy steps, and, peering out of the booking-office door, watched his proceedings; then he turned and beckoned to me.

"There he goes," said he, pointing to an iron footbridge that spanned the line; and, as I looked, I saw, clearly defined against the dim night sky, a flying figure racing towards the "up" side.

It was hardly two-thirds across when the guard's whistle sang out its shrill warning.

"Quick, Jervis," exclaimed Thorndyke; "she's off!"

He leaped down on to the line, whither I followed instantly, and, crossing the rails, we clambered up together on to the foot-board opposite an empty first-class compartment. Thorndyke's magazine knife, containing, among other implements, a railway-key, was already in his hand. The door was speedily unlocked, and, as we entered, Thorndyke ran through and looked out on to the platform.

"Just in time!" he exclaimed. "He is in one of the forward compartments."

He relocked the door, and, seating himself, proceeded to fill his pipe.

"And now," said I, as the train moved out of the station, "perhaps you will explain this little comedy."

"With pleasure," he replied, "if it needs any explanation. But you can hardly have forgotten Mr. James's flattering remarks in his report of the Greek Street incident, clearly giving the impression that the mysterious document was in my possession. When I read that, I knew I must look out for some attempt to recover it, though I hardly expected such promptness. Still, when Mr. Barton called without credentials or appointment, I viewed him with some suspicion. That suspicion deepened when he wanted us both to come.

"It deepened further when I found an impossible quantity of arsenic in his sample, and it gave place to certainty when, having allowed him to select the trains by which we were to travel, I went up to the laboratory and examined the time-table; for I then found that the last train for London left Rexford ten minutes after we were due to arrive. Obviously this was a plan to get us both safely out of the way while he and some of his friends ransacked our chambers for the missing document."

"I see; and that accounts for his extraordinary anxiety at the lateness of the train. But why did you come, if you knew it was a 'plant'?"

"My dear fellow," said Thorndyke, "I never miss an interesting experience if I can help it. There are possibilities in this, too, don't you see?"

"But supposing his friends have broken into our chambers already?"

"That contingency has been provided for; but I think they will wait for Mr. Barton—and us."

Our train, being the last one up, stopped at every station, and crawled slothfully in the intervals, so that it was past eleven o'clock when we reached Liverpool Street. Here we got out cautiously, and, mingling with the crowd, followed the unconscious Barton up the platform, through the barrier, and out into the street. He seemed in no special hurry, for, after pausing to light a cigar, he set off at an easy pace up New Broad Street.

Thorndyke hailed a hansom, and, motioning me to enter, directed the cabman to drive to Clifford's Inn Passage.

"Sit well back," said he, as we rattled away up New Broad Street. "We shall be passing our gay deceiver presently—in fact, there he is, a living, walking illustration of the folly of underrating the intelligence of one's adversary."

At Clifford's Inn Passage we dismissed the cab, and, retiring into the shadow of the dark, narrow alley, kept an eye on the gate of Inner Temple Lane. In about twenty minutes we observed our friend approaching on the south side of Fleet Street. He halted at the gate, plied the knocker, and after a brief parley with the night-porter vanished through the wicket. We waited yet five minutes more, and then, having given him time to get clear of the entrance, we crossed the road.

The porter looked at us with some surprise.

"There's a gentleman just gone down to your chambers, sir," said he. "He told me you were expecting him."

"Quite right," said Thorndyke, with a dry smile, "I was. Good-night."

We slunk down the lane, past the church, and through the gloomy cloisters, giving a wide berth to all lamps and lighted entries, until, emerging into Paper Buildings, we crossed at the darkest part to King's Bench Walk, where Thorndyke made straight for the chambers of our friend Anstey, which were two doors above our own.

"Why are we coming here?" I asked, as we ascended the stairs.

But the question needed no answer when we reached the landing, for through the open door of our friend's chambers I could see in the darkened room Anstey himself with two uniformed constables and a couple of plain-clothes men.

"There has been no signal yet, sir," said one of the latter, whom I recognised as a detective-sergeant of our division.

"No," said Thorndyke, "but the M.C. has arrived. He came in five minutes before us."

"Then," exclaimed Anstey, "the ball will open shortly, ladies and gents. The boards are waxed, the fiddlers are tuning up, and—"

"Not quite so loud, if you please, sir," said the sergeant. "I think there is somebody coming up Crown Office Row."

The ball had, in fact, opened. As we peered cautiously out of the open window, keeping well back in the darkened room, a stealthy figure crept out of the shadow, crossed the road, and stole noiselessly into the entry of Thorndyke's chambers. It was quickly followed by a second figure, and then by a third, in which I recognised our elusive client.

"Now listen for the signal," said Thorndyke. "They won't waste time. Confound that clock!"

The soft-voiced bell of the Inner Temple clock, mingling with the harsher tones of St. Dunstan's and the Law Courts, slowly tolled out the hour of midnight; and as the last reverberations were dying away, some metallic object, apparently a coin, dropped with a sharp clink on to the pavement under our window.

At the sound the watchers simultaneously sprang to their feet.

"You two go first," said the sergeant, addressing the uniformed men, who thereupon stole noiselessly, in their rubber-soled boots, down the stone stairs and along the pavement. The rest of us followed, with less attention to silence, and as we ran up to Thorndyke's chambers, we were aware of quick but stealthy footsteps on the stairs above.

"They've been at work, you see," whispered one of the constables, flashing his lantern on to the iron-bound outer door of our sitting-room, on which the marks of a large jemmy were plainly visible.

The sergeant nodded grimly, and, bidding the constables to remain on the landing, led the way upwards.

As we ascended, faint rustlings continued to be audible from above, and on the second-floor landing we met a man descending briskly, but without hurry, from the third. It was Mr. Barton, and I could not but admire the composure with which he passed the two detectives. But suddenly his glance fell on Thorndyke, and his composure vanished. With a wild stare of incredulous horror, he halted as if petrified; then he broke away and raced furiously down the stairs, and a moment later a muffled shout and the sound of a scuffle told us that he had received a check. On the next flight we met two more men, who, more hurried and less self-possessed, endeavoured to push past; but the sergeant barred the way.

"Why, bless me!" exclaimed the latter, "it's Moakey; and isn't that Tom Harris?"

"It's all right, sergeant," said Moakey plaintively, striving to escape from the officer's grip. "We've come to the wrong house, that's all."

The sergeant smiled indulgently. "I know," he replied. "But you're always coming to the wrong house, Moakey; and now you're just coming along with me to the right house."

He slipped his hand inside his captive's coat, and adroitly fished out a large, folding jemmy; whereupon the discomfited burglar abandoned all further protest.

On our return to the first-floor, we found Mr. Barton sulkily awaiting us, handcuffed to one of the constables, and watched by Polton with pensive disapproval.

"I needn't trouble you tonight, Doctor," said the sergeant, as he marshalled his little troop of captors and captives. "You'll hear from us in the morning. Good-night, sir."

The melancholy procession moved off down the stairs, and we retired into our chambers with Anstey to smoke a last pipe.

"A capable man, that Barton," observed Thorndyke—"ready, plausible, and ingenious, but spoilt by prolonged contact with fools. I wonder if the police will perceive the significance of this little affair."

"They will be more acute than I am if they do," said I.

"Naturally," interposed Anstey, who loved to "cheek" his revered senior, "because there isn't any. It's only Thorndyke's bounce. He is really in a deuce of a fog himself."

However this may have been, the police were a good deal puzzled by the incident, for, on the following morning, we received a visit from no less a person than Superintendent Miller, of Scotland Yard.

"This is a queer business," said he, coming to the point at once—"this burglary, I mean. Why should they want to crack your place, right here in the Temple, too? You've got nothing of value here, have you? No 'hard stuff,' as they call it, for instance?"

"Not so much as a silver teaspoon," replied Thorndyke, who had a conscientious objection to plate of all kinds.

"It's odd," said the superintendent, "deuced odd. When we got your note, we thought these anarchist idiots had mixed you up with the case—you saw the papers, I suppose—and wanted to go through your rooms for some reason. We thought we had our hands on the gang, instead of which we find a party of common crooks that we're sick of the sight of. I tell you, sir, it's annoying when you think you've hooked a salmon, to bring up a blooming eel."

"It must be a great disappointment," Thorndyke agreed, suppressing a smile.

"It is," said the detective. "Not but what we're glad enough to get these beggars, especially Halkett, or Barton, as he calls himself—a mighty slippery customer is Halkett, and mischievous, too—but we're not wanting any disappointments just now. There was that big jewel job in Piccadilly, Taplin and Horne's; I don't mind telling you that we've not got the ghost of a clue. Then there's this anarchist affair. We're all in the dark there, too."

"But what about the cipher?" asked Thorndyke.

"Oh, hang the cipher!" exclaimed the detective irritably. "This Professor Poppelbaum may be a very learned man, but he doesn't help us much. He says the document is in Hebrew, and he has translated it into Double Dutch. Just listen to this!" He dragged out of his pocket a bundle of papers, and, dabbing down a photograph of the document before Thorndyke, commenced to read the professor's report. "'The document is written in the characters of the well-known inscription of Mesha, King of Moab' (who the devil's he? Never heard of him. Well known, indeed!) 'The language is Hebrew, and the words are separated by groups of letters, which are meaningless, and obviously introduced to mislead and confuse the reader.

"The words themselves are not strictly consecutive, but, by the interpellation of certain other words, a series of intelligible sentences is obtained, the meaning of which is not very clear, but is no doubt allegorical. The method of decipherment is shown in the accompanying tables, and the full rendering suggested on the enclosed sheet. It is to be noted that the writer of this document was apparently quite unacquainted with the Hebrew language, as appears from the absence of any grammatical construction.' That's the professor's report, Doctor, and here are the tables showing how he worked it out. It makes my head spin to look at 'em."

He handed to Thorndyke a bundle of ruled sheets, which my colleague examined attentively for a while, and then passed on to me.

"This is very systematic and thorough," said he. "But now let us see the final result at which he arrives."

"It may be all very systematic," growled the superintendent, sorting out his papers, "but I tell you, sir, it's all BOSH!" The latter word he jerked out viciously, as he slapped down on the table the final product of the professor's labours. "There," he continued, "that's what he calls the 'full rendering,' and I reckon it'll make your hair curl. It might be a message from Bedlam."

Thorndyke took up the first sheet, and as he compared the constructed renderings with the literal translation, the ghost of a smile stole across his usually immovable countenance.

"The meaning is certainly a little obscure," he observed, "though the reconstruction is highly ingenious; and, moreover, I think the professor is probably right. That is to say, the words which he has supplied are probably the omitted parts of the passages from which the words of the cryptogram were taken. What do you think, Jervis?"

	Space	Word	Space	Word	Space	Word
Moabite	Y∃	H7A9	∆7	4Zo	9A	ZYA
Hebrew		בגרים		עיר		אוי
Translation		LIES		CITY		WOE
Moabite	۶٦	6Yφ	6¥7	74x		6ᴵ٦
Hebrew		קל		שרף		גזל
Translation		NOISE		PREY		ROBBERY
Moabite	w4	۶7Y&	φ๒	woq	70ǂ	xYw
Hebrew		אופן		רעש		שוט
Translation		WHEEL		RATTLING		WHIP
Moabite	Y∃	ϽYᴵ	∆٦	۶۹٠Y�9٦	94x	ǂY◈
Hebrew		יום		מרכבה		סוס
Translation		DAY		CHARIOT		HORSE

THE PROFESSOR'S ANALYSIS.
Handwritten: Analysis of the cipher with translation into modern
square Hebrew characters + a translation into English.
N.B. The cipher reads from right to left.

He handed me the two papers, of which one gave the actual words
of the cryptogram, and the other a suggested reconstruction, with
omitted words supplied. The first read:

"Woe city lies robbery prey noise whip rattling wheel horse chariot day darkness gloominess cloud darkness morning mountain people
strong fire them flame."

Turning to the second paper, I read out the suggested rendering:
"'Woe to the bloody city! It is full of lies and robbery; the prey de-
parteth not. The noise of a whip, and the noise of the rattling of the
wheels, and of the prancing horses, and of the jumping chariots.

"'A day of darkness and of gloominess, a day of clouds, and of thick
darkness, as the morning spread upon the mountains, a great people
and a strong.

"'A fire devoureth before them, and behind them a flame bur-
neth.'"

Here the first sheet ended, and, as I laid it down, Thorndyke looked
at me inquiringly.

"There is a good deal of reconstruction in proportion to the original matter," I objected. "The professor has 'supplied' more than three-
quarters of the final rendering."

262

"Exactly," burst in the superintendent; "it's all professor and no cryptogram."

"Still, I think the reading is correct," said Thorndyke. "As far as it goes, that is."

"Good Lord!" exclaimed the dismayed detective. "Do you mean to tell me, sir, that that balderdash is the real meaning of the thing?"

"I don't say that," replied Thorndyke. "I say it is correct as far as it goes; but I doubt its being the solution of the cryptogram."

"Have you been studying that photograph that I gave you?" demanded Miller, with sudden eagerness.

"I have looked at it," said Thorndyke evasively, "but I should like to examine the original if you have it with you."

"I have," said the detective. "Professor Poppelbaum sent it back with the solution. You can have a look at it, though I can't leave it with you without special authority."

He drew the document from his pocket-book and handed it to Thorndyke, who took it over to the window and scrutinized it closely. From the window he drifted into the adjacent office, closing the door after him; and presently the sound of a faint explosion told me that he had lighted the gas-fire.

"Of course," said Miller, taking up the translation again, "this gibberish is the sort of stuff you might expect from a parcel of crackbrained anarchists; but it doesn't seem to mean anything."

"Not to us," I agreed; "but the phrases may have some pre-arranged significance. And then there are the letters between the words. It is possible that they may really form a cipher."

"I suggested that to the professor," said Miller, "but he wouldn't hear of it. He is sure they are only dummies."

"I think he is probably mistaken, and so, I fancy, does my colleague. But we shall hear what he has to say presently."

"Oh, I know what he will say," growled Miller. "He will put the thing under the microscope, and tell us who made the paper, and what the ink is composed of, and then we shall be just where we were." The superintendent was evidently deeply depressed.

We sat for some time pondering in silence on the vague sentences of the professor's translation, until, at length, Thorndyke reappeared, holding the document in his hand. He laid it quietly on the table by the officer, and then inquired: "Is this an official consultation?"

"Certainly," replied Miller. "I was authorised to consult you respecting the translation, but nothing was said about the original. Still, if you want it for further study, I will get it for you."

"No, thank you," said Thorndyke. "I have finished with it. My theory turned out to be correct."

"Your theory!" exclaimed the superintendent, eagerly. "Do you mean to say—?"

"And, as you are consulting me officially, I may as well give you this."

He held out a sheet of paper, which the detective took from him and began to read.

"What is this?" he asked, looking up at Thorndyke with a puzzled frown. "Where did it come from?"

"It is the solution of the cryptogram," replied Thorndyke.

The detective re-read the contents of the paper, and, with the frown of perplexity deepening, once more gazed at my colleague.

"This is a joke, sir; you are fooling me," he said sulkily.

"Nothing of the kind," answered Thorndyke. "That is the genuine solution."

"But it's impossible!" exclaimed Miller. "Just look at it, Dr. Jervis."

I took the paper from his hand, and, as I glanced at it, I had no difficulty in understanding his surprise. It bore a short inscription in printed Roman capitals, thus:

THE PICKERDILLEY STUF IS UP THE CHIMBLY 416 WARDOUR ST 2ND FLOUR BACK IT WAS HID BECOS OF OLD MOAKEYS JOOD MOAKEY IS A BLITER.

"Then that fellow wasn't an anarchist at all?" I exclaimed.

"No," said Miller. "He was one of Moakey's gang. We suspected Moakey of being mixed up with that job, but we couldn't fix it on him. By Jove!" he added, slapping his thigh, "if this is right, and I can lay my hands on the loot! Can you lend me a bag, doctor? I'm off to Wardour Street this very moment."

We furnished him with an empty suitcase, and, from the window, watched him making for Mitre Court at a smart double.

"I wonder if he will find the booty," said Thorndyke. "It just depends on whether the hiding-place was known to more than one of the gang. Well, it has been a quaint case, and instructive, too. I suspect our friend Barton and the evasive Schoenberg were the collaborators who produced that curiosity of literature."

"May I ask how you deciphered the thing?" I said. "It didn't appear to take long."

"It didn't. It was merely a matter of testing a hypothesis; and you ought not to have to ask that question," he added, with mock severity, "seeing that you had what turn out to have been all the necessary facts, two days ago. But I will prepare a document and demonstrate to you tomorrow morning."

★★★★★★★★

"So Miller was successful in his quest," said Thorndyke, as we smoked our morning pipes after breakfast. "The 'entire swag,' as he calls it, was 'up the chimbly,' undisturbed."

He handed me a note which had been left, with the empty suitcase, by a messenger, shortly before, and I was about to read it when an agitated knock was heard at our door. The visitor, whom I admitted, was a rather haggard and dishevelled elderly gentleman, who, as he entered, peered inquisitively through his concave spectacles from one of us to the other.

"Allow me to introduce myself, gentlemen," said he. "I am Professor Poppelbaum."

Thorndyke bowed and offered a chair.

"I called yesterday afternoon," our visitor continued, "at Scotland Yard, where I heard of your remarkable decipherment and of the convincing proof of its correctness. Thereupon I borrowed the cryptogram, and have spent the entire night in studying it, but I cannot connect your solution with any of the characters. I wonder if you would do me the great favour of enlightening me as to your method of decipherment, and so save me further sleepless nights? You may rely on my discretion."

"Have you the document with you?" asked Thorndyke.

The professor produced it from his pocket-book, and passed it to my colleague.

"You observe, professor," said the latter, "that this is a laid paper, and has no water-mark?"

"Yes, I noticed that."

"And that the writing is in indelible Chinese ink?"

"Yes, yes," said the *savant* impatiently; "but it is the inscription that interests me, not the paper and ink."

"Precisely," said Thorndyke. "Now, it was the ink that interested me when I caught a glimpse of the document three days ago. 'Why,' I asked myself, 'should anyone use this troublesome medium'—for this appears to be stick ink—'when good writing ink is to be had?' What advantages has Chinese ink over writing ink? It has several advantages as a drawing ink, but for writing purposes it has only one: it is quite unaffected by wet. The obvious inference, then, was that this document was, for some reason, likely to be exposed to wet. But this inference instantly suggested another, which I was yesterday able to put to the test—thus."

He filled a tumbler with water, and, rolling up the document, dropped it in. Immediately there began to appear on it a new set of characters of a curious grey colour. In a few seconds Thorndyke lifted out the wet paper, and held it up to the light, and now there was plainly visible an inscription in transparent lettering, like a very distinct water-mark. It was in printed Roman capitals, written across the other writing, and read:

"THE PICKERDILLEY STUF IS UP THE CHIMBLY 416 WARDOUR ST 2ND FLOUR BACK IT WAS HID BECOS OF OLD MOAKEYS JOOD MOAKEY IS A BLITER."

The professor regarded the inscription with profound disfavour.

"How do you suppose this was done?" he asked gloomily.

"I will show you," said Thorndyke. "I have prepared a piece of paper to demonstrate the process to Dr. Jervis. It is exceedingly simple."

He fetched from the office a small plate of glass, and a photographic dish in which a piece of thin notepaper was soaking in water.

"This paper," said Thorndyke, lifting it out and laying it on the glass, "has been soaking all night, and is now quite pulpy."

He spread a dry sheet of paper over the wet one, and on the former wrote heavily with a hard pencil, "Moakey is a bliter." On lifting the upper sheet, the writing was seen to be transferred in a deep grey to the wet paper, and when the latter was held up to the light the inscription stood out clear and transparent as if written with oil.

"When this dries," said Thorndyke, "the writing will completely disappear, but it will reappear whenever the paper is again wetted."

The professor nodded.

"Very ingenious," said he—"a sort of artificial palimpsest, in fact. But I do not understand how that illiterate man could have written in the difficult Moabite script."

"He did not," said Thorndyke. "The 'cryptogram' was probably written by one of the leaders of the gang, who, no doubt, supplied copies to the other members to use instead of blank paper for secret communications. The object of the Moabite writing was evidently to divert attention from the paper itself, in case the communication fell

266

into the wrong hands, and I must say it seems to have answered its purpose very well."

The professor started, stung by the sudden recollection of his labours.

"Yes," he snorted; "but I am a scholar, sir, not a policeman. Every man to his trade."

He snatched up his hat, and with a curt "Good-morning," flung out of the room in dudgeon.

Thorndyke laughed softly.

"Poor professor!" he murmured. "Our playful friend Barton has much to answer for."

Phyllis Annesley's Peril

"One is sometimes disposed to regret," said Thorndyke, as we sat waiting for the arrival of Mr. Mayfield, the solicitor, "that our practice is so largely concerned with the sordid and the unpleasant."

"Yes," I agreed. "Medical Jurisprudence is not always a particularly delicate subject. But it is our line of practice and we have got to take it as we find it."

"A philosophic conclusion, Jervis," he rejoined, "and worthy of my learned friend. It happens that the most intimate contact of Law and Medicine is in crimes against the person and consequently the proper study of the Medical Jurist is crime of that type. It is a regrettable fact, but we must accept it."

"At the same time," said I, "there don't seem to be any Medico-legal issues in this Bland case. The woman was obviously murdered. The only question is, who murdered her? And the answer to that question seems pretty obvious."

"It does," said Thorndyke. "But we shall be better able to judge when we have heard what Mayfield has to tell us. And I think I hear him coming up the stairs now."

I rose to open the door for our visitor, and, as he entered, I looked at him curiously. Mr. Mayfield was quite a young man, and the mixture of deference and nervousness in his manner as he entered the room suggested no great professional experience.

"I am afraid, sir," said he, taking the easy-chair that Thorndyke offered him, "that I ought to have come to you sooner, for the inquest, or, at least, the police court proceedings."

"You reserved your defence, I think?" said Thorndyke.

"Yes," replied the solicitor, with a wry smile. "I had to. There seemed to be nothing to say. So I put in a plea of Not Guilty and reserved the defence in the hope that something might turn up. But

I am gravelled completely. It looks a perfectly hopeless case. I don't know how it strikes you, sir."

"I have seen only the newspaper reports," said Thorndyke. "They are certainly not encouraging. But let us disregard them. I suggest that you recite the facts of the case and I can ask any questions that are necessary to elucidate it further."

"Very well, sir," said Mayfield. "Then I will begin with the disappearance of Mrs. Lucy Bland. That occurred about the eighteenth of last May. At that time she was living, apart from her husband, at Wimbledon, in furnished lodgings. After lunch on the eighteenth she went out, saying that she should not be home until night. She was seen by someone who knew her at Wimbledon Station on the down side about three o'clock. At shortly after six probably on the same day, she went to the Post Office at Lower Ditton to buy some stamps.

"The postmistress, who knew her by sight, is certain that she called there, but cannot swear to the exact date. At any rate, she did not go home that night and was never seen alive again. Her landlady communicated with her husband and he at once applied to the police. But all the inquiries that were made led to nothing. She had disappeared without leaving a trace.

"The discovery was made four months later, on the sixteenth of September. On that day some workmen went to 'The Larches,' a smallish, old-fashioned, riverside house just outside Lower Ditton, to examine the electric wiring. The house was let to a new tenant, and as the meter had shown an unaccountable leakage of current during the previous quarter, they went to see what was wrong.

"To get at the main, they had to take up part of the floor of the dining-room; and when they got the boards up, they were horrified to discover a pair of feet—evidently a woman's feet—projecting from under the next board. They immediately went to the police station and reported what they had seen, whereupon the inspector and a sergeant accompanied them back to the house and directed them to take up several more boards—which they did; and there, jammed in between the joists, was the body of a woman who was subsequently identified as Mrs. Lucy Bland. The corpse appeared to be perfectly fresh and only quite recently dead; but at the postmortem it was discovered that it had been embalmed or preserved by injecting a solution of *formaldehyde* and might have been dead three or four months. The cause of death was given at the inquest as suffocation, probably preceded by the forcible administration of chloroform."

"The house, I understand," said Thorndyke, "belongs to one of the accused?"

"Yes. Miss Phyllis Annesley. It is her freehold, and she lived in it until recently. Last autumn, however, she took to travelling about and then partly dismantle the house and stored most of the furniture; but she kept two bedrooms furnished and the kitchen and dining, room in just usable condition, and she used to put up there for a day or two in the intervals of her journeys, either alone or with her maid."

"And as to Miss Annesley's relations with the Blands?"

"She had known them both for some years. With Leonard Bland she was admittedly on affectionate terms, though there is no suggestion of improper relations between them. But Bland used to visit her when she lived there and they used to go for picnics on the river in the boat belonging to the house. Mrs. Bland also occasionally visited Miss Annesley, and they seem to have been on quite civil terms. Of course, she knew about her husband's affection for the lady, but she doesn't seem to have had any strong feeling about it."

"And what were the relations of the husband and wife?" asked Thorndyke.

"Rather queer. They didn't suit one another, so they simply agreed to go their own ways. But they don't seem to have been unfriendly, and Mr. Bland was most scrupulous in regard to his financial obligations to his wife. He not only allowed her liberal maintenance but went out of his way to make provision for her. I will give you an instance, which impressed me very much.

"An old acquaintance of his, a Mr. Julius Wicks, who had been working for some years in the film studio at Los Angeles, came to England about a year ago and proposed to Bland that they should start one or two picture theatres in the provinces, Bland to find the money—which he was able to do—and Wicks to provide the technical knowledge and do the actual management. Bland agreed, and a partnership was arranged on the basis of two-thirds of the profits to Bland and one-third to Wicks; with the proviso that if Bland should die, all his rights as partner should be vested in his wife."

"And supposing Wicks should die?"

"Well, Wicks was not married, though he was engaged to a film actress. On his death, his share would go to Bland, and similarly, on Bland's death, if he should die after his wife, his share would go to his partner."

"Bland seems to have been a fairly good business man," said I.

271

"Yes," Mayfield agreed. "The arrangement was all in his favour. But he was the capitalist, you see. However, the point is that Bland was quite mindful of his wife's interests. There was nothing like enmity."

"Then," said Thorndyke, "one motive is excluded. Was the question of divorce ever raised?"

"It couldn't be," said Mayfield. "There were no grounds on either side. But it seems to have been recognised and admitted that if Bland had been free he would have married Miss Annesley. They were greatly attached to one another."

"That seems a fairly solid motive," said I.

"It appears to be," Mayfield admitted. "But to me, who have known these people for years and have always had the highest opinion of them, it seems—Well, I can't associate this atrocious crime with them at all. However, that is not to the point. I must get on with the facts.

"Very soon after the discovery at 'The Larches,' the police learned that there had been rumours in Lower Ditton for some time past of strange happenings at the house and that two labourers named Brodie and Stanton knew something definite. They accordingly looked up these two men and examined them separately, when both men made substantially identical statements, which were to this effect:

"About the middle of May—neither of them was able to give an exact date—between nine and ten in the evening, they were walking together along the lane in which 'The Larches' is situated when they saw a man lurking in the front garden of the house. As they were passing, he came to the gate and beckoned to them, and when they approached he whispered: 'I say, mates, there's something rummy going on in this house.'

"'How do you know?' asked Brodie.

"'I've been looking in through a hole in the shutter,' the man replied. 'They seem to be hiding something under the floor. Come and have a look.'

"The two men followed him up the garden to the back of the house, where he took them to one of the windows of a ground-floor room and pointed to two holes in the outside shutters.

"'Just take a peep in through them,' said he.

"Each of the men put an eye to one of the holes and looked in; and this is what they both saw: There were two rooms, communicating, with a wide arch between them. Through the arch and at the far end of the second room were two persons, a man and a woman. They were on their hands and knees, apparently doing something to the

272

floor. Presently the man, who had on a painter's white blouse, rose and picked up a board which he stood on end against the wall. Then he stooped again and seemed to lay hold of something that lay on the floor—something that looked like a large bundle or a roll of carpet.

"At this moment something passed across in front of the holes and shut out the view—so that there must have been a third person in the room. When the obstructing body moved away again, the man was kneeling on the floor looking down at the bundle and the woman had come forward and was standing just in the arch with a pair of pincers in her hand. She was dressed in a spotted pinafore with a white sailor collar, and both the men recognised her at once as Miss Annesley."

"They knew her by sight, then?" said Thorndyke.

"Yes. They were Ditton men. It is a small place and everybody in it must have known Miss Annesley and Bland, too, for that matter. Well, they saw her standing in the archway quite distinctly. Neither of the men has the least doubt as to her identity. They watched her for perhaps half a minute. Then the invisible person inside moved in front of the peepholes and shut out the scene.

"When the obstruction moved away, the woman was back in the farther room, kneeling on the floor. The bundle had disappeared and the man was in the act of taking the board, which he had rested against the wall, and laying it in its place in the floor. After this, the obstruction kept coming and going, so that the watchers only got occasional glimpses of what was going on. They saw the man apparently hammering nails into the floor and they heard faint sounds of knocking. On one occasion, towards the end of the proceedings, they saw the man standing in the archway with his face towards them, apparently looking at something in his hand.

"They couldn't see what the thing was, but they clearly recognised the man as Mr. Bland, whom they both knew well by sight. Then the view was shut out again, and when they next saw Mr. Bland, he was standing by Miss Annesley in the farther room, looking down at the floor and taking off his blouse. As it seemed that the business was over and that Bland and Miss Annesley would probably be coming out, the men thought it best to clear off, lest they should be seen.

"As they walked up the lane, they discussed the mysterious proceedings that they had witnessed, but could make nothing of them. The stranger suggested that perhaps Miss Annesley was hiding her plate or valuables to keep them safe while she was travelling, and hinted that it might be worth someone's while to take the floor up later on and see what was there. But this suggestion Brodie and Stanton, who are most respectable men, condemned strongly, and they agreed that, as the affair was no concern of theirs, they had better say nothing about it. But they evidently must have talked to some extent, for the affair got to be spoken about in the village, and, of course, when the body was discovered under the floor, the gossip soon reached the ears of the police."

"Has the third man come forward to give evidence?" Thorndyke asked.

"No, he has not been found yet. He was a stranger to both the men; apparently a labourer or farm-hand or tramp. But nothing is known about him. So that is the case; and it is about as hopeless as it is possible to be. Of course, there is the known character of the accused; but against that is a perfectly intelligible motive and the evidence of two eye-witnesses. Do you think you would be disposed to undertake the defence, sir? I realise that it is asking a great deal of you."

"I should like to think the matter over," said Thorndyke, "and make a few preliminary inquiries. And I should want to read over the depositions in full detail. Can you let me have them?"

"I have a *verbatim* report of the police court proceedings and of the inquest. I will leave them with you now. And when may I hope to have your decision?"

"By the day after tomorrow at the latest," was the reply, on which the young solicitor produced a bundle of papers from his bag, and having laid them on the table, thanked us both and took his leave.

"Well, Thorndyke," I said when Mayfield had gone, "I am fairly mystified. I know you would not undertake a merely formal defence, but what else you could do is, I must confess, beyond my imagination. It seems to me that the prosecution have only to call the witnesses and the verdict of 'Guilty' follows automatically."

"That is how it appears to me," said Thorndyke. "And if it still appears so when I have read the reports and made my preliminary investigations, I shall decline the brief. But appearances are sometimes misleading."

With this he took the reports and the notebook, in which he had made a few brief memoranda of Mayfield's summary of the case, and drawing a chair to the table, proceeded, with quiet concentration, to read through and make notes on the evidence. When he had finished, he passed the reports to me and rose, pocketing his note book and glancing at his watch.

"Read the evidence through carefully, Jervis," said he, "and tell me if you see any possible way out. I have one or two calls to make, but I shall not be more than an hour. When I come back, I should like to hear your views on the case."

During his absence I read the reports through with the closest attention. Something in Thorndyke's tone had seemed to hint at a possible flaw in the case for the prosecution. But I could find no escape from the conviction that these two persons were guilty. The reports merely amplified what Mayfield had told us; and the added detail, especially in the case of the eye witnesses, only made the evidence more conclusive. I could not see the material for even a formal defence.

In less than an hour my colleague re-entered the room, and I was about to give him my impressions of the evidence when he said, "It is rather early, Jervis, but I think we had better go and get some lunch. I have arranged to go down to Ditton this afternoon and have a look at the house. Mayfield has given me a note to the police sergeant, who has the key and is virtually in possession."

"I don't see what you will gain by looking at the house," said I.

"Neither do I," he replied. "But it is a good rule always to inspect the scene of a crime and all the evidence as far as possible."

"Well," I said, "it is a forlorn hope. I have read through the evidence and it seems to me that the accused are as good as convicted. I can see no line of defence at all. Can you?"

"At present I cannot," he replied. "But there are one or two points that I should like to clear up before I decide whether or not to undertake the defence. And I have a great belief in first-hand observation."

We consumed a simplified lunch at one of our regular haunts in Fleet Street and from thence were conveyed by a taxi to Waterloo, where we caught the selected train to Lower Ditton. I had put the reports in my pocket, and during our journey I read them over again, to see if I could discover any point that would be cleared up by an inspection of the premises.

For, in spite of the rather vague purpose implied by Thorndyke's explanation, something in my colleague's manner, coupled with long experience of his method made me suspect that he had some definite object in view. But nothing was said by either of us during the journey, nor did we discuss the case; indeed, so far as I could see, there was nothing to discuss.

Our reception at the Lower Ditton Police Station was something more than cordial. The sergeant recognised Thorndyke instantly—it appeared that he was an enthusiastic admirer of my colleague—and after a brief glance at Mayfield's note, took a key from his desk and put on his helmet.

"Lord bless you, sir," said he, "I don't need to be told who you are. I've seen you in court, and heard you. I'll come along with you to the house myself."

I suspected that Thorndyke would have gladly dispensed with this attention, but he accepted it with genial courtesy, and we went forth through the village and along the quiet lane in which the ill-omened house was situated. And as we went, the sergeant commented on the case with curiously unofficial freedom.

"You've got your work cut out, sir, if you are going to conduct the defence. But I wish you luck. I've known Miss Annesley for some years—she was well known in the village here—and a nicer, gentler, more pleasant lady you wouldn't wish to meet. To think of her in connection with a murder—and such a murder, too—such a brutal, callous affair! Well, it's beyond me. And yet there it is, unless those two men are lying."

"Is there any reason to suppose that they are?" I asked.

"Well, no; there isn't. They are good, sober, decent men. And it would be such an atrociously wicked lie. And they both knew the prisoners, and liked them. Everybody liked Mr. Bland and Miss Annesley, though their friendship for one another may not have been quite in order. But I can tell you, sir, these two men are frightfully cut up at having to give evidence. This is the house!"

He opened a gate and we entered the garden, beyond which was a smallish, old-fashioned house, of which the ground-floor windows were protected by outside shutters. We walked round to the back of the house, where was another garden with a lawn and a path leading down to the river.

"Is that a boat-house?" Thorndyke asked, pointing to a small gable that appeared above a clump of lilac bushes.

"Yes," replied the sergeant. "And there is a boat in it; a good, beamy, comfortable tub that Miss Annesley and her friend used to go out picnicking in. This is the window that the men peeped in at, but you can't see much now because the room is all dark."

I looked at the two French windows, which opened on to the lawn, and reflected on this new instance of the folly of wrong-doers. Each window was fitted with a pair of strong shutters, which bolted on the inside, and each shutter was pierced, about five feet from the sill, by a circular hole a little over an inch in diameter. It seemed incredible that two sane persons, engaged in the concealment of a murdered body, should have left those four holes uncovered for any chance eavesdropper to spy on their doings.

But my astonishment at this lack of precaution was still greater when the sergeant admitted us and we stood inside the room, for both the windows, as well as the pair in the farther room, were furnished with heavy curtains.

"Yes," said the sergeant, in answer to my comment, "it's a queer thing how people overlook matters of vital importance. You see, they drew the drawing-room curtains all right, but they forgot these. Is there anything in particular that you want to see, sir?"

"I should like to see where the body was hidden," said Thorndyke, "but I will just look round the rooms first."

He walked slowly to and fro, looking about him and evidently fixing the appearance of the rooms on his memory. Not that there was much to see or remember. The two nearly square rooms communicated through a wide arch, once closed by curtains, as shown by the brass curtain-rod. The back room had been completely dismantled with the exception of the window curtains, but the front room, although the floor and the walls, were bare, was not entirely unfurnished. The sideboard was still in position and bore at each end a tall electric light standard, as did also the mantelpiece. There were three dining chairs and a good-sized gate-leg table stood closed against the wall.

"I see you have not had the floor-boards nailed down," said Thorndyke.

"No, sir; not yet. So we can see where the body was hidden and where the electric main is. The electricians took up the wrong board at first—that is how they came to discover the body. And one of them said that the boards over the main had been raised recently, and he thought that the—er—the accused had meant to hide the body there, but when they got the floor up they struck the main and had to choose a fresh place."

He stooped, and lifting the loose boards, which he stood on end against the mantelpiece, exposed the joists and the earth floor about a foot below them. In one of the spaces the electric main ran and in the adjoining one the apparently disused gas main.

"This is where we found poor Mrs. Bland," said the sergeant, pointing to an empty space. "It was an awful sight. Gave me quite a turn. The poor lady was lying on her side jammed down between the joists and her nose flattened up against one of the timbers. They must have been brutes that did it, and I can't—I really can't believe that Miss Annesley was one of them."

"It looks a narrow place for a body to lie in," said I.

"The joists are sixteen inches apart," said Thorndyke, laying his pocket rule across the space, "and two and a half inches thick. Heavy timber and wide spaces."

He stood up, and turning round, looked towards the windows of the back room. I followed his glance and noted, almost with a start, the two holes in the shutter of the left-hand window (the right-hand window, of course, from outside) glaring into the darkened room like a pair of inquisitive, accusing eyes. The holes in the other window were hardly visible, and the reason for the difference was obvious. The one window had small panes and thick muntins, or sash-bars, whereas the other was glazed, with large sheets of plate glass and had no muntins.

"Of course it would be dark at the time," I said in response to his unspoken comment, "and this room would be lighted up, more or less."

"Not so very dark in May," he replied. "There is a furnished bed-room, isn't there, sergeant?"

"Two, sir," was the reply; and the sergeant forthwith opened the door and led the way across the hall and up the stairs.

"This is Miss Annesley's room," he said, opening a door gingerly and peering in.

We entered the room and looked about us with vague curiosity. It was a simply-furnished room, but dainty and tasteful, with its small four-post bedstead, light easy-chair and little, ladylike writing-table.

"That's Mr. Bland," said the sergeant, pointing to a double photograph-frame on the table, "and the lady is Miss Annesley herself."

I took up the frame and looked curiosity at the two portraits. For a pair of murderers they were certainly uncommonly prepossessing. The man, who looked about thirty-five, was a typical good-looking, middle-class Englishman, while the woman was distinctly handsome, with a thoughtful, refined and gentle cast of face.

"She has something of a Japanese air," said I, "with that coil on the top of the head and the big ivory hairpin stuck through it."

I passed the frame to Thorndyke, who regarded each portrait attentively, and then, taking both photographs out of the frame, closely examined each in turn, back and front, before replacing them.

"The other bedroom," said the sergeant as Thorndyke laid down the frame, "is the spare room. There's nothing to see in it."

Nevertheless he conducted us into it, and when we I had verified his statement we returned downstairs.

"Before we go," said Thorndyke, "I will just see what is opposite those holes."

He walked to the window and was just looking out through one of the holes when the sergeant, who had followed him closely, suddenly slid along the floor and nearly fell.

"Well, I never!" he exclaimed, recovering himself and stooping to pick up some small object. "There's a dangerous thing to leave lying about the floor. Bit of slate pencil—at least, that is what it looks like."

He handed it to Thorndyke, who glanced at it and remarked, "Yes, things that roll under the foot are apt to produce broken bones; but I think you had better take care of it. I may have to ask you something about it at the trial."

We bade the sergeant farewell at the bottom of the lane, and as we turned into the footpath to the station I said: "We don't seem to have picked up very much more than Mayfield told us—excepting that bit of slate pencil. By the way, why did you tell the sergeant to keep it?"

"On the broad principle of keeping everything, relevant or irrelevant. But it wasn't slate pencil; it was a fragment of a small carbon rod."

"Presumably dropped by the electricians who had been working in the room," said I, and then asked, "Have you come to any decision about this case?"

"Yes; I shall undertake the defence."

"Well," I said, "I can't imagine what line you will take. Strong suspicion would have fallen on these two persons even if there had been no witnesses; but the evidence of those two eye-witnesses seems to clench the matter."

"Precisely," said Thorndyke. "That is my position. I rest my case on the evidence of those two men—as I hope it will appear under cross-examination."

This statement of Thorndyke's gave me much food or reflection during the days that followed. But it was not very nourishing food, for the case still remained perfectly incomprehensible. To be sure, if the evidence of the two eye-witnesses could be shown to be false, the ease against the prisoners would break down, since it would bring another suspected person into view. But their evidence was clearly not false. They were men of known respectability and no one doubted the truth of their statements.

Nor was the obscurity of the case lightened in any way by Thorndyke's proceedings. We called together on the two prisoners, but from neither did we elicit any fresh facts. Neither could establish a clear alibi or suggest any explanation of the eye-witnesses' statements. They gave a simple denial of having been in the house at that time or of having ever taken up the floor.

Both prisoners, however, impressed me favourably. Bland, whom we interviewed at Brixton, seemed a pleasant, manly fellow, frank and straightforward though quite shrewd and business-like; while Miss Annesley, whom we saw at Holloway, was a really charming young lady—sweet-faced, dignified and very gracious and gentle in manner. In one respect, indeed, I found her disappointing. The picturesque coil had disappeared from the top of her head and her hair had been shortened ("bobbed" is, I believe, the correct term) into a mere fringe. Thorndyke also noticed the change, and in fact commented on it.

"Yes," she admitted, "it is a disimprovement in my case. It doesn't suit me. But I really had no choice. When I was in Paris in the spring I had an accident. I was having my hair cleaned with petrol when it caught fire. It was most alarming. The hairdresser had the presence of mind to throw a damp towel over my head, and that saved my life. But my hair was nearly all burnt. There was nothing for it but to have it trimmed as evenly as possible. But it looked horrid at first. I had my photograph taken by Barton soon after I came home, just as a record, you know, and it looks awfully odd. I look like a Bluecoat boy."

"By the way," said Thorndyke, "when did you return?"

"I landed in England about the middle of April and went straight to my little flat at Paddington, where I have been living ever since."

"You don't remember where you were on the eighteenth of May?"

"I was living at my flat, but I can't remember what I did on that day. You don't, as a rule, unless you keep a diary, which I do not."

This was not very promising. As we came away from the prison, I felt, on the one hand, a conviction that this sweet, gracious lady could have had no hand in this horrible crime, and on the other an utter despair of extricating her from the web of circumstances in which she had become enmeshed.

From Thorndyke I could gather nothing, except that he was going on with his investigations—a significant fact, in his case. To my artfully disguised questions he had one invariable reply: "My dear Jervis, you have read the evidence, you have seen the house, you have all the facts.

Think the case over and consider the possibilities of cross-examination." And that was all I could get out of him.

He was certainly very busy, but his activities only increased my bewilderment. He sent a well-known architect down to make a scale-plan of the house and grounds; and he dispatched Polton to take photographs of the place from every possible point of view. The latter, indeed, was up to his eyes in work, and enjoying himself amazingly, but as secret as an oyster. As he went about, beaming with happiness and crinkling with self-complacency, he exasperated me to that extent that I could have banged his little head against the wall. In short, though I had watched the development of the case from the beginning, I was still without a glimmer of understanding of it even when I took my seat in court on the morning of the trial.

It was a memorable occasion, and every incident in it is still vivid in my memory. Particularly do I remember looking with a sort of horrified fascination at the female prisoner, standing by her friend in the dock, pale but composed and looking the very type and picture of womanly beauty and dignity; and reflecting with a shudder that the graceful neck—looking longer and more slender from the shortness of the hair—might very probably be, within a matter of days, encircled by the hangman's rope. These lugubrious reflections were interrupted by the entrance of two persons, a man and a woman, who were apparently connected with the case, since as they took their seats they both looked towards the dock and exchanged silent greetings with the prisoners.

"Do you know who those people are, Mayfield?" I asked.

"That is Mr. Julius Wicks, Mr. Bland's partner, and his *fiancée*, Miss Eugenia Kropp, the film actress," he replied.

I was about to ask him if they were here to give evidence when, the preliminaries having come to an end, the counsel for the Crown, Sir John Turville, rose and began his opening speech.

It was a good speech and eminently correct; but its very moderation made it the more damaging. It began with an outline of the facts, almost identical with Mayfield's summary, and a statement of the evidence which would presently be given by the principal witnesses.

"And now," said Sir John, when he had finished his recital, "let us bring these facts to a focus. Considered as a related group, this is what they show us. On the sixteenth of September there is found, concealed under the floor of a certain room in a certain house, the body of a woman who has evidently been murdered. That woman is the separated wife of a man who is on affectionate terms with another woman whom he would admittedly wish to marry and who would be willing to marry him. This murdered woman is, in short, the obstacle to the marriage desired by these two persons. Now the house in which the corpse is concealed is the property of one of those two persons, and both of them have access to it; and no other person has access to it. Here, then, to begin with, is a set of profoundly suspicious circumstances.

"But there are others far more significant. That unfortunate lady, the unwanted wife of the prisoner, Bland, disappeared mysteriously on the eighteenth of last May; and witnesses will prove that the body was deposited under the floor on or about that date. Now, on or about that same date, in that same house, in that same room, in the same part of that room, those two persons, the prisoners at the bar, were seen by two eminently respectable witnesses in the act of concealing some large object under the floor. What could that object have been? The floor of the room has been taken up and nothing whatever but the corpse of this poor murdered lady has been found under it. The irresistible conclusion is that those two persons were then and there engaged in concealing that corpse.

"To sum up, then, the reasons or believing that the prisoners are guilty of the crime with which they are charged are threefold. They had an intelligible and strong motive to commit that crime; they had the opportunity to commit it; and we have evidence from two eyewitnesses which makes it practically an observed fact that the prisoners did actually commit that crime."

As the Crown counsel sat down, pending the swearing of the first witness, I turned to Thorndyke and said anxiously: "I can't imagine what you are going to reply to that."

"My reply," he answered quietly, "will be largely governed by what I am able to elicit in cross-examination." Here the first witness was called—the electrician who discovered the body—and gave his evidence, but Thorndyke made no cross-examination. He was followed by the sergeant, who described the discovery in more detail. As the Crown counsel sat down, Thorndyke rose, and I pricked up my ears.

"Have you mentioned everything that you saw or found in this room?" he asked.

"Yes, at that time. Later—on the second of October—I found a small piece of a carbon pencil on the floor of the front room near the window."

He produced from his pocket an envelope from which he extracted the fragment of the alleged "slate pencil" and passed it to Thorndyke, who, having passed to the judge with the intimation that he wished it to be put in evidence, sat down. The judge inspected the fragment curiously and then cast an inquisitive glance at Thorndyke—as he had done once or twice before. For my colleague's appearance in the role of counsel was a rare event, and one usually productive of surprises.

To the long succession of witnesses who followed Thorndyke listened attentively but did not cross-examine, I saw the judge look at him curiously from time to time and my own curiosity grew more and more intense. Evidently he was saving himself up for the crucial witnesses. At length the name of James Brodie was called, and a serious-looking elderly workman entered the box. He gave his evidence clearly and confidently, though with manifest reluctance, and I could see that his vivid description of that sinister scene made a great impression on the jury. When the examination in chief was finished, Thorndyke rose, and the judge settled himself to listen with an air of close attention.

"Have you ever been inside 'The Larches'?" Thorndyke asked.

"No, sir. I've passed the house twice every day for years, but I've never been inside it."

"When you looked in through the shutter, was the room well lighted?"

"No, 'twas very dim. I could only just see what the people were doing."

"Yet you recognised Miss Annesley quite clearly?"

"Not at first, I didn't. Not until she came and stood in the archway. The light seemed quite good there."

"Did you see her come out of the front room and walk to the arch?"

"No. I saw her in the front room and then something must have stopped up the hole, for 'twas all dark. Then the hole got clear again and I saw her standing in the arch. But I only saw her for a moment or two. Then the hole got stopped again and when it opened she was back in the front room."

"How did you know that the woman in the front room was Miss Annesley? Could you see her face in that dim light?"

"No, but I could tell her by her dress. She wore a striped pinafore with a big, white sailor-collar. Besides, there wasn't nobody else there."

"And with regard to Mr. Bland. Did you see him walk out of the front room and up to the arch?"

"No. 'Twas the same as with Miss Annesley. Something kept passing across the hole. I see him in the front room; then I see him in the arch and then I see him in the front room again."

"When they were in the archway, were they moving or standing still?"

"They both seemed to be standing quite still."

"Was Miss Annesley looking straight towards you?"

"No. Her face was turned away a little."

"I want you to look at these photographs and tell us if any of them shows the head in the position in which you saw it."

He handed a bundle of photographs to the witness, who looked at them, one after another, and at length picked out one.

"That is exactly how she looked," said he. "She might have been standing for this very picture."

He passed the photograph to Thorndyke, who noted the number written on it and passed it to the judge, who also noted the number and laid it on his desk. Thorndyke then resumed: "You say the light was very dim in the front room. Were the electric lamps alight?"

"None that I could see were alight."

"How many electric lamps could you see?"

"Well, there was three hanging from the ceiling and there was two standards on the mantelpiece and one on the sideboard. None of them was alight."

"Was there only one standard on the sideboard?"

"There may have been more, but I couldn't see 'em because I could only see just one corner of the sideboard."

"Could you see the whole of the mantelpiece?"

"Yes. There was a standard lamp at each end."

"Could you see anything on the near side of the mantelpiece?"

"There was a table there: a folding table with twisted legs. But I could only see part of that. The side of the arch cut it off."

"You have said that you could see Miss Annesley quite clearly and could see how she was dressed. Could you see how her hair was arranged?"

"Yes. 'Twas done up on the top of her head in what they calls a bun and there was a sort of a skewer stuck through it."

As the witness gave this answer, a light broke on me. Not a very clear light, for the mystery was still unsolved. But I could see that Thorndyke had a very definite strategic plan. And, glancing at the dock, I was immediately aware that the prisoners had seen the light, too.

"You have described what looked like a hole in the floor," Thorndyke resumed, "where some boards had been raised, near the middle of the room. Was that hole nearer the sideboard or nearer the mantelpiece?"

"It was nearer the mantelpiece," the witness replied; on which Thorndyke sat down, the witness left the box, and both the judge and the counsel for the prosecution rapidly turned over their notes with evident surprise.

The next witness was Albert Stanton and his evidence was virtually a repetition of Brodie's; and when, in cross Thorndyke put over again the same series of questions, he elicited precisely the same answers even to the recognition of the same photograph. And again I began to see a glimmer of light. But only a glimmer.

Stanton being the last of the witnesses for the Crown, his brief re-examination by Sir John Turville completed the case for the prosecution. Thereupon Thorndyke rose and announced that he called witnesses, and forthwith the first of them appeared in the box. This was Frederick Stokes, A.R.I.B.A., architect, and he deposed that he had made a careful survey of the house called "The Larches" at Lower Ditton and prepared a plan on the scale of half an inch to a foot. He swore that the plan—of which he produced the original and a number of lithographed duplicates—was true and exact in every respect. Thorndyke took the plans from him and passing them to the judge asked that the original should be put in evidence and the duplicates handed to the jury.

The next witness was Joseph Barton of Kensington, photographer. He deposed to having taken photographs of Miss Annesley on various occasions, the last being on the twenty-third of last April. He produced copies of them all with the date written on each. He swore that the dates written were the correct dates. The photographs were handed up to the judge, who looked them over, one by one. Suddenly he seemed, as it were, to stiffen and turned quickly from the photographs to his notes; and I knew that he had struck the last portrait—the one with the short hair.

As the photographer left the box, his place was taken by no less a person than our ingenious laboratory assistant; who, having taken his place, beamed on the judge, the jury and the court in general, with a face wreathed in crinkly smiles. Nathaniel Polton, being sworn, deposed that, on the fifteenth of October, he proceeded to "The Larches" at Lower Ditton and took three photographs of the ground-floor rooms. The first was taken through the right-hand hole of the shutter marked A in the plan; the second through the left-hand hole, and the third from a point inside the back room between the windows and nearer to the window marked B. He produced those photographs with the particulars written on each. He had also made some composite photographs showing the two prisoners dressed as the witnesses, Brodie and Stanton, had described them.

The bodies in those photographs were the bodies of Miss Winifred Blake and Mr. Robert Anstey, K.C., respectively. On these bodies the heads of the prisoners had been printed; and here Polton described the method of substitution in detail. The purpose of the photographs was to show that a photograph could be produced with the head of one person and the body of another. He also deposed to having seen and taken possession of two photographs, one of each of the two prisoners, which he found in the bedroom and which he now produced and passed to the judge. And this completed his evidence.

Thorndyke now called the prisoner, Bland, and having elicited from him a sworn denial of the charge, proceeded to examine him respecting the profits from his three picture theatres; which, it appeared, amount to over six thousand pounds *per annum*.

"In the event of your death, what becomes of this valuable property?"

"If my wife had been alive it would have gone to her, but as she is dead, it goes to my partner and manager, Mr. Julius Wicks."

"In whose custody was the house at Ditton while Miss Annesley was in France?"

"In mine. The keys were in my possession."

"Were the keys ever out of your possession?"

"Only for one day. My partner, Mr. Wicks, asked to be allowed to use the boat for a trip on the river and to take a meal in the house. So I lent him the keys, which he returned the next day."

After a short cross-examination, Bland returned to the dock and was succeeded by Miss Annesley, who, having given a sworn denial of the charge, described her movements in France and in London about the period of the crime. She also described, in answer to a question, the circumstances under which she had lost her hair.

"Can you remember the date on which this accident happened?" Thorndyke asked.

"Yes. It was on the thirtieth of March. I made a note of the date, so that I could see how long my hair took to grow."

As Thorndyke sat down, the counsel for the prosecution rose and made a somewhat searching cross-examination, but without in any way shaking the prisoner's evidence. When this was concluded and Miss Annesley had returned to the dock, Thorndyke rose to address the court for the defence.

"I shall not occupy your time, gentlemen," he began, "by examining the whole mass of evidence nor by arguing the question of motive. The guilt or innocence of the prisoners turns on the accuracy or inaccuracy of the evidence of the two witnesses, Brodie and Stanton; and to the examination of that evidence I shall confine myself.

"Now that evidence, as you may have noticed, presents some remarkable discrepancies. In the first place, both witnesses describe what they saw in identical terms. They saw exactly the same things in exactly the same relative positions. But this is a physical impossibility, if they were really looking into a room; for they were looking in from different points of view; through different holes, which were two feet six inches apart. But there is another much more striking discrepancy. Both these men have described, most intelligently, fully and clearly, a number of objects in that room which were totally invisible to both of them; and they have described as only partly visible other objects which were in full view.

"Both witnesses, for instance, have described the mantelpiece with its two standard lamps and a table with twisted legs on the near side of it; and both saw one corner only of the sideboard. But if you look at the architect's plan and test it with a straight-edge, you will see that neither the mantelpiece nor the table could possibly be seen by either. The whole of that side of the room was hidden from them by the jamb of the arch. While as to the sideboard, the whole of it, with its two standards, was visible to Brodie, and to Stanton the whole of it excepting a small portion of the near side.

"But further, if you lay the straight-edge on the point marked C and test it against the sides of the arch, you will see that a person standing at that spot would get the exact view described by both the witnesses. I pass round duplicate plans with pencil lines ruled on them; but in case you find any difficulty in following the plans, I have put in the photographs of the room taken by Polton. The first photograph was taken through the hole used by Brodie, and shows exactly what he would have seen on looking through that hole; and you see that it agrees completely with the plan but disagrees totally with his description. The second photograph shows what was visible to Stanton; and the third photograph, taken from the point marked C, shows exactly the view described by both the witnesses, but which neither of them could possibly have seen under the circumstances stated.

"Now what is the explanation of these extraordinary discrepancies? No one, I suppose, doubts the honesty of, these witnesses. I certainly do not. I have no doubt whatever that they were telling the truth to the best of their belief. Yet they have stated that they saw things which it is physically impossible that they could have seen. How can these amazing contradictions be reconciled?"

He paused, and in the breathless silence, I noticed that the judge was gazing at him with an expression of intense expectancy; an expression that was reflected on the jury and indeed on every person present.

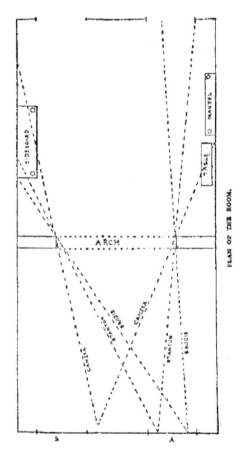

"Well, gentlemen," he resumed, "there is one explanation which completely reconciles these contradictions; and that explanation also reconciles all the other strange contradictions and discrepancies which you may have noticed. If we assume that these two men, instead of looking through an arch into a room, as they believed, were really looking at a moving picture thrown on a screen stretched across the arch, all the contradictions vanish. Everything becomes perfectly plain, consistent and understandable."

"Thus both men, from two different points of view, saw exactly the same scene; naturally, if they were both looking at the same picture, but otherwise quite impossible. Again, both men, from the point A, saw a view which was visible only from the point C. Perfectly natural if they were both looking at a picture taken from the point C; for a picture is the same picture from whatever point of view it is seen. But otherwise a physical impossibility.

"You may object that these men would have seen the difference between a picture and a real room. Perhaps they would, even in that

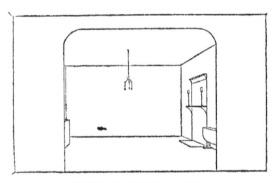

THE ROOM AS DESCRIBED BY BRODIE.

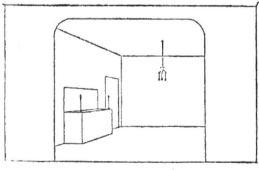

THE ROOM AS SEEN FROM BRODIE'S SPYHOLE.

289

dim light—if they had looked at the scene with both eyes. But each man was looking with only one eye—through a small hole. Now it requires the use of both eyes to distinguish between a solid object and a flat picture. To a one-eyed man there is no difference—which is probably the reason that one-eyed artists are such accurate draughtsmen—they see the world around them as a flat picture, just as they draw it, whereas a two-eyed artist has to turn the solid into the flat. For the same reason, if you look at a picture with one eye shut it tends to look solid, really because the frame and the solid objects around it have gone flat. So that, if this picture was coloured, as it must have been, it would have been indistinguishable, to these one-eyed observers, from the solid reality.

"Then, let us see how the other contradictions disappear. There is the appearance of the prisoner Annesley. She was seen—on or after the eighteenth of May—with her long hair coiled on the top of her head. But at that date her hair was quite short. You have heard the evidence and you have the photograph taken on the twenty-third of April showing her with short hair, like a man's. Here is a contradiction which vanishes at once if you realise that these men were not looking at Miss Annesley at all, but at a photograph of her taken more than a year previously.

"And everything agrees with this assumption. The appearance of Miss Annesley has been declared by the witnesses to be identical with that photograph—a copy of which was in the house and could have been copied by anyone who had access to the house. Her figure was perfectly stationary. She appeared suddenly in the arch and then disappeared; she was not seen to come or to go. And the light kept coming and going, with intervals of darkness which are inexplicable, but that exactly fitted these appearances and disappearances. Then the figure was well lighted, though the room was nearly dark. Of course it was well lighted. It had to be recognised. And of course the rest of the room was dimly lighted, because the film-actors in the background had to be unrecognised.

"Then there is the extraordinary dress; the striped pinafore with the great white collar and the painter's blouse worn by Bland. Why this ridiculous masquerade? Its purpose is obvious. It was to make these observers believe that the portraits in the arch—which they mistook for real people—were the same persons as the film-actors in the background, whose features they could not distinguish. And Mr. Polton has shown us how the clothing of the portraits was managed.

"Then there is the lighting of the room. How was it lighted? None of the electric lamps was alight. But—a piece of a carbon pencil from an arc lamp, such as kinematographers use, has been found near the point C, from which spot the picture would have been taken and exhibited; and the electric light meter showed, about this date, an unaccountable leakage of current such as would be explained by the use of an arc lamp.

"Then the evidence of the witnesses shows the hole in the floor in the wrong place. Of course it could not have been a real hole, for the gas and electric mains were just underneath. It was probably an oblong of black paper. But why was it in the wrong place? The explanation, I suggest, is that the picture was taken before the murder (and probably shown before the murder, too); that the spot shown was the one in which it was intended to bury the body, but that when the floor was taken up after the murder, the mains were found underneath and a new spot had to be chosen.

"Finally—as to the discrepancies—what has become of the third spectator? The mysterious man who came to the gate and called in these two men from the lane—along which they were known to pass every day at about the same time? Who is this mysterious individual? And where is he? Can we give him a name? Can we say that he is at this moment in this court, sitting amongst the spectators, listening to the pleadings in defence of his innocent victims, the prisoners who stand at the bar on their deliverance? I affirm, gentlemen, that we can. And more than that it is not permitted to me to say."

He paused, and a strange, impressive hush fell on the court. Men and women furtively looked about them; the jury stared openly into the body of the court, and the judge, looking up from his notes, cast a searching glance among the spectators. Suddenly my eye lighted on Mr. Wicks and his *fiancée*. The man was wiping away the sweat that streamed down his ashen, ghastly face; the woman had rested her head in her hands, and was trembling as if in an ague-fit.

I was not the only observer. One after another—spectators, ushers, jurymen, counsel, judge—noticed the terror-stricken pair, until every eye in the court was turned on them. And the silence that fell on the place was like the silence of the grave.

It was a dramatic moment. The air was electric; the crowded court tense with emotion. And Thorndyke, looking, with his commanding figure and severe impassive face, like a personification of Fate and Justices stood awhile motionless and silent, letting emotion set the coping-stone on reason.

At length he resumed his address. "Before concluding," he began, "I have to say a few words on another aspect of the case. The learned counsel for the prosecution, referring to the motive for this crime, has suggested a desire on the part of the prisoners to remove the obstacle to their marriage. But it has been given in evidence that there are other persons who had a yet stronger and more definite motive for getting rid of the deceased Lucy Bland. You have heard that in the event of Bland's death, his partner, Julius Wicks, stood to inherit property of the value of six thousand pounds *per annum*, provided that Bland's wife was already dead.

"Now, the murder of Lucy Bland has fulfilled one of the conditions for the devolution of this property; and if you should convict and his lordship should sentence the prisoner, Bland, then his death on the gallows would fulfil the other condition and this great property would pass to his partner, Julius Wicks—This is a material point; as is also the fact that Wicks is, as you have heard, an expert film-producer and kinema operator; that he has been proved to have had access to the house at Ditton, and that he is engaged to a film-actress.

"In conclusion, I submit that the evidence of Brodie and Stanton makes it certain that they were looking at a moving picture, and that all the other evidence confirms that certainty. But the evidence of this moving picture is the evidence of a conspiracy to throw suspicion on the prisoners. But a conspiracy implies conspirators. And there can be no doubt that those conspirators were the actual murderers of Lucy Bland. But if this be so, and I affirm that there can be no possible doubt that it is so, then it follows that the prisoners are innocent of the crime with which they are charged, and I accordingly ask you for a verdict of 'Not Guilty.'"

As Thorndyke sat down a faint hum arose in the court; but still all eyes were turned towards Wicks and Eugenia Kropp. A moment later the pair rose and walked unsteadily towards the door. But here, I noticed, Superintendent Miller had suddenly appeared and stood at the portal with a uniformed constable. As Wicks and Miss Kropp reached the door, I saw the constable shake his head. With, or without authority, he was refusing to let them leave the court. There was a brief pause. Suddenly there broke out a confused uproar; a scuffle, a loud shriek, the report of a pistol and the shattering of glass; and then I saw Miller grasping the man's wrists and pinning him to the wall, while the shrieking woman struggled with the constable to get to the door.

After the removal of the disturbers—in custody—events moved swiftly. The Crown counsel's reply was brief and colourless, practically abandoning the charge, while the judge's summing-up was a mere précis of Thorndyke's argument with a plain direction for an acquittal. But nothing more was needed; for the jury had so clearly made up their minds that the clerk had hardly uttered his challenge when the foreman replied with the verdict of "Not Guilty." A minute later, when the applause had subsided and after brief congratulations by the judge, the prisoners came down from the dock, into the court, moist-eyed but smiling, to wring Thorndyke's hands and thank him for this wonderful deliverance.

"Yes," agreed Mayfield—himself disposed furtively to wipe his eyes—"that is the word. It was wonderful And yet it was all so obvious—when you knew."

The Missing Mortgagee

PART 1

Early in the afternoon of a warm, humid November day, Thomas Elton sauntered dejectedly along the Margate esplanade, casting an eye now on the slate-coloured sea with its pall of slate-coloured sky, and now on the harbour, where the ebb tide was just beginning to expose the mud. It was a dreary prospect, and Elton varied it by observing the few fishermen and fewer promenaders who walked foot to foot with their distorted reflections in the wet pavement; and thus it was that his eye fell on a smartly-dressed man who had just stepped into a shelter to light a cigar.

A contemporary joker has classified the Scotsmen who abound in South Africa into two groups: those, namely, who hail from Scotland, and those who hail from Palestine. Now, something in the aspect of the broad back that was presented to his view, in that of the curly, black hair and the exuberant raiment, suggested to Elton a Scotsman of the latter type. In fact, there was a suspicion of disagreeable familiarity in the figure which caused him to watch it and slacken his pace.

The man backed out of the shelter, diffusing azure clouds, and, drawing an envelope from his pocket, read something that was written on it. Then he turned quickly—and so did Elton, but not quickly enough. For he was a solitary figure on that bald and empty expanse, and the other had seen him at the first glance. Elton walked away slowly, but he had not gone a dozen paces when he felt the anticipated slap on the shoulder and heard the too well-remembered voice.

"Blow me, if I don't believe you were trying to cut me, Tom," it said.

Elton looked round with ill-assumed surprise. "Hallo, Gordon! Who the deuce would have thought of seeing you here?"

Gordon laughed thickly. "Not you, apparently; and you don't look

295

as pleased as you might now you have seen me. Whereas I'm delighted to see you, and especially to see that things are going so well with you."

"What do you mean?" asked Elton.

"Taking your winter holiday by the sea, like a blooming duke."

"I'm not taking a holiday," said Elton. "I was so worn out that I had to have some sort of change; but I've brought my work down with me, and I put in a full seven hours every day."

"That's right," said Gordon. "'Consider the ant.' Nothing like steady industry! I've brought my work down with me too; a little slip of paper with a stamp on it. You know the article, Tom."

"I know. But it isn't due till tomorrow, is it?"

"Isn't it, by gum! It's due this very day, the twentieth of the month. That's why I'm here. Knowing your little weakness in the matter of dates, and having a small item to collect in Canterbury, I thought I'd just come on, and save you the useless expense that results from forgetfulness."

Elton understood the hint, and his face grew rigid.

"I can't do it, Gordon; I can't really. Haven't got it, and shan't have it until I'm paid for the batch of drawings that I'm working on now."

"Oh, but what a pity!" exclaimed Gordon, taking the cigar from his thick, pouting lips to utter the exclamation. "Here you are, blueing your capital on seaside jaunts and reducing your income at a stroke by a clear four pounds a year."

"How do you make that out?" demanded Elton.

"Tut, tut," protested Gordon, "what an unbusinesslike chap you are! Here's a little matter of twenty pounds quarter's interest. If it's paid now, it's twenty. If it isn't, it goes on to the principal and there's another four pounds a year to be paid. Why don't you try to be more economical, dear boy?"

Elton looked askance at the vampire by his side; at the plump blue-shaven cheeks, the thick black eyebrows, the drooping nose, and the full, red lips that embraced the cigar, and though he was a mild tempered man he felt that he could have battered that sensual, complacent face out of all human likeness, with something uncommonly like enjoyment. But of these thoughts nothing appeared in his reply, for a man cannot afford to say all he would wish to a creditor who could ruin him with a word.

"You mustn't be too hard on me, Gordon," said he. "Give me a little time. I'm doing all I can, you know. I earn every penny that I am able, and I have kept my insurance paid up regularly. I shall be paid for this work in a week or two and then we can settle up."

Gordon made no immediate reply, and the two men walked slowly eastward, a curiously ill-assorted pair: the one prosperous, jaunty, over-dressed; the other pale and dejected, and, with his well-brushed but napless clothes, his patched boots and shiny-brimmed hat, the very type of decent, struggling poverty.

They had just passed the pier, and were coming to the base of the jetty, when Gordon next spoke.

"Can't we get off this beastly wet pavement?" he asked, looking down at his dainty and highly-polished boots. "What's it like down on the sands?"

"Oh, it's very good walking," said Elton, "between here and Fore-ness, and probably drier than the pavement."

"Then," said Gordon, "I vote we go down;" and accordingly they descended the sloping way beyond the jetty. The stretch of sand left by the retiring tide was as smooth and firm as a sheet of asphalt, and far more pleasant to walk upon.

"We seem to have the place all to ourselves," remarked Gordon, "with the exception of some half-dozen dukes like yourself."

As he spoke, he cast a cunning black eye furtively at the dejected man by his side, considering how much further squeezing was possi-ble, and what would be the probable product of a further squeeze; but he quickly averted his gaze as Elton turned on him a look eloquent of contempt and dislike. There was another pause, for Elton made no reply to the last observation; then Gordon changed over from one arm to the other the heavy fur overcoat that he was carrying. "Needn't have brought this beastly thing," he remarked, "if I'd known it was going to be so warm."

"Shall I carry it for you a little way?" asked the naturally polite Elton.

"If you would, dear boy," replied Gordon. "It's difficult to manage an overcoat, an umbrella and cigar all at once."

He handed over the coat with a sigh of relief, and having straight-ened himself and expanded his chest, remarked: "I suppose you're be-ginning to do quite well now, Tom?"

Elton shook his head gloomily. "No," he answered, "it's the same old grind."

"But surely they're beginning to recognise your talents by this time," said Gordon, with the persuasive air of a counsel.

"That's just the trouble," said Elton. "You see, I haven't any, and they recognised the fact long ago. I'm just a journeyman, and journeyman's work is what I get given to me."

"You mean to say that the editors don't appreciate talent when they see it."

"I don't know about that," said Elton, "but they're most infernally appreciative of the lack of it."

Gordon blew out a great cloud of smoke, and raised his eyebrows reflectively. "Do you think," he said after a brief pause, "you give 'em a fair chance? I've seen some of your stuff. It's blooming prim, you know. Why don't you try something more lively? More skittish, you know, old chap; something with legs, you know, and high shoes. See what I mean, old chap? High with good full calves and not too fat in the ankle. That ought to fetch 'em; don't you think so?"

Elton scowled. "You're thinking of the drawings in 'Hold Me Up,'" he said scornfully, "but you're mistaken. Any fool can draw a champagne bottle upside down with a French shoe at the end of it."

"No doubt, dear boy," said Gordon, "but I expect that sort of fool knows what pays."

"A good many fools seem to know that much," retorted Elton; and then he was sorry he had spoken, for Gordon was not really an amiable man, and the expression of his face suggested that he had read a personal application into the rejoinder. So, once more, the two men walked on in silence.

Presently their footsteps led them to the margin of the weed-covered rocks, and here, from under a high heap of bladder-wrack, a large green shore-crab rushed out and menaced them with uplifted claws. Gordon stopped and stared at the creature with Cockney surprise, prodding it with his umbrella, and speculating aloud as to whether it was good to eat. The crab, as if alarmed at the suggestion, suddenly darted away and began to scuttle over the green-clad rocks, finally plunging into a large, deep pool. Gordon pursued it, hobbling awkwardly over the slippery rocks, until he came to the edge of the pool, over which he stooped, raking inquisitively among the weedy fringe with his umbrella.

He was so much interested in his quarry that he failed to allow for the slippery surface on which he stood. The result was disastrous. Of a sudden, one foot began to slide forward, and when he tried to recover his balance, was instantly followed by the other. For a moment he struggled frantically to regain his footing, executing a sort of splashing, stamping dance on the margin. Then, the circling sea birds were startled by a yell of terror, an ivory-handled umbrella flew across the rocks, and Mr. Solomon Gordon took a complete header into the deepest part of the pool. What the crab thought of it history does not relate. What Mr. Gordon thought of it is unsuitable for publication; but, as he rose, like an extremely up-to-date merman, he expressed his sentiments with a wealth of adjectives that brought Elton in the verge of hysteria.

"It's a good job you brought your overcoat, after all," Elton remarked for the sake of saying something, and thereby avoiding the risk of exploding into undeniable laughter. The Hebrew made no reply— at least, no reply that lends itself to *verbatim* report—but staggered towards the hospitable overcoat, holding out his dripping arms. Having inducted him into the garment and buttoned him up, Elton hurried off to recover the umbrella (and, incidentally, to indulge himself in a broad grin), and, having secured it, angled with it for the smart billycock which was floating across the pool.

It was surprising what a change the last minute or two had wrought. The positions of the two men were now quite reversed. Despite his shabby clothing, Elton seemed to walk quite jauntily as compared with his shuddering companion who trotted by his side with short miserable steps, shrinking into the uttermost depths of his enveloping coat, like an alarmed winkle into its shell, puffing out his cheeks and anathematising the Universe in general as well as his chattering teeth would let him.

For some time they hurried along towards the slope by the jetty without exchanging any further remarks; then suddenly, Elton asked: "What are you going to do, Gordon? You can't travel like that."

"Can't you lend me a change?" asked Gordon. Elton reflected. He had another suit, his best suit, which he had been careful to preserve in good condition for use on those occasions when a decent appearance was indispensable. He looked askance at the man by his side and something told him that the treasured suit would probably receive less careful treatment than it was accustomed to. Still the man couldn't be allowed to go about in wet clothes.

"I've got a spare suit," he said. "It isn't quite up to your style, and may not be much of a fit, but I daresay you'll be able to put up with it for an hour or two."

"It'll be dry anyhow," mumbled Gordon, "so we won't trouble about the style. How far is it to your rooms?"

The plural number was superfluous. Elton's room was in a little ancient flint house at the bottom of a narrow close in the old quarter of the town. You reached it without any formal preliminaries of bell or knocker by simply letting yourself in by a street door, crossing a tiny room, opening the door of what looked like a narrow cupboard, and squeezing up a diminutive flight of stairs, which was unexpectedly exposed to view. By following this procedure, the two men reached a small bed-sitting-room; that is to say, it was a bed room, but by sitting down on the bed, you converted it into a sitting-room.

Gordon puffed out his cheeks and looked round distastefully.

"You might just ring for some hot water, old chappie," he said.

Elton laughed aloud. "Ring!" he exclaimed. "Ring what? Your clothes are the only things that are likely to get wrung."

"Well, then, sing out for the servant," said Gordon.

Elton laughed again. "My dear fellow," said he, "we don't go in for servants. There is only my landlady and she never comes up here. She's too fat to get up the stairs, and besides, she's got a game leg. I look after my room myself. You'll be all right if you have a good rub down."

Gordon groaned, and emerged reluctantly from the depths of his overcoat, while Elton brought forth from the chest of drawers the promised suit and the necessary undergarments. One of these latter Gordon held up with a sour smile, as he regarded it with extreme disfavour.

"I shouldn't think," said he, "you need have been at the trouble of marking them so plainly. No one's likely to want to run away with them."

The undergarments certainly contrasted very unfavourably with the delicate garments which he was peeling off, excepting in one respect; they were dry; and that had to console him for the ignominious change.

The clothes fitted quite fairly, notwithstanding the difference between the figures of the two men; for while Gordon was a slender man grown fat, Elton was a broad man grown thin; which, in a way, averaged their superficial area.

Elton watched the process of investment and noted the caution with which Gordon smuggled the various articles from his own pockets into those of the borrowed garments without exposing them to view; heard the jingle of money; saw the sumptuous gold watch and massive chain transplanted and noted with interest the large leather wallet that came forth from the breast pocket of the wet coat. He got a better view of this from the fact that Gordon himself examined it narrowly, and even opened it to inspect its contents.

"Lucky that wasn't an ordinary pocketbook." he remarked. "If it had been, your receipt would have got wet, and so would one or two other little articles that wouldn't have been improved by salt water. And, talking of the receipt, Tom, shall I hand it over now?"

"You can if you like," said Elton; "but as I told you, I haven't got the money;" on which Gordon muttered: "Pity, pity," and thrust the wallet into his, or rather, Elton's breast pocket.

A few minutes later, the two men came out together into the gathering darkness, and as they walked slowly up the close, Elton asked: "Are you going up to town tonight, Gordon?"

"How can I?" was the reply. "I can't go without my clothes. No, I shall run over to Broadstairs. A client of mine keeps a boarding-house there. He'll have to put me up for the night, and if you can get my clothes cleaned and dried I can come over for them tomorrow."

These arrangements having been settled, the two men adjourned, at Gordon's suggestion, for tea at one of the restaurants on the Front; and after that, again at Gordon's suggestion, they set forth together along the cliff path that leads to Broadstairs by way of Kingsgate.

"You may as well walk with me into Broadstairs," said Gordon; "I'll stand you the fare back by rail;" and to this Elton had agreed, not because he was desirous of the other man's company, but because he still had some lingering hopes of being able to adjust the little difficulty respecting the instalment.

He did not, however, open the subject at once. Profoundly as he loathed and despised the human spider whom necessity made his associate for the moment, he exerted himself to keep up a current of amusing conversation. It was not easy; for Gordon, like most men whose attention is focussed on the mere acquirement of money, looked with a dull eye on the ordinary interests of life. His tastes in art he had already hinted at, and his other tastes lay much in the same direction. Money first, for its own sake, and then those coarser and more primitive gratifications that it was capable of purchasing. This was the horizon that bounded Mr. Solomon Gordon's field of vision.

Nevertheless, they were well on their way before Elton alluded to the subject that was uppermost in both their minds.

"Look here, Gordon," he said at length, "can't you manage to give me a bit more time to pay up this instalment? It doesn't seem quite fair to keep sending up the principal like this."

"Well, dear boy," replied Gordon, "it's your own fault, you know. If you would only bear the dates in mind, it wouldn't happen."

"But," pleaded Elton, "just consider what I'm paying you. I originally borrowed fifty pounds from you, and I'm now paying you eighty pounds a year in addition to the insurance premium. That's close on a hundred a year; just about half that I manage to earn by working away like I do. If you stick it up any farther you won't leave me enough to keep body and soul together; which really means that I shan't be able to pay you at all."

There was a brief pause; then Gordon said dryly: "You talk about not paying, dear boy, as if you had forgotten about that promissory note."

Elton set his teeth. His temper was rising rapidly. But he restrained himself.

"I should have a pretty poor memory if I had," he replied, "considering the number of reminders you've given me."

"You've needed them, Tom," said the other. "I've never met a slacker man in keeping to his engagements."

At this Elton lost his temper completely.

"That's a damned lie!" he exclaimed, "and you know it, you infernal, dirty, blood-sucking parasite."

Gordon stopped dead.

"Look here, my friend," said he; "none of that. If I've any of your damned sauce, I'll give you a sound good hammering."

"The deuce you will!" said Elton, whose fingers were itching, not for the first time, to take some recompense for all that he had suffered from the insatiable usurer. "Nothing's preventing you now, you know, but I fancy *cent. per cent.* is more in your line than fighting."

"Give me any more sauce and you'll see," said Gordon.

"Very well," was the quiet rejoinder. "I have great pleasure in informing you that you are a human maw-worm. How does that suit you?"

For reply, Gordon threw down his overcoat and umbrella on the grass at the side of the path, and deliberately slapped Elton on the cheek.

The reply followed instantly in the form of a smart left-hander, which took effect on the bridge of the Hebrew's rather prominent nose. Thus the battle was fairly started, and it proceeded with all the fury of accumulated hatred on the one side and sharp physical pain on the other. What little science there was appertained to Elton, in spite of which, however, he had to give way to his heavier, better nour-ished and more excitable opponent. Regardless of the punishment he received, the infuriated Jew rushed at him and, by sheer weight of onslaught, drove him backward across the little green.

Suddenly, Elton, who knew the place by daylight, called out in alarm.

"Look out, Gordon! Get back, you fool!"

But Gordon, blind with fury, and taking this as attempt to escape, only pressed him harder. Elton's pugnacity died out instantly in mortal terror. He shouted out another warning and as Gordon still pressed him, battering furiously, he did the only thing that was possible: he dropped to the ground. And then, in the twinkling of an eye came the catastrophe. Borne forward by his own momentum, Gordon stumbled over Elton's prostrate body, staggered forward a few paces, and fell. Elton heard a muffled groan that faded quickly, and mingled with the sound of falling earth and stones. He sprang to his feet and looked round and saw that he was alone.

For some moments he was dazed by the suddenness of the awful thing that had happened. He crept timorously towards the unseen edge of the cliff, and listened.

There was no sound save the distant surge of the breakers, and the scream of an invisible sea-bird. It was useless to try to look over. Near as he was, he could not, even now, distinguish the edge of the cliff from the dark beach below. Suddenly he bethought him of a narrow cutting that led down from the cliff to the shore. Quickly crossing the green, and mechanically stooping to pick up Gordon's overcoat and umbrella, he made his way to the head of the cutting and ran down the rough chalk roadway. At the bottom he turned to the right and, striding hurriedly over the smooth sand, peered into the darkness at the foot of the cliff.

Soon there loomed up against the murky sky the shadowy form of the little headland on which he and Gordon had stood; and, almost at the same moment, there grew out of the darkness of the beach a darker spot amidst a constellation of smaller spots of white. As he drew nearer the dark spot took shape; a horrid shape with sprawling limbs and a head strangely awry. He stepped forward, trembling, and spoke the name that the thing had borne. He grasped the flabby hand, and laid his fingers on the wrist; but it only told him the same tale as did that strangely misplaced head. The body lay face downwards, and he had not the courage to turn it over; but that his enemy was dead he had not the faintest doubt.

He stood up amidst the litter of fallen chalk and earth and looked down at the horrible, motionless thing, wondering numbly and vaguely what he should do. Should he go and seek assistance? The answer to that came in another question. How came that body to be lying on the beach? And what answer should he give to the inevitable questions? And swiftly there grew up in his mind, born of the horror of the thing that was, a yet greater horror of the thing that might be.

A minute later, a panic-stricken man stole with stealthy swiftness up the narrow cutting and set forth towards Margate, stopping *anon* to listen, and stealing away off the path into the darkness, to enter the town by the inland road.

Little sleep was there that night for Elton in his room in the old flint house. The dead man's clothes, which greeted him on his arrival, hanging limply on the towel-horse where he had left them, haunted him through the night. In the darkness, the sour smell of damp cloth assailed him with an endless reminder of their presence, and after each brief doze, he would start up in alarm and hastily light his candle; only to throw its flickering light on those dank, drowned-looking vestments. His thoughts, half-controlled, as night thoughts are, flitted erratically from the unhappy past to the unstable present, and thence to the incalculable future.

Once he lighted the candle specially to look at his watch to see if the tide had yet crept up to that solitary figure on the beach; nor could he rest again until the time of high water was well past. And all through these wanderings of his thoughts there came, recurring like a horrible refrain, the question what would happen when the body was found? Could he be connected with it and, if so, would he be charged with murder? At last he fell asleep and slumbered on until the landlady thumped at the staircase door to announce that she had brought his breakfast.

As soon as he was dressed he went out. Not, however, until he had stuffed Gordon's still damp clothes and boots, the cumbrous overcoat and the smart billy-cock hat into his trunk, and put the umbrella into the darkest corner of the cupboard. Not that anyone ever came up to the room, but that, already, he was possessed with the uneasy secretiveness of the criminal. He went straight down to the beach; with what purpose he could hardly have said, but an irresistible impulse drove him thither to see if it was there. He went down by the jetty and struck out eastward over the smooth sand, looking about him with dreadful expectation for some small crowd or hurrying messenger.

From the foot of the cliffs, over the rocks to the distant line of breakers, his eye roved with eager dread, and still he hurried eastward, always drawing nearer to the place that he feared to look on. As he left the town behind, so he left behind the one or two idlers on the beach, and when he turned Foreness Point he lost sight of the last of them and went forward alone. It was less than half an hour later that the fatal headland opened out beyond Whiteness.

Not a soul had he met along that solitary beach, and though, once or twice, he had started at the sight of some mass of drift wood or heap of seaweed, the dreadful thing that he was seeking had not yet appeared. He passed the opening of the cutting and approached the headland, breathing fast and looking about him fearfully. Already he could see the larger lumps of chalk that had fallen, and looking up, he saw a clean, white patch at the summit of the cliff. But still there was no sign of the corpse. He walked on more slowly now, considering whether it could have drifted out to sea, or whether he should find it in the next bay. And then, rounding the headland, he came in sight of a black hole at the cliff foot, the entrance to a deep cave.

He approached yet more slowly, sweeping his eye round the little bay, and looking apprehensively at the cavity before him. Suppose the thing should have washed in there. It was quite possible. Many things did wash into that cave, for he had once visited it and had been as-tonished at the quantity of seaweed and jetsam that had accumulated within it. But it was an uncomfortable thought. It would be doubly horrible to meet the awful thing in the dim twilight of the cavern. And yet, the black archway seemed to draw him on, step by step, until he stood at the portal and looked in. It was an eerie place, chilly and damp, the clammy walls and roof stained green and purple and black with encrusting lichens.

At one time, Elton had been told, it used to be haunted by smug-glers, and then communicated with an underground passage; and the old smuggler's look-out still remained; a narrow tunnel, high up the cliff, looking out into Kingsgate Bay; and even some vestiges of the rude steps that led up to the look-out platform could still be traced, and were not impossible to climb. Indeed, Elton had, at his last visit, climbed to the platform and looked out through the spy-hole. He recalled the circumstance now, as he stood, peering nervously into the darkness, and straining his eyes to see what jetsam the ocean had brought since then.

At first he could see nothing but the smooth sand near the opening; then, as his eyes grew more accustomed to the gloom, he could make out the great heap of seaweed on the floor of the cave. Insensibly, he crept in, with his eyes riveted on the weedy mass and, as he left the daylight behind him, so did the twilight of the cave grow clearer. His feet left the firm sand and trod the springy mass of weed, and in the silence of the cave he could now hear plainly the rain-like patter of the leaping sand-hoppers. He stopped for a moment to listen to the unfamiliar sound, and still the gloom of the cave grew lighter to his more accustomed eyes.

And then, in an instant, he saw it. From a heap of weed, a few paces ahead, projected a boot; his own boot; he recognised the patch on the sole; and at the sight, his heart seemed to stand still. Though he had somehow expected to find it here, its presence seemed to strike him with a greater shock of horror from that very circumstance.

He was standing stock still, gazing with fearful fascination at the boot and the swelling mound of weed, when, suddenly, there struck upon his ear the voice of a woman, singing.

He started violently. His first impulse was to run out of the cave. But a moment's reflection told him what madness this would be. And then the voice drew nearer, and there broke out the high, rippling laughter of a child. Elton looked in terror at the bright opening of the cavern's mouth, expecting every moment to see it frame a group of figures. If that happened, he was lost, for he would have been seen actually with the body. Suddenly he bethought him of the spy-hole and the platform, both of which were invisible from the entrance; and turning, he ran quickly over the sodden weed till he came to the remains of the steps.

Climbing hurriedly up these, he reached the platform, which was enclosed in a large niche, just as the reverberating sound of voices told him that the strangers were within the mouth of the cave. He strained his ears to catch what they were saying and to make out if they were entering farther. It was a child's voice that he had first heard, and very weird were the hollow echoes of the thin treble that were flung back from the rugged walls. But he could not hear what the child had said. The woman's voice, however, was quite distinct, and the words seemed significant in more senses than one.

"No, dear," it said, "you had better not go in. It's cold and damp. Come out into the sunshine."

Elton breathed more freely. But the woman was more right than she knew. It was cold and damp, that thing under the black tangle of weed. Better far to be out in the sunshine. He himself was already longing to escape from the chill and gloom, of the cavern. But he could not escape yet. Innocent as he actually was, his position was that of a murderer. He must wait until the coast was clear, and then steal out, to hurry away unobserved.

He crept up cautiously to the short tunnel and peered out through the opening across the bay. And then his heart sank. Below him, on the sunny beach, a small party of visitors had established themselves just within view of the mouth of the cave; and even as he looked, a man approached from the wooden stairway down the cliff, carrying a couple of deck chairs. So, for the present his escape was hopelessly cut off.

He went back to the platform and sat down to wait for his release; and, as he sat, his thoughts went back once more to the thing that lay under the weed. How long would it lie there undiscovered? And what would happen when it was found? What was there to connect him with it? Of course, there was his name on the clothing, but there was nothing incriminating in that, if he had only had the courage to give information at once. But it was too late to think of that now.

Besides, it suddenly flashed upon him, there was the receipt in the wallet. That receipt mentioned him by name and referred to a loan. Obviously, its suggestion was most sinister, coupled with his silence. It was a deadly item of evidence against him. But no sooner had he realised the appalling significance of this document than he also realised that it was still within his reach. Why should he leave it there to be brought in evidence—in false evidence, too—against him?

Slowly he rose and, creeping down the tunnel, once more looked out. The people were sitting quietly in their chairs, the man was reading, and the child was digging in the sand. Elton looked across the bay to make sure that no other person was approaching, and then, hastily climbing down the steps, walked across the great bed of weed, driving an army of sand-hoppers before him. He shuddered at the thought of what he was going to do, and the clammy chill of the cave seemed to settle on him in a cold sweat.

He came to the little mound from which the boot projected, and began, shudderingly and with faltering hand, to lift the slimy, tangled weed. As he drew aside the first bunch, be gave a gasp of horror and quickly replaced it. The body was lying on its back, and, as he lifted the weed he had uncovered—not the face, for the thing had no face. It had struck either the cliff or a stone upon the beach and—but there is no need to go into particulars: it had no face. When he had recovered a little, Elton groped shudderingly among the weed until he found the breast-pocket from which he quickly drew out the wallet, now clammy, sodden and loathsome. He was rising with it in his hand when an apparition, seen through the opening of the cave, arrested his movement as if he had been suddenly turned into stone.

A man, apparently a fisherman or sailor, was sauntering past some thirty yards from the mouth of the cave, and at his heels trotted a mongrel dog. The dog stopped, and, lifting his nose, seemed to sniff the air; and then he began to walk slowly and suspiciously towards the cave. The man sauntered on and soon passed out of view; but the dog still came on towards the cave, stopping now and again with upraised nose.

The catastrophe seemed inevitable. But just at that moment the man's voice rose, loud and angry, evidently calling the dog. The animal hesitated, looking wistfully from his master to the cave; but when the summons was repeated, he turned reluctantly and trotted away.

Elton stood up and took a deep breath. The chilly sweat was running down his face, his heart was thumping and his knees trembled, so that he could hardly get back to the platform. What hideous peril had he escaped and how narrowly! For there he had stood; and had the man entered, he would have been caught in the very act of stealing the incriminating document from the body. For that matter, he was little better off now, with the dead man's property on his person, and he resolved instantly to take out and destroy the receipt and put back the wallet. But this was easier thought of than done. The receipt was soaked with sea water, and refused utterly to light when he applied a match to it. In the end, he tore it up into little fragments and deliberately swallowed them, one by one.

But to restore the wallet was more than he was equal to just now. He would wait until the people had gone home to lunch, and then he would thrust it under the weed as he ran past. So he sat down again and once more took up the endless thread of his thoughts.

The receipt was gone now, and with it the immediate suggestion of motive. There remained only the clothes with their too legible markings. They certainly connected him with the body, but they offered no proof of his presence at the catastrophe. And then, suddenly, another most startling idea occurred to him. Who could identify the body—the body that had no face? There was the wallet, it was true, but he could take that away with him, and there was a ring on the finger and some articles in the pockets which might be identified. But—a voice seemed to whisper to him—these things were removable, too. And if he removed them, what then? Why, then, the body was that of Thomas Elton, a friendless, poverty-stricken artist, about whom no one would trouble to ask any questions.

He pondered on this new situation profoundly. It offered him a choice of alternatives. Either he might choose the imminent risk of being hanged for a murder that he had not committed, or he might surrender his identity for ever and move away to a new environment.

He smiled faintly. His identity! What might that be worth to barter against his life? Only yesterday he would gladly have surrendered it as the bare price of emancipation from the vampire who had fastened on to him.

He thrust the wallet into his pocket and buttoned his coat. Thomas Elton was dead; and that other man, as yet unnamed, should go forth, as the woman had said, into the sunshine.

PART 2
(Related by Christopher Jervis, M.D.)

From various causes, the insurance business that passed through Thorndyke's hands had, of late, considerably increased. The number of societies which regularly employed him had grown larger, and, since the remarkable case of Percival Bland, the Griffin had made it a routine practice to send all inquest cases to us for report.

It was in reference to one of these latter that Mr. Stalker, a senior member of the staff of that office, called on us one afternoon in December; and when he had laid his bag on the table and settled himself comfortably before the fire, he opened the business without preamble.

"I've brought you another inquest case," said he; "a rather queer one, quite interesting from your point of view. As far as we can see, it has no particular interest for us excepting that it does rather look as if our examining medical officer had been a little casual."

"What is the special interest of the case from our point of view?" asked Thorndyke.

"I'll just give you a sketch of it," said Stalker, "and I think you will agree that it's a case after your own heart.

"On the 24th of last month, some men who were collecting seaweed, to use as manure, discovered in a cave at Kingsgate, in the Isle of Thanet, the body of a man, lying under a mass of accumulated weed. As the tide was rising, they put the body into their cart and conveyed it to Margate, where, of course, an inquest was held, and the following facts were elicited. The body was that of a man named Thomas Elton. It was identified by the name-marks on the clothing, by the visiting-cards and a couple of letters which were found in the pockets. From the address on the letters it was seen that Elton had been staying in Margate, and on inquiry at that address, it was learnt from the old woman who let the lodgings, that he had been missing about four days. The landlady was taken to the mortuary, and at once identified the body as that of her lodger.

"It remained only to decide how the body came into the cave; and this did not seem to present much difficulty; for the neck had been broken by a tremendous blow, which had practically destroyed the face, and there were distinct evidences of a breaking away of a portion of the top of the cliff, only a few yards from the position of the cave. There was apparently no doubt that Elton had fallen sheer from the top of the overhanging cliff on to the beach. Now, one would suppose with the evidence of this fall of about a hundred and fifty feet, the smashed face and broken neck, there was not much room for doubt as to the cause of death. I think you will agree with me, Dr. Jervis?"

"Certainly," I replied; "it must be admitted that a broken neck is a condition that tends to shorten life."

"Quite so," agreed Stalker; "but our friend, the local coroner, is a gentleman who takes nothing for granted—a very Thomas Didymus, who apparently agrees with Dr. Thorndyke that if there is no post mortem, there is no inquest. So he ordered a post mortem, which would have appeared to me an absurdly unnecessary proceeding, and I think that even you will agree with me, Dr. Thorndyke."

But Thorndyke shook his head.

"Not at all," said he. "It might, for instance, be much more easy to push a drugged or poisoned man over a cliff than to put over the same man in his normal state. The appearance of violent accident is an excellent mask for the less obvious forms of murder."

"That's perfectly true," said Stalker; "and I suppose that is what the coroner thought. At any rate, he had the post-mortem made, and the result was most curious; for it was found, on opening the body, that the deceased had suffered from a smallish thoracic aneurism, which had burst. Now, as the aneurism must obviously have burst during life, it leaves the cause of death—so I understand—uncertain; at any rate, the medical witness was unable to say whether the deceased fell over the cliff in consequence of the bursting of the aneurism or burst the aneurism in consequence of falling over the cliff. Of course, it doesn't matter to us which way the thing happened; the only question which interests us is, whether a comparatively recently insured man ought to have had an aneurism at all."

"Have you paid the claim?" asked Thorndyke.

"No, certainly not. We never pay a claim until we have had your report. But, as a matter of fact, there is another circumstance that is causing delay. It seems that Elton had mortgaged his policy to a money lender, named Gordon, and it is by him that the claim has been made, or rather, by a clerk of his, named Hyams. Now, we have had a good many dealings with this man Gordon, and hitherto he has always acted in person; and as he is a somewhat slippery gentleman we have thought it desirable to have the claim actually signed by him. And that is the difficulty. For it seems that Mr. Gordon is abroad, and his whereabouts unknown to Hyams; so, as we certainly couldn't take Hyams's receipt for payment, the matter is in abeyance until Hyams can communicate with his principal. And now, I must be running away. I have brought you, as you will see, all the papers, including the policy and the mortgage deed."

As soon as he was gone, Thorndyke gathered up the bundle of papers and sorted them out in what be apparently considered the order of their importance. First he glanced quickly through the proposal form, and then took up the copy of the coroner's depositions.

"The medical evidence," he remarked, "is very full and complete. Both the coroner and the doctor seem to know their business."

"Seeing that the man apparently fell over a cliff," said I, "the medical evidence would not seem to be of first importance. It would seem to be more to the point to ascertain how he came to fall over."

"That's quite true," replied Thorndyke; "and yet, this report contains some rather curious matter. The deceased had an aneurism of the arch; that was probably rather recent. But he also had some slight, old-standing aortic disease, with full compensatory hypertrophy. He also had a nearly complete set of false teeth. Now, doesn't it strike you, Jervis, as rather odd that a man who was passed only five years ago as a first-class life, should, in that short interval, have become actually uninsurable?"

"Yes, it certainly does look," said I, "as if the fellow had had rather bad luck. What does the proposal form say?"

I took the document up and ran my eyes over it. On Thorndyke's advice, medical examiners for the Griffin were instructed to make a somewhat fuller report than is usual in some companies. In this case, the ordinary answers to questions set forth that the heart was perfectly healthy and the teeth rather exceptionally good, and then, in the summary at the end, the examiner remarked: "the proposer seems to be a completely sound and healthy man; he presents no physical defects whatever, with the exception of a bony *ankylosis* of the first joint of the third finger of the left hand, which he states to have been due to an injury."

Thorndyke looked up quickly. "Which finger, did you say?" he asked.

"The third finger of the left hand," I replied.

Thorndyke looked thoughtfully at the paper that he was reading. "It's very singular," said he, "for I see that the Margate doctor states that the deceased wore a signet ring on the third finger of the left hand. Now, of course, you couldn't get a ring on to a finger with bony *ankylosis* of the joint."

"He must have mistaken the finger," said I, "or else the insurance examiner did."

"That is quite possible," Thorndyke replied; "but, doesn't it strike you as very singular that, whereas the insurance examiner mentions the *ankylosis*, which was of no importance from an insurance point of view, the very careful man who made the post-mortem should not have mentioned it, though, owing to the unrecognisable condition of the face, it was of vital importance for the purpose of identification?"

I admitted that it was very singular indeed, and we then resumed our study of the respective papers. But presently I noticed that Thorndyke had laid the report upon his knee, and was gazing speculatively into the fire.

"I gather," said I, "that my learned friend finds some matter of interest in this case."

For reply, he handed me the bundle of papers, recommending me to look through them.

"Thank you," said I, rejecting them firmly, "but I think I can trust you to have picked out all the plums."

Thorndyke smiled indulgently. "They're not plums, Jervis," said he; "they're only currants, but they make quite a substantial little heap."

I disposed myself in a receptive attitude (somewhat after the fashion of the juvenile pelican) and he continued: "If we take the small and unimpressive items and add them together, you will see that a quite considerable sum of discrepancy results, thus:

"In 1903, Thomas Elton, aged thirty-one, had a set of sound teeth. In 1908, at the age of thirty-six, he was more than half toothless. Again, at the age of thirty-one, his heart was perfectly healthy. At the age of thirty-six, he had old aortic disease, with fully established compensation, and an aneurism that was possibly due to it. When he was examined he had a noticeable incurable malformation; no such malformation is mentioned in connection with the body.

"He appears to have fallen over a cliff; and he had also burst an aneurism. Now, the bursting of the aneurism must obviously have occurred during life; but it would occasion practically instantaneous death. Therefore, if the fall was accidental, the rupture must have occurred either as he stood at the edge of the cliff, as he was in the act of falling, or on striking the beach.

"At the place where he apparently fell, the footpath is some thirty yards distant from the edge of the cliff.

"It is not known how he came to that spot, or whether he was alone at the time.

"Someone is claiming five hundred pounds as the immediate result of his death.

"There, you see, Jervis, are seven propositions, none of them extremely striking, but rather suggestive when taken together."

"You seem," said I, "to suggest a doubt as to the identity of the body."

"I do," he replied. "The identity was not clearly established."

"You don't think the clothing and the visiting-cards conclusive."

"They're not parts of the body," he replied. "Of course, substitution is highly improbable. But it is not impossible."

"And the old woman—" I suggested, but he interrupted me.

"My dear Jervis," he exclaimed; "I'm surprised at you. How many times has it happened within our knowledge that women have identified the bodies of total strangers as those of their husbands, fathers or brothers? The thing happens almost every year. As to this old woman, she saw a body with an unrecognisable face, dressed in the clothes of her missing lodger. Of course, it was the clothes that she identified."

"I suppose it was," I agreed; and then I said: "You seem to suggest the possibility of foul play."

"Well," he replied, "if you consider those seven points, you will agree with me that they present a cumulative discrepancy which it is impossible to ignore. The whole significance of the case turns on the question of identity; for, if this was not the body of Thomas Elton, it would appear to have been deliberately prepared to counterfeit that body. And such deliberate preparation would manifestly imply an attempt to conceal the identity of some other body.

"Then," he continued, after a pause, "there is this deed. It looks quite regular and is correctly stamped, but it seems to me that the surface of the paper is slightly altered in one or two places and if one holds the document up to the light, the paper looks a little more transparent in those places." He examined the document for a few seconds with his pocket lens, and then passing lens and document to me, said: "Have a look at it, Jervis, and tell me what you think."

I scrutinised the paper closely, taking it over to the window to get a better light; and to me, also, the paper appeared to be changed in certain places.

"Are we agreed as to the position of the altered places?" Thorndyke asked when I announced the fact.

"I only see three patches," I answered. "Two correspond to the name, Thomas Elton, and the third to one of the figures in the policy number."

"Exactly," said Thorndyke, "and the significance is obvious. If the paper has really been altered, it means that some other name has been erased and Elton's substituted; by which arrangement, of course, the correctly dated stamp would be secured. And this—the alteration of an old document—is the only form of forgery that is possible with a dated, impressed stamp."

"Wouldn't it be rather a stroke of luck," I asked, "for a forger to happen to have in his possession a document needing only these two alterations?"

"I see nothing remarkable in it," Thorndyke replied. "A money-lender would have a number of documents of this kind in hand, and you observe that he was not bound down to any particular date. Any date within a year or so of the issue of the policy would answer his purpose. This document is, in fact, dated, as you see, about six months after the issue of the policy."

"I suppose," said I, "that you will draw Stalker's attention to this matter."

"He will have to be informed, of course," Thorndyke replied; "but I think it would be interesting in the first place to call on Mr. Hyams. You will have noticed that there are some rather mysterious features in this case, and Mr. Hyams's conduct, especially if this document should turn out to be really a forgery, suggests that he may have some special information on the subject." He glanced at his watch and, after a few moments' reflection, added: "I don't see why we shouldn't make our little ceremonial call at once. But it will be a delicate business, for we have mighty little to go upon. Are you coming with me?"

If I had had any doubts, Thorndyke's last remark disposed of them; for the interview promised to be quite a sporting event. Mr. Hyams was presumably not quite newly-hatched, and Thorndyke, who utterly despised bluff of any kind, and whose exact mind refused either to act or speak one hair's breadth beyond his knowledge, was admittedly in somewhat of a fog. The meeting promised to be really entertaining.

Mr. Hyams was "discovered," as the playwrights have it, in a small office at the top of a high building in Queen Victoria Street. He was a small gentleman, of sallow and greasy aspect, with heavy eyebrows and a still heavier nose.

"Are you Mr. Gordon?" Thorndyke suavely inquired as we entered.

Mr. Hyams seemed to experience a momentary doubt on the subject, but finally decided that he was not. "But perhaps," he added brightly, "I can do your business for you as well."

"I daresay you can," Thorndyke agreed significantly; on which we were conducted into an inner den, where I noticed Thorndyke's eye rest for an instant on a large iron safe.

"Now," said Mr. Hyams, shutting the door ostentatiously, "what can I do for you?"

"I want you," Thorndyke replied, "to answer one or two questions with reference to the claim made by you on the Griffin Office in respect of Thomas Elton."

Mr. Hyams's manner underwent a sudden change. He began rapidly to turn over papers, and opened and shut the drawers of his desk, with an air of restless preoccupation.

"Did the Griffin people send you here?" he demanded brusquely.

"They did not specially instruct me to call on you," replied Thorndyke.

"Then," said Hyams bouncing out of his chair, "I can't let you occupy my time. I'm not here to answer conundrums from Tom, Dick or Harry."

Thorndyke rose from his chair. "Then I am to understand," he said, with unruffled suavity, "that you would prefer me to communicate with the Directors, and leave them to take any necessary action."

This gave Mr. Hyams pause. "What action do you refer to?" he asked. "And, who are you?"

Thorndyke produced a card and laid it on the table. Mr. Hyams had apparently seen the name before, for he suddenly grew rather pale and very serious.

"What is the nature of the questions that you wished to ask?" he inquired.

"They refer to this claim," replied Thorndyke. "The first question is, where is Mr. Gordon?"

"I don't know," said Hyams.

"Where do you think he is?" asked Thorndyke.

"I don't think at all," replied Hyams, turning a shade paler and looking everywhere but at Thorndyke.

"Very well," said the latter, "then the next question is, are you satisfied that this claim is really payable?"

"I shouldn't have made it if I hadn't been," replied Hyams.

"Quite so," said Thorndyke; "and the third question is, are you satisfied that the mortgage deed was executed as it purports to have been?"

"I can't say anything about that," replied Hyams, who was growing every moment paler and more fidgety, "it was done before my time."

"Thank you," said Thorndyke. "You will, of course, understand why I am making these inquiries."

"I don't," said Hyams.

"Then," said Thorndyke, "perhaps I had better explain. We are dealing, you observe, Mr. Hyams, with the case of a man who has met with a violent death under somewhat mysterious circumstances. We are dealing, also, with another man who has disappeared, leaving his affairs to take care of themselves; and with a claim, put forward by a third party, on behalf of the one man in respect of the other. When I say that the dead man has been imperfectly identified, and that the document supporting the claim presents certain peculiarities, you will see that the matter calls for further inquiry."

There was an appreciable interval of silence. Mr. Hyams had turned a tallowy white, and looked furtively about the room, as if anxious to avoid the stony gaze that my colleague had fixed on him.

"Can you give us no assistance?" Thorndyke inquired, at length.

Mr. Hyams chewed a pen-holder ravenously, as he considered the question. At length, he burst out in an agitated voice: "Look here, sir, if I tell you what I know, will you treat the information as confidential?

"I can't agree to that, Mr. Hyams," replied Thorndyke. "It might amount to compounding a felony. But you will be wiser to tell me what you know. The document is a side-issue, which my clients may never raise, and my own concern is with the death of this man."

Hyams looked distinctly relieved. "If that's so," said he, "I'll tell you all I know, which is precious little, and which just amounts to this: Two days after Elton was killed, someone came to this office in my absence and opened the safe. I discovered the fact the next morning. Someone had been to the safe and rummaged over all the papers. It wasn't Gordon, because he knew where to find everything; and it wasn't an ordinary thief, because no cash or valuables had been taken. In fact, the only thing that I missed was a promissory note, drawn by Elton."

"You didn't miss a mortgage deed?" suggested Thorndyke, and Hyams, having snatched a little further refreshment from the penholder, said he did not.

"And the policy," suggested Thorndyke, "was apparently not taken?"

"No," replied Hyams "but it was looked for. Three bundles of policies had been untied, but this one happened to be in a drawer of my desk and I had the only key."

"And what do you infer from this visit?" Thorndyke asked.

"Well," replied Hyams, "the safe was opened with keys, and they were Gordon's keys—or at any rate, they weren't mine—and the person who opened it wasn't Gordon; and the things that were taken—at least the thing, I mean—chiefly concerned Elton. Naturally I smelt a rat; and when I read of the finding of the body, I smelt a fox."

"And have you formed any opinion about the body that was found?"

"Yes, I have," he replied. "My opinion is that it was Gordon's body: that Gordon had been putting the screw on Elton, and Elton had just pitched him over the cliff and gone down and changed clothes with the body. Of course, that's only my opinion. I may be wrong; but I don't think I am."

As a matter of fact, Mr. Hyams was not wrong. An exhumation, consequent on Thorndyke's challenge of the identity of the deceased, showed that the body was that of Solomon Gordon. A hundred pounds reward was offered for information as to Elton's whereabouts. But no one ever earned it. A letter, bearing the post mark of Marseilles, and addressed by the missing man to Thorndyke, gave a plausible account of Gordon's death; which was represented as having occurred accidentally at the moment when Gordon chanced to be wearing a suit of Elton's clothes.

Of course, this account may have been correct, or again, it may have been false; but whether it was true or false, Elton, from that moment, vanished from our ken and has never since been heard of.

Milton Keynes UK
Ingram Content Group UK Ltd.
UKHW030855151124
451262UK00001B/135